Tell England

A Study in a Generation

Ernest Raymond

Contents

TELL ENGLAND
A STUDY IN A GENERATION

BY

Ernest Raymond

NEW YORK
GEORGE H. DORAN COMPANY
1922

For all emotions that are tense and strong,
  And utmost knowledge, I have lived for these—
Lived deep, and let the lesser things live long,
  The everlasting hills, the lakes, the trees,
Who'd give their thousand years to sing this song
  Of Life, and Man's high sensibilities,
Which I into the face of Death can sing—
O Death, then poor and disappointed thing—

Strike if thou wilt, and soon; strike breast and brow;
For I have lived: and thou canst rob me now
Only of some long life that ne'er has been.
The life that I have lived, so full, so keen,
Is mine! I hold it firm beneath thy blow

And, dying, take it with me where I go.

A PROLOGUE BY PADRE MONTY

Sec.1

In the year that the Colonel died he took little Rupert to see the swallows fly away. I can find no better beginning than that. When there devolved upon me as a labour of love the editing of Rupert Ray's book, "Tell England," I carried the manuscript into my room one bright autumn afternoon, and read it during the fall of a soft evening, till the light failed, and my eyes burned with the strain of reading in the dark. I could hardly leave his ingenuous tale to rise and turn on the gas. Nor, perhaps, did I want such artificial brightness. There are times when one prefers the twilight. Doubtless the tale held me fascinated because it revealed the schooldays of those boys whom I met in their young manhood, and told afresh that wild old Gallipoli adventure which I shared with them. Though, sadly enough, I take Heaven to witness that I was not the idealised creature whom Rupert portrays. God bless them, how these boys will idealise us!

Then again, as Rupert tells you, it was I who suggested to him the writing of his story. And well I recall how he demurred, asking:

"But what am I to write about?" For he was always diffident and unconscious of his power.

"Is Gallipoli nothing to write about?" I retorted. "And you can't have spent five years at a great public school like Kensingtowe without one or two sensational things. Pick them out and let us have them. For whatever the modern theorists say, the main duty of a story-teller is certainly to tell stories."

"But I thought," he broke in, "that you're always maintaining that the greatest fiction should be occupied with Subjective Incident."

"Don't interrupt, you argumentative child," I said (you will find Rupert is impertinent enough in one place to suggest that I have a tendency to be rude and a tendency to hold forth). "Surely the ideal story must contain the maximum of Objective Incident with the maximum of Subjective Incident. Only give us the exciting events of your schooldays, and describe your thoughts as they happened, and you will unconsciously reveal what sort of scoundrelly characters you and your friends were. And when you get to the Gallipoli part, well, you can give us chiefly your thoughts, for Gallipoli, as far as dramatic incident is concerned, is well able to shift for itself."

Little wonder that I was fascinated to read Rupert's final manuscript. And, when I had finished the last words, I announced aloud a weighty decision: "We must have a Prologue, Rupert,"—though, to be sure, my study was empty at the time—"and it must give pictures of what your three heroes were like, when they were small, abominable boys."

And thereafter I busied myself in seeking information of the early childhood of Rupert Ray, Archibald Pennybet, and Edgar Gray Doe. Not without misgiving do I offer the result of these researches, for I fear all the time lest my self-conscious hand should profane Rupert's artless narrative.

In the year that the Colonel died he took little Rupert to see the swallows fly away. Colonel Ray was a stately, grey-bearded grandfather; and Rupert his flushed and blue-eyed grandson of six years old; and the two stood side by side and watched. Behind them lay the French town, Boulogne; beside them went the waters of the French river, the Liane. Suddenly Rupert, who had kept his blue eyes on a sky but little bluer, cried out excitedly: "There they are!" For him at that moment the most interesting thing in the world was the flight of swallows overhead. The Colonel, also, looked at the birds till they were out of sight, and then, after keeping silence awhile, uttered a remark which was rather sent in pursuit of the birds than addressed to his young companion. "I shall not see the swallows again," he said.

Colonel Rupert Ray was no ordinary person. He was one of those of whom tales are told; and such people are never ordinary. The most treasured of these tales is the story of the swallows; and it goes on to tell, as you would expect, how the Colonel died that year, before the swallows came flying north and home again. He was buried, while little Rupert and Rupert's mother looked on, in that untidy corner of the

Boulogne Cemetery, where many another English half-pay officer had been laid before him.

Of course the burial of the Colonel was very sad for Rupert; but he soon forgot it all in the excitement of preparing for the journey back to London. The Colonel, you see, had known that his old life would break up soon, and had summoned from their home in London the widow and child of his favourite son, "that Rupert, the best of the lot," as he used to call him. And now the Colonel was dead. So his grandson, the last of the Rupert Rays, could look forward to all the jolly thrills of steaming across the Channel to Folkestone and bowling in a train to London. Really life was an excellent thing.

The day of the venturesome voyage began with excited sleeplessness and glowing health, and ended with a headache and great tiredness. There was the bustle of embarkation on to the boat; the rattle and bang of falling luggage; the jangle of French and English tongues; the unstraining of mighty ropes; the "hoot! hoot!" from the funnel, a side-splitting incident; the *suff-suff-lap-suff* of the ploughed-up sea; the spray of the Channel, which sprinkling one's cheeks, caused one to roar with laughter, till more moderation was enjoined; the incessant throb of the engines; the vision of white cliffs, and the excitement among the passengers; the headache; the landing on a black old pier; the privilege of guarding the luggage by sitting upon as much of one trunk as six years' growth of boy will cover, and pressing firmly upon two other trunks with either hand, while Mrs. Ray (that capable lady) changed francs into shillings; there was the wearisome and rolling train-journey, wherein one slept, first against the window and then against the black sleeve of an unknown gentleman; and lastly there was the realisation that pale and sunny France had withdrawn into the past to make room for pale and smutty London.

Now the Captain of all these manoeuvres, as the meanest intelligence will have observed, was Mrs. Ray. Mrs. Ray was Rupert's mother, and as beautiful as every mother must be, who has an only son, and is a widow. Moreover she was a perfect teller of stories: all really beautiful mothers are. And, for years after, she used at evening time to draw young Rupert against her knees, and tell him the traditional stories of that old half-pay officer at Boulogne. And grandfather was indeed a hero in these stories. We suspect—but who can sound the artful depths of a woman who is at once young, lovely, a mother, and a widow?—that Mrs. Ray, knowing that Rupert could never recall his father, was determined that at least one soldierly figure should loom heroic in his childish memories. She would tell again and again how he asked repeatedly, as he lay dying, for "that Rupert, the best of the lot." And her son would say: "I s'pose he meant Daddy, mother." "Yes," she would answer. "You see, you were all Ruperts: Grandfather Rupert Ray, Daddy Rupert Ray, and Sonny Rupert Ray, my own little Sonny Ray." (Mothers talk in this absurd fashion, and Mrs. Ray was the chief of such offenders.)

But quite the masterpiece of all her tales was this. One summer morning, when the Boulogue promenade was bright and crowded and lively, the Colonel was seated with his grandson beside him. A little distance away sat Rupert's mother, who was just about as shy of the Colonel as the Colonel was shy of her (which fact accounts, probably, for Rupert Ray's growing up into the shy boy we knew). Well, all of a sudden, the boy got up, stood immediately in front of his grandsire, and leaned forward against his knees. There was no mistaking the meaning in the child's eyes; they said plainly: "This is entirely the best attitude for story-telling, so please."

The officer, with military quickness, summed up the perilous situation on his front; he had suffered himself to be bombarded by a pair of patient eyes. And now he must either acknowledge his incompetence by a shameful retreat, or he must stir up the dump of his imagination and see what stories it contained. So with no small apprehension, he drew upon his inventive genius.

A wonderful story resulted—wonderful as a prophetic parable of things which the Colonel would not live to see. Perhaps it was only coincidence that it should be so; perhaps the approach of death endowed the old gentleman with the gift of dim prophecy—did he not know that he would follow the swallows away?—perhaps all the Rays, when they stand in that shadow, possess a mystic vision. Certainly the boy Rupert—but there! I knew I was in danger of spoiling his story.

If the Colonel's tale this morning was wonderful to the listener, the author suspected that he was plagiarising. The hero was a knight of peculiar grace, who sustained the spotless name of Sir R—— R——. He was not very handsome, having hair that was neither gold nor brown, and a brace of absurdly sea-blue eyes. But he was distinguished by many estimable qualities; he was English, for example, and not French, very brave, very sober, and quite fond of an elderly relation. And one day he was undoubtedly (although the Colonel's conscience pricked him) plunging on foot through a dense forest to the aid of a fellow-knight who had been captured and imprisoned.

"What was the other knight like?" interrupted Rupert.

"What, indeed?" echoed the Colonel, temporising till he should evolve an answer. "Yes, that's a very relevant question. Well, he was a good deal fairer than Sir R—— R——, but about the same age, only with brown eyes, and he was a very nice little boy—young fellow, I mean."

"What was his name?"

"His name? Oh, well—" and here the Colonel, feeling with some taste that "Smith," or "Jones," or "Robinson" was out of place in a forest whose mediaeval character was palpable, and being quite unable at such short notice to recall any other English names, gained time by the following ingenious detail: "Oh, well, he lost his good name by being captured. And then—and then to his aid came the stalwart Sir R——, with his sword drawn, and his—er—"

"Revoller," suggested the listener.

"Yes, his revolver fixed to his chain-mail—"

In this strain the Colonel proceeded, wondering whether such abominable nonsense was interesting the child, whose gaze had now begun to reach out to sea. In reality Rupert was thrilled, and did not like to disturb the flow of a story so affecting. But the strength of his feelings was too much. He was obliged to suggest an amendment.

"Are you sure I didn't go upon a horse?" he asked.

"Why, of course, the unknown knight in question did, and the sheath of his sword clanked against his horse's side, as he dashed through the thicket."

"Had the fair-haired knight anything to eat all this time?"

This important problem was duly settled, and several others which were seen to be involved in such an intricate story; and a very happy conclusion was reached, when Mrs. Ray decided that it was time for Rupert to be taken home. She was about to lead him away, when the Colonel, who seldom spoke to her much, abruptly murmured:

"He has that Rupert's eyes."

For a moment she was quite taken aback, and then timorously replied: "Yes, they are very blue."

"Very blue," repeated the Colonel.

Mrs. Ray thereupon felt she must obviate an uncomfortable silence, and began with a nervous laugh:

"He was born when we were in Geneva, you know, and we used to call him 'our mountain boy,' saying that he had brought a speck of the mountain skies away in his eyes."

The Colonel conceded a smile, but addressed his reply to the child: "A mountain boy, is he?" and, placing his hand on Rupert's head, he turned the small face upward, and watched it break into a smile. "Well, well. A mountain boy, eh?—from the lake of Geneva. H'm. ***Il a dans les yeux un coin du lac.***"

At this happy description the tears of pleasure sprang to the foolish eyes of Mrs. Ray, while Rupert, thinking with much wisdom that all the conditions were favourable, gazed up into the Colonel's face, and fired his last shot.

"What really was the fair-haired knight's name?"

"Perhaps you will know some day," answered the Colonel, half playfully, half wearily.

Sec.2

In the course of the same summer Master Archibald Pennybet, of Wimbledon, celebrated his eighth birthday. He celebrated it by a riotous waking-up in the sleeping hours of dawn; he celebrated it by a breakfast which extended him so much that his skin became unbearably tight; and then, in a new white sailor-suit and brown stockings turned over at the calves to display a couple of magnificent knees, he celebrated some more of it in the garden. There on the summer lawn he stood, unconsciously deliberating how best to give new expression to the personality of Archibald Pennybet. He was dark, gloriously built, and possessed eyes that lazily drooped by reason of their heavy lashes; and, I am sorry to say, he evoked from a boudoir window the gurgling admiration of his fashionable mother, who, while her hair was being dressed, allowed her glance to swing from her hand-mirror, which framed a gratifying vision of herself, to the window, which framed a still more gratifying vision of her son. "He gets his good looks from me," she thought. And, having noticed the drooping of his eyelids, over-weighted with lashes, she brought her hand-mirror into play again. "He is lucky," she added, "to have inherited those lazy eyes from me."

Soon Archie retired in the direction of the kitchen-garden. The kitchen-garden, with its opportunities of occasional refreshment such as would not add uncomfortably to his present feeling of tightness, was the place for a roam. Five minutes later he was leaning against the wire-netting of the chicken-run, and offering an old cock, who asked most pointedly for bread, a stone. To know how to spend a morning was no easier on a birthday than on any ordinary day.

Suddenly, however, he overheard the gardener mentioning a murder which had been committed on Wimbledon Common, a fine tract of wild jungle and rolling prairie, that lay across the main road. Without waiting to prosecute inquiries which would have told him that, although the confession was only in the morning papers, the murder was twenty years old, he escaped unseen and set his little white figure on a walk through the common. He was out to see the blood.

But, for a birthday, it was a disappointing morning. He discovered for the first time that Wimbledon Common occupied an interminable expanse of country; and really there was nothing unusual this morning about its appearance, or about the looks of the people whom he passed. So he gave up his quest and returned homeward. Then it was that his lazy eyes looked down a narrow, leafy lane that ran along the high wall of his own garden. Now all Wimbledon suspects that this lane was designed by the Corporation as a walk for lovers. There is evidence of the care and calculation that one spends on a chicken-run. For the Corporation, knowing the practice of lovers, has placed in the shady recesses of the lane a seat where these comical people can intertwine. At the sight of the lane and the seat, Master Pennybet immediately decided how he would occupy his afternoon. He would move that seat along his garden wall, till it rested beneath some ample foliage where he could lie hidden. Then he would wait the romantic moments of the evening.

This idea proved so exciting that the luncheon of which he partook was (for a birthday) regrettably small. And no sooner was it finished than he rushed into the lane, and addressed his splendid muscles to removing the seat.

To begin with he tried pushing. This failed. The more he pushed the more his end of the seat went up into the air, while the other remained fast in the ground. The only time he succeeded in making the seat travel at all it went so fast that it laid him on his stomach in the lane. So he tried pulling from the other end. This was only partially successful. The seat moved towards him with jerks, at one time arriving most damnably on his shins, and at another throwing him into a sitting position on to the ground. And there is a portion of small boys which is very sensitive to stony ground. At these repeated checks the natural child in Mr. Pennybet caused his eyes to become moist, whereupon the strong and unconquerable man in him choked back a sob of temper, and pulled the seat with a passionate determination. I tell you, such indomitable grit will always get its way, and the seat was well lodged against Mr. Pennybet's wall and beneath his green fastness, before the afternoon blushed into the lovers' hour. He returned into his garden, and, climbing up the wall by means of the mantling ivy, reached his chosen observation-post. Through curtains of greenery he watched the arrival of a pair of lovers, and held his breath, as they seated themselves beneath him.

They were an even more ridiculous couple than their kind usually are. And, when the gentleman squeezed the lady, she laughed so foolishly that Archie Pennybet was within an ace of forgetting himself and heartily laughing too. It was worse still, when they began the pernicious practice of "rubbing noses." For the operation was so new and unexpected, and withal so congenial to Archie, that he risked discovery by craning forward to study it. He watched with jaws parted in a wide gape of amazement, and then said to himself: "Well, I'm damned!" There is but one step (I am told) from rubbing noses to the real business of the kiss. And it was when the gentleman brought the lady's lips into contact with his own, and the peculiar sound was heard in the lane, that Mr. Pennybet's moment had come.

"Hem! Hem! Oh, I say!" he suggested loudly, and sought safety by slipping rapidly down his side of the wall, scratching his hands and bare knees as he fell.

This fine triumph had been at a cost. Archie surveyed himself. His new suit was clearly disreputable. And, in his mother's eyes, the one crime punishable by whipping was to make a new suit disreputable. The more he studied the extent of the damage, the more he felt convinced that, in the expiation of this potty little offence, his body would be commandeered to play a painful and rather passive part.

His brain, therefore, worked rapidly and well. It was more than possible, thought he, that his mother's sympathy could be induced to exceed her indignation. She was really an affectionate woman; and this was the line to go upon. So he squeezed the scratches in his knees to expedite the issue of blood, and bravely entered the house.

"Mother," he called, introducing suitable pathos into his tones, "Mother, I've fallen all down the wall!"

This effective opening, should it seem successful, it was his intention to follow up with seasonable allusions to his birthday. But alas! one glimpse of Mrs. Pennybet's face when she saw his suit, showed him the folly of remaining on the scene, and with the speed of a fawn, he was out in the garden, and up an elm tree, swaying about like a crow's nest. And there, a minute later, was Mrs. Pennybet standing below, her skirts held up in one hand, a small cane in the other.

"Come down, Archie," she said. "Come down."

"Not a bit of it," replied her son. "You come up!"

*   *   *   *   *

At least Mrs. Pennybet, a vivacious *raconteuse*, always declared to me that such was his reply. I do not trust these mothers, however, and regard it as a piece of her base embroidery. At any rate, it is certain that her effort to secure Archie for punishment was quite unsuccessful. And, an hour afterwards, a small figure came quietly down the trunk of the tree, and, entering the room where his mother was, sat quickly in a big arm-chair, and held on tightly to its arms. This position prevented access to that particular area of Archie Pennybet, which, in the view of himself, his mother, and all sound conservatives, must be exposed, if corporal punishment is to be the standard thing. Mrs. Pennybet, good woman, admitted her defeat, and kissed him repeatedly, while he still held himself tight in his chair.

Such was Archie Pennybet, whom Mrs. Pennybet considered a remarkably fine boy, and the son of a remarkably fine woman. In this battle of wits he undoubtedly won. And it is a fact that throughout life he made a point of winning, as all shall see, who read Rupert Ray's story.

He was a mischievous, tumbling scamp, I suppose; but what are we to say? All young animals gambol, and are saucy. Only this morning I was watching a lamb butt its mother in the ribs, and roll in the grass, and dirty its wool—the graceless young rascal!

Sec.3

But come, we are keeping Edgar Gray Doe waiting.

If you have ever steamed up the Estuary of the Fal, that stately Cornish river, and gazed with rapture at the lofty and thick-wooded hills, through which the wide stream runs, you have probably seen on the eastern bank the splendid mansion of Graysroof. You have admired its doric facade and the deep, green groves that embrace it on every side. Perhaps it has been pointed out to you as the home of Sir Peter Gray, the once-famous Surrey bowler, and the parent of a whole herd of young cricketing Grays.

It was in this palatial dwelling that little Edgar Gray Doe awoke to a consciousness of himself, and of many other remarkable things; such things as the broad, silver mouth of the Fal; the green slopes, on which his house stood; the rather fearsome woods that surrounded it; and, above all, the very obvious fact that he was not as other boys. For instance, his cricketing cousins, these Gray boys, were sons with a visible mother and father, and, in being so, appeared to conform to a normal condition, while *he* was a nephew with an uncle and aunt. Again these fellows were blue-eyed and drab, and, as such, were decent and reasonable, while *he* was brown-eyed and preposterously fair-haired. To be sure, it was only his oval face that saved him from the horrible indignity of being called "Snowball."

One morning of that perfect summer, which was the sixth of Rupert Ray, and the eighth of Archie Pennybet, Edgar Gray Doe felt some elation at the prospect of a visit from a very imposing friend. This person was staying down the stream at Falmouth; and he and his mother had been invited by Lady Gray to spend the day at Graysroof. His name was Archie Pennybet. And the power of his personality lay in these remarkable qualities: first, he enjoyed the distinction of being two years older than Master Doe; secondly, he had a genius for games that thrilled, because they were clearly sin; and thirdly, his hair was dark and glossy, so he could legitimately twit other people with being albinos.

And to-day this exciting creature would have to devote himself entirely to Edgar Doe, as the Gray boys were safely billeted in public and preparatory schools, and there was thus no sickening possibility of his chasing after them, or going on to their side against Edgar.

Edgar Doe knew that Mrs. Pennybet and Archie were coming in a row-boat from Falmouth, and it was a breathless moment when he saw them stepping on to the Graysroof landing-stage, and Lady Gray walking down the sloping lawn to meet them.

"Hallo, kid," shouted Archie. "Mother, there's Edgar!"

Rather startled by this sudden notoriety, Edgar approached the new arrivals.

"Hallo, kid," repeated Master Pennybet; and then stopped, his supply of greetings being exhausted.

"Hallo," answered Edgar, slowly and rather shyly, for he was two years younger than anyone present.

"Welcome to the Fal," said Lady Gray to Mrs. Pennybet. "Archie, are you going to give me a kiss?"

"No," announced Archie firmly. "I don't kiss mother's friends now."

Lady Gray concealed the fact that she thought her guest's little boy a hateful child, and, having patted his head, sent him off with Edgar Doe to play in the Day-nursery.

Of course the Master of the Ceremonies in the Day-nursery was Master Pennybet. Master Doe was his devoted mate. The first game was a disgusting one, called "Spits." It consisted in the two combatants facing each other with open umbrellas, and endeavouring to register points by the method suggested in the title of the game; the umbrella was a shield, with which to intercept any good shooting. Luckily for their self-respect in later years, this difficult game soon yielded place to an original competition, known as "Fire and Water." You placed a foot-bath under that portable gas-stove which was in the Day-nursery; you lit all the trivets in the stove to represent a house on fire; and you had a pail, ready to be filled from the bathroom, which, need we say, was the fire-station. The rules provided that the winner was he who could extinguish the conflagration raging in the foot-bath in the shortest possible time, and with the least expenditure of water. But the natural desire to win and to record good times meant that you were apt, in the haste and enthusiasm of the moment, to miss the bath entirely, and to flood quite a different part of the nursery. It was this flaw in an otherwise simple game, which brought the play to an end. Intimations that an aquatic tourney of some sort was the feature in the Day-nursery began to leak through to the room below. The competitors were apprehended and brought for judgment before the ladies, who were sitting in the garden and watching the Fal as it streamed by to the sea.

"They had better go and play in the Beach Grove," sighed Lady Gray.

This ruling Archie did not veto or contest, for he had wearied of indoor amusements, and felt that the well-timbered groves would afford new avenues for play. So the boys departed like deer among the trunks of the trees.

It was a cosy conversation which the ladies enjoyed after this. Any conversation would be cosy that had been reared in the glory of such a garden, and in the comfort of those lazy chairs. Mrs. Pennybet began by declaring, as these shameless ladies do, that her hostess's fair-haired nephew was quite the most beautiful child she had ever seen; she could hug him all day; nay, she could eat him. And, thereupon Lady Gray told her the whole story of Edgar Gray Doe; how his mother had been Sir Peter's sister, and the loveliest woman in Western Cornwall; how she had paid with her life for Edgar's being; and how her husband, the chief of lovers, had quickly followed his young bride.

"They're an emotional lot, these Does," said Lady Gray. "As surely as they come fair-haired, they are brilliantly romantic and blindly adoring. And Edgar's every inch a Doe. Anybody can lead him into mischief. And anybody who likes will do so."

"Oh, I suppose he's troublesome like all boys," suggested Mrs. Pennybet, with a rapid mental survey of the existence of Archie. "He will grow into a fine man some day."

"Perhaps," said Lady Gray, staring over the tranquil water of the Fal, as though it represented the intervening years. "We shall see."

"And Archie," continued Mrs. Pennybet, "though he's a plague now, will be a brilliant and dominating man, I think. He's not easily mastered, and I don't believe adverse circumstances will ever beat him.... Isn't it funny to think that these restless boys are here to inherit the world? We old fogies"—Mrs. Pennybet laughed, for she didn't mean what she said—"are really done for and shelved. These boys are the interesting ones, whose tales have yet to be told."

The speaker dropped her voice, as she found herself moralising; and Lady Gray perceived that an atmosphere of tender speculation had risen around their conversation. She turned her face away, and looked over that part of the inheritable world which met her gaze. From her feet perfect lawns sloped down to a gracious waterway, which shuddered occasionally in a gentle wind; on every side pleasing trees were massed into shady and grateful woods; overhead the noonday sun lit up a deep-blue sky. Perhaps the sublimity of the scene played upon her softer emotions. Perhaps all intense beauty is pathetic, and makes one think of poor illusions and un-availing dreams. Lady Gray wondered why she could not feel, on this serene morn-ing, the same confidence in Edgar Doe's future, as her friend felt in Archie's; why she should rather be conscious of a romantic foreboding. But she only murmured:

"Yes, we must bow before sovereign youth."

And that was the last word uttered, till the sound of hearty boys' voices, com-ing from the trunks of the trees, prompted Mrs. Pennybet to say cheerfully:

"Here they come, the heirs to the world."

As she spoke, Archie Pennybet, dark and dictatorial, and Edgar Doe, fair and enthusiastic, came into view.

"Yes," replied Lady Gray, "but only two of them. There are others they must share it with. Shall we go indoors?"

And indoors or out-of-doors, that was a very delightful day spent at Graysroof. And, when the sun's rays began to grow ruddy, there came the pleasant journey down the Estuary to Falmouth Town. Mrs. Pennybet and her son were rowed homeward by Baptist, that sombre boatman employed at Graysroof, in Master Doe's own particular boat. "*The Lady Fal*," men called it, from the dainty conceit that it was the spouse of the lordly Estuary. Edgar Doe accompanied them, as the master of his craft.

Nobody talked much during the voyage. Baptist was always too solemn for speech. Master Doe, on these occasions, liked to dream with one hand trailing in the water. Master Pennybet, in the common way of tired children, finished the day in listless woolgathering. And his mother, recalling the conversation in the stately garden up the stream, fell to wondering whither these boys were tending.

So the passage down the full and slumbery Fal seemed nearly a soundless thing. But all the real river-noises were there; the birds were singing endlessly in the groves; the gulls with their hoarse language were flying seawards from the mud-flats of Truro; the water was gently lapping the sides of the boat; and voices could be heard from the distances higher up and lower down the stream. And behind all this prattle of the Estuary hung the murmur of the sea.

It was a very quiet boat that unladed the Pennybets on the steps of a stone pier at Falmouth, and then swung round and carried Edgar up its own wake. Baptist was a glorious hand with the paddles, and, as the **Lady Fal** swept easily over the glassy water, Edgar gazed at the familiar things coming into view. There, at last, was the huge house of Graysroof, belittled by the loftiness of the quilted hill, on whose slope it stood, and by the extent of its surrounding woods. And there in the water lay mirrored a reflection of house and trees and hillside. Baptist rested on his oars, and, turning round on his seat, drank in the loveliness of England and the Fal. His oars remained motionless for a long time, till he suddenly commented:

"H'm."

This encouraging remark Master Doe interpreted as a willingness to converse, and he let escape a burst of confidence.

"You know, I like Archie Pennybet very much indeed. In fack, I think I like him better than anyone else in the world, 'septing of course my relations."

Watching his hearer nervously to see how he would receive this important avowal, Master Doe flushed when he saw no signs of emotion on Baptist's countenance. He didn't like thinking he had made himself look a fool. Probably Baptist perceived this, for he felt he must contrive a reply, and, abandoning "H'm" as too uncouth and too unflavoured with sympathy, gave of his best, muttering:

"Ah, he's one of we."

Then, realising that the sun had gone in a blaze of glory, and that he must waste no further time in prolonged gossip, he dipped his blade into the still water, and turned the head of the boat for the Graysroof bank; and for the things that should be.

BOOK I
FIVE GAY YEARS OF SCHOOL

Part I: Tidal Reaches

CHAPTER I
RUPERT RAY BEGINS HIS STORY

Sec.1

I'm the best-looking person in this room," said Archibald Pennybet. "Ray's face looks as though somebody had trodden on it, and Doe's—well, Doe's would be better if it had been trodden on."

It was an early morning of the Kensingtowe Summer Term, and the three of us, Archie Pennybet, Edgar Gray Doe, and I, Rupert Ray, were waiting in the Junior Preparation Room at Bramhall House, till the bell should summon us over the playing fields to morning school. Kensingtowe, of course, is the finest school in England, and Bramhall its best house. Now, Pennybet, though not himself courteous, always insisted that Doe and I should treat him with proper respect, so, since he was senior and thus magnificent, I'll begin by describing him.

He was right in saying that he was the handsomest. He was a tall boy of fifteen years, with long limbs that were saved from any unlovely slimness by their full-fleshed curves and perfect straightness. His face, whose skin was as smooth as that of a bathed and anointed Greek, was crowned by dark hair, and made striking by a pair of those long-lashed eyes that are always brown. And in character he was the most remarkable. Though two years our senior, he deliberately lagged behind the boys of his own age, and remained the oldest member of our form. Thoughtless masters called him a dunce, but abler ones knew him to be only idle. And Pennybet cared little for either opinion. He had schemed to remain in a low form; and that was enough. It was better to be a field-marshal among the "kids" than a ranker among his peers. Like Satan, for whom he probably felt a certain admiration, he found it better to reign in hell than serve in heaven.

The personal attendants of this splendid sultan consisted of Edgar Doe and myself. We were not allowed by him to forget that, if he could total fifteen years, we could only scrape together a bare thirteen. We were mere children. Doe and I, being thirteen and an exact number of days, were twins, or we would have been, had it not been for the divergence of our parentage. We often expressed a wish that this divergence were capable of remedy. It involved minor differences. For instance, while Doe's eyes were brown, mine were blue; and while Doe's hair was very fair, mine was a tedious drab that had once been gold. Moreover, in place of my wide mouth, Doe possessed lips that were always parted like those of a pretty girl. Indeed, if Archie Pennybet was the handsomest of us three, it is certain that Edgar Gray Doe was the prettiest.

We came to be discussing our looks this morning, because Pennybet, having discovered that among other accomplishments he was a fine ethnologist, was about to determine the race and tribe of each of us by an examination of our features and colouring.

"I'm a Norman," he decided, and threw himself back on his chair, putting his thumbs into the armholes of his waistcoat, as though that were a comely Norman attitude, "a pure Norman, but I don't know how my hair got so dark, and my eyes such a spiffing brown."

"What am I?" I interrupted, as introducing a subject of more immediate interest.

"You, Ray? Oh, you're a Saxon. Your name's Rupert, you see, and you've blue eyes and a fair skin, and all that rot."

I was quite satisfied with being a pure Saxon, and left Doe to his examination.

"What am I?" he eagerly asked, offering his oval face and parted lips for scrutiny.

"You? Oh, Saxon, with a dash of Southern blood. Brown eyes, you see, and that sloppy milk-and-coffee skin. And there's a dash of Viking in you—that's your fair hair. Adulterated Saxon you are."

At this Doe loudly protested that he was a pure Saxon, a perfect Cornish Saxon from the banks of the Fal.

Penny always discouraged precocious criticism, so he replied:

"I'm not arguing with you, my child."

"*You?* Who are you?"

Penny let his thumbs go further into his armholes, and assured us with majestic suavity:

"I? I'm *Me*."

"No, you're not," snapped Doe. "You're not me. I'm me."

"Well, you're neither of you me," interrupted the third fool in the room. "I'm me. So sucks!"

"Now you two boys," began our stately patron, "don't you begin dictating to *me*. Once and for all, Doe is Doe, Ray is Ray, and I'm Me. Why, by Jove! Doe-Ray-Me! It's a joke; and I'm a gifted person."

This discovery of the adaptability of our names was so startling that I exclaimed:

"Good Lord! How mad!"

Penny only shrugged his shoulders, and generally plumed himself on his little success. And Doe said:

"Has that only just dawned on you?"

"Observe," sneered Penny. "The Gray Doe is jealous. He would like the fame of having made this fine jest. So he pretends he thought of it long ago. He bags it."

"Not worth bagging," suggested Doe, who was pulling a lock of his pale hair over his forehead, and trying with elevated eye-brows to survey it critically. His feet were resting on a seat in front of him, and his trousers were well pulled up, so as to show a certain tract of decent sock. Penny scanned him as though his very appearance were nauseating.

"Well, why did you bag it?"

"I didn't."

"I say, you're a bit of a liar, aren't you?"

"Well, if I'm a bit of a liar, you're a lot of one."

"My dear little boy," said Penny, with intent to hurt, "we all know the reputation for lying you had at your last school."

As we had all been at Kensingtowe's Preparatory School together, I was in a position to know that this was rather wild, and remonstrated with him.

"I say, that's a bit sticky, isn't it?"

The nobility of my interference impressed me as I made it. Meanwhile the angry blood mounted to Doe's face, but he carelessly replied:

"You show what a horrible liar you are by your last remark. I never said your beastly idea was mine; and because you accused me of doing so, and I said I didn't, you call me a liar: which is a dirty lie, if you like. But of course one expects lies from you."

"That may be," rejoined Pennybet. "But you know you don't wash."

Doe parried this thrust with a sarcastic acquiescence.

"No, I know I don't—never did—don't believe in washing."

Now Penny was out to hurt. A mere youngster had presumed to argue and be cheeky with him: and discipline must be maintained. To this end there must be punishment; and punishment, to be effective, must hurt. So he adopted a new line, and with his clever strategy strove to enlist my support by deigning to couple my name with his.

"At any rate," he drawled, "Ray and I don't toady to Radley."

This poisonous little remark requires some explanation. Mr. Radley, the assistant house-master at Bramhall House, was a hard master, who would have been hated for his insufferable conceptions of discipline, had he not been the finest bat in the Middlesex team. Just about this time there was a libel current that he made a favourite of Edgar Doe because he was pretty. "Doe," I had once said, "Radley's rather keen on you, isn't he?" And Doe had turned red and scoffed: "How absolutely silly—but, I say, do you really think so?" Seeing that he found pleasure in the insinuation, I had followed it up with chaff, upon which he had suddenly cut up rough, and left me in a pique.

This morning, as Penny pricked him with this poisoned fang, Doe began to feel that for the moment he was alone amongst us three; and odd-man-out. He put a tentative question to me, designed to see whether I were siding with him or with the foe.

"Now, Ray, isn't that the dirtiest lie he's told so far?"

"No," I said. I was still under the glamour of having been appealed to by the forceful personality of Pennybet; and, besides, it certainly wasn't.

"Oh, of course you'd agree with anything Penny said, if he asked you to. But you know you don't really believe I ever sucked up to Radley."

This rejoinder was bad tactics, for by its blow at my face it forced me to take sides against him in the quarrel. So I answered:

"Rather! Why, you always do."

"Dir-dirty liar!"

"Ha-ha!" laughed Penny. He saw that he had been successful in his latest thrust, and set himself to push home the advantage. The dominance of his position must be secured at all costs. He let down his heavy-lashed eyelids, as though, for his part, he only desired a peaceful sleep, and said: "Ha-ha! Ray, that friend of yours is losing his temper. He's terribly vicious. Mind he doesn't scratch."

Doe's parted lips came suddenly together, his face got red, and he moved impatiently as he sat. But he said nothing, either because the words would not come, or lest something more unmanly should.

"Ray," pursued the tormentor, "I think that friend of yours is going to blub."

Doe left his seat, and stood upon his feet, his lips set in one firm line. He tossed his hair off his forehead, and, keeping his face averted from our gaze lest we should detect any moisture about the eyes, opened a desk, and selected the books he would require. They were books over which he had scrawled with flourishes:

> "Mr. Edgar Gray Doe, Esq.,"
> "E. Gray Doe, M.A.,"
> "Rev. Edgar G. Doe, D.D.,"
> "E. G. Doe, Physician and Surgeon,"

and, when he had placed them on his arm, he walked towards the door with his face still turned away from us.

"Oh, don't go, Doe. Don't be a sloppy ass," I said, feeling that I had been fairly trapped into deserting a fellow-victim, and backing our common tyrant.

My appeal Doe treated as though he had not heard it; and Penny, certain that his victory was won, and that he had no further need of my support, kicked it away with the sneer: "Hit Doe, and Ray's bruised! What a David and Jonathan we're going to be! How we agree like steak and kidney!... Rather a nice expression, that."

Penny's commentary was thus turned inwards upon himself, in an affectionate criticism of his vocabulary, to show the utter detachment of his interest from the pathetic exit of Edgar Doe. For now Doe had reached the door, which he opened, passed, and slammed. In a twinkling I had opened it again, and was looking down the corridor. There was no sign of my friend anywhere. The moment he had slammed the door he must have run.

I returned to the preparation room, and Penny sighed, as much as to say: "What a pity little boys are so petulant and quarrelsome." But the victory was his, as it always was, and he could think of other things. There was a clock on the wall behind him, but, too comfortable to turn his head, he asked me:

"What's the beastly?"

I glanced at the clock, and intimated, sulkily enough, that the beastly was twenty minutes past nine. He groaned.

"Oh! Ah! An hour's sweat with Radley. Oh, hang! Blow! Damn!"

He stood up, stretched himself, yawned, apologised, got his books, and occasionally tossed a remark to me, as if he were quite unaware that I was not only trying to sulk, but also badly wanted him to know it. As I looked for my books, I sought for the rudest and most painful insult I could offer him. My duty to Doe demanded that it should be something quite uncommon. And from a really fine selection I had just chosen: "You're the biggest liar I've ever met, and, for all I know, you're as big a thief," when I turned round and found he was gone. Pennybet always left the field as its master.

Sec.2

Within Radley's spacious class-room some twenty of us took our way to our desks. Radley mounted his low platform, and, resting his knuckles on his writing-table, gazed down upon us. He was a man of over six feet, with the shoulders, chest, and waist of a forcing batsman. His neck, perhaps, was a little too big, the fault of a powerful frame; and the wrist that came below his cuff was such that it made us wonder what was the size of his forearm. His mouth was hard, and set above a squaring chin, so that you thought him relentless, till his grey eyes shook your judgment.

"Let me see," he said, as he stood, looking down upon us, "you should come to me for both periods this morning. Well, I shall probably be away all the second period. You will come to this class-room as usual, and Herr Reinhardt will take you in French."

"Oh, joy!" I muttered. Boys whom Radley could not see flipped their fingers to express delight. Others lifted up the lids of their desks, and behind these screens went through a pantomime that suggested pleasure at good news. The fact was that the announcement that we were to have second period with the German, Reinhardt, was as good as promising us a holiday. Nay, it was rather better; for, in an unexpected holiday, we might have been at a loss what to do, whereas under Reinhardt we had no doubt—we played the fool.

"And now get on with your work," concluded Radley.

We got on with it, knowing that it was only for a short time that we need work that morning.

It was writing work I know, for, after a while, I had a note surreptitiously passed to me between folded blotting-paper. The note bore in Doe's ambitiously ornate writing the alarming statement: "I shall never like you so much after what you said this morning Yours Edgar Gray Doe." There was room for me to pen an answer, and in my great round characters I wrote: "I never really meant anything and after you left I tried to be rude to Penny but he'd gone and will you still be my chum Yours S. Ray." (My real name was Rupert, but I was sometimes nicknamed "Sonny Ray" from the sensational news, which had leaked out, that my mother so called me, and I took pleasure in signing myself "S. Ray.") My handsome apology was passed back to the offended party, and in due course the paper returned to me, bearing his reply: "I don't know We must talk it over, but don't tell anyone Yours Edgar Gray Doe." That was the last sentence destined to be written on this human document, for Radley, without looking up from the exercise he was correcting, said quietly:

"In the space of the last five minutes Doe has twice corresponded with Ray, and Ray has once replied to Doe. Now both Ray and Doe will come up here with the letters."

To the accompaniment of a titter or two, Ray and Doe came up, I trying to look defiantly indifferent to the fact that he was going to read my silly remarks, and Doe with his lips firmly together, and his fair hair the fairer for the blush upon his forehead and cheeks.

Radley left us standing by his desk, while at his leisure he finished his correcting; then, still without looking up, he ordered:

"Hand over the letters."

A little doggedly I passed over the single sheet of paper feeling some absurd satisfaction that, since he evidently thought there were several sheets involved, his uncanny knowledge was at least wrong in one particular. Doe, on my right hand, turned redder and redder to see the paper going beneath the master's eye, and made a few nervous grimaces. Radley read the correspondence pitilessly; and, with his hard mouth unrelaxed, turned first on Doe, as though sizing him up, and then on me. He stared at my face till I felt fidgety, and my mind, which always in moments of excitement ran down most ridiculous avenues, framed the sentence: "Don't stare, because it's rude," at which involuntary thought I scarcely restrained a nervous titter. After this critical inspection, Radley murmured:

"Yes, talk your quarrel over. The bands of friendship mustn't snap at a breath."

As he said this, Doe edged closer to me, and I wondered if Radley was a decent chap.

"But why do you sign yourself 'S. Ray'?"

Now my blush outclassed anything Doe had yet produced, and I looked in dumb confusion towards my friend. Radley refrained from forcing the question, but pursued with brutal humour:

"Well, there's nothing like suffering together to cement a friendship. Doe, put out your knuckles."

Radley was ever a man of surprises. This was the first time he had invited the use of our knuckles for his punitive practices. Doe proffered four of those on the back of his narrow, cream-coloured right hand. He did it readily enough, but trembled a little, and the blush that had disappeared returned at a rush to his neck. Radley took his ruler, and struck the knuckles with a very sharp rap. Doe's lips snapped together and remained together,—and that was all.

"And Ray," invited Radley.

I offered the back of my right hand, and, copying my friend, kept my lips well closed. My eyes had shut themselves nervously, when I heard a clatter, and realised that Radley had dropped his ruler. Leaving my right hand extended for punishment, I stooped down, picked up the ruler with my left, and gave it back to Radley. Perhaps the blood that now coloured my face was partly due to this stooping. Radley smiled. It was his habit to become suddenly gentle after being hard. One second, his hard mouth would frame hard things; another second, and his grey eyes would redress the balance.

"Ray, you disarm me," he said. "Go to your seats, both of you."

Back we walked abreast to our places, Doe palpably annoyed that he had not been the one to pick up the ruler. He was a romantic youth and would have liked to occupy my picturesque and rather heroic position.

"Why didn't you let me pick up the ruler?" he whispered. "You knew I wanted to."

This utterly senseless remark I had no opportunity of answering, so I determined to sulk with Doe, as soon as the interval should arrive. When, however, the bell rang for that ten-minutes' excitement, I forgot everything in the glee of thinking that the second period would be spent with Herr Reinhardt. Ten minutes to go, and then—and then, Mr. Caesar!

Sec.3

In the long corridor, on to which Radley's class-room opened, gathered our elated form, awaiting the arrival of Herr Reinhardt. He was late. He always was: and it was a mistake to be so, for it gave us the opportunity, when he drew near, of asking one another the time in French: "Kell er eight eel? Onze er ay dammy. Wee, wee."

Caesar Reinhardt, the German, remains upon my mind chiefly as being utterly unlike a German: he was a long man, very deaf, with drooping English moustaches, and such obviously weak eyes that now, whenever Leah's little eye-trouble is read in Genesis, I always think of Reinhardt. But I think of him as "Mr. Caesar." Why "Mr. Caesar" and not purely "Caesar" I cannot explain, but the "Mr." was inseparable from the nickname. Good Mr. Caesar was misplaced in his profession. Had he not been obliged to spend his working life in the position of one who has just been made to look a fool, he would have been an attractive and lovable person. He had the most beautiful tenor voice, which, when he spoke was like liquid silver, and, when he sang elaborate opera passages, made one see glorious wrought-steel gateways of heavenly palaces. This inefficient master owed his position to the great vogue enjoyed by his books: "Reinhardt's German Conversation," "Reinhardt's French Pieces," and others. But the boys, by common consent, decided not to identify this "Caesar Reinhardt, Modern Language Master at Kensingtowe School" with their own dear Mr. Caesar. Thus, you see, in their ignorance, they were able to bring up the Reinhardt works to Mr. Caesar, and say with worried brows: "Here, sir. This bally book's all wrong"; "I could write a better book than this myself, sir"; "The Johnny who wrote this book, sir—well, *st. st.*" Pennybet, however, used to tremble on the brink of identification, when he made the idiotic mistake of saying: "Shall I bring up my Caesar, sir,—I mean, my Reinhardt?"

The jubilation of our class, as we lolled or clog-danced in the corridor, had need to be organised into some systematic fooling; and for once in a way, the boys accepted a suggestion of mine.

"Let's all hum 'God Save the King' exactly at twelve o'clock. Mr. Caesar won't hear; he's too deaf."

Immediately several boys started to sing the popular air in question, and others went for a slide along the corridor, both of which performances are generally construed as meaning: "Right-ho!"

"It's crude," commented Penny, "but I'll not interfere. I might even help you—who knows? And here comes Mr. Caesar. Ah, wee, wee."

It was our custom to race in a body along the corridor to meet Mr. Caesar, and to arrive breathless at his side, where we would fight to walk, one on his right hand, and another on his left. In the course of a brilliant struggle several boys would be prostrated, not unwillingly. We would then escort him in triumph to his door, and all offer to turn the lock, crying: "Let *me* have the key, sir." "Do let *me*, sir." "You never let *me*, sir—dashed unfair." When someone had secured the key, he would fling wide the door, as though to usher in all the kings of Asia, but promptly spoil this courtly action by racing after the door ere it banged against the wall, holding it in an iron grip like a runaway horse, and panting horribly at the strain. This morning I was honoured with the key. I examined it and saw that it was stuffed up with dirt and there would be some delay outside the class-room door while the key underwent alterations and repairs.

"Has any boy," I asked, "a pin?"

None had; but Pennybet offered to go to Bramhall House in search of one. He could do it in twenty minutes, he said.

"Dear me, how annoying!" I shook the key, I hammered it, I blew down it till it gave forth a shrill whistle, and Penny said: "Off side." And then I giggled into the key.

Don't think Mr. Caesar tolerated all this without a mild protest. I distinctly remember his saying in his silvery voice: "Give it to me, Ray. I'll do it," and my replying, as I looked up into his delicate eyes: "No, it's all right, sir. You leave it to me, sir."

In due course I threw open the door with a triumphant "There!" The door hit the side-wall with a bang that upset the nervous systems of neighbouring boys, who felt a little faint, had hysterics, and recovered. Mr. Caesar, feeling that the class was a trifle unpunctual in starting, hurriedly entered.

Then Pennybet distinguished himself. He laid his books unconcernedly on the master's desk, and walked with a dandy's dignity to the window. Having surveyed the view with a critical air, he faced round and addressed Mr. Caesar courteously: "May I shut the window for you, sir?" adding in a lower tone that he was always willing to oblige. Without waiting for the permission to be granted, he turned round again and, pulling up each sleeve that his cuffs might not be soiled in the operation, proceeded to turn the handle, by means of which the lofty window was closed.

Now there were four long windows in a row, and they all needed shutting—this beautiful summer morning. None of us was to be outdone in politeness by Penny; and all rushed to the coveted handles so as to be first in shutting the remaining windows. The element of competition and the steeplechasing methods necessary, if we were to surmount the intervening desks, made it all rather exciting. Several boys, converging from different directions, arrived at the handles at the same time. It was natural, then, that a certain amount of discussion should follow as to whose right it was to shut the windows, and that the various little assemblies debating the point should go and refer the question simultaneously to Mr. Caesar.

Mr. Caesar gave his answer with some emphasis:

"Will—you—all—sit—down?"

This rhetorical question being in the nature of a command, we sullenly complied, tossing our heads to show our sense of the indignity to which we had been submitted. Pennybet, meanwhile, continued to turn his handle in a leisurely fashion and touch his forehead like an organ-grinder.

Mr. Caesar looked at him angrily and pathetically, conscious of his powerlessness.

"Que faites vous, Pennybet? Asseyez vous toute suite!"

"Yes, sir," answered Penny, who had no sympathy with German, French, or any of these ludicrous languages. "Yes, sir, we had two, and one died."

"Que voulez vous dire? Allez a votre place!"

"It's all right, sir, if you cross your fingers," suggested Penny.

Poor Mr. Caesar made a movement, as though he would go and push the mutineer to his place.

"You will go to your seat immediately, Pennybet," he ordered.

Penny cocked his head on one side. "Oh, *sir*," said he reproachfully.

Our friend always expressed his sense of injustice with this sad "Oh, *sir*," and, as he generally detected a vein of injustice in any demand made upon him, the expression was of frequent occurrence.

Mr. Caesar first moved his lips incompetently, and then, with a studied slowness that was meant to sound imperious, began:

"When I say 'Sit'—"

"You mean 'Sit,'" explained Penny promptly.

"That's impertinence."

But Penny had his head thrown back, and was gazing out of eyes, curtained by the fall of heavy-fringed lids, at the ceiling.

"Pennybet," cried his master, his very voice apprehensive, "will you have the goodness to attend?"

"Oh, ah, yes, sir," agreed Penny, awaking from his reverie.

"You haven't the manners of a savage, boy."

"Oh, *sir*."

Mr. Caesar bit his lip, and his silver voice would scarcely come.

"Or of a pig!"

"Would a pig have manners, sir?" corrected Penny.

"That's consummate impudence!"

"Oh, is it, sir?" Penny's tone suggested that he was grateful for the enlightenment. Henceforth he would not be in two minds on the subject.

Mr. Caesar, repulsed again by the more powerful character of the boy, tried to cover the feebleness of his position by sounding as threatening as possible.

"Go to your seat at once! The impudence of this class is insufferable!"

Loud murmurs of dissent from twenty boys greeted this aspersion. The class resolved itself into an Opposition, inspired by one object, which was to repudiate aspersions. Penny excellently voiced their resentment.

"Oh, *sir*." (Opposition cheers.)

Mr. Caesar hurled his chair behind him, and approached very close to Penny.

"Will you go to your seat at once?"

Penny, with all his power, was still a boy; and for a moment the child in him flinched before the exceedingly close approach of Mr. Caesar. But the next minute he looked up at the still open window; shivered, and shuddered; rubbed his cold hands (this beautiful summer morning); buttoned himself up warmly; went to the master's desk for his books; dropped them one after another; blew on his numbed fingers to infuse a little warmth into them, contriving a whistle, and all the time looking most rebukingly at his tyrannical master; picked up four books and dropped two of them; picked up those and dropped one more; walked to his seat in high sorrow, and banged the whole lot of the books down upon the desk and floor in an appalling cataract, as the full cruelty of Mr. Caesar's treatment came suddenly home to him.

When we recovered from this shattering explosion of Penny's books, a little quiet work would have begun, had not Doe, with his romantic imagination lit by the glow of Penny's audacity, started to crave the notoriety of being likewise a leader of men. He rose from his desk, approached Mr. Caesar, and extended his hand with a belated "Good morning, sir."

Poor Mr. Caesar, in the kindliness of his heart, was touched by Doe's graceful action, and grasped the proffered hand, saying: "Good morning, Doe." By this time the whole class was arranged in a tolerably straight line behind Doe, and waiting to go through the ceremony of shaking hands.

Work commenced at about twenty minutes to twelve, and, when twelve should come, we were to render, according to programme, "God Save the King," with some delicate humming. For want of something better to do, I wrote a clause of the exercise set. Mr. Caesar's back was now turned and he was studying a wall-map.

"Shall I?"

"Yes, rather!"

These two whispered sentences I heard from behind me. Inquisitively I turned round to see what simmered there.

"Keep working, you fool!" hissed my neighbour.

Events of some moment were happening in the rear. It had occurred to several that the hands of the clock might be encouraged with a slight push to hasten their journey over the next few minutes. Doe, half anxious to be the daring one to do it, half nervous of the consequences, had whispered: "Shall I?" And his advisers had answered: "Yes, rather!" He threw down a piece of blotting paper, and tip-toed towards it, as though to pick it up. Seeing with a side-glance that Mr. Caesar's back was still turned, he mounted a form, and pushed on the clock's hands. Then, hurriedly getting down, he flew back nervously to his seat, where he pretended to be rapidly writing.

Hearing these slithy and suggestive movements, I declined to remain any longer ignorant of their meaning. After all, I had suggested the "whole bally business," and was entitled to know the means selected for its conduct. So round went my inquisitive head. Then I shook in my glee. Someone had pushed on the hands of the clock, and it was three minutes to twelve. There was a rustle of excitement in the room. The silence of expectancy followed. "Two-minutes-to" narrowed into "One-minute-to"; and after a premonitory click, which produced sufficient excitement to interfere with our breath, the clock struck twelve.

Inasmuch as I occupied a very favourable position, I got up to conduct proceedings. I faced the class, stretched out my right hand, which held a pen by way of a baton, and whispered: "One. Two. *Three*."

It began. I have often wondered since how I could have been so wrong in my calculations. I had estimated that, if we all hummed, there would result a gentle murmur. I never dreamt that each of the twenty boys would respond so splendidly to my appeal. Instead of a gentle murmur, the National Hymn was opened with extraordinary volume and spirit.

My first instinct was the low one of self-preservation. Feeling no desire to play a leading part in this terrible outbreak, I hastily sat down with a view to resuming my studies. Unfortunately I sat down too heavily, and there was the noise of a bump, which served to bring the performance to an effective conclusion. My books clattered to the floor, and Mr. Caesar turned on me with a cry of wrath.

"Ray, what are you doing?"

It was a sudden and awkward question; and, for a second, I was at a loss for words to express to my satisfaction what I was doing. Penny seemed disappointed at my declension into disgrace, and murmured reproachfully: "O Rupert, my little Rupert, *st. st.*" I saw that the game was up. Mr. Caesar had inquired what I was doing; and a survey of what I was doing showed me that, between some antecedent movements and some subsequent effects, my central procedure was a conducting of the class. So, very red but trying to be impudent, I said as much, after first turning round and making an unpleasant face at Penny.

"Conducting, sir," I explained, as though nothing could be more natural at twelve o'clock.

"Conducting!" said Mr. Caesar. "Well, you may be able to conduct the class, but you certainly cannot conduct yourself."

This resembling a joke, the class expressed its appreciation in a prolonged and uproarious laugh. It was a stupendous laugh. It had fine crescendo and diminuendo passages, and only died hard, after a chain of intermittent "Ha-ha's." Then it had a glorious resurrection, but faded at last into the distance, a few stray "Ha-ha's" from Pennybet bringing up the rear.

Mr. Caesar trembled with impotent passion, his weak eyes eloquent with anger and suffering.

"Are you responsible for this outrage, Ray?"

I looked down and muttered: "It was my suggestion, sir."

"Then you shall suffer for it. Who has tampered with the clock?"

There was no answer, and every boy looked at the remainder of the class to show his ignorance of the whole matter. Doe glanced from one to another for instructions. Some by facial movements suggested an avowal of his part, but he whispered: "Not yet," and waited, blushing.

"Then the whole class shall do two hours' extra work."

The words were scarcely out of Mr. Caesar's mouth, before every boy was protesting. I caught above the confusion such complaints as: "Oh, sir!" "But *really*, sir," or a more sullen: "I never touched the beastly clock!" or even a frank: "I won't do it." I observed that Penny was taking advantage of the noise to deliver an emotional sermon, which he accompanied with passionate gestures and concluded by turning eastward and profanely repeating the ascription: "And now to God the Father—"

A sudden silence, and every boy sits awkwardly in his place. Radley's tall figure stood in the room: and the door was being shut by his hand. I kept my eyes fixed on him. I was changed. I no longer felt disorderly nor impudent: for disorderliness and impudence in me were but unnatural efforts to copy Pennybet, that master-fool. I dropped into my natural self, a thing of shyness and diffidence. I was not conscious of any ill-will towards Radley for returning to his class-room, when he was not expected; it was just a piece of bad fortune for me. I was about to be "whacked," I knew; and, though I did not move, I felt strange emotions within me. Certainly I was a little afraid, for Radley whacked harder than they all.

And then, as usual, my brain ran down a wildly irrelevant course. I reflected that the height of my ambition would be reached, if I could grow into as tall a man as Radley. My frame, at present, gave no promise of developing into that of a very tall man; but henceforth I would do regular physical exercises of a stretching character, and eschew all evils that retarded the growth. In the enthusiasm of a new aim, towards which I would start this very day, I almost forgot my present embarrassing position. Hasty calculations followed as to how much I would have to grow each year. Let me see, how old was I? Just thirteen. How many years to grow in?

"Who is the ringleader of this?" asked Radley..

I stood up and whispered: "Me, sir."

Somehow a ready acknowledgment seemed to agree with my latest ambition.

"Then come and stand out here. You know you ought to be caned, so you'll thoroughly enjoy it. In fact, being a decent boy, you'd be miserable without it."

Here Mr. Caesar, who bore no grudge against Radley for assuming the reins of command, whispered to him; and Radley asked the class:

"Who touched the clock?"

"I did, sir."

It was Doe's voice.

"Why didn't you say so before?"

"I was just going to when you came in."

Radley looked straight into the brown eyes of the boy who was supposed to be his favourite, and Doe looked back unshiftingly; he had heard those condemned, who did not look people straight in the face, and I fancy he rather exaggerated his steady return gaze.

"I'm sure you were," said Radley.

Then the foreman of the other boys got up.

"Some of us suggested it to Doe, sir."

"Very well, you will have the punishment of seeing him suffer for it."

And thereupon, without waiting to be told, Doe left his desk, and came and stood by me. It was a theatrical action, such as only he would have done, and our master concealed his surprise, if he felt any, by an impassive face.

"I shall now cane these two boys," he said with cold-blooded directness.

"Certainly," whispered Penny.

Both corners of my mouth went down in a grim resignation. Doe's lips pressed themselves firmly together, and his eyelids trembled. Mr. Caesar, ever generous, looked through the window over green lawns and flower-beds. Radley went to his cupboard, and took out a cane.

"Bend over, Ray."

"Certainly," muttered Penny again. "Bend over."

I bent over, resting my hands on my knees. Radley was a cricketer with a big reputation for cutting and driving; and three drives, right in the middle of the cane, convinced me what a first-class hitter he was. At the fourth, an especially resounding one, Penny whistled a soft and prolonged whistle of amazement, and murmured: "Well, *that's* a boundary, anyway." And I heard suppressed giggles, and knew that my class-fellows were enjoying the exquisite agony of forcing back their laughter.

When my performance was over, the second victim, Edgar Doe, with the steel calm of a French aristocrat, which he affected under punishment, walked to the spot where I had been operated on. He bent over (again without being told to do so), and only spoiled his proud submission by telegraphing to Radley one uncontrolled look of pathetic appeal like the glance of a faithful dog. Radley, not noticing these unnerving actions, or possibly a little annoyed by them, administered justice severely enough for Doe, proud as he was, to wince slightly at every cut. Then he put his cane away, and issued, as before, his little ration of gentleness.

"You're two plucky boys," he said.

Sec.4

That night I measured my barefoot height against the dormitory wall, and made a deep pencil-mark thereon: which done, I reached up to a great height, and made a mark to represent Radley. After these preliminaries there was nothing to do but to wait developments. One practice which aided growth was to lie full-length in bed instead of curled up. So, after I had cut with nail-scissors the few fair hairs from my breast and calves, in an endeavour to encourage a plentiful crop like that which added manliness to Pennybet's darker form—after this delicate, operation, I got between the sheets, and straightened out my limbs with a considerable effort of the will. Later on I forced them down again, when I found that my knees had once more strayed up to my chin.

Our dormitory at Bramhall House was a long many-windowed room, containing thirty beds, Edgar Doe's being on my left. He suddenly made reference to our punishment of the morning.

"I wonder why he gave me a worse dose than you."

"Yes, he did let into you," I said cheerfully.

Doe flushed, and continued talking so as to be heard only by me.

"If it had been any other master, I'd have been mad with him. Fancy, practically two whackings in a morning; one on the knuckles and one on the—and the other. But you can't hate Radley, can you?"

"Oh, I don't know," I said, with grave doubts.

There was a pause. But a desire to tell confidences had been begotten of warm bed and darkness, and my friend soon proceeded:

"It's funny, Rupert, but I like talking to you better than to any of the other chaps. I feel I can tell you things I wouldn't tell anybody else. Do you know, I really think I like Radley better than anyone else in the world. I simply loved being whacked by him."

I pulled the clothes off my head that I might see the extraordinary creature that was talking to me. A dim light always burned near our beds, and by it I was able to see that Doe was very red and clearly wishing he had not made his last remark. My immediate desire, on witnessing his discomfiture, was to put him at his ease by pretending that I saw nothing unusual in the words. So I quickly evolved a very casual question.

"What! Better than your father and mother?"

"Well, you see—" and he shifted uneasily—"you know perfectly well that my father and mother are dead."

"O law!" I said.

Awkwardly the conversation dropped. And, as I lay upon my pillow, down went my brain along a line of wandering thoughts. Doe's remark, I reflected, was like that of a school-girl who adored her mistress. Perhaps Doe was a girl. After all, I had no certain knowledge that he wasn't a girl with his hair cut short. I pictured him, then, with his hair, paler than straw, reaching down beneath his shoulders, and with his brown eyes and parted lips wearing a feminine appearance. As I produced this strange figure, I began to feel, somewhere in the region of my waist, motions of calf-love for the girl Doe that I had created. But, as Doe's prowess at cricket asserted itself upon my mind, his gender became conclusively established, and—ah, well, I was half asleep.

But, so strange were the processes of my childish mind that this feeling of love at first sight for the girl Doe, who never existed, I count as one of the strongest forces that helped to create my later affection for the real Edgar Gray Doe.

"I think you and I must have been intended to come together, Rupert," I heard him saying later on, as I was fast dozing off. "I s'pose that's why we were called Doe and Ray."

"Er," I dreamily assented from beneath the bedclothes.

And still later a voice said:

"It was rather fun being whacked side by side, being twins."

From a great distance I heard it, as I listened upon the frontier of sleep. And, recalling without any effort Radley's words: "There's nothing like suffering together to cement a friendship," I crossed the frontier. All coiled up again, my knees nearly touching my chin, I passed into the country of dreams.

CHAPTER II
RUPERT OPENS A GREAT WAR

Sec.1

P oor Mr. Caesar, with the weak eyes! He had left his class-room door un-locked. *Golly*, so he had! And since the bell had only just ceased to echo, and Mr. Caesar would certainly be some minutes late, what was to stop us from conducting a few operations within the class-room? Under the command of Pennybet, we entered the room and with due respect lifted the master's large writing-desk from its little platform, and carried it to the further end of the room. We left him his armchair, decently disposed upon the platform, thinking it would be ungenerous to keep him standing through an hour's lesson.

Then we guiltily stole out of the class-room, closed the door, and lined up in the corridor, as smartly as a squad of regulars. Aided by Penny's hand, we right-dressed. We kept our eyes front, heads erect, and heels together. We braced ourselves up still better when Mr. Caesar appeared at the end of the corridor. None of us spoke nor moved. A few fools like myself giggled nasally, and were promptly subdued: "Don't spoil it all, you stinking fish!"

On came the gallant Mr. Caesar, his eyes mutely inquiring the reason for this ominous quiet. He reached the door with no sign from any of us that we were aware of a new arrival. He tried the lock with his key and, after an expression of surprise to find it already turned, opened the door and walked in. Immediately, in accordance with a pre-arranged code of signals, Penny dropped *one* book. We right-turned. We did it in faultless time, turning as one man, and each of us bringing his left foot with a brisk stamp on the floor. Then, a suitable silence having ensued, Penny dropped two books. Instantly we obeyed. In single file, our left feet stamping rhythmically, with heads erect and eyes front, we marched after Mr. Caesar, and gradually diverged from one another till each man stood marking time at his particular desk. At this point Penny tripped over his left heel, and in an unfortunate accident flung all his books on to the floor. Abruptly, and like machines, we sat down. The room shook.

It was difficult for our master to know what to do; as there was no real reason to associate our military movements with Penny's series of little accidents, and there was certainly no fault to find with our orderly entry into the class-room. So he did nothing beyond sadly sweeping us with his eyes. And then he inquired:

"Where's my desk?"

Goodness gracious, where could his great desk be? We got out of our seats, foreseeing a long search. We began by opening our own desks and looking inside. Certain high lockers that stood against the wall we opened. It was in none of them. We pulled ourselves up and looked along the top of these lockers. It was not there. Penny did three or four of these "pull-ups" by way of extending his biceps. We looked along the walls and under the forms. Penny created a little excitement by declaring that "he thought he saw it then." And Doe opened the door and looked up and down the corridor.

"It's not anywhere in the corridor," said he. The whole class felt he might be mistaken, and went to the door to satisfy themselves.

Mr. Caesar affected a little sarcasm.

"Is not that it at the other end of the room?"

We turned round and gazed down the direction in which he was looking. Yes, there was surely something there. Penny flung up his hand and cried:

"Please, teacher, I've found it."

"Well," began Mr. Caesar, "if one or two of you would bring the desk up here—"

If one or two of us would! Why, we all would—all twenty of us. We took off our coats and, folding them carefully, laid them on the desks. We rolled up our shirt-sleeves above the elbows, disclosing a lot of white, childish forearms. We spat on our hands and rubbed them together. We did a little spitting on one another's hands. Then we hustled and crowded round the desk. We lifted it off the ground, brought it a foot or two, and dropped it heavily. Phew! it was hard work. We took out our handkerchiefs, and wiped the sweat from our brows. Anyone who had no handkerchief borrowed from someone who had finished with his. Returning to our task, we carried the desk a little nearer and dropped it. Doe got a serious splinter in his hand, and we all pulled it out for him. Puffing and groaning as we dragged the unwieldy desk, we approached the dais on which it must be placed. We all stepped upon the dais (slightly incommoding Mr. Caesar, who was standing there), and lifted up one end of the desk so that the pens and pencils rattled inside. One pull, my lads, and the desk was half on the platform and half on the floor. Leaving it in this inclined position, we stepped down to the floor again, and three of us placed our shoulders against the lower end, while the rest scrummed down, Rugby fashion, in row upon row behind one another. A good co-operative shove, accompanied by murmurs of "Coming on your right, forwards; heel it out, whites; break away, forwards!" and up she went, a diagonal route into the air. Unfortunately, we all raised our heads at the same time to see how much further she had to go, and back she tobogganed again on to the shins of the boys in the front row. They declared they were henceforth incapacitated for life.

We got it on to the platform at last with a good run, but the enthusiasm of the back row of scrummers, who apparently thought the task could not be completed till they were off the floor and on the platform, was so strong that the desk was pushed much too far, and toppled over the further side of the platform.

This was too much. My suppressed giggling burst like a grenade into uncontrolled laughter. Then I said: "I'm sorry, sir."

Sec.2

But this disorder is a strong dish, and we've talked about quite as much as is good for us. So let us change the hour and visit another class-room, where there are no rebellions, but nevertheless arithmetic and trouble—and Ray and Doe and Pennybet. And here is a dear little master in charge. It is Mr. Fillet, the housemaster of Bramhall House, where, as you know, we were paying guests—a fat little man with a bald pate, a soft red face, a pretty little chestnut beard, and an ugly little stutter in his speech. Bless him, the dear little man, we called him Carpet Slippers. This was because one of his two chief attributes was to be always in carpet slippers. The other attribute was to be always round a corner.

Fillet, or Carpet Slippers, disliked his young boarder, Rupert Ray. The reason is soon told. One night, when I was out of my bed and gambolling in pyjamas about the first story of his house, I looked up the well of the staircase and saw the little shadow of someone parading the landing above. Thinking it to be a boy, I called out in a stage-whisper: "Is that old pig, Carpet Slippers, up there?" And a dear little chestnut beard and a smile came over the balusters, accompanied by a voice: "Yes, h-h-here he is. Wh-what do you want with him?"

It was Fillet, in carpet slippers, and round a corner.

And then in his class-room, this day, I got a sum wrong. I deduced that in a certain battle "point 64" of a soldier remained wounded on the field, while "point 36" escaped with the retreating army unhurt. This did not seem a satisfactory conclusion either to the sum or to the soldier, and I was not surprised, on looking up the answer, to find that I was wrong. There were two methods of detecting the error: one was to work through the sum again, the other was to submit it to Fillet for revision. The latter seemed the less irksome scheme, and in a sinister moment—heavens! how pregnant with consequences it was—I left my desk, approached Carpet Slippers, and laid the trouble before him.

Now Fillet was in the worst of tempers, having been just incensed by a boy who had declared that two gills equalled one pint, two pints one quart, and two quarts one rod, pole, or perch. So, when I brought my sum up and giggled at the answer, he looked at me as if he neither liked me nor desired that I should ever like him. Then he indulged in cheap sarcasms. This he was wont to do, and, after emitting them through his silky beard, he would draw in his breath through parted teeth, as a child does when it has the taste of peppermint in its mouth.

"I-I-I t-tell you, a boy in a kindergarten could get it right—a g-g-guttersnipe could. I-I-I-I—"

This was so much like what they yell from a fire-engine that, though I struggled hard, I could not contain a giggle.

"I-I-I'll do it for you."

He got it wrong, which elicited a bursting giggle from me. Fillet turned on me like a barking dog.

"Go to your place, boy, and take your vulgar guffaws with you!"

Surprised at Fillet's taking it to heart in this way, I went, much abashed, to my seat, and tried to control my fit of giggling. But it so possessed me that finally it made a very horrible noise in my nose. Carpet Slippers raised his little head that was a hybrid between a peach and a billiard ball—a peach as to the face, and a billiard ball as to the cranium—and when he saw me sitting with lips tightly set and my desk trembling with my internal laughter, anger put a fresh coating of red upon both peach and ball. But he took no action at present.

"I-I'll d-do one of these sums on the board for you."

Getting up, he turned his back on us and, facing the board, wrote with his chalk the number 10. Now, as he wrote on a level with his eyes, his fat little head quite eclipsed his writing. So, simply to show that I was no longer laughing, I called out loudly:

"What number, sir?"

Round swung Carpet Slippers, his peach-face assuming the tint of a tomato.

"What number? I-I'll t-teach you to ask 'what number' when I've written '10' on the board. I-I've heard what you do in other class-rooms. D-don't think you're going to introduce your hooliganism here. Go and ask the p-porter to let me have a cane."

The boys pricked up their ears and looked at me. Penny let his jaw drop in amazement and, leaving his mouth open, maintained an expression like that of the village idiot. I stared, flabbergasted, into Carpet Slippers' face.

"But, sir—" I ventured. Tears and temper began to rise in me.

"D-don't argue. Do what you're told."

"But, sir—" And then, like a cloud, sullen obstinacy came down upon me. I was certain that he had been longing for an excuse to flog me. The pride and the relish of the martyr supported me as, without telling him that his head had obstructed my view, I walked out to do my message.

Finding the porter in his office, I politely inquired if he could spare a cane for Mr. Fillet; and, at my query, he grinned—the blithering idiot. The cane that he handed me I took, and, being at that moment a youngster who wouldn't have let his spirits sink for all the Fillets in the world, I offered back the cane and suggested:

"I say, are you sure you couldn't lose this?"

"Quite sure, sir."

"Well, look here, do you really think you can manage to part with it?"

"Quite sure, sir."

"Well, don't you think that, for a man of your age, you look rather a fool standing up there and saying 'Quite sure' to everything that's said to you? Don't you think it's rather a fat and silly thing to do?"

I put it to him as man to man.

"Quite sure, sir," he replied with a laugh.

"Go to blazes," I said, "and take your vulgar guffaws with you."

On my way back I stayed to admire the classical busts and statues that lined the deserted corridors like exhibits in a museum. All the life-size ones I whacked with my cane. I took a wistful pleasure in giving the naked ones two good strokes each. As I drew near the class-room door I certainly felt uncomfortable, for I knew Fillet intended to sting. But my sense of martyrdom carried me through. I gathered my dignity about me and knocked heavily on the door. Annoyed that my hand had trembled and spoilt the effect, I opened the door briskly and shut it briskly. With a calm step and fearless look, both studied, for I copied Doe in these matters, I walked towards Carpet Slippers. The little man was pretending he had forgotten all about me, while really he had prepared a sarcasm with which to poison my wounds.

"Oh, indeed. You've b-been a long time gone; but thrashings are like good wine—they improve with keeping."

He sucked in his breath with satisfaction.

"Yes, sir," replied I. If there was any trembling about me it was inside and not visible.

He took the cane from my hand and examined its effectiveness. Then, intending a pretty little jest, he faced the class and commanded:

"St-stand out, that boy who asked the number of the sum after I had put it on the board."

"Swine!" hissed somebody. I fancy it was Edgar Doe.

"I'm here, sir," replied I from his side, white.

Pennybet, who all this time had kept his mouth agape and impersonated the village idiot, laid down his pen, closed his book, and disposed himself to watch out the matter. He was always callous when in pursuit of his object; and his object now was to suck the humour out of my painful position. He put his elbow on the desk, rested his head at a graceful angle on the palm of his hand, and half closed his Arab eyes. He looked like an earnest parson posing for a photograph.

Our engaging little master, having bent me over and arranged me for punishment, gave me ten strokes instead of the usual six—the number of the sum had been "ten."

When I rose from my bended posture, how I hated Carpet Slippers, and was happy in my hate! I hated the silkiness of his chestnut beard; I hated the sheen of his pink cranium; I hated his soft rotundity and his little curvilinear features; I hated, above all, his poisonous speeches. As I walked to my seat, my body stinging still, I resolved to go to war with Fillet. I declared with all a child's power of make-believe that a state of war existed between Rupert Ray and Carpet Slippers. War, then, war, open or understood!

And when that class closed, no boy was more forcedly loud and lively than I: no boy shut his books with greater claps; no boy banged his desk more carelessly. Nor would I listen to sympathising friends, but laughed out in Fillet's hearing: "You don't think I care, do you?"

Fillet noticed my ostentatious display of indifference and perhaps felt apprehensive of the latent devil that he had aroused, but his inward comment, I doubt not, was: "We'll see who's going to be master here. He can feel the weight of my hand again, if he likes. We can't let a bad-spirited little boy have all his own way. I think we'll break his defiance. I think we will." And possibly, as he said it, he sucked in his breath with satisfaction. Fillet realised that it was War and the first shots had been exchanged.

Sec.3

This was the preliminary skirmish. Real and bloody battle was joined twenty-four hours later. But, in the meantime, there was an early-evening lull which enclosed a delightful cricket match. A team of junior Kensingtonians, that included Doe and myself, was going across Kensingtowe High Road to play the First Eleven of the Preparatory School, an academy flippantly known as the "Nursery," its boys being "Suckers." Edgar Doe had been a certain choice. Brought up in the midst of a great cricketing family, the Grays of Surrey tradition, in his beautiful Falmouth home which boasted cricket pitches of its own, he was as polished a bat as the Nursery had ever known. I came to be selected as a promising change-bowler.

We were walking in our flannels towards the Nursery gates, when Doe, referring with bad taste to the Fillet incident just closed, began to chastise me with his cricket bat. I returned the treatment with a pair of pads. So we went along, full in the public view, each trying to "get in a good one" on the other. I managed to knock Doe's bat out of his hand, and, as he stooped to pick it up, he received my pads upon his person. This was actually in the middle of the High Street. He laughed loudly, and crying "O you young beast!" started to belabour me with his fists. Suddenly we stopped, let our hands fall to our sides, and began to walk like nuns in a cloister. Radley had joined us.

"If you're so anxious to whack each other," said he pleasantly, "won't you commission me to do it in both cases?"

We grinned sheepishly and said nothing. My mind formulated the sentence "Good Lord, no!" and, quickly constructing what would have happened had I uttered it aloud, I tittered uncomfortably and looked away. There was an awkward pause as we walked along with our master between us.

"Well, Ray," he said, endeavouring to put us at our ease, "are you a great batsman?"

"No, sir," replied I. "Doe is."

"So I've heard. I'm coming to see what he's made of."

Doe could find nothing to say in reply, but lifted up his face and looked at Radley with the gratitude of a dog. For my part I felt a pleasing, squirmy excitement to think that we were to walk on to the Nursery field in the company of the great Middlesex amateur; and, incidentally, I took the opportunity of measuring myself against him.

We arrived on the ground, creating less sensation than I would have liked. Radley took a deck-chair in front of the pavilion next to Dr. Chapman, or "Chappy," surely the stoutest and jolliest of school doctors. The fact that Chappy, occupying so withdrawn a position as medical officer to the two schools, should have been such a memorable figure in the life of the boys testifies to the largeness of his personality. And, not being the most modest of stout and hearty doctors, he was always willing himself to testify to the largeness of his personality. He dearly loved cricket, he would tell you, for he had been a cricketer himself and seen many worse; and he dearly loved boys, for he had been a boy himself and never seen any worse: so, where there was a boys' cricket match, there, old man, you would find Dr. Chapman. Besides, when boys played cricket, it was well to have a doctor on the field, and he was a doctor and had never met a better. Would you have a cigar? All tobacco, in his opinion, led to the overthrow of body and soul—believe him; it did—but you would never see him without a cigar. Not he!

Such was Chappy, the medicine man. He was right, about the cigar. As I figure him in my mind, the things that I immediately associate with his stout, jolly presence are a chewed cigar drooping from his mouth and a huge white waistcoat soiled by the tumbled ash. I sum him up as a genial soul whose religion was to seek comfort, to find popularity a comfortable thing, and to love popularity among young things as the most comfortable of all. And, if that last dogma of his be not Heaven's truth, then my outlook on life is all wrong, and this book's a failure!

As Radley placed his muscular frame in the deck-chair, Chappy greeted him with these regrettable remarks: "Hallo, Radley, aren't you dead yet? How the devil are you? My word, how you've grown!"

The match started, Doe and our captain opening the Kensingtowe innings. I left the other boys and lay down upon the grass a little behind Radley's chair. Converging reasons led me there: one—I desired that my old friends, the Suckers, should know of my intimacy with S.T. Radley, of Middlesex; two—I felt Chappy's conversation would certainly be entertaining; and three—I should soon have to go in to bat, and was feeling too nervous to talk to offensively happy boys who were unworried by such imminent publicity.

"So they've sent us a cricketer in young Doe," Radley was saying to Dr. Chapman.

Chappy turned in his chair, which creaked alarmingly, and composed himself to talk comfortably.

"Oh, the Gray Doe—yes, charming little squirt—best bat the Nursery had last year. And, though nobody but myself recognised it, the Gem was the best bowler."

"The Gem?" queried Radley. "Who was the 'Gem'?"

"Don't you know the Gem? Why, Ray, the little snipe with eyes something between a diamond and a turquoise. The ladies here called him 'The Gem' because of this affliction. He'd be a great bowler, only he's too shy."

At this point I rolled on to my stomach so as to appear unaware of their conversation, which was even more entertaining than I had hoped. Radley turned round and, having seen me, said something in an undertone to Chappy. I imagine he drew attention to my proximity, for Chappy laughed out: "O law! Glory be!" and continued in a lower voice.

My sense of honour was not so nice that it prevented me from trying to catch the rest of their conversation. They had opened so promisingly: and now Chappy was getting quite enthusiastic, and the rapid motion of his lips was causing the cigar to be so restless that it constantly changed its position and scattered ash down his expanse of white waistcoat. I had no need, however, to strain my ears, for Chappy was incapable of speaking softly for any length of time. I caught him proceeding:

"He's clever, his masters say, and got a big future. Handsome little rogue, too. He's none of your ordinary boys. He's a twig from the cedar-top."

For two reasons—first, that this was a fine rhetorical flourish on which to close; and secondly, that his breath was giving out—Chappy concluded his remarks, swept his waistcoat, and re-arranged his position in the deck-chair. I was feeling horribly anxious lest I should die without knowing whether it was of Doe or of me that he had spoken, when Radley cleared up the matter by saying:

"He's playing a straight bat, isn't he?"

So it was Doe. Well, he was clever, I supposed, but not as clever as all that.

"Straight bat, rather!" agreed Chappy.

"Does he play a straight bat in all things?"

"My dear fellow, what the la-diddly-um do you mean?"

"Why, he seems to be a bit of an actor—to do things because he wants to appear in a favourable light."

"I say, that's doocid ungenerous of you," said Chappy. "And, by jove, if he likes to imagine himself very noble and heroic, and tries to act accordingly, very fine of him."

"Very," endorsed Radley, cryptically.

"I've a great liking for him."

"So have I."

"Good. Now, what first attracted you—his good looks or his virtues?"

"Neither. His vices."

"Here, hang me, Radley," said Chappy, "you want examining. You're not only a shocking bad conversationalist, but also a little mad. That's your doctor's opinion; that'll be a guinea, please."

After this I ceased to listen. The talk was all about Doe, and rather silly. And I wanted to think over the little fact, which Chappy had let fall, that certain ladies called me the "Gem." I chewed a blade of grass and ruminated. That flattering little disclosure balanced the weight of Fillet's dislike. I wished it could be brought to his knowledge; and I imagined conversations in which he was told. This was the first time that it dawned upon me that there was anything in my looks to admire. Pennybet I conceived to be dark and handsome, Doe fair and pretty, and myself drab and plain. But now I got up and took myself, completely thrilled, to a mirror in the changing room to have a look at these same eyes. I was prepared for something good. The result was that I became almost sick with disappointment. A close examination showed them to be quite commonplace. I could not really detect that they were blue. I even thought they looked a little foolish. And, as I gazed at them, they certainly turned very sad.

I strolled back to the pavilion just as a burst of applause announced a fine drive by Doe.

"Oh, pretty stroke!" shouted Chappy, sprinkling quantities of ash. "Pretty play! By jove, the little fool's a genius!"

"He may be a genius of some other sort," said Radley, "but he's not a genius at cricket. Look at his diffidence in the treatment of swift balls. He's a cricketer *made*, not born. He has imagination and a sense of artistic effect, and a natural grace—that's all. They'll make him a poet, perhaps, but not a cricketer."

"Don't talk such flapdoodle!" grumbled Chappy. "Look at that!"

All that Doe did then was to direct the ball with perfect ease between Point and Short Slip and to glance quickly towards the pavilion to see if the stroke had been noticed. The sight of him batting there made me feel another squirmy sensation at the thought that he was my especial friend. He had given, I recall, his grey hat to the umpire to hold, and the wind was playing with his hair. His shirt-sleeves were rolled up, showing arms smooth and round like a woman's.

Just then, however, my attention was attracted by a new arrival. The boy

Freedham, having listlessly wandered across from Kensingtowe, slouched on to the Nursery playground. He was a tall, weedy youth of sixteen; and the unhealthiness of his growth was shown by the long, graceless neck, the spare chest, and the thin wrists. There was a weakness, too, at his knees which caused me to think that they had once worked on springs which now were broken. But the greatest abnormality was seen in his eyes. Startlingly large, startlingly bright, they were sometimes beautiful and always uncanny.

This Freedham, with his slack gait and carriage, strolled towards a railing and, resting both elbows on it, watched Doe at his cricket. The whole picture is very clear on my mind. A sunny afternoon seemed to have forgotten the time and only just made up its mind to merge into a mellow evening: the boys, watching the game, were sending their young and lively sounds upon the air; those of the smaller cattle, whose interest had waned, were engaging with the worst taste in noisy French cricket: the flannelled figures of the players, with their wide little chests, neat waists, and round hips, promised fine things for the manhood of England ten years on: at the wicket stood the attractive figure of Edgar Doe in an occupation very congenial to him—that of shining: and Chappy had just said: "I say, Radley, don't you think this generation of boys is the most shapely lot England has turned out? I wonder what use she'll make of them," when he saw Freedham's entry and opened a new conversation.

"That's old Freedham's boy over there, isn't it?" he asked. "Shocking specimen."

"Yes, he's a day-boy. You know his father, the doctor?"

"Doctor be damned!" answered Chappy. "He's no more a doctor than a Quaker's a Christian. Old Freedham's surgery is a bally schism-shop. He's one of those homoeopathic Johnnies, and would be blackballed on societies of which I'm a vice-president. You know—just as I can never go into dissenting chapels without feeling certain of the presence of evil spirits—my wife says it's the stuffiness of the atmosphere, but I say: 'No, my dear, it's evil spirits; I know what's evil spirits and what's bad air'—well, just so I could never go into old Freedham's—but I'm not likely to be asked. Doctor—bah!"

And Chappy flung away the moist and masticated end of his cigar and all such nonsensical ideas with it. Then he took a new cigar from his case, proceeding:

"And the man's not only a nonconformist in the Medicine Creed, but he's actually a deacon in a Presbyterian chapel—or something equally heathen—and a fluent one at that, I expect. I make a point of never trusting those people. Look at his sickening son and heir yonder. Did you ever see an orthodox doctor produce a cockchafer like that? That's homoeopathy, that is—"

And Chappy flourished his new cigar towards Freedham.

Doe, too, had seen Freedham's entry, and some sign of recognition passed between them. The next ball came swiftly and threateningly down upon the leg side, and Doe, perhaps with the nervousness consequent upon the arrival of a new critic before whom he would fain do well, stepped back. A shout went up as it was seen that the ball had taken the leg bail. Doe looked flurried at this sudden dismissal and a bit upset. He involuntarily shot a glance at Freedham and after some hesitation left the crease. He rather dragged his bat and drooped his head as he walked to the pavilion, till, realising that this might be construed into an ungracious acceptance of defeat, he brought his head erect and swung his bat with a careless freedom.

"Heavens!" murmured Radley. "Isn't he self-conscious?"

Chappy didn't hear. He was taken up in applauding the stylish innings of the retiring batsman, and swearing he would stand the boy a liquor.

"Bravo, Doe!" he shouted. "Don't think you can play cricket, 'cos you can't. So there!"

Doe entered blushing and stood nervously by an empty chair near Radley, who read his meaning and said: "Sit there, if you like."

My friend put the chair very close to his hero and, having sat in it, began to remove his pads. I think Radley was pleased with this action and liked having the worshipping youth beside him. The fall of Doe's wicket had brought my innings nearer and started a fresh attack of stage-fright. In my agitation movement seemed imperative. So I came and reclined on the ground by Edgar, intruding myself on his notice by asking:

"That beastly tapeworm Freedham spoilt your game, didn't he?"

Edgar heard my question, and his lips fumbled with a reply. The face that he turned upon me was a deep plum-pink from recent running and surmounted with fair hair whose disordered ends were darkened with moisture.

"No," he said; "at least, I don't know him. But what's it to do with you?"

This remark was sufficiently discouraging to impel me on to my feet and to send me to districts where I should be less unpopular. I conceived the idea of examining Freedham at nearer range. Perhaps I was jealous of him. Though as yet I had no unordinary love for Doe, I had a sense of proprietorship in him which was quickened the minute it was disturbed. So I moored myself on the railing about three yards from Freedham. This could easily be managed, Freedham being one of those boys who were always alone. For a little I pretended to watch the game and then stole a furtive, sideways glance at his lank profile. I had immediate cause to wish I had done nothing of the sort, for he turned his unholy eyes on mine and so disconcerted me that I swung my face back upon the cricket field and affected complete indifference. I even hummed a little ditty to show that if any mind was free from the designs of the private detective, mine was. But my acting was not made easier by the certainty that Freedham's eyes were steadily examining my burning cheek. And, if it be possible to see a question in eyes which you are only imagining, I saw in Freedham's: "What the blazes do you want?" After giving him time to forget me, I turned again to look at him. But once more I caught his weird orbs full upon mine, and muttering. "Oh, dash!" concentrated my attention on the cricket.

A few minutes later the heavy wooden rail on which I was leaning began to vibrate horribly. I looked in alarm at Freedham. He was standing rigid, as though sudden death had stiffened him upright. His left hand was grasping the railing, and through this channel an electric trembling of his whole frame had communicated itself to the wood. His face was unnaturally red, and his right hand had passed over his heart which it was pressing. His eyes were fixed on the cricket match.

My first sensation, I confess, was one of pride at being the boy to discover Freedham in what appeared to be a fit. I went quickly to him and said: "I say, Freedham. Freedham, what's the matter?"

"N-nothing," he replied, still stiff and trembling. "But it's all—right. I shall be quite—fit again in a minute. Don't look at me."

"But shall I get you water or something?"

"No. It's all right. I've had these attacks before. In class sometimes and—I've conquered them, and—no one's known anything about them. So don't tell anyone about this. Promise."

It cost me something to throw away the prospect of telling this thrilling story of which I had exclusive information, but the man in pain is master of us all, so I readily promised.

"All right, Freedham. That's all right."

Though some years his junior, I said it much as a mother would soothe a frightened child to sleep.

"Thanks awfully," said Freedham gratefully.

"Oh, by the by, there's old Dr. Chapman over there. Should I fetch him?"

"No, damn you!" cried my patient with extraordinary conviction. "Can't you mind your own infernal business and leave me to mind mine?"

This was so rude that I felt quite justified in leaving him to mind his own infernal business, whatever it might be. I strolled away.

Now, with this interesting performance of Freedham's, my desire to describe this cricket match ends. There was a hot finish, but, in spite of some fortunate overs from myself, the Suckers won. The last wicket down, Chappy got out of his deck-chair with a sudden quickness which suggested that such was the only method of successfully getting his fat self upon his feet; and, when he had shaken down his white waistcoat and said: "Bye-bye, Radley. Reg'lar meals, no smoke, and you may grow into a fine lad yet," carried himself off with the awkward leg-work of a heavy-bodied man, cheerily acknowledging the greetings of the little Sucker boys, and prodding the fattest of them in the ribs. Radley strolled away, followed by the wondering looks of boys who were told that this big man was S.T. Radley, of Middlesex. Freedham, quite recovered, returned to his day-boy roof among the endless roofs of Kensingtowe Town. And I plied homeward to Bramhall House, depressed by the prospect of Preparation for the rest of the evening, and by the restored consciousness of Fillet's hostility, which, forgotten during the cricket match, now came back upon me like a sense of foreboding.

CHAPTER III
AWFUL ROUT OF RAY

Sec.1

The following afternoon I was looking rather glumly out of a window at the broad playing fields which, in the greyness of a rainy day, seemed as deserted as myself. From my place I could see nearly all the red-brick wall that surrounds Kensingtowe grounds; I could see the iron railings which, at long intervals, break the monotony of the wall. Now the railings of Kensingtowe, like all places with sad memories, have an honourable place in my heart.

Naturally it was a rule, strictly enforced, that boys must make their exit from the fields by going through the Bramhall gate rather than over the railings. Naturally, too, this rule was sometimes disregarded, for the architect, whom I deem a desirable soul, had made the passage over the railings invitingly possible by means of some well-placed cross-pieces, which he sketched into his designs, saying (I imagine): "We shall have the lads climbing over at this point—well, God bless 'em—I hope they're not caught and whopped for it." Right at the farthest corner of the field was the Bramhall gate, which—But the Bramhall gate needn't interest us: *we* leave by the railings.

The noise of a footstep disturbing the gravel caused me to look down. A boy, hatless, ran across to the wall and walked guiltily beneath it till he reached the railings. The fairness of his hair arrested my attention. And, while I was wondering what any boy might be doing hatless in the rain, my friend Doe had grasped the railings, pulled himself to their top, and dropped on to the pavement beyond.

Now, my dear Watson, here was a case of exceptional interest. In all the annals of criminal investigation I know of none that presented possibilities more bizarre, none that called more urgently for the subtlest qualities of the private detective. I rushed out of the building, letting doors slam behind me. Quickly I reached the railings, raised myself to the top, and glanced down the road in time to see Doe join the lank and sinister figure of Freedham at the corner.

But alas! just over the road was Bramhall House, Fillet's own kingdom, and even at that moment I saw a bald head emerge from its central doorway. A feeling that was partly terror and partly temper manacled me to the top of the railings; and after a few tense seconds I was gazing fascinated into a little bearded face which was staring with interest up at me. It was Carpet Slippers, and he may be said to have been round a corner.

"Oh, dash!" I muttered. And then, as I stared down at him, thinking it right that he, by virtue of his seniority, should open the conversation, I gradually began to feel better, for I remembered that it was War.

"Hallo, Ray," said Fillet, "what may you be d-d-doing up there?"

"Climbing over, sir." (Indeed, what more obvious?)

"Oh, you-you are climbing over, are you?"

"Yes, sir."

"Oh, indeed."

When I saw that he was trifling with me, I determined that he should know it was War. Defiantly I answered:

"Yes, sir. Climbing over. YES, SIR. *YES, SIR*."

Fillet went white, but he only sucked in his breath and said:

"Oh, indeed. And d-d-do you contemplate coming down?"

I borrowed a favourite word of Penny's. "Ultimately, sir."

"Ah! you do, do you? Well, wh-when you 'ultimately' come down, you will go straight to my study."

"Delighted, sir." The blood rushed to my face as I realised my own impudence, but I was glad that I had said it.

Fillet went his way, and I came down from my railing, combating the sickening certainty that I had made a fool of myself, and determining to believe in the splendour of my attitude and to carry it through to victory. Carry on, Rupert, carry on. Onward, Christian soldiers.

I sauntered over to Bramhall House and climbed the stairs to the house-master's study. Hearing Fillet grunt at my knock, I walked in to execution.

"Oh, let's see, Ray, you were cl-climbing over, weren't you?"

"I believe so, sir."

"Oh, indeed. Then you shall write five hundred lines of Cicero. You'll play no games till they're done."

Five hundred Latin lines! God! I had nerved myself for physical punishment, but for nothing so dreadful as this. This meant long days of confinement with hard, hard labour. A great mass of tears rose from somewhere and came dangerously near the surface. But I kept them down and tried to show, though there was a catch in my voice, that I was still unbroken.

"Yes, sir. Anything further?"

"Yes indeed." Carpet Slippers sucked in his breath. "A further hundred lines. P-p-perhaps that'll teach you that rebellion is expensive."

I swallowed the tears. "No, sir. That won't teach me."

"So? Well, let's say yet another hundred."

Mentally stunned and bleeding, but ready to do battle with the Day of Judgment itself, I retorted:

"That won't teach me either, sir."

"Oh, indeed. Then we'll add another *three* hundred—eh?—making a thousand in all."

And at that point I shamefully broke off the fight. It wasn't fair—he had all the artillery. I held back the tears, fast gathering in volume, and gave up the unequal contest. One day my own guns would come. Quite respectfully I said "Yes, sir," and walked out. The vanguard of that mighty array of tears had forced its way as far as my eyes, which felt suspiciously moist. In fact, as I shut the door and found myself alone—absolutely alone—they nearly came forth in full cataract. But I saved the situation by thinking hard of other things and whistling loudly.

I went to an open window in the corridor and, looking out, saw that the sun had just dispelled the rain. The railings of Kensingtowe over the roadway were still burnished and glistening with wet, as were the leaves of shrubs and trees. And the air that touched my cheek was all soft and sweet-smelling after rain. Resting my elbows on the window-sill, I told myself that I hated Carpet Slippers; that I hated Doe and it was all his fault; that I wouldn't do the lines—I wouldn't do them; that

I didn't care if I was expelled; Kensingtowe was a beastly school, and Bramhall was its filthiest house.

The sound of a step in the corridor behind me arrested my thoughts. I leaned farther out of the window and muttered: "Oh, I hope he won't speak to me. I hope he'll pass by. I hate him, whoever he is. O God, make him pass by," for I knew there was a moisture in my eyes. I hurriedly held them wide open, that they might dry in the sun.

"Ray?" It was Radley's voice, but I wilfully paid no attention.

In a second he had laid violent hands on me and swung me round, so that I was held facing him.

"What? Crying, Ray? That's a luxury we men must deny ourselves."

It seems, as I recall it, a fine sentence, but at that moment, when I wanted to be a wild ass among men, it was a *lie*. The hot blood flooded my forehead. "I'm *not* crying!" I snapped, keeping my face upturned, my eyes fixed on his, and my teeth firmly set, that he might see that he had lied.

"No, of course you're not. But come, now, Ray, what's the matter? Out with it! There's nobody but me to hear you. And I understand."

I didn't want him to speak kindly to me, for I hated him. So I said in a rapid, trembling voice:

"I've got a thousand lines from Mr. Fillet. I didn't deserve them and I'm not going to do them!"

Immediately I felt that a catastrophe had occurred—that an edifice, which had been standing a second ago, was now no more. Before that sentence I had faced a kindly friend, now I faced an offended master. But, though I knew the ruin my words had wrought, I indulged a glow of self-righteousness and was prepared to relate my defiance to an approving world.

"Come with me," commanded Radley. Swinging round, he walked towards his room. At first I remained at the window without moving, and waited for him to turn his head and tell me a second time to come. But he walked on, never entertaining the thought of my not obeying him. And I followed, armed with indifference. It was a pity that walking behind him should give me so fine a view of his splendid proportions and inflate me with strange aspirations, for I hated the man and *wanted* to do so. I hated him—let no other thought replace that.

He led me to his room and said "Come in." I entered and, when I had closed the door, looked aimlessly about, taking little interest in the suggestive fact that Radley was opening a cupboard. There was little change in my countenance when he placed himself opposite me with his cane in his hand.

"You have been very rude to me in speaking defiantly of your house-master. Do you understand?"

There was no alternative for me but to say "Yes, sir." The answer came huskily. I was annoyed that my voice sounded hoarse.

"Put out your hand."

I obeyed, stretching out my right hand as far as I could and displaying no perturbation, though I was wondering what it would be like to be caned on the hand. This was one of Radley's surprises, and he followed it with one of his brutal remarks:

"Put that right hand down. You'll need it to be in good condition for writing your lines. Put up your left."

I held out my left hand. The cane sang in the air and whistled on to my open palm. A spasm of pain passed up my arm, my hand closed convulsively, my elbow drooped, and that vast array of tears made a tremendous effort to carry everything before them. But with all the strength at my command I got the better of them. Angry at having closed my hand, I extended the scorching palm again, and, very pale and trembling perceptibly, looked with set features straight at Radley.

He threw the cane away and, sitting on the edge of his table, took hold of the hand that he had struck and drew me towards him.

"Don't you think, Ray, that you, who can take a licking so pluckily, ought to face bad luck in a less cowardly fashion than you have this afternoon? You'll meet worse things than lines before you're ten years older; and, Ray, I want you always to face your fate, whatever it may be, as you faced my cane—teeth set, no wincing."

It was a stroke of master play. His gentleness, following immediately upon his severity, burst the dam. His words were an "Open Sesame" to the leaky floodgates I had held so tightly closed. I hung my head and the huge throng of tears broke forth. Wo-ho, what a cascade! My eyes overflowed with salt tears and my nose wanted wiping. Oh, waly, waly. Radley seemed indisposed to let go of my left hand, so I was compelled to search for my handkerchief with my right. After sounding the depths of four pockets, I found it, a singularly dirty one, in the fifth. And, while great internal sobs shook my frame with the regularity of minute-guns, Radley spoke so nicely that I determined I would be everything he wanted, a really beautiful character—always providing that it didn't interfere with my war with Fillet. For one day—one great and distant day—I would terribly overthrow that little old pantaloon.

"Now, Ray, we must get someone to dictate a few of these lines to you."

I looked up and smiled. "Thank you very much, sir," and I unconsciously pressed his hand.

"Doe is your friend. We'll test his metal and see whether he thinks friendship is something more than getting into scrapes together." He touched a bell. "I'll send for him."

I gave a sudden shiver. Doe was out in the world with Freedham, probably without an "exeat," and certainly without a hat. I began to wonder whether by a dramatic ***denouement*** I was to be the cause of Doe's capture.

"You rang, sir?" inquired the manservant.

"Yes; find Master Doe. He's in the house."

"Yes, sir." The door closed, and it was too late. Too late for what? I was sure I didn't know, for there was nothing I could have done to prevent the search for Doe. Late emotion had left, I suppose, my imagination in an overwrought state. And I had reason to wonder if I was moving in a dream, when, after a knock at the door, Doe walked in, his eyes sparkling at having been sent for by the object of his worship.

"Now, Doe," began Radley, with a smile—

> "This life's mostly froth and bubble.
>   Two things stand like stone:
> Kindness in another's trouble,
>   Courage in your own.

Ray's just got a thousand lines of Cicero. But he understands all about 'courage in your own,' and you understand all about 'kindness in another's trouble.'"

"Yes, sir," agreed Doe, a bit bewildered, but instantly prepared to live up to this noble reputation.

"Well, what do you say to dictating some of the lines to him?"

"Rather, sir. I'll dictate them.... Besides, sir," he added, as if this explained everything, "Ray and I are twins."

Sec.2

And not a game did Doe play until he had dictated all those lines. It occupied a week and two days. When I dropped my pen, having written the last word, the relief of thinking that I had no more lines to write was almost painful. I felt suddenly ill. My loins, aching alarmingly, reminded me that I had been in a sitting posture for many a weary hour; and my fingers, suffering from what I judged to be rheumatism or gout, fidgeted to go on writing. My mind, too, was confused so that I found myself repeating whole lines of Cicero, sometimes aloud; and my face was pale, save for a dangerous pink flush on the forehead.

Life, however, seemed brightened by the sense of a task completed, and I began to think of someone else besides myself.

"I say, Doe," I asked, "aren't you going to tell me where you were going when you joined that knock-kneed idiot Freedham?"

"No," announced Doe.

"But look here," I began, and was just about to tell him that Freedham was an unwholesome creature who had mysterious fits like a demoniac, when I remembered my promise of silence: so I went on lamely: "You will tell me one day, won't you?"

"No," he repeated, feeling very firm and adamant and Napoleonic.

"But, my darling blighter, why not?"

"Because I don't choose to."

"Then you're a pig. But you might, Doe. Out with it. There's nobody but me to hear you. And I understand."

"No."

"Well, tell me, how did you get back so early?"

"You see," answered Doe, cryptically, "the sun came out; and when the sun came out, I came in."

It was a romantic sentence such as would delight this rudimentary poet. Why he condescended to break his mighty silence even to this extent, I don't know. It was perhaps a boyish love of hinting at a secret which he mustn't disclose. An awful idea struck me. I say it was awful because, though stirring in itself, it brought the thought that I was left out of it.

"Oh, Doe, have you—have you a SECRET SOCIETY?"

"No."

"Here, hang me, Doe," I said, "you're not only a shocking bad conversationalist, but also a little mad. That's your doctor's opinion. That'll be a guinea, please."

And I got up to take the lines to Fillet.

"I say, Rupert," said Doe, blushing and looking away.

"Well?" I asked, with my hand on the door-knob.

"I say," he stuttered, "you—you might just mention to Radley that I dictated *all* the lines. It would sort of—I mean—Oh, but you needn't, if you don't want to."

Sec.3

That night there happened in Bramhall House one of those strange events that are best chronicled in a few cold sentences. That night, I say, while honest men and boys slept, Mr. Fillet sat up in bed and listened. He distinctly heard movements in his study below. Jumping up, he slided into his carpet slippers and crept downstairs. There was a light in his study. He looked round the half-open door and saw the back view of a boy in pyjamas. The whole incident is much too sinister for me to remind you frivolously that little Carpet Slippers was once again round his corner. He began: "Wh-what are you doing?" and the boy at once did what any properly constituted midnight visitor should do—switched off the electric light. When Mr. Fillet, with a heart going like a motor engine, found the switch and flooded the room with light, there was, of course, no one there. But on his writing-table lay his cane, broken into pieces, and my own copy of the thousand lines torn into little bits.

CHAPTER IV
THE PREFECTS GO OVER TO THE ENEMY

Sec.1

What more exciting than for the whole school to learn by rumour the next morning that all the prefects of Bramhall House had been mysteriously withdrawn from their Olympian class-rooms to a special cabinet meeting under the presidency of Stanley, the gorgeous house-captain? Clearly some awful crime had been committed at Bramhall, and there would be a public whacking and an expulsion. We humans may or may not be brutal, but life is certainly more stimulating when there is an execution in the air.

Chattering, prophesying, and wondering who was the criminal, we found our way to our various class-rooms. It being First Period, Doe, Penny, and I were under Radley's stern rule and obliged to sit quietly in our desks, knowing that he would allow no more licence on this exciting day than on any other. Our heads were bent over our work when Bickerton, the junior prefect of Bramhall, entered the room, approached the master's desk, and spoke in an undertone to Radley.

I saw—for I was gazing at the new arrival over my work—Radley look astonished, and turn his eyes in my direction.

"Ray."

"Yes, sir."

"You're wanted in the Prefects' Room."

I remember the universal flutter of excitement and surprise; I remember Doe raising his head like a startled deer as I went out and shut the door; I remember catching, from outside, Radley's sharp rebuke, "Get on with your work." His voice sounded strangely distant, and seemed to be on the happier side of a closed door.

Bickerton, who was enjoying himself, walked in front; and I followed behind, bringing my attention to bear upon keeping in step. Rearranging my stride now and then, I marched through the empty corridors, listening to the drone of masters' voices teaching in their class-rooms, and wondering at the loudness of our foot-steps. The sight of the prefects' door gave me my first sense of fear.

Being a prefect and thus mightily privileged, Bickerton turned the door-handle of the room without knocking. It was like laying a hand upon the Ark. Into the holy place Doe and I had passed before, not as prisoners, but as patronised pets who were suffered to amuse the august tenants with our "lip" until we became too disrespect-ful, when we would be ejected with a kick. This morning it struck strange and cold to hear Bickerton say:

"Here's the little bounder."

I entered, and saw the whole array of Bramhall prefects assembled, Stanley, their senior, presiding. Bickerton shut the door ceremoniously.

There were twelve of them, and every man was a blood. They had reached a solemn age and, in the dignity of their bloodhood, were quite unaware that they were playing at a mock-trial and enjoying it. I'm sure none of them would have missed it. Were Stanley alive now, instead of lying beneath the sea off Gallipoli, he would be twenty-seven years of age, very junior in his profession, and therefore much younger than when he was a house-captain of nineteen: and he would admit that on this famous occasion he and his fellow-prefects were highly pleased with the transaction entrusted to them. For at twenty-seven we are people who have been old and now are young again.

His team sat down two sides of a long table, and himself was enthroned at the top in front of foolscap and blotting-paper. It was a splendid tribunal.

I tried to persuade myself that I was perfectly comfortable, and could, if need be, show my easy conscience by a little old-time impudence. In reality my heart was fluttering, and a perspiration had broken out upon my head and the palms of my hands. My brows I wiped on my sleeve, and my hands I rubbed on the seat of my trousers. Nor had I lost the headache which asserted itself directly my long im-position was done. My forehead felt as if it had swollen and extended the skin across it like elastic. And for the last twelve hours my face had been warm and burning.

"Now, Rupert Ray," said Stanley, "we want you to own up to this blooming business of last night. So fire away."

"I don't know what you're gassing about," said I.

"Now don't be sulky. You'll only make matters worse by trying to bluff us. And goodness knows they're bad enough as it is."

"Oh, to think how we've been disappointed in you!" interposed Bickerton, who had taken up a position on the fender. "To think how we've cherished this viper in our bosom!" And he raised his hands in mock despair.

"Now don't be an ass, Bicky," said Stanley, who deemed that a Court of Inquiry over which he presided was much too weighty an affair to be approached with levity; "it's no joking matter. The kid's in a beastly mess, and, when he owns up, we must try to get him off as lightly as possible. I think perhaps we've let this youth and his chum, the Gray Doe, get too cheeky, and to that extent we're to blame.... Now, Ray, answer me some questions. Did you get a thousand lines from our revered housemaster, Carpet—Mr. Fillet?"

"Yes."

"When did you complete them?"

"Yesterday afternoon."

"In short, on the afternoon immediately preceding the tragedy which took place in the microscopic hours of this morning?"

"Yes, I s'pose so."

"That's a remarkable coincidence, isn't it?"

"I'm bothered if I see why."

"My dear child, you really mustn't be 'bothered' in here. It's gross disrespect to my brother-prefects—my colleagues. Besides, you knew perfectly well that in the stilly night a malicious attempt was made upon—not upon the life—but upon the cane of Mr. Fillet, which is, after all, the life and soul of the little man."

There was laughter in court, in which his worship joined.

"O law!" ejaculated I, as things began to fall into shape.

"Really, child, such expressions as 'O law!' are out of order, especially when they're only so much bluff.... I must now approach a subject which may have sordid recollections for you, but in the interest of the law I am bound to allude to it. Were you whacked—ahem!—chastised a few days ago by the aforesaid Mr. Fillet?"

"Yes."

"When did the old gaffer—when did Mr. Fillet whack you?"

"Yes, tell the gentleman that," put in Kepple-Goddard, a prefect who felt that he was not playing a sufficiently imposing part and wished to have his voice heard.

"A week ago last Monday," I answered.

"Where did he whack you?" pursued Stanley.

"On the recognised spot."

"Now, don't be cheeky. In what place did he whack you?"

"Why, in his class-room, of course," I retorted. "Where do you think he'd do it? In the High Street?" As I said this I was seized with a nervous fit of giggling.

"Look here, sonny," said Kepple-Goddard, rapping on the table, "you're going the right way towards getting a prefects' whacking for contempt of court."

Stanley raised his hand for silence.

"Why did he whack you?"

"Because he couldn't get my sum right."

Here Banana-Skin, a large and overbearing prefect, so called because of his yellowish complexion, burst in with the skill of a prosecuting counsel:

"Oh, then, are we to understand that you were whacked unjustly and had reason for vindictiveness?"

"Go easy, Banana-Skin," protested Stanley. "Don't bully the kid."

"But," I said, beginning to feel that horrid array of tears mobilising again, "that was some time before he gave me the lines—"

"Don't beat about the bush," interrupted Banana-Skin. "Did you feel that you hated him?"

The question was not answered at once. I cannot explain how it was, but the figure of Radley stood very clearly before my mind's eye, and this helped me to speak the truth, though my voice broke a bit.

"Yes."

"Ah!" Everybody considered Banana-Skin to have elicited a damning admission.

"Now," continued Stanley, his curiosity superseding his sense of what was relevant, "how many cuts did he give you?"

"Ten."

"Poor little beggar! Didn't that seem to you rather a lot?"

I shrugged my shoulders.

"Now answer the Coroner that," commanded Kepple-Goddard.

"Yes," I replied.

"H'm!" grunted Stanley. "How did you know where you could find your thousand lines so that you could tear them up?"

"I don't know what you mean. *You're* bluffing now."

"Hallo!" cried Banana-Skin. "Didn't you hear him say ' *You're* bluffing now'? That shows that *he* was bluffing before."

"Oh, that's a bit *too* clever!" objected Stanley. "Give the kid a chance."

There's nothing like sympathy for provoking misery and starting tears, and, as Stanley uttered that sentence, I decided that God had gone over to the prefects, and I would very much like to cry. To drive back the tears I called to my aid all the callousness and sulkiness which I possess. My face was the portrait of a sulky schoolboy as Stanley continued:

"Now, Ray, which door did you leave the dormitory by?"

"I didn't leave it."

"I say," suggested Kepple-Goddard, "couldn't we send Bickerton to ask all the boys who sleep in the same dormitory whether they saw him leave it?"

"But they'd have been asleep, you ox!" put in Banana-Skin.

"Not necessarily."

"But it doesn't follow that, if they didn't see him leave the dormitory, he didn't do it," objected Banana-Skin, the self-constituted prosecuting counsel, who didn't want to see his case fall to the ground.

"Not quite. But if they *did* see him, it proves him a liar and pretty well shows that he did."

"There's more sense in Kepple's idea than one would expect," gave Stanley as his decision. "Dash away, Bicky, and find out."

So Bickerton—or shall I call him Mercury, the messenger of the gods?—went, and I remained. It was no matter to me what news he brought back. I stood there, in the lions' den, and counted the cracks in the ceiling. I counted, also, the number of corners that the room possessed, and remembered how these same prefects had often (as when gods disport themselves) tried to make Doe and me stand in them for what they termed "unmitigated cheek"; how, giggling, we would fight them and kick them till they surrounded us and held us with our faces to the wall; and how we would call them all the rude names we could think of till they stuffed handkerchiefs in our mouths as a gag. One of their favourite pastimes had been to do Doe's hair, which they darkened with their wet brushes. It was usually a difficult business, as Doe would treat the whole operation in a disorderly spirit and declare that it tickled.

Presently Bickerton was heard running up the corridor (rather undignified for a prefect) and came bursting into the room.

"Now listen," said he, somewhat out of breath, and looking at a sheet of paper which he held in his hand. "Two boys saw Ray get up and leave the dormitory last night. They sleep on either side of him, and their names are Pennybet and Doe. The latter isn't sure whether he dreamt it."

"Well, Ray, what have you got to say to that?" asked Stanley.

"Nothing," I answered, "except that, if it's true, I must have been walking in my sleep. I did once, when I was a small boy."

Stanley ignored my feeble defence. He submitted to his colleagues that it was all his eye and Betty Martin; and the others nodded assent. Then the Chairman, recovering from his slight relapse into the vernacular of the Fourth Form, enunciated the following remarkable sentence:

"This inquest has, you will agree, been conducted by me in a strictly impartial and disinterested way, and the proceedings have been conspicuous for the absence of any bias, prejudice, or bigotry."

"Whew!" whistled several boys. Stanley let a grin hover in a well-bred way about his lips as he recommenced, the sentence being well-prepared and worth repeating:

"There has been no bias, prejudice, or bigotry. Well, gentlemen, is the corpse guilty or not guilty?"

"Guilty, the little beast!"

I went out of that cruel room resolved that "beneath all the bludgeonings of chance my head should be bloody but unbowed." I was unconquerable! I walked along the corridor, blown out with injured virtue—a King among men. We assure you, our beloved subjects, we were Rupert Head-in-Air.

Sec.2

I returned to Radley's class-room and entered jauntily. All eyes turned and followed me as I walked to the master's desk. The excitement experienced by each boy seemed communicated to me. Radley feigned indifference.

"Well?" said he.

"I've come back, sir."

"Right. Go and sit down."

Scarcely had I reached my seat before the bell rang loudly for the Interval. The boys in their anxiety to hear the latest news flowed out hurriedly. I lingered apprehensively behind. At last I summoned up courage to venture into the corridor, where I found a group of boys awaiting me. Through these I broke at a rush and went and hid.

All that Interval lip tossed to lip such remarks as: "Ray did it." "I say, have you heard Ray's the culprit?" "What'll be done to him?" "Oh, the prefects have issued an edict that anyone who holds communication with him will get a Prefects' Whacking." "Ray did it." "What? that kid? Little devil—it's good-bye to him, I suppose." "What'll Radley say? He's one of his latest bally pets." "Ray did it."

After ten minutes the Second Period began. As our form went to Herr Reinhardt, the great Mr. Caesar, and he would certainly be late, I dawdled in my hiding-place, not having the courage to face the boys in the corridor. I waited till I conjectured that Mr. Caesar must be safe in his class-room, and the boys in their desks. Then I entered his room, famous character as I was, and apologised for being late. Mr. Caesar wrote my name in the Imposition Book, but, having raised his face and given one look at my swollen, tearful eyes, he deliberately crossed the name out again. And, indeed, throughout that period he so consistently refused to see that the boys were showing detestation of my degrading presence, and was so inexpressibly gentle in his manner towards me, that now I always think of this weak-eyed German master as a quiet and Christian gentleman.

When school-hours were over I went to a window, and there, leaning on the sill, thought how badly my war was going. Fillet was winning; he had won when he caned me for asking the number of the sum; he had won when he gave me the thousand lines; and now he was assaulting in mass formation with the whole school as his allies. Ah, well! as Wellington said at Waterloo—it depended who could stand this pounding longest, gentlemen.

And, as Wellington did, I would charge at the end of the day. One splendid way of charging, I thought, would be to die immediately. That would be most effective. How Fillet would prick up his ears on Monday morning when he heard the Head Master say to the school assembled in the Great Hall: "Your prayers are asked for your schoolfellow, Rupert Ray, who is lying at the point of death." And on Tuesday, when he should say in a shaking voice: "Your schoolfellow, Ray, died early this morning. His passing was beautiful; and may my last moments be like his." And then there would be the Dead March.

Having no one to talk to, I drew out from among the crumbs and rubbish in my pockets a letter that had arrived from my mother that morning. My young mother's love for me was always of the extravagant kind, and the words with which she closed this letter were:

> "I do hope you are having a magnificent time and that everybody
> is fond of you and nice to you. I must stop now, so good-bye,
> my darling little son, and God bless you. With heaps of love
> from your ever devoted and affectionate Mother."

It was funny that I had not even noticed those words when I hurriedly read them in the morning. But now I found them strangely comforting, strangely satisfying.

A slap on the back awoke me from my reverie. It was Doe.

"Come along, Rupert. I know you didn't do it. Or, if you did, I don't care. We're twins."

"Go away. You'll get into a dreadful row if you're caught talking to me."

"I don't care. They won't think any the worse of me, whatever they do."

"Go away, I tell you. Or, if you don't, I shall have to, and I'm very comfortable here."

"I shan't. And if you try to escape me I'll follow you."

"Oh, why can't you go away?" I grumbled with something like a sob. "Go away. Go away."

But Doe persisted. In full view of the prefects he chatted gaily to me. Once, as Radley passed, he slipped his arm into mine. And when the master was out of hearing he asked:

"I s'pose Radley knows you're in Coventry?"

"Of course. Everybody does."

"Do you think he saw I had my arm in yours?"

"I should think so. You made it pretty obvious."

"I wonder what he thought."

All this time the skin on my forehead seemed to tighten and my cheeks to tingle with warmth. Towards evening my temples began to beat regularly. At these symptoms I was rather thrilled than otherwise, for I felt there was a distinct prospect of my turning the tables on everybody by dying.

At preparation the boys, with that lust to punish to which a crowd is always susceptible, slid along the form to get as far from me as possible and to leave plenty of room for myself and my contamination.

In the dormitory no one spoke to me, but as I was getting into my pyjamas one of the dormitory prefects burst in and addressed a senior boy:

"I say, talking about this row of Rupert Ray's, isn't the Gray Doe going to catch it to-morrow, by jove?"

In my anxiety about Doe I forgot that I was banned.

"What's he going to get?" My voice sounded husky and strange. The boys didn't answer me or show that they had heard. They ostentatiously proceeded with their conversation. Even Pennybet had his back turned. I flung myself into my bed in a way that nearly broke the springs, and, pulling the clothes furiously over my head, left my bare feet showing, at which several boys laughed contemptuously.

Oh, the horrid activity of my wide-awake brain! I couldn't sleep, and even found difficulty in keeping my eyes shut. Once, as I raised my weary lids, I found that the lights had gone out since I last opened my eyes. And my headache, which had spread to the back of my neck, was getting but little relief from my frequent changes of position. Oh, the horrible conglomeration of ideas that crowded my mind! Recent scenes and conversations entangled themselves in one another. Ray did it—Ray did it—my darling little son—good-bye and God bless you—there has been no bias, prejudice, or bigotry, but heaps of love from your devoted and affectionate mother—Ray did it—it's good-bye to him, I suppose—good-bye and God bless you—

"*Good-night, Ray*."

That must be Doe's voice; it came from reality and not from dreams: it came loudly out of the silence of the dormitory and not from the chorus of conflicting sentences droning in my mind: it was a real voice, but I was too tired and too far lost in stupor to answer it: good-night, Ray—it's good-bye to him, I suppose—heaps of love—there was some comfort in that—heaps of love from your devoted and affectionate mother. Ah! when shall I get properly off to sleep? Let me turn over on to my other side and put my hand under the pillow—but it was young Ray—Ray did it—Ray did it—how that detestable sentence swells till it packs my head!—and I must be asleep now, for I see Fillet fitting a rope across the door of an unknown bedroom wherein I am confined with some invisible Terror which drives me out of my bed: as I rush into the passage the rope trips me up, and I fall forwards but am saved from injury by my mother's arms: she catches me in the dark and says something about my darling little son. And she remonstrates with Fillet, who is standing by that dreadful bedroom door, till he merges into Stanley listening shame-facedly to my mother's silvery, chiding laugh and assuring her that the inquest was conducted in a strictly impartial and disinterested way. He changes into old Doctor Chapman, who tells her that Freedham died early this morning. For everything changes in the dream except one thing: which is that there is a head aching somewhere; now it is my own, now someone else's. I draw my mother along a passage to a window and explain that the pencil-mark on the glass is the register of my height. I put my back against the wall to let her see that I can just reach the mark, when lo! it is a great distance above me. I get on the cold stone window-sill that I may reach it, and would fall a thousand feet, only something in my breast goes "click"—and the dream was gone. With my return to consciousness came the knowledge that the headache had been my own throughout.

But it was terribly cold—and what a draught! Perhaps it was because I was lying so dreadfully straight, whereas I generally lay curled up. I wanted to bring my knees towards my chest, but couldn't move my legs. How cold my chest was! Why had the bedclothes fallen away and left it exposed to this horrible draught? I would have liked to pull them right over my head that I might get warm again, but I was too tired to make the effort. At last, however, the cold was more than I could bear. So I put out both hands to pull up the blankets—but could find none anywhere. God! I wasn't in bed at all, but was standing!

The horror of that moment! A wild heart beat lawlessly at my side. One more touch of terror, and it would rebel in utter panic. Why was the dormitory so dark? Why had the little night-lamp gone out? And the wooden floors were stone-cold like the window-sill in my dream. I couldn't see if my bed were close to me or far away because of the impenetrable darkness; but I was so very, very tired, and my eyes were so uncomfortably warm with interrupted sleep that I must try to feel my way. I put out my hand and touched a ***padlock***. Like a flash, it came with all its terror upon me: I was not in the dormitory nor anywhere near it, but right away in a cellar below the ground where there were some old lockers and play-boxes. Flinging myself first to one side of the cellar and then to the other, I tore at the walls in an agonised endeavour to get out. The last thing that I remember was shrieking loudly and feeling a moisture rise to my dry lips and pass down my chin.

Sec.3

I awoke with a dull sense of impending trouble to find myself abed in the Bramhall sick-room, into which long shafts of noonday sunlight were streaming from behind drawn blinds. Looking down upon me was Dr. Chapman, with his usual white waistcoat and moist cigar.

"Ah ha!" he said. "Now, Gem, what the dooce do you think is the matter with you?"

I replied that I didn't know, and, just to see what he would say, asked him why he called me "Gem."

"Gem? Whoever called you 'Gem'? Did I? Yes, of course I did—it's short for Jeremiah."

"The gifted old liar!" I thought, while I demanded aloud his reason for calling me "Jeremiah."

"Why, because you look so dam—miserable, as though your eyes would gush out with water."

And partly at this idea, partly at his skill in getting out of a difficulty, Chappy laughed so heartily that I laughed too, only with this difference—that, whereas his laugh was like sounding brass, mine was like a tinkling cymbal. Then he sat down by my bed and, taking my wrist in one hand, pushed up the sleeve of my pyjama jacket and felt my smooth, firm forearm. "Good enough," he said, and proceeded to open the jacket down the front, and feel my chest and waist, thumping me in both of them, and expecting me to gurgle thereat like a sixpenny toy.

"You're all right," he decided, "except that you're an ass. Take your medical man's word for it—you're an ass. My prescription is 'Cease to be lunatic three times daily and after eating.' My fee'll be a guinea, please."

I said nothing, but looked at him for further advice.

"Confound you! Don't look at me with those Jeremiad eyes. What have you been doing, moping indoors for the last ten days instead of playing in the fresh air?"

"I wasn't moping—" I began sullenly.

"Now, sulky—sulky!" interrupted Chappy.

"I wasn't moping. I went and got a thousand lines from Mr. Fillet—"

"Yes, I know. The damned old stinker!" said Chappy, always coarse and delightful.

I think I loved him for those words. I felt that my allies were swinging into line for the great war against Carpet Slippers. There was Doe, and now Chappy.

"I know all about it," continued the new ally, "and then you filled your excitable mind with thoughts of revenge—eh?"

"Yes," I admitted, and looked down at the clean white sheet.

"And off you go on your midnight perambulations—the cold wakes you up—and there's the devil to pay—and the old doctor to pay! One guinea, please. And now I'm off."

"Oh, don't go," I pleaded, before I was aware of saying it. I didn't want him to go, for he was an entertaining apothecary and a sympathetic person, before whom I could act my sullenness and aggrievement.

"Don't go? Why shouldn't I?" demanded Chappy, who seemed, however, touched at my wanting him. "Now, my son, don't you run away with the idea that you're of the slightest importance. All boys are the most useless, burdensome, and expensive animals in the world. It wouldn't matter twopence if they were all wiped out of existence—there'd be a sigh of relief. So don't think it interesting that you're ill. Because it isn't. And you ain't ill. So good-bye."

He disappeared into the matron's room next door, and his hearty voice could be heard haranguing the lady:

"The Gem's got a healthy young constitution, but his brain's a ticklish instrument. His *corpore* is as *sano* as you like, but his *mens* is rather too *excitabilis*. Ah ha! Matron, what it is to move in this classic atmosphere! Certain sproutings of his imagination must be repressed—push 'em down, Matron. Young beggar, I'd sit on him and crush him. But then, it's all the fault of that stuttering old barbarian slave-driver, Fillet."

Here the matron must have been speaking, for I heard no more till Chappy began again:

"He's got a tough little breast, fine stomach-muscles, and limbs firm and round enough to get him a prize in a Boy Show. But the beast is spoiled as a specimen by his little Vesuvius of a mind. And oh, Matron, I lied to him like an under-secretary. I said that boys were the least important arrangements in the world, when, dammit—I mean, God bless my soul—they're the most important things in Creation, and this particular hotbed of the vermin has some of the finest editions of them all. But never let the little blades know it—never let 'em know it."

With that he must have taken his leave, for quiet assumed possession of everything. I settled down to the boredom of the afternoon, letting my eyes travel up and down the stripes of the wall-paper. Up one stripe I went, down the next, and up the third, till I had covered the whole of one wall. Then I tossed myself on to my other side with an audible groan that gave me but little relief, since there was no one to hear. The day wore on, and the long streaks of light worked their way round the room, grew ruddier, and climbed up the wall.

Oh, wearisome, wearisome afternoon! I began to sing quietly to myself such songs as I knew: "Rule, Brittania," "God save the King," and "A Life on the Ocean Wave." This I gave up at last, and thought out *corking* replies that I might have made to the prefects, had my wit been readier.

"Ding-ding-ding!" That was tea. Would Doe be any less happy when he saw my vacant place, and wonder if I were very ill? How was Penny feeling, who had lifted up his heel against me? Might he, together with Stanley and his colleagues, think me dying! What would Stanley and the prefects do to Doe for his flagrant breach of their edict? Perhaps at this moment he was being tried by the great Stanley and his Tribunal. Perhaps even now they had him bent over a chair and were giving him a Prefects' Whacking. At any rate, I wished he would walk in his sleep or do something that would bring him to this monotonous sick-room. Why shouldn't he? Like me, he had been immured indoors for ten days; like me, also, he had reasons for being unhealthily excited.

"Ding-ding-ding!" I had closed my eyes when this bell sounded. It meant Preparation, so it must be getting dark. I would open my eyes and see. I did so, and saw nothing except darkness, which made me think I must have dozed. The sudden view of the darkness frightened me, for I remembered the terror of the preceding night and that, before many hours, the whole world would be silenced in sleep, while I might be wandering in the fearful cellars. At the thought my lips formed the words: "O God, don't make me wake again in the Old Locker Room. O God, don't. I wish I had somebody to talk to."

As I mechanically uttered this prayer, I began to feel rather strongly that, if I were going to ask God to make this arrangement for me, I ought to do something for Him. Clearly I must get out of bed and say my prayers properly. So I stepped on to the floor, reeling dizzily from my enforced recumbence, and knelt by the side of the bed. Falling into prayers that I knew by heart, and scarcely heeding what I was saying, I prayed (as my mother had taught me to do when I was a little knickerbockered boy) for the whole chain of governesses who had once taken charge of me. I enumerated them by their nicknames: "Tooby and Dinky and Soaky and Miss Smith." Trapping myself in this mistake, I actually blushed as I knelt there. I realised that I must be more up to date. So I prayed for Penny, Freedham, Stanley, Bickerton, and Banana-Skin, but I drew up abruptly at Carpet Slippers. I couldn't forgive him. I felt I ought to, but I couldn't. There, on my knees, I thought it all out; and at last light broke upon me. To forgive didn't necessarily mean to forgo the punishment. Yes, I would forgive him and pray for him, but his punishment would go on just the same.

After this satisfactory compromise I got back into bed, happy at being spiritually solvent, and repeating: "O God, don't make me wake in the Old Locker Room; I wish I had someone to talk to."

And almost immediately, as if my prayers were to be answered, I heard the noise of feet running towards my door. It opened, and Bickerton, taking no notice of me, walked to the middle of the room, struck a match, and lit the gas. Returning quickly, he said to someone else who was approaching: "Oh, there you are. I've lit the gas. Bring him and get him to bed. Put him beside the other ass for company." I sat up in my excitement, and with a thrill—first of elation and then of dismay—saw Stanley enter, bearing a boy, who, with arms and legs hanging limply downwards, was apparently lifeless: his fair head was a contrast with Stanley's dark blue sleeve on which it rested, and his brown eyes, wide open, were shining in the gas like glass.

Sec.4

In committee that morning Stanley and his colleagues had decided that Doe had deliberately asked for a Prefects' Whacking, and must therefore be given an extra severe dose. He should be summoned to judgment after games. So, just as Doe, who was standing bare-chested in the changing room, had pushed his head into his vest, a voice, shouting to him by name, obliged him to withdraw it that he might see his questioner. It was Pennybet, acting as Nuncius from the prefects.

"You're in for it, Edgar Doe," said this graceful person, leisurely taking a seat and watching Doe dress. "I'm Cardinal Pennybet, papal legate from His Holiness Stanley the Great. Bickerton had the sauce to send for me and to describe me as a ringleader in all your abominations. I represented to him that he was a liar, and had been known to be from his birth, and that he probably cheated at Bridge; and he told me to jolly well disprove his accusation by fetching you along. I explained they were making beasts of themselves over this Ray business—"

"It would have been more sporting of you," said Doe, drawing on his trousers and thanking Heaven that he was not as other men, nor even as this Pennybet, "if you'd stuck by Rupert and defied the prefects."

"My dear Gray Doe," this statesman expounded, "I go in for nothing that I can't win. And if you want to win, you must always make sure that the adverse conditions are beatable. I like to tame circumstances to my own ends (hear, hear), but if they aren't tamable I let them alone. So now you know. But about these prefects. They've got their cane ready, so push your shirt well down."

Doe studiously refused to hurry over his dressing, and, having assumed his jacket, went to a mirror and took great pains with his hair. At this moment, though the hand which held the brush trembled, he was almost happy: for he was play-ing, I know, at being a French Aristocrat going to the guillotine dressed like a gentleman.

"My time is valuable," hinted Penny. "Still, by all means let us be spotless.... That's right. Now you look ripping. Come along, and I'll stand you a drink when it's over."

For Penny, the callous opportunist, had a sort of patronising tenderness for his two acolytes.

Doe followed his conductor in a silence which not only saved him from betray-ing timidity by a trembling voice, but also suited the dignity of a French Aristocrat. But no—at this point, I think, he was a Christian martyr walking to the lions.

"Come, my lamb, to the slaughter-house," said Penny, in the best of spirits, "and don't try that looking-defiant game, 'cos it won't pay. They're not taking any to-day, thank you. That's their tone.... There's the door. Now remember not to say a word on your own behalf, for with these bally prefects anything that you say will be taken down in evidence against you.... Enter the prisoner, gentlemen. Sorry to be so long, but we had to make ourselves presentable. Anything else in the same line to-day?"

Penny paused for breath, but showed no desire to leave the Prefects' Room. He wanted to see at least the commencement of judicial proceedings. They looked so promising. All the Bramhall prefects were there—Bickerton, Kepple-Goddard, and the prosecuting counsel, Banana-Skin; and Stanley—Stanley by the grace of God.

"Bring the boy Doe in," ordered Stanley, "and kick that gas-bag Pennybet out. If he were a year younger we'd whack him too."

No one thought himself specifically addressed, and Penny was left in posses-sion of the floor. But Stanley's curt treatment rankled in his heart. So, placing his feet wide apart and his hands in his waistcoat pockets, he respectfully drew atten-tion to the opprobrious epithet "gas-bag" which had been employed in requesting him to retire from this Chamber of Horrors, and asked that the offensive remark might be withdrawn.

Stanley scorned communication with an impertinent junior. He telegraphed a glance to Bickerton.

"Turf him out, Bicky."

But Penny, perceiving that rough treatment would ensue, gracefully removed himself from the room, so timing his motions that he closed the door from outside just as Bickerton from within arrived at the handle. Bickerton, defeated, swung round upon the assembly and asked if he should follow the fugitive.

"That kid's too smart to live," said Stanley, more generous than his peers. "Let him be. He'd best you and a good many more of us. Besides, it's nearly tea-time, and we've got to get this Doe business over."

Bickerton accordingly took up his place on the fender and considered himself empanelled upon the jury. Doe stood with his hands behind his back, his cheeks very flushed, and his knees slightly shivering, but upheld by the thought of his resemblance to Charles I. He would scorn to plead before this unjust tribunal.

"Now, Edgar Doe," began Stanley, and his voice was the signal for silence in the court and for all eyes to be concentrated on the prisoner. "You've made a little fool of yourself. You've openly set us all at defiance and, no doubt, thought yourself mighty clever. I don't think you'd have been so ready to do it if we hadn't been decent and had you in here sometimes. But that's beside the point, only I may say in passing that we shan't have you here any more."

"I don't care," said Doe. "I don't want to come, and I wouldn't come if you asked me."

"Yes, we all know that. It was the obvious thing to say, Mr. Edgar Gray Doe. Now we aren't bullies, and perhaps, had you comforted your friend on the Q.T., and been copped doing so, we'd have let you off. But it's the beastly blatancy of it all that constitutes the gravity of your offence and detracts from its value as a self-denying act of friendship. Do I express myself clearly?" concluded Stanley, turning to his colleagues.

"Perfectly," said Kepple-Goddard.

"Well, Doe, did you grasp the drift of all I said?"

"I wasn't listening."

Stanley, nonplussed, looked round upon the jury. Banana-Skin muttered: "The little devil!" Bickerton from the fender sighed: " *St. St.* Ah, me! to think how we've swept and garnished the Gray Doe! 'I never loved a dear gazelle, But what it turned and stung me well.'"

"Dry up, Bicky," came the president's rebuke, "and go and turn away those kids who are making a row with their feet in the corridor. Remain on guard out there, if you don't mind. It's behaviour like Doe's that makes these kids so uppish. Thanks, Bicky."

There was a sound of scurrying feet and repressed impish laughter, as Bickerton opened the door and shut it behind him.

"Now, Doe," resumed Stanley, "what have you to say for yourself before we leave the talking and get to business?"

"Nothing," replied Doe, "except that I'll go on being pally with Ray whatever you do, you—you set of cads!"

"I say"—Stanley was keeping his temper—"don't play the persecuted hero defying the world. It won't wash here."

"I'm not playing the persecuted hero," retorted Doe loudly, but with drowned eyes. "I didn't think myself mighty clever—I—"

"I thought you hadn't been listening," put in Banana-Skin in a quiet and torturing way.

"And I thought you'd nothing to say for yourself," added another.

"Steady, Banana," remonstrated Stanley, "don't tease the kid."

"They're not teasing me. I don't care what they say or what any of you do."

"What a little liar it is!" taunted Banana-Skin, "when he's fairly blubbing there."

"I'm not!"

"Fetch the cane out," pursued Banana-Skin, unheeding. "It's no good talking. Get him over that chair, Kepple."

"You shan't!" said Doe, trembling terribly.

"By jove!" cried Stanley, jumping up. "He's going to show fight, is he? Pass over that cane. Now, bend over that chair, youngster."

"I won't."

"Look here, you unutterable fool. Here's the cane. See it? If you do what you're told you'll get a stiff whacking, but if you don't, by God, there's no saying what you'll get."

Doe sprang forward, seized the cane, smashed it, and hurled the pieces into their midst. "Now then, you cads, you can't lick me, you brutes, you fools! Come for me—you lot of great devils!" He roared this at them, and the last words were shouted in a burst of hysterical crying. With head down he charged into Stanley, crashing his fist on the senior prefect's chin.

The outraged prefects lost their heads. They surrounded him as he fought. Above the turmoil came the cries: "Get hold of the little devil!" "Pin his hands to his sides!" "He shan't forget this!" "Trip him up, if you can't do anything else!" "It's not pluck, it's temper!" "He's down—he's up again!" "By jove, the little blackguard is going to beat the lot of you!" "Get him on the ground—don't be afraid to go for him—he's asked for it." "That's right—got his wrist? Twist it!" "Devil take it, he's wrenched it free again." "Get out of the light—I'll settle him!" "I've got him—no, by God, I haven't!"

Stanley, the first to recover himself, fell away from the rest.

"Come away, you fools. There are ten of you. Leave him alone."

"Can't help it!" yelled back Banana-Skin. "It's his fault. Let him have it. That's right. Get him against the wall."

"Come away, you fools!" And Stanley began to pull them off and fling them away furiously. Banana-Skin had a shock when he found himself seized and hurled against the opposite wall.

It had been well had Stanley done this earlier, for Doe, turning very white, fell forwards.

"Heaven save us!" exclaimed Stanley, as white as Doe. "We've done it now. What brutes we are! Lock the door. He's fainted. By heaven, I wish this had never happened!"

Doe had not fainted. He was in a state of semi-unconsciousness when he knew where he was, but it was a long way off—when he heard all that was said, but it came from a great distance—when neither his position nor the sound of voices was of any interest to him, and his only desire was to pass into complete unconsciousness, which would bring rest and sleep. He felt them catch hold of him, one by the armpits and another by the ankles, and knew that he was being lifted on to a table.

Then the voices began from the top of a great well, while he lay at the bottom. He could hear what they said; but why would they persist in talking and keeping him awake? He was indifferent to them: they were like voices in a railway carriage to a dozing traveller.

"I wouldn't have thought he had so much in him."

"Oughtn't we to undo his collar?"

Then the remarks evaporated into nonsense, but only for a space, after which the nonsense solidified into sentences again.

"Don't you think we ought to send for Chappy?"

"Wait and see if he'll come round. His colour's returning."

Doe was ascending from the bottom of his great well: the voices were becoming distincter, a pain in his head and body worse.

"Yes, he's less white. Sprinkle water over his forehead."

Doe was coming up and must have reached the top, for it was raining. How silly! That wasn't rain, but the water being sprinkled over his forehead. How hard the top of the well was! But there—he was nowhere near a well, but in the Prefects' Room, lying on a deal table. Or was he at the bottom of the sea?

"He's looking better now."

Up he came from the bottom of the ocean. Above him he could see the surface, a broad expanse of pale green, through which the sun was trying to shine and succeeding better every second. Though all the while conscious that his eyes were closed, he saw dancing on the green rippling veil, beneath which he lay, little spots of colour that grew in number till they became a dazzling kaleidoscope.

"Doe, are you all right now?"

The kaleidoscope was gone; and the top of the sea was above him, getting steadily closer and brighter. Good—he was above the surface now, and the water seemed out of his ears, so that he heard with perfect clearness the voice of Stanley saying:

"That's right—you're round again."

Though his eyes were still shut he felt he must be awake, because the Prefects' Room with its furniture had crowded his mental vision. So he opened his eyes, and there, sure enough, were the prefects' chairs and cupboards; they seemed, however, to have moved with a jump from the positions they had occupied in his mental picture.

If you wake and see faces looking down on you, the natural thing to do is to smile round upon them all; and this Doe did, so that his persecutors were touched, and Stanley said:

"How are you feeling now, kid? We're all of us beastly sorry."

"And I'm beastly sorry if I cheeked you."

"Well, never mind about that; but tell us if you're feeling putrid, because then we'll tell old Dr. Chapman and make a clean breast of it. My colleagues and I are determined to do the right thing."

"Oh, I'm all right. Don't say anything to anyone."

Ding-ding-ding!

"Are you fit for walking in to tea?" asked Stanley.

"Rather! I'm quite the thing now. Thanks awfully."

So Doe, sustained by a pride in his determination to conceal what had happened and screen the prefects, walked with racking head and aching limbs into tea, where he made a show of eating and drinking, though periodically the room went spinning round him.

Tea over, he staggered into the Preparation room and sat at his desk with his brows on his hand and his eyes on his book. The print danced before his gaze: letter rushed into letter, word merged mistily into word, line into line, till all was a grey blur. A blink of the eyes—an effort of the will—a sort of "squad, shun!" to the type before him—and the words jumped back into their places, letters separated from their entanglement and stood like soldiers at spruce attention. A relaxing of the effort—and dismiss! helter-skelter, pell-mell went letter, word, and line. It was all a blur again. Once more he made the necessary exercise of his will and was able to read a line or two; but, if the mistiness were not to come before his eyes, the effort had to be sustained, and that made his head feel very heavy. It proved too much for him; the will to do it expired, and away went the letters into the fog. Some boys whispered that he was sighing for his friend Ray; others teased him by muttering: "Diddums get whacked by the prefects? Diddums get a leathering?"

Poor Doe! He must have been strongly tempted to retort: "I wasn't whacked, so sucks!" and to describe that picturesque incident when he smashed the prefects' cane, for his milk was the praise of men. But he had to choose whether, by a little honourable bragging, he should gratify his desire for glory, or by a martyr's silence he should give himself the satisfaction of playing a fine hero. The latter was the stronger motive. He kept silence, and only hoped that his valorous deeds would leak out.

Tell England

85

Preparation was nearly over when there came one of those heart-stopping crashes which all who hear know to be the total collapse of a human being. A faint—aye, and a faint in the first degree, when life goes out like a candle.

"Who's that? What's that?" cried the master-in-charge, quickly rising.

"It's Doe, sir. He's fainted."

"Oh, ah, I see," said he, leaving his desk and hastening to the spot. "Sit down, all of you. There's nothing very extraordinary in a boy fainting. Here, Stanley, pick him up and take him to the sick-room; and, Bickerton, go with him. The rest of you get on with your work."

Thereafter Pennybet—or, at least, so he assured us—expended his spare time in knocking his head against walls and holding his breath in the hope that he, too, might faint and have a restful holiday in the sick-room.

"For," said he, "where Doe and Ray are, there should Me be also."

Sec.5

It's funny that we do everything together," said Doe that same evening, as we lay in our beds and watched each other's eyes in the light of the turned-down gas. "First we're twins; then we get whacked together; then we both get rowed by prefects; and I do a faint and you do a sort of fit.... But, I say, Rupert, look here; I want to ask you something: will people think I was a fool in everything I did, or will they think—well, the other thing? I mean, let's put it like this—what would Radley think?"

"I don't know," said I, not very helpfully.

"I s'pose he's heard all about it. I hope he has—at least, I mean, I'd like him to think I stuck by you. Only, when the prefects were talking about defiance, it struck me that Radley might call it 'insubordination.'"

There was a pause, and then he proceeded: "I wonder if he'll be sorry when he hears we are both laid up."

"Who?"

"Why, Radley, of course."

"*Mr.* Radley," said a voice, "if you please."

Radley, who had walked softly lest the invalids should be wakened from sleep, was standing in the room and looking at us in the glimmer. We were very surprised, and Doe's blushes at being caught were only exceeded by the pleasure-sparkling of his eyes.

Radley approached my bed and placed the clothes carefully over my chest. I didn't know whether to thank him for this, and only smiled and reddened. And after he had done the same for Doe he sat at the foot of his bed.

"When the world turns against you, always go sick," said he, smiling. "It's an excellent rule for changing ill-will to sympathy. If you're sent to Coventry, go straight to bed there. Oh, you're a subtle pair, aren't you?"

We were both too shy to answer.

"Well, Ray, I've come to tell you to sleep with an easy mind. The Head Master is satisfied that, if you were conducting operations in Mr. Fillet's room, you were not conscious of it. It was Dr. Chapman who worked all this for you. He threatened to go on strike if any other conclusion were come to. He asked the Head whether he'd ever dreamt he was doing most impossible things. The Head said 'Yes,' and the doctor replied triumphantly: 'Well, don't let your brain get as excited as a child's, or, maybe, if you're feverish and run down, you'll go and do them.' He even suggested that possibly it was not you but the Head who had committed the crime. He asked him if he could imagine 'a silly and excitable kid' (which is an excellent description of Ray) dreaming that he had done what actually was done.... The Head was incredulous at first, but the doctor talked so learnedly about the Subliminal Consciousness and Alternating Personalities that the Head, if only for fear of getting out of his depth, began to yield. I drove home the advantage by saying that I believed you didn't generally lie—which was true, wasn't it?"

"Good Lord, no!" I replied.

"Well, it will be some day." Radley rose and strolled to the door. "Yes, there's been a slump in Rupert Ray recently, but I'm afraid there'll be a boom in him when he comes back to work, and he'll get too big for his boots. It's a pity. Good-night."

And though Stanley, as we learnt later, had manfully revealed the full story of Doe's sufferings at the hands of the prefects, Radley walked away without giving the young hero one word of admiration. And as the door shut Doe turned round in his bed, so that his face was away from me, and maintained a wonderful silence.

CHAPTER V
CHEATING

Sec.1

Time carried us a year nearer the shadow of the Great War. It brought us to our fourteenth year, at which period Doe's mysterious intrigue with Freedham still awaited solution, and my Armageddon with Fillet still languished in a sort of trench-warfare.

It was now that our abominable form took to cheating once a week in Fillet's class-room. A Roman History lesson left invitingly open the opportunity to do so. For Fillet's method of examining our acquaintance with the chapter he had set to be learnt in Preparation was invariably the same. He asked twenty questions, whose answers we had to write on paper. He would then tell us the answers and allow us to correct our own work. After this he would take down our marks.

Now, our form had been organised by the all-powerful statesman, Pennybet, who had lately been reading the Progressive Papers, into a Trade Union, of which the President was Mr. Archibald Pennybet. He had decided (as it is the business of all trade unions to decide) that we were worked too hard. We must organise to effect an improvement in the conditions of living. To demand from the Head Master an instant reduction in the hours of labour didn't seem feasible to our union of twenty members, but it would be quite easy by a co-operative effort to modify the extent of our Preparation. At a mass-meeting of the workers Penny outlined his scheme—Penny loved scheming, moving forces, and holding their reins.

It was a marvellous scheme. We were to leave undone our Preparation for the Roman History lesson, and, when Fillet told us the answers, we were to write them down and credit ourselves with the marks. "It's not cheating," explained our leader in his speech (and we were all very glad, I think, to hear that it wasn't cheating), "because it's not an effort to take an unfair advantage of each other. It's just a cordial understanding, by which we all lessen one another's burdens.

"I and my executive," continued Penny, "have all the details worked out to a nicety. Here is a table for the whole term, showing how many marks each worker will give up week by week. It is so graduated that the clever fellows will end up at the top, and those who would naturally slack will end up at the bottom. My executive has decided that Doe is about the brainiest, so he comes out first"—blushes from Doe—"and I myself am willing to stand at the bottom."

By this revelation of astonishing magnanimity Penny came out of the transaction, as he did out of most things that he put his hand to, with nothing but credit.

For half a term this comfortable scheme ran as merrily as a stream down hill. And then a strange thing happened to me. I was talking one afternoon to Penny on the absurdities of the Solar System, when I became conscious that my mind had closed upon seven words: "That Rupert, the best of the lot."

"That Rupert, the best of the lot." What on earth had resuscitated those words? I politely bowed them out and continued my conversation. But the phrase had entered like a bailiff into possession of my mind. Even as I put it from me, believing it would be lost in the flow of an absorbing conversation, I knew that there had appeared upon the horizon a cloud no bigger than a man's hand.

"That Rupert, the best of the lot." The words, as first told to me by my mother, had been the dying words of my grandfather, Colonel Rupert Ray, with which he asked repeatedly for his dead son, my father. So the words were uttered by the first Rupert Ray, applied to the second, and recalled by the third at a most inopportune moment. And the third would have bowed them out. Why? Because he was a cheat? No—let us not be ridiculous—because he was in the midst of an important conversation.

I pretended to listen to Penny, but really I was reasoning something else. I was admitting that, now that this little phrase had popped up through some trap-door of my mind, my conscience, long dormant on the cheating theme, would have to be talked round again. And, as something like suspense set in, I was anxious to join issue at once.

I left Penny abruptly and retired to a window (as you will have observed it was my fashion to do), where I leant upon the sill and prepared to argue out the problem.

Our co-operative effort to avoid preparing our lesson, was it wrong? Yes. In spite of the old sophistry I knew it to be so. But what attitude should one adopt? To refuse publicly to have any part in the system would seem like mock-heroics. The only course open was to learn the work and earn the marks. Inevitably I had arrived at the conclusion which I dreaded. To learn the work seemed a task surprisingly difficult and menacing after half-a-term's freedom. I hugged that freedom. I wished my calm acquiescence in the system had not been ruffled.

To learn the work—it was a little thing surely: to learn it unseen and alone, while other boys went free of the labour, and gave themselves the marks, notwithstanding. But no, I could no more persuade myself that it was a little thing than I could believe that any other course was the right one. I felt it was big—too big for *me*.

Then the old thought, probably not an hour younger than sin itself, was quick to take advantage of my indecision: I would go on as I was a little while longer— till the end of the term—and then begin with a clean sheet. There was much to be said in favour of this: for see, if I were to do the thing thoroughly this term, I ought to forgo all the marks that I had already come by dishonestly. To do that was impossible. The confession involved would court expulsion. Expulsion! As the word occurred to me, I realised the enormity of my offence. How could I go on with that which, if detected, would mean expulsion? To answer this question I went the whole dreary round of reasoning once more and arrived at the conviction that the straight action was incumbent upon me; which conviction I hastened to explain away with the same dull casuistry. Sick and weary, I left the window-sill and ceased to think any more. My conscience had given battle to evil and neither lost nor won. Indecisive as the issue was, I knew in my heart of hearts that it partook of the nature of a defeat.

Later on, I wrote to my mother quite an effective analysis of this spiritual difficulty: and I wrote it, so she loves to say, on a postcard, and signed it "yours truly, Rupert Ray." Her reply I could not expect till Wednesday morning, the morning of the lesson. Of that I was glad. For to this extent I had temporised: I would wait till I heard from her before attempting to learn the work. If necessary, I could cram it up on Wednesday morning. And with this settlement I was satisfied in a sickly way.

Sec.2

While Tuesday is passing in silence and inaction, and the issue of this crisis is in the bag of the postman, let me tell you something of my relations with my mother. Her love for me, I have said, was of the extravagant kind. It was ever and actively present. Though she discharged her social duties with a peculiar grace, yet I am certain that the thought she bestowed on them was an intruder amongst her thoughts of me. My figure was present to her in the drawing-room, the ball-room, or the theatre.

I fear I was not demonstrative in my affection for her. Perhaps, when we sat alone at dinner on holiday evenings, and her dress was one that left her arms bare, I would think that the softness of the limbs was such as to make one wish to touch them; and I would stroke them; or, when she laid her hand upon the table, I would rest my own hot palm upon it. But I am certain that it was not till our stories marched into the shadow of the Great War that I became at all demonstrative.

Enough of that, then—the postman's feet are on the steps of Bramhall House. May I just ask you to think of my mother as a very gracious lady, gracious in form and feature and character?

Sec.3

When breakfast was over on Wednesday morning, I repaired to the Steward's Room, where letters had to be sought. I was attacked by a feverish nervousness, which increased as I passed other boys returning with letters in their hands. Anxiety seemed to be a physical thing deflating my breast and loins. My heart, too, was affected when I asked the Steward with feigned unconcern if there were any letters for Ray. It beat rapidly as I awaited the reply.

None. I was stupefied: but soon stupefaction became anger; anger hardened into sulkiness; and, as more sinister feelings grew, sulkiness lost itself in guilty belief. Now I knew what course I would take—I would go on cheating.

I turned to go out. Since that afternoon when the choice between good and evil came so plainly before me, I had been dilly-dallying at the spot where the two ways met. The more I hesitated, the greater had become the desire to take the easier road. And now in open rebellion against my scruples I stepped firmly upon it. My reasoning was played out, and, as I walked back along the corridor, I felt like one released from irksome fetters. Oh, it was good to be free! At the same time, however, with the obstinacy of one who seeks to justify himself, I muttered: "She might have written, I think, she might have written."

Then a step sounded behind me, a hand touched my shoulder, so that my heart jumped like a startled frog, and Radley said:

"Come and have a talk with me a minute."

Sec.4

My mother had written, but not to her son. The postman, who disappointed me, brought a graceful note to Radley:

> "I am most sorry for this trespass upon your time, and yet I
> have little hesitation in asking your help in a matter that
> concerns my son. Rupert, in his talks during the holidays, so
> often mentions your name, that it is not difficult to see that
> he owes you a good deal. Although he is too reserved to say so,
> I fancy he is quite devoted to you. His postcard, which I
> enclose, will explain all.
>
> "May I take this opportunity of expressing my thanks, and of
> saying how grateful his father would have been for all that you
> are doing for our son?"

Radley, when we reached the privacy of his room, took up his favourite position of sitting on the edge of the table. Before him stood I, all reasoning suspended.

"Well, how's the cheating going on?" he asked.

"What ch—?"

"Stop! Don't say 'What cheating?' because that would be acting a lie. I tell you what we'll do. We'll wait a whole minute before you answer me. We'll collect our thoughts and think whether we'll act straightly or crookedly." He took his watch off his chain and placed it upon the table beside him. "Right, we're off."

As the seconds sped by I tried to find some excuses. But, bewildered and sick, I could only wonder how he came to know of it all. I had found no answer when I saw him replacing his watch on his chain.

"Well, Ray, how's the cheating going on?"

"I didn't think it exactly cheating."

"Ray, don't." Radley protruded and withdrew his lower jaw with irritation. "You know it was cheating. If you didn't, why did you know what I was referring to? Well, we'll have another sixty seconds' interval. We must have time to think, or else we lie."

Out came the watch again. The pantomime of waiting in silence and of replacing the watch was re-enacted. Then Radley, half smiling, as if he knew the worst was over, took up his question once more.

"Well, how's the cheating going on?"

Since I was not allowed to prevaricate, all that remained for me to do was to return no reply. But there was stubbornness in my silence; I should have liked to say pettishly: "But you won't let me explain, you won't let me explain."

And then—quickly—Radley grasped me by the elbow and looked straight down at me. For a second I resisted and tried to pull the elbow away. His grip, however, was too strong, and I yielded.

I know now that his feeling for all the boys, as he gazed down upon them from his splendid height, was love—a strong, active love. We were young, human things, of soft features gradually becoming firmer as of shallow characters gradually deepening. And he longed to be in it all—at work in the deepening. We were his hobby. I have met many such lovers of youth. Indeed, I think this is a book about them.

And, as I am certain of his feelings for us all, so am I certain of his feelings for myself. Those who were most pliant to his touch loomed, of course, largest in his thoughts: and my mother's letter, giving him the proof of my affection, which, since it was less obtrusive than Doe's, had been probably less clear to him, brought me in the foreground of his view. Be it right or wrong, this man with the hard chin and kind eyes had his favourites; and I date from this moment my usurping of Doe's position as Radley's foremost favourite. The way in which he took hold of my elbow, my willing submission of the army to his grasp told me that something was given by him and taken by me. And my eyes, as was to be expected of them, became suddenly moist and luminous.

"Time's going," he said, "and this Roman History lesson is upon us. Have you learnt it?"

"No, sir."

"Well, the issue is simple: either you continue cheating, or you give up no marks. Shall you cheat any more?"

"N-no, sir."

"Good, then you give up no marks."

"All right, sir."

"Well, hurry away. And if, when the big moment comes, you succeed in doing what's right, come and see me again."

Sec.5

The big moment came. Fillet opened his mark-book and read the names in the order of last term's examination-list, which brought Doe's name first. Doe was mending a nib when his name was called, and, without raising his head, replied "100, sir."

Other names followed, and the boys gave up the marks allotted them by Penny's system. Then came mine.

"Ray?"

For a second my voice or will failed me, so I pretended I had not heard, and let him ask again.

"Ray?"

"*None, sir.*"

Every boy turned towards me, and my cheeks burned to maroon. I caught mutters of "Well, I'm hanged!" "Ye gods!" "Good-night!"

"Wh-what did you say?" stuttered Carpet Slippers.

I was irritated and nervous and replied rather too loudly:

"*None, sir.*"

"None? Why none?"

"I didn't learn it."

The mutterings began again: "Oh, I say, stow it!" "Lie down."

"You didn't learn it? St-stand up when I question you. Wh-why didn't you learn it?"

Here I failed. I had answered the first two questions truthfully because I had reasoned about them. The third took me unawares. And, such is the result of trifling with conscience, I had lost the knack of doing right without premeditation. "We must have time to think," Radley had said bitterly, "or else we lie." Obliged to answer without delay, I lied.

"I hadn't time, sir."

No sooner had I uttered the words than the dull and sickening sense of failure came over me. In spite of all—in spite of the fact that I had dealt honourably with the first two questions—I had ended by lying. I sat down slowly, and stared vacantly in front of me. The big moment had come and passed, and I had missed it. I couldn't believe it. I had been determined, and yet I had failed. My breath became tremulous, and across my brows went the sudden invasion of a headache.

Little it matters what Fillet said. Destiny ordains for our correction that there shall be some people before whom we shall always appear at our worst. Fillet occupied that place in my schooldays.

Little would it matter, either, what my fellow trade-unionists thought of this black-leg in the camp, were it not for the remarkable deed of Pennybet. He, I am convinced, felt that he must rise to the occasion. There were few things he liked better than rising to an occasion. Here was an opportunity for a ***coup d'etat***. Here, praise the gods, were circumstances to be tamed. So he at once threw all his weight on my side, knowing full well that he had but to do that to secure me from all persecution or contempt.

"P-pennybet?"

"Oh—er—none, sir."

"None? Another boy with none? Why none?"

Penny admired the nails on his right hand and then said:

"I didn't exactly learn it."

"Oh, indeed? And wh-why, pray?"

As though deploring such tactless persistency, Penny pursed up his mouth, laid his head on one side, shrugged his shoulders, and held his peace.

"Had you, too, no time?"

"Well, not a great deal, sir."

There were some titters, and Penny looked deprecatingly in the direction whence they came. Fillet passed judgment so severe that Penny made a shocking grimace and said: "Thank you, sir. It shall not occur again," which, to be sure, might have meant anything.

I think the characters of both my friends stood out, clearly defined, in the words with which they referred to this incident afterwards. Doe was generous in his praise. "Golly," he said, "I wish I could feel I had done it as you can now. I cursed my luck that my name didn't come after yours, so that I could have stood by you, as Penny did. I could have throttled him with jealousy. Do you know, I almost wished the other boys had mobbed you a bit, so that I could have stuck by you." And Penny said: "You didn't really think I was going to throw the weight of my trade union on to the side of that foul, caitiff knave of a Carpet Slippers? Why, the man's a low fellow—the sort of person one simply doesn't know. He'd drink his own bath-water."

Sec.6

"If you succeed in doing what is right, come and see me again." I decided to stay away. Many times that morning I passed Radley in the school buildings, and, pretending not to have seen him, went by with a hum or a whistle. In the afternoon he came and coached our game at cricket; and after tea he bowled at the Bramhall Nets where I was practising. When he instructed me he spoke as though there were nothing between us. But he was watching me, I knew; wondering why I had not come, and longing for me: and I rather overplayed my part.

It had been a grey, dull day, but, just before retiring, the sun came out and shamed the clouds into a sullen withdrawal. Then it went under, leaving behind it a glorious red glow and the hope of better things in the morning. All this I was in the mood to notice, for, though trying to be indifferent to destiny, I was heavy and dispirited. I did not see how I could ever do right again, since Radley's determination and my own had been insufficient to brace me for the onslaught. It was evident that mine was the stuff from which criminals were made.

And, as the red glow departed and the darkness gathered, if there was one lonely boy in the world, languidly despairing, it was I. Many times I found myself uttering aloud such slang expressions as: "Oh, my hat! If only I had told the beastly truth for the third time! Dash it, why didn't I? Why the deuce didn't I?" I addressed myself as: "You blithering, blithering fool!" And my temples began to ache and now and then to hammer. For, always in these my early days of puberty, excitement and worry produced such immediate sensuous results.

Radley sent for me at last, and it was a relief to go. He was very kind. Frankly, I believe he was pleased to have his new favourite in his room again. I was indeed his hobby at present.

"Have I ever bullied you at the nets," he said, "for stepping back to a straight ball?"

"Yes, sir."

"Well, the universal habit of 'stepping back' is exactly parallel to that of arguing with conscience. The habit grows; one's wicket always falls after a few straight balls; and one's batting goes from bad to worse. Never mind, you stood up splendidly to the first two straight balls and scored boundaries off both. That shows you are getting into your old form. You are out of practice a bit, that's all."

And I went out of his room, feeling sure that for some time I would be very good.

Sec.7

I always left Radley's room, feeling that I could blast a way through every mountain. And it was not long after he had received my mother's letter with its allusion to my lack of a father, that he addressed himself to a bigger mountain than any of these little trumpery hills that you have watched me conquering. He invited me to his room one evening, and sat me in an armchair opposite him: and then he talked, while I watched the fire getting redder, as the room grew darker. Soon he came unhesitatingly to a subject that I was just at an age to understand. He spoke so fearlessly as to be quite unrestrained and natural. Nevertheless, I was glad that the room was getting darker, as I felt that my cheeks were red and hot. And when he said: "You mustn't mind my talking to you like this," I could only reply: "Oh, it's all right, sir."

But, once again, I left his room feeling that, though already I had had my reverses in the moral contest of which he spoke, I would win through in the end.

CHAPTER VI
AN INTERLUDE

In the summer holidays of that year I received a letter from Doe inviting me to spend a few days with him at his Cornish home on the Fal. Radley, he told me, was already his guest.

There was some excitement the morning I left home for this adventure into the West Country. My mother had clothed me in a new dark-blue suit. Her son must look his best, she said. She insisted on my wearing a light-blue tie, for "it matched the colour of my eyes." I rather opposed this on the ground that it was "all dashed silly." But she disarmed me by pointing out that I was *her* doll and not my own, and the only one she had had since she was my age, which was a century ago—a terrible lie, as she looked about twenty-seven. She carried her point with a kiss, called me her Benjamin, tied the tie very gingerly, and subsequently disarranged it completely by hugging me to say good-bye, as though I were off for a lifetime.

Alone in my corner seat I was rolled over the Trail of Beauty that the line of the Great Western follows. And I watched the telegraph wires switchbacking from post to post, as we sped along.

When we steamed into Falmouth station, I easily distinguished Radley's majestic figure standing on the platform, with Doe actually hanging on his arm—a thing I would never have dared to do. In fact, I guessed that Doe was doing it for my benefit. Our young host was in a light grey suit that would have brought tears to the eyes of Kensingtowe's administrators, who stipulate for dark garments only: and, evidently, he had been allowed to dictate to his tailor, for the suit was an exact copy of one that Radley had worn during the previous term. He looked more than ever like his nickname, "the Gray Doe."

Next morning the sun blazed out over England's loveliest stream, the Fal, as, widening, it flowed seaward. We hurried down to the foot of Doe's garden, where a rustic boat-house sheltered his private vessel, the ***Lady Fal***. Doe stepped into its stern, and I into its bows, and Radley took the oars. With a few masterly manoeuvres he turned the boat into midstream, and then pulled a rapid and powerful stroke towards Tresillian Creek, where we had decided to bathe. We touched the bank at a suitable landing-place, disembarked, and prepared to undress.

The events of this day linger with me like a string of jewels; and the bathe was one of the brightest of them all. There was a race between Doe and myself to be first in the water. As I tossed off my clothes, the excitement of anticipation was inflating me. I would surprise them with my swimming.

My mother had taught me to swim. We began our studies in the bath, when I was still a baby, she leaning over the side and directing my splashing limbs. We achieved the desired result some years later in the French seas off Boulogne. She never could swim a stroke herself, but was splendid in the book-work of the thing. Since those days she had given me unlimited opportunities to acquire perfection. So now, Radley and Doe, my masters, you should learn a thing or two!

The undressing race resulted in a dead-heat, but whereas Doe contented himself with a humble jump into the stream, I contrived to execute a racing dive. Glorious immersion! It was lovely, oh, lovely! The embrace of the cool river seemed entrancing, and I remained a fathom down, experiencing one continuous delight. Unfortunately I was under water longer than my breath would hold out, and came to the view of Radley and Doe, choking and spluttering and splashing. Anxious to retrieve my reputation, for I was detestably conceited about my art, I started off for a long, speedy swim, displaying my best racing stroke. Back again, at an even faster pace, I got entangled with Doe, who greeted me a little jealously with: "Gracious! Where did you learn to swim like that?" Radley's mouth was set, and he remained mercilessly silent. He wasn't going to teach me conceit.

Soon we were clothed again, and back in the boat with untidy wet hair and stinging eyes, but with the glow of health warming our bodies.

Throughout the day we plied our craft over the Fal, lunching up King Harry Reach, and taking tea not far from Truro. When we turned the head of the ***Lady Fal*** for home, the sun was sinking fast, and Radley pulled his swiftest, as he wished to be at Graysroof before dark. So I lay in the bows and wondered at the straightness of his back, and Doe nestled in the stern and admired the width of his chest.

We glided over the surface: and there were no sounds anywhere, save the rushes kissing the reeds, the water lapping the sides of the boat, the little fishes chattering beneath, and the rhythmic music of Radley's graceful feathering, which sounded like the flutter of a bird upon the wing.

To dwell upon this beautiful evening is to recover a little of its serene exaltation. I like to recall it as one of those days about which we ask ourselves why we did not value them more when we had them. I speak of it here, because, in the soothing peace of the Fal that twilight, the AEsthetic seemed to stir in me—not so as to wake, but so as to wake soon. I felt some vague premonition of all the love, the sentiment, and the sorrow which would be mine in the manhood that was brightening to a pale, but tinted, dawn.

Part II: Long, Long Thoughts

CHAPTER VII
CAUGHT ON THE BEATEN TRACK

Sec.1

I am sixteen now, and the marks on the dormitory wall show me that I am many inches nearer the height of my ambition, which is the height of Radley. Second in importance, Kensingtowe has a new headmaster, an extraordinary phenomenon in the scholastic heavens, a long man of callow years and restless activity, with a stoop and a pointing forefinger. He has a quaint habit, when addressing a bewildered pupil, of prefacing his remarks, be they gracious or damnatory, with the formula: "Ee, bless me, my man." (Nowadays none of us speaks to a schoolfellow without beginning: "Ee, bless me, my man.") "Salome" we call the entertaining creature. This nickname adhered like a barnacle to him, immediately after he had employed, in his exegesis of the Greek narrative of Herodias' daughter, the expression: "Now, if I had been Salome—"

Ill fares it with a youth, if he has his hands in his pockets and is seen by Salome. Before he is aware of the great presence, that stoop overhangs him, that forefinger points to the tip of his nose, and a drawling voice says with rhythmic emphasis: "Ee, bless me, my man, you've *got*—your *hands*—in your *pockets*. Take off your spectacles, sir. I'm *going*—to *smack*—your *face*."

And he can put his foot down, too. The Bramhallites recently organised a very successful punitive raid on the local errand boys, who were getting too uppish, and now he has stopped all "exeats" for the members of Bramhall House. The town is out of bounds.

Third in importance is my quarrel with Edgar Doe. It began, I think, with his jealousy of me as Radley's new favourite. Then he has apparently thrown over all desire for glory in the cricket world and decided that, for an elect mind such as his, a reputation for intellectual brilliance is the only seemly fame. He delights to shock us by boldly saying that he would rather win the Horace Prize than his First Eleven Colours; and is actually at work, I believe, on a translation of the Odes into English verse. At any rate, he is two forms ahead of Penny and me, and has joined the Intellectuals. He has views on the Pre-Raphaelites, Romanticism, and the Housing Question.

Maybe, too, I have been very willing for the quarrel to proceed, because he will persist in his collusion with that mystery-man, Freedham.

Archibald Pennybet is the same as ever, unless, perhaps, his eyelids are drooping a little more in satisfaction with himself, and his nostrils becoming more sensitive to the inferiority of everybody else.

In a rash moment, one half-holiday, Penny and I made use of the privilege, to which we became entitled when we completed two years at Kensingtowe, of strolling across to the Preparatory School and organising a cricket match between some of the younger "Sucker-boys." Not being allowed to go down to the town, we thought there might be fun in playing the heavy autocrat at the "Nursery."

"We'll make these beastly little maggots sit up, unless they play properly," said Penny. "There shall be no fooling when *we* umpire."

The Suckers received us with gratifying awe. One of them in a moment of forgetfulness called Pennybet "sir." He accepted it without remark, as his due.

For half-an-hour we did well. Six balls went to every "over," no more and no less. Our decisions, when we were appealed to, were given promptly and decisively. But the boys were so small, and the play was so bad, that the novelty soon wore off. Our feeling of importance died away, when we realised we were umpiring in a match where the stumps were kept in position by the bails, and there was no one who could bowl a straight ball, or anyone who could hit it, if he did. The wicket-keeper, also, gave Penny much trouble; and sulked because he had been forbidden to stop the swift bowler's deliveries by holding a coat in front of him and allowing the ball to become entangled in its folds. My fellow-umpire had occasion to speak very seriously to him. "Really," he said, "you're a stench in my nostrils. Mr. Ray, who's kindly umpiring for you at the other end, never gave me half the cheek you do, when *he* was a kid." For a second the little boy wondered if he had made a mistake and Penny was really a master.

Having given eight balls to an over, I got bored and retired to my position at square-leg, displeased with the condition on which our privilege was granted that, having organised a game, we were to remain at our posts to the end. Someone awoke Penny, who walked with a yawn to the bowler's wicket, and, graciously putting into his mouth a huge green fruit-ball, offered by one of the more minute players, said with this obstruction on his tongue:

"Plo-ay."

When the twenty-eighth ball of that over had been bowled, I went across to Penny, presented my compliments, and intimated that six balls constituted an over. In a reply of some length he showed that he had a sucked fruit-ball in his mouth, which he must of necessity finish before he called "over," as the word required a certain rounding of the lips, and the confectionery might shoot out of his mouth at the effort. An impertinent little junior echoed my criticism.

"Yes," he protested, "there are six balls to an over."

Penny placed the fruit-ball between his gums and his cheek, and answered magnificently:

"There are not. There are just as many as I choose to give."

Then he took the fruit-ball on his tongue again and added:

"We-soom your plo-ay."

The bowler having exerted himself twenty-nine times, was a little tired and erratic, and the thirtieth ball hit Square-leg in the stomach.

"Wide," announced Penny, without a smile.

The thirty-first ball, amid disorderly laughter, was caught by Point before it pitched. The batsman meanwhile sat astride his bat: he was the only person who seemed out of harm's way. Point held up the ball triumphantly and yelled to Penny: "What's that, umpire?"

"I think it would not be unreasonable," answered Penny, "to call that a wide."

This was a long sentence, and the fruit-ball shot out about half-way through.

Relieved of this confectionery, Penny proceeded to give a practical illustration of "How to bowl." I fear he intended to show off, and to send down a ball at express speed which should shatter the stumps. At any rate, while the Suckers watched with breathless interest, he took a long run and let fly. One thing in favour of Penny's ball was that it went straight. But it flew two feet over the head of the batsman, who flung himself upon his face. It pitched opposite Long-stop.

"Run!" yelled the batsman, picking himself up. "*Bye!* Run, you fool! Bye, idiot!" This was addressed to the batsman at the other end, who was swinging his bat like an Indian club and paying no attention to the game. He pulled himself together on being appealed to, and ran, but it was evident that he could not reach his crease, as Long-stop had accidentally stopped the lightning-ball—much to his own chagrin—and was hurling it back to the wicket-keeper with all the enthusiasm of acute agony.

Our unhappy batsman did what excitable little boys always do—flung in his bat and sprawled on the ground. The bat struck the wicket-keeper, who had just knocked off the bails. It hit him, so he said, on his bad place.

"Out," ruled I.

"Over," proclaimed Penny victoriously, as who should say: "There! I've got a man out for you"; and he retired honourably to the leg position, where he composed himself for a happy day-dream.

The new bowler at my end began by bowling swift. The wicket-keeper jumped out of the way, as his mother would have wished him to do, and Long-stop shut his eyes and hoped for the best. The batsman blindly waved his bat, and, inasmuch as the ball hit it, and rebounded some distance, called to his partner, who was mending the binding on his bat-handle.

"Will you come? Osborne, you fool! Yes. *Yes*. YES! No, no. YE-E-ES! No—go back, you fool. All right, come. No-no-no. O, Osborne, why didn't you run that? It was an easy one."

"Silly ass, Osborne," roared Cover-point, quite gratuitously, for no one had addressed him for the last twenty minutes.

The batsman ran wildly out to the next ball and missed it. The wicket-keeper successfully stumped him. It was a clear case of "out," and a shout went up: "How's that?"

"That," said Penny, who had been in a dream and seen nothing, "is Not Out."

I was disheartened to learn on this occasion that little boys could be so rude to those who were sacrificing their spare time to teach them cricket.

"Really," sighed Penny, adjusting his tie, "unless you treat me with due respect, I will not come and coach you again."

This was greeted with an unmannerly cheer.

"Resume your play," commanded Pennybet. "It was Not Out."

"Why?" loudly demanded the bowler.

Penny seized the only escape from his sensational error.

"Because, you horrid little tuberculous maggot, it was a no-ball. Besides, you smell."

The little boy looked defiantly at him, and, pointing to me, said:

"Bowler's umpire didn't give 'no-ball.'"

"Then," said Penny promptly, "he ought to have done."

I was so shocked at this unscrupulous method of sacrificing me to save his reputation that I shouted indignantly: "You're a liar!"

Later a warm discussion arose between the batsman and the bowler as to whether the former could be out, if "centre" had not been given to him properly. I took no part in it, but looked significantly at Pennybet. He gazed reproachfully at me, as much as to say: "How could you suggest such a thing?" I walked over to him, ostensibly to ask his advice. The quarrel continued, most of the fieldsmen asserting that the batsman was out: they wanted an innings. Unperceived, we strolled leisurely away and disappeared round a corner. The last thing that I heard was the batsman's voice shouting: "I'm not an ass. I haven't got four legs, so sucks for you!"

Sec.2

Reaching the road, we linked arms with the affection born of sharing a crime and the risk of detection.

"Where are we going to?" asked I.

"Ee, bless me, my man. Down town, of course."

"But it's out of bounds."

"Ee, bless me, my man, don't you know that to me all rules are but gossamer threads that I break at my will? I'm off to buy sausages. I haven't had anything worth eating since the holidays."

And so, arm in arm, we marched briskly down the Beaten Track. The Beaten Track, I must tell you, was a route into the town which Penny, Doe, and I regarded as our private highway. We would have esteemed it disloyalty to an inanimate friend to approach the town by any other channel. It led through the residential district of Kensingtowe, past a fashionable church, and down a hill. Dear old Beaten Track! How often have I mouched over it, alone and dreamy, adjusting my steps to the cracks between its pavement-flags! How often have I sauntered along it, arm in arm with one of my friends, talking those great plans which have come to nothing!

We always became confidential on the Beaten Track; and to-day I suddenly pressed Penny's arm and opened the subject that, though I would not have admitted it, was the most pressing at the moment.

"I say, why does Doe avoid us now?"

"The Gray Doe," sneered Penny. "Oh, he—She's in love, I suppose. With Radley."

"Don't drivel," I commanded; "why does he hang about with that awful Freedham?"

"When you're my age, Rupert," began Penny, in kind and accommodating explanation, "you'll know that there are such things as degenerates and decadents. Freedham is one. And very soon Doe will be another."

"Well, hang it," I said, "if you think that, how can you joke about it, and leave him to go his way?"

"Oh, the young fellow must learn wisdom. And he's not in any danger of being copped. I'm the only one that suspects; and I guessed because I'm exceptionally brilliant. Besides, if he wants to go to the devil for a bit, you can't take his arm and go with him."

"No," said I, "but you can take his arm and lug him back."

"There are times, Rupert," conceded Penny graciously, "when you show distinct promise. I have great hopes of you, my boy."

"Oh, shut up!" I said, mentally overthrown to find that, without forewarning of any kind, something had filled my throat like a sob of temper. What was the matter with me? I unlinked my arm and walked beside Penny in moody silence, determining that at an early opportunity I would bring about a quarrel between us which should not be easily repaired. He, however, was disposed to continue being humorous, and frequently cracked little jokes aloud to himself. "Here's the butcher's shop," he explained, pointing to an array of carcasses; "hats off! We're in the presence of death." And, when he had purchased his sausages, he stepped gaily out of the place, saying: "Come along, Rupert, my boy. Home to tea! Trip along at Nursie's side." Just as I, thoroughly sulky, was wondering how best to break with him, and deciding to let him walk on alone a hundred yards, before I resumed my homeward journey, I heard his voice saying:

"Talking about Doe, there he is. And the naughty lad has been strictly forbidden to enter the town. Dear, dear!"

It was an acute moment. There, far ahead of us, was Doe in the company of Freedham, with whom he was turning into a doorway. A pang of jealousy stabbed me, and with a throb, that was as pleasing as painful, I realised that I loved Doe as Orestes loved Pylades.

The truth is this: ever since our form had been engaged on Cicero's "De Amicitia," I had wanted to believe that my friendship for Doe was on the classical models. And now came the gift of faith. It was born of my sharp jealousy, my present weariness of Pennybet, and my heroic resolution to rescue Doe from the degenerate hands of Freedham. Only go nobly to someone's assistance, and you will love him for ever. Love! It was an unusual word for a shy boy to admit into his thoughts, but I was even taking a defiant and malicious pleasure in using it. I was Orestes, and I loved Pylades.

In the glow of this romantic discovery, I no longer thought Penny worth any anger or resentment, so I slipped my arm back into his. He patted my hand with just such an action as an indulgent father would use in welcoming a sulky child who has returned for forgiveness. After this we climbed the slope of the Beaten Track at a faster pace. And then—what an afternoon of strange moods and tense moments this was!—I encountered on the other side of the road the surprised gaze of Radley.

It was a very awkward recognition, and I hope he felt half as uncomfortable as I did. I pinched Penny's arm and hurried him on quickly.

"Don't push me," he grumbled. "The damage is done. And it's all your fault for leading me astray. Radley'll tell. He never spares anyone; least of all, his pets, like you. There's one comfort; I can't be whacked; I'm too old. But you'll get it, Rupert. Salome's already done several of the sixteen-year-olds. Cheer up, Rupert!"

"Hang you, I don't want your sympathy," I retorted sullenly. And as I said it, I passed through Kensingtowe's gates to the punishment that awaited me within.

Sec.3

We were not summoned for judgment for several uneasy hours. It was dreary, waiting. About six o'clock I paid a lonesome visit to the swimming baths, and was glad to find them deserted. Even Jerry Brisket, the professional instructor, was not in his little private room. Jerry Brisket, that supreme swimmer, loomed as an heroic figure to me who fancied myself no common devotee of his art. I had often thought that my ideal would be to build a private swimming bath and to employ Jerry at a salary of some thousands as my own particular coach. But to-night, in spite of this lavish worship, I was relieved to find him absent. I flung off my clothes and took a long, splashless dive into the shallow end.

Water was my favourite element, especially the clear, green water of the baths. I loved to feel that it was covering every part of my body. With my breast nearly touching the tiled bottom, I swam under water for a long spell. And, moving down there, like a young eel, I compared this dip with that in the beautiful Fal of a year ago. Certainly there was still pleasure, glorious pleasure, in complete submersion, but on that bejewelled day there was joy above as well as below the surface. This evening all that awaited me, when I rose from the transparent water, was punishment and indignity.

"Hang it," I said to myself. "I think I'll stay in the baths. They can't dive after me here."

With the unreasonableness of guilt I stigmatised all those plotting my hurt as "they." I did not specialise individuals, possibly because Radley was one. They were "they"—a contemptible "they."

"They are brutes," I concluded, "and I don't care a hang for any of them."

Then, in the luxury of defiance, I swam my fastest and most furious racing-stroke, till my breath gave out with a gasp, my breast felt like bursting, and my heart beat heavily on my ribs. So I lay supine upon the water, closed my eyes, and derived a surfeit of joy from this rest after fatigue.

And, while I was doing that, I suffered a queer thing. Through my closed lids I saw a yellow atmosphere that was fast whitening. It seemed to smell very sweet; and the sensation of seeing it and smelling it was intoxicatingly delightful. It was like an opiate. What Freedham was doing in the atmosphere I know not, but I saw him, as one would in a dream. An exquisite sleepiness was entrancing me, when the cold water rushed in at my ears and mouth, and with an "Oh!" and a choking, I struggled to the rope. Dizzily, and feeling a pain in my head and neck, I scrambled out and lay upon the cold sides of the baths.

"Heavens!" thought I. "That was a close shave. I must have strained myself and nearly fainted. Why have I got that ass, Freedham, on the brain?"

At that moment the sound of Jerry Brisket's return caused me to jump up and dress. I was quite recovered, but tired and depressed. And, as a result of the curious conditions of the evening, there seemed to be gathering about me a presentiment of disaster.

When I passed Jerry's door on my way out of the building, I thought I would like to hear a friendly voice, so I called:

"Good-night, Jerry."

He came to the door in his white sweater and white trousers.

"Good-night, Mr. Ray. Where are you off to now?"

"Well, to tell the truth, I'm off to be walloped."

Jerry was too courteous to seek particulars.

"Oh, bad luck," he said. "Come to the baths this time to-morrow, and it'll be all over."

"Oh, I don't mind, it, Jerry," I replied. "Good-night"; and, letting the door swing behind me, I passed out of the baths.

"Good old Jerry," I murmured sentimentally. "By Jove, if I could only swim like him! Dear—old—Jerry."

An unaccountable melancholy overcame me, as I rambled in this strain. I sighed: "I think I'm getting too old to be whacked."

And, as I phrased the thought, walking dreamily outside the baths, the strangest thing of this evening happened. There seemed to be thrown over me, far more heavily than on that evening up the Fal, the shadow of my oncoming manhood. And with it came ineffable longings—longings to live, and to feel; to do, and to be. The vague wish to avoid the indignity of corporal punishment threw off its cloak and showed itself to be Aspiration. There, outside the baths, the AEsthetic awoke in me. The sensation, infinitely sad and yet pleasing, was so complete that it left me hot-cheeked and wondering....

In truth, so warm and all-pervading was it that the other day, when during a short leave from France I stood on the gravel that sweeps to the entrance of the baths, I felt the memory of that moment of yearning egoism hanging over the spot like a restless spirit of the past.

Sec. 4

The whole period of Preparation passed in suspense. And, when the bell had gone, Penny and I found our way to one of the Bramhall class-rooms, where I sat upon the hot-water pipes (the wisdom of which proceeding I have since doubted). After about five minutes there rushed in a bad little boy who, having more relish in the thought of his message than breath to deliver it, puffed out: "Oh, there you are. I've searched for you everywhere." Then he paused, recovered his breath, and actually pointed a finger at us, saying:

"Ee, bless me, my men, Salome wants you in Radley's room."

Penny took the small boy's head and banged it three times on a desk.

In Radley's familiar room we found Salome, who no sooner saw me than he cried:

"Ee, bless me, my man. Will you *take*—your *hand*—out of your *pocket*?"

This was such a surprise that I blushed and—oh, accursed nervousness!—began to giggle. My terror at giggling in the Presence was so real that I compressed my lips to secure control. But control was as impossible as concealment. Salome came very close, pointed at my mouth, and said:

"I think you're *giggling*. Take off that ridiculous expression, my man. I'm *going*—to *smack*—your *face*."

Sobered in a moment, I composed my features for the punishment and received it, stinging and burning, on my reddened cheek.

Salome again pointed at me.

"You're a ***sportsman***, sir, a ***sportsman***, and I ***like*** you," an affection which I at once reciprocated.

"Ee, bless me, my man," he pursued. "What's your horrible name?"

"Ray, sir."

"Well, Ray, I'm going to cane you hard"—(rather crudely expressed, I thought)—"because your offence is serious, bless me, my man"—(an unreasonable request at this stage).

He took out his cane and turned first to Pennybet.

"I find, Mr. Pennybet, that, when you were breaking bounds, you should have been with your ***company***—your ***company***, sir—at shooting practice. It's ***desertion***, sir—and punishable by ***death***. But I shan't shoot you. You're not ***worth*** it—not ***worth*** it. I shan't even cane you, sir. You're too ***old***—too ***old***."

Penny looked at him, as much as to say he thought his point of view was very sensible.

"But ee, bless me, my man, take off that complacent expression, or I feel I may certainly smack your face."

Poor Penny, for once in a way, was rather at a loss, which was all Salome desired, so he turned to me.

"Ray—I think ***that*** was your detestable name—I shall now cane you. Get ***over***, my man—get ***over***."

When the ceremony was completed, Salome talked to us so nicely, although periodically asking us to bless him, that I told myself I would never break bounds again; thereby making one of those good resolutions which pave, we are told, another Beaten Track.

CHAPTER VIII
THE FREEDHAM REVELATIONS

Sec.1

The next half-holiday I was walking towards the tuck-shop and gloomily deciding that Doe's wilful estrangement from me was fast being frozen into tacit enmity, when I felt an arm tucked most affectionately into mine. It was done so quietly and quickly that I nearly leapt a yard at the shock. The arm belonged to Doe.

"Ray, you old ass," he began.

Doe, now sixteen, was not so very different from the small fawning creature of three years before. Although the perfect curve of the cheek-line had given place to a perceptible depression beneath the cheek-bone; although the usual marks of a boy's adolescence—the slight pallor, the quick blush of diffidence, the slimness of limb—were all very noticeable in Doe, there was yet much of the original Baby about his appearance. It could be marked in his soft, indeterminate mouth, whose flower-like lips seemed always parted; in his inquiring eyes and unkempt hair; and, at the present moment, in an artless excitement that I had not seen for many a day.

I tried to drag my arm away, but he held it too tight, and proceeded to make the remarkable statement:

"You old ass! Surely you've been sulking long enough."

"Well, I like that," replied I, with an empty laugh. "You drop me, sulk like a pig, and then say it's the other way round—"

"Rot!" he interrupted. "Didn't you deliberately cut me out with Radley?"

"I don't know what you mean," I said, although the hint that I was Radley's favourite always gave me a flush of pleasure.

"And haven't you been hanging on to Penny, just to make me jealous?"

"Never entered my head," I replied promptly, and with truth. "I leave that sort of thing to schoolgirls like you. But it evidently did make you jealous."

"*Yes*, it did," he admitted with an engaging smile. This softened me; and my affection for him began at once to throb into activity.

"*Yes*, it did; and now that you've said you're sorry, I feel frightfully lively. Let's go and smash a window or something."

His spirits were infectious, and he dragged me off to the study which his intellectual eminence had recently secured for him. When we arrived there, he tossed me a bag of sweets, which had clearly been bought as a means to sugar the reconciliation, and, dropping into his armchair, stretched his legs in front of him, and said:

"Let's talk as we used to."

I was relieved from the necessity of finding some opening remark by the bursting into the room of "Moles" White.

If you look up the Latin word "Moles" in the dictionary, you will find that it means "a huge, shapeless mass"; and all of us had been very quick to see that this was an excellent description of our junior house-prefect, White. Moles White was as enormous and ugly in his dimensions as he was genial and simple in face. You saw at a glance that he possessed all the traditional kindliness and generosity of the giant. As he crashed into Doe's study, he was swinging some books on the end of a strap.

"Found you, Doe," said he. "Look here, Bramhall's got to make the best house-team it can, which means you must give up slacking at cricket. You'll play at the nets this evening."

"Heavens! Ray," Doe murmured in mock dismay, as he stared out of eyes that sparkled with impudence at White's huge frame, "what on earth is this coming in?"

White smiled meaningly.

"Don't be cheeky now, Doe," he suggested. "No lip, please."

Doe's reply was a laugh, and the question addressed to me:

"I say, Ray, do you think it's an Iguanodon?"

"Well," said White, striding forward and beginning to swing his books ominously, "if you're asking for trouble, you shall have it."

Doe ducked down and raised his right hand to protect his head.

"I never said it, White," he affirmed, giggling. "Really, I didn't. You thought I did. I never called you an Iguanodon—I've too much respect for you."

"Yes, you did. Take your hand away. I'm determined to swing these books on to your head."

"Ray," shouted Doe between his giggles, "take him away. Don't bully, Moles! You great beast! Ray, he's bullying me."

White paused. Bullying, even in fun, was a horrible idea. The books fell limply to his side.

"Be sensible, if you can, Doe. You've got to play this evening."

The change in White's voice prompted Doe to raise his head and look up from under his arm at his attacker.

"Great Scott, Ray," he blurted out. "If it's not an Iguanodon, it's a prehistoric animal of some sort."

"My hat!" exclaimed White. "You young devil! Put that hand down while I smite you over the head with these books." And he made as though to execute his threat. Doe accordingly retired still further down into his chair, and placed his elbow to ward off the swinging books.

"I didn't say it, White, you liar! Shut up, will you? You might hurt me seriously. Go away. I hate you! Oh, hang it!"—(this was when the books struck him on the elbow),—"it hurts, Moles. Leave off, while I rub my elbow."

The gentle giant responded to this reasonable request; the books dropped; and Doe, looking reproachfully at his executioner, set about massaging his elbow.

"Ray," he said, when the operation was complete, "is there any known means of removing this nightmare?"

Immediately his uplifted arm was seized in White's huge paw. Doe's eyes were sparkling, his cheeks red, and his hair tumbled. His right arm being now held, he laughed more loudly and nervously and raised his left.

"By Jove, White," he cried, "if you rouse my ire, I'll get up and lick you. Let go of my hand—it's not yours. Oh, shut up, you great swine! Hang it, Ray"—(this with a shriek, half of laughter, half of anticipation)—"he's got my left hand as well—O, White, I'm sorry."

White held both his victim's wrists in one hand. Too honourable to take advantage of this, he swung his books at a distance and said:

"You've got to play at the nets, do you hear?"

My friend simulated anger. Struggling to get free, he ejaculated:

"I'll not be ordered about by an Iguanodon. I'm not that sort of man. O, White, I said I was—he, he, ha!—sorry. I didn't mean to be rude. I didn't see it in that light—"

"Whack" came the books gently on his back.

"Oh, please, Moles White, please stop. There's a dear old Iguanodon. Ow—Ow—Ow!"

By this time Doe was much out of breath, and his sentences were short and broken: "It doesn't hurt. It's lovely! Ray, don't stand there grinning like this chimpanzee, White."

Suddenly at an upward swing the slender strap broke, and the books crashed through the window.

"Damn!" said White.

Doe, flushed and dishevelled, picked himself out of his chair.

"That's what comes of bullying, Moles White. I'll pay for it. It was my beastly fault!"

"No, you won't," said White.

"Don't presume to contradict me, Moles White, or I'll lick you! I have stated that I'll pay for it."

"No," White decided. "We'll split the difference and go shags."

I felt the old fellow was not displeased at this compromise, for his purse had its limitations. He withdrew from the scene and left us to our confidential chat.

When he had gone, there set in a reaction from the excited liveliness of his visit. Doe looked sadly through the broken pane and said:

"Isn't Moles a corking old thing? The sort of chap who's naturally good, and couldn't be anything else if he tried."

Something wistful in the words caused me to see a vision of the gravel-path sweeping to the doorway of the baths.

"I say, Doe," I began, "have you ever felt that you'd like to be—something different from the ordinary run?"

Doe swung round on me.

"Have I ever? Why, you know, Rupert, that I'm the most ambitious person in the world. And, by Jove! I believe I might have done something great—"

"*Might* have done!" interrupted I, surprised that he should have decided at sixteen that his life was earmarked for a failure. "You'll probably live quite ten years more, so there's still time."

Doe turned again and sent his gaze through the broken window, replying in a little while:

"Oh, I've lived long enough to know that I'm the sort that's destined to make a mess of his life. I—oh, hang it, you wouldn't understand..."

Evidently in Doe, as in me, his manhood had come down the corridor of the future and met his childhood face to face. One minute before this he was an irresponsible baby "cheeking" Moles White; now he was the germinal man, borne down with the weight of life. He paused for me to plead my understanding, and invite his confidence. But an awkwardness held me dumb, and he was obliged to continue:

"I wish you could understand, because—Do you know, Rupert, why I made it up with you this afternoon?" He came away from the window and sat in a chair opposite me. "It was because I was glowing with a new resolution. It was the rippingest feeling in the world. I—I had just decided to cut with Freedham."

Up to this point I had been looking into his face, but now I turned away. Instinctively I felt that, if he were going to, speak of his transactions with Freedham, he would be abashed by my gaze. He rested his elbows on his knees, and began to tie knot after knot in a piece of string.

"Freedham's an extraordinary creature," he proceeded. "He first got hold of me when I was at the Nursery. He would get me in a dark corner, and alternately pet and bully me. I remember his once holding me in a frightful grip and saying: 'You're so—' (I'm only telling you what he said, Rupert)—'You're so pretty that I'd love to see you cry.' He's *that* type, you know."

For a while Doe, whose cheeks and neck were crimson, knotted his string in silence.

"Then he used to give me money to encourage me to like him, and dash it, Ray! I *do* like him. He's got such weird, majestic ideas that are different from anyone else's,—and he attracts me. His great theory is that Life is Sensation, and there must be no sensation—a law, or no law—which he has not experienced. I believed him to be right (as I do still, in part) and we—we tried everything together. We—we got drunk on a beastly occasion in his room. We didn't like it, but we pushed on, so as to find out what the sensation was. And then—oh! I wish I'd never started telling you all this—"

He tied a knot with such viciousness that few would have had the patience to untie it.

"Go on, old chap," I said encouragingly. I was proud of playing the sympathetic confidant; but, less natural than that, a certain abnormality in the conversation had stimulated me; I was excited to hear more.

"Well, he told me that years before he had wanted to see what taking drugs was like, and he had been taking them ever since. He was mad keen on the subject and had read De Quincey and those people from beginning to end. I've tried them with him.... There are not many things we haven't done together."

Doe tossed the string away.

"I know I might have done well in cricket, but Freedham used to say that excelling in games was good enough for Kipling's 'flannelled fools' and 'muddied oafs.' We thought we were superior, chosen people, who would excel in mysticism and intellectualism."

As he said it, Doe looked up and smiled at me, while I sat, amazed to discover how far he, with his finer mind, had outstripped me in the realms of thought. I had no idea what mysticism was.

"And I still think," he pursued, "that Freedham's got hold of the Truth, only perverted; just as he himself is a perversion. Life *is* what feeling you get out of it; and the highest types of feeling are mystical and intellectual. I only knew yesterday what a perversion he really was. I saw something that I'd never seen before—he had a sort of paroxysm—like a bad *rigor*; something to do with the drug-habit, I s'pose—"

A powerful desire came over me to say: "I knew all about his fits years ago," but it melted before the memory of a far-away promise. At this point, too, I became perfectly sure that, although Doe's sudden self-revelation was an intense and genuine outburst, yet he was sufficiently his lovable self to feel pride in his easy use of technical terms like *paroxysm* and *rigor*.

"It frightened me," continued he. "It's only cowardice that's made me cut with him. I know my motives are all rotten, but no matter; I was gloriously happy half-an-hour ago, when I had made the resolution. And now I'm melancholy. That's why I'm talking about being a great man. You must be melancholy to feel great."

As he said the words, Doe leapt to his feet and unconsciously struck his breast with a fine action.

"And I sometimes *know* I could be great. I feel it surging in me. But I shall only dream it all. I haven't the cold, calculating power of Penny, for instance. He's the only one of us who'll set the Thames on fire. At present, Rupert, I've but one goal; and that is to win the Horace Prize before I leave. If I can do that, I'll believe again in my power to make something of my life."

Sec.2

I fear I'm a very ignoble character, for this conversation, instead of filling me with pain at Doe's deviations, only gave me a selfish elation in the thought that I had utterly routed my shadowy rival, Freedham, and won back my brilliant twin, who could talk thus familiarly about mysticism. And now there only remained the very concrete Fillet to be driven in disorder from the field.

CHAPTER IX
WATERLOO OPENS

Sec.1

And here begins the record of my Waterloo with Fillet.

One June morning of the following year all we Bramhallites were assembled in the Preparation Room for our weekly issue of "Bank" or pocket-money; we were awaiting the arrival of Fillet, our house-master, with his jingling cash-box. Soon he would enter and, having elaborately enthroned himself at his desk, proceed to ask each of us how much "Bank" he required, and to deliberate, when the sum was proposed, whether the boy's account would stand so large a draft. The boy would argue with glowing force that it would stand that and more; and Fillet would put the opposing case with irritating contumacy.

This morning he was late; the corridors nowhere echoed the rattle of his cash-box. So it occurred to me to entertain the crowd with a little imitation of Fillet. Seating myself at his desk, I frowned at a nervous junior, and addressed him thus:

"N-now, my boy, how much b-b-bank do you want? Shilling? B-b-bank won't stand it. T-take sixpence. Sixpence not enough? Take ninepence and run away."

The Bramhallites enjoyed my impersonation.

"N-now, Moles—White, I mean—how much b-b-bank do you want? Two shillings? B-bank won't stand it. Take three halfpence—take it, Moles, and toddle away."

There were roars of laughter, and a grin from White like the smile of a brontosaurus.

"N-now, Doe, you don't want any this week—you've come to pay in some, I suppose. You—oh, damn!"

This whispered oath, accompanied by a dismayed stare at the door, turned the heads of all in that direction. Fillet, in his carpet slippers, had come round the corner and was an interested critic of my little imitation.

Very red, I vacated the seat to its owner and stepped down among the boys. Without a word he took it in my stead, placed his cash-box on the desk, and opened his book.

"N-now, White, how much b-b-bank do you want?"

Having heard this before, several boys tittered. Out of nervousness I tittered too, and cursed myself as I did so. Fillet looked at me as though he would have liked to repeat the flogging he had given me many years before. But the blushing boy in front of him was now seventeen, and taller than he.

When the last account had been duly debited, the Bramhallites dispersed to their classes. Throughout that day the incident was a painful recollection for me. I felt I could beat Fillet with cleaner weapons than an exploiting of his affliction: and the more I thought of it, the more I decided that I must go and apologise to him. The sentence to be used crystallised in my mind: "Please, sir, I came to say I was sorry I was imitating you this morning."

With this little offering I walked in the fall of the evening upstairs to his study. My knock eliciting a "C-come in," I entered and began:

"Please, sir, I came to say—" I got no further, for, with a sour look, he interrupted testily:

"Run away, b-boy, run away."

This rejection of my apology I had never contemplated, and it was with a sinking heart that I persisted:

"Please, sir, I wanted to—"

" *Run away, boy.* I'm accustomed to dealing with gentlemen."

At once my attitude of submission was changed at Fillet's clumsy touch into one of hot defiance.

"Indeed, sir," I retorted. "I'm not always so fortunate." I went quickly out and managed to slam the door. Blood up, I muttered:

"Brute! Beast! Swine! Devil!"

Sec.2

Moles White, who was now the house-captain, was occupied two afternoons later in discussing with the bloods of Bramhall the composition of the House Swimming Four for the Inter-house relay races.

"Erasmus House have a splendid Four," he said. "We've only got three so far: there's myself and Cully and Johnson."

"And a precious rotten three too," said Doe.

"Well," grumbled White, "there's nobody else in the House who can swim a stroke; a good many think they can."

"Not so sure," whispered Doe, obscurely. "Come along with me. No, Moles alone." And he dragged White towards the baths.

Within that beloved building I was trying to see how many lengths I could swim. It was rather late, and I had the water to myself. I was doing my sixth length when I saw entering the baths the ungainly carcass of White with the graceful form of Doe hanging affectionately on his arm. The latter was explaining that no one knew how well I could swim, as I had once nearly fainted when extending myself to the utmost and had gone easy ever since. "But Rupert can really swim at ninety miles an hour," he concluded.

So White called: "Come here, Ray."

"When you say 'please,'" shouted I, swimming about.

Doe thereupon took the matter in hand and addressed me:

"Now, Ray, I want you to swim your best. Here's a little kiddy friend of mine I've brought to see you. Mr. Ray, this is Master Moles."

White ignored his companion's playfulness and asked me:

"Can you swim sixty yards?"

I hurled about five pints of water at him to show that I detected the insult.

"You old Moles!" said Doe. "Serves you right. Why, he's just finished swimming about seventy thousand yards."

"Well, sheer off and let's see you do it," ordered White.

I accordingly swam my fastest to the deep end and back.

"My word!" gasped White. "I didn't know you could swim like that."

Doe laughed in his face.

"You loon! He could swim before you were born."

Moles seized Doe by the throat and pretended to push him into the water, but characteristically saved him from falling by placing an arm round his waist.

"Apologise," he hissed, "or I'll drop you."

"Moles," replied Doe reproachfully. "At once let me go; or I'll push you in." I rendered my friend immediate assistance by filling White's shoes with water.

"Shut up that!" said he, quickly releasing Doe, who retired from the baths shouting: "Moles, you ugly old elephant, Ray could give you eighty yards in a hundred, and beat you."

This last impertinence suggested an idea to White. He arranged that Cully, Johnson, he, and I should have a private race, "in camera," as he put. The event came off the following day, and I won it with some yards to spare. My three defeated opponents were generous in their praise.

"Golly!" said Johnson. "I thought we'd be last for the Swimming Cup. But snakes alive! we'll get in the semi-final."

"Why, man," declared Cully. "I see us in the final with Erasmus."

"Final be damned!" said White. "Train like navvies and we'll lift the Cup!"

Sec.3

Never did human boy have three more sporting associates in a swimming four than I had in White, Cully, and Johnson. Because I was a year younger than they it was their pleasure to call me the "Baby of the Team," and to take a pride in my successes. They would, in order to pace me, take half-a-length's start in a two-lengths' practice race, and make me strain every nerve to beat them. Or they would time me with their watches over the sixty yards, and, all arriving at different conclusions as to my figures, agree only in the fact that I was establishing records. Once, when according to a stop-watch I really did set up a record, Cully, forgetting his dignity as a prefect in his enthusiasm as a Bramhallite, cried "Alleluia! alleluia!" and hurled Johnson's hat into the air, so that it fell into the water.

The members of Erasmus' Four were at first incredulous.

"Heard of Bramhall's find?" said they. "They've discovered a young torpedo in Ray. He's quite good and they'll probably get into the final. But we needn't be afraid. They've a weak string in Johnson, while we haven't a weakness anywhere. However, we'll take no risks." And so they started a savagely severe system of training.

Meantime White constituted himself my medical adviser, and some such dialogue as this would take place every morning:

"Now, Ray, got any pain under the heart?"

"No."

"Do you feel anything like a stomach-ache?"

"Only when I see your face."

"Look here, I'd knock your face through your head, if I didn't want your services so badly. Are you at all stiff?"

"Yes, bored stiff with your conversation."

It was true that there had been no trace of the faintness which had attacked me a year before. Had there been, I should have kept quiet about it, for, in that time of excitement, I would willingly have shortened my life by ten years, if I could have made certain of securing the Cup for Bramhall. Only one thing marred this period of my great ascendency; Radley, Bramhall's junior house-master, never gave me a word of praise or flattery.

That wound to my self-love festered stingingly. I persisted in letting my thoughts dwell on it. I would frame sentences with which Radley would express his surprise at my transcendent powers, such as: "Ray, you're a find for the house"; "I'm glad Bramhall possesses you, and no other house"; "I don't think I've ever seen a faster boy-swimmer"; "You're the best swimmer in the school by a long way." I would turn any conversation with him on to the subject of the race, and suffer a few seconds' acute suspense, while I waited for his compliment. I would depreciate my own swimming to him, feeling in my despair that a murmured contradiction would suffice: but this method I gave up, owing to the horror I experienced lest he should agree.

And, when he mercilessly refused to gratify me, I would wander away and review all the occasions on which he had seen me swim, recalling how I then acquitted myself; or I would laboriously enumerate all the people who must have told him in high terms of my performances. A growing annoyance with him pricked me into a defiant determination, so that I reiterated to myself: "I'll do it. I'll win it. I swear I will!"

Bramhall passed easily into the final. Erasmus, too, romped home in their first and second rounds. So on the eve of the great race it was known throughout Bramhall that the house must be prepared to measure itself against Erasmus' famous four.

Betting showed Erasmus as firm favourites, the school critics looking askance at Johnson, our weakest man. Only the Bramhallites laid nervous half-crowns on the house, and hoped a mighty hope. That excellent fellow, White, displayed his unfortunate features glowing with an expression that was almost beautiful.

As the day of the race led me, steadily and without pity, to the time of ordeal, I sickened so from nerves that I could scarcely swallow food; and what I did swallow I couldn't taste. I was glad when at five o'clock something definite could be done like going to the baths, selecting a cabin, and beginning to undress. Four minutes were scarcely sufficient for me to undo my braces, such was the trembling of my hand. I longed for the moments to pass, so that the time to dive in could come; every delay ruffled me; I wished the whole thing were over. It didn't lessen my suffering to watch the gallery filling with excited boys, and to see the crowd on the ground-floor make way for Salome himself, followed by Fillet and Radley as representatives of Bramhall, and Upton as house-master of Erasmus. Perspiration beaded my forehead. My heart fluttered, and I began to fear some failure in that quarter. At one moment, when I was *in extremis*, I would willingly have exchanged positions with the humblest of the onlookers: at another I caught a faint gleam of hope in the thought that the end of the world might yet come before I was asked to do anything publicly. And I conceived of happier boys who had died young.

The baths were prepared for the event. Across the water, thirty feet from the diving-station, a large beam was fixed, which the competitors must reach and touch, before turning round and swimming back to the starting point. More boys were allowed to crowd into the gallery and the cabins. Very conspicuous was the expansive white waistcoat of old Dr. Chapman, who was busy backing Erasmus when talking to the boys of Erasmus, and Bramhall when questioned by Bramhallites. Fillet, as master of Bramhall; Upton, as master of Erasmus; and Jerry Brisket, as a neutral, were appointed judges.

White gathered the Bramhall four into his cabin and arranged with sanguine comments that we should swim in this order:

1. Himself—to give us a good start.
2. Johnson—to lose as little as possible of the fine lead established.
3. Ray—to make the position absolutely certain.
4. Cully—to maintain the twenty-yards' lead secured by Ray.

"See, Ray," he said to me, after he had dismissed the others, "you swim third—last but one."

"Ye—es," I stuttered.

"Nervous?" he inquired softly.

I smiled and made a grimace. "Beastly."

He gripped my hand in his powerful fist and whispered: "Rot! you are certain to do everything for us. My heart is set on winning this and staggering the school."

I smiled again. "You're a ripping chap, and I'm sorry if I've ever cheeked you."

Sudden cheering told us that the great Erasmus four had emerged from their cabins. They were as fine a little company of Saxon boys as ever school could show; comely, tall, and fair-skinned. On the left side of the diving-boards they took up their pre-arranged positions: Atwood, first; Southwell Primus, behind him; Lancelot, third (and therefore my opponent); and then Southwell Secundus. And all four had tied on their heads the black and white polo-caps of the school. Upton looked with satisfaction upon his house's representatives; while Dr. Chapman, standing near, exclaimed: "Fine young shoots of yours, Uppy. I tell you, this is England's best generation. Dammit, there are three things old England *has* learnt to make: ships, and poetry, and boys."

Now, amid less resounding but still enthusiastic applause, the Bramhall four assumed positions on the right. White stood on the diving-mat; behind him, Johnson, frowning; next myself; and lastly Cully. We were of very varying heights, from White, whose huge proportions exaggerated the difference, to little thick-set Cully, who was the shortest of all. And only these two wore the polo-cap. So both fours stood before the multitude, inviting comparison: Erasmus, a team; Bramhall, a scratch lot.

Behind me Cully observed the contrast, and, striving with courage to belie his agitation, murmured: "Look at Erasmus. Did you ever see such a measly lot? If we can't beat that crew, Ray, my boy, we must be duffers," to emphasise which remark he tickled me under both armpits, so that, nearly jumping out of my skin, I fell forward on to Johnson, who fell forward on to White, who, having nobody to fall forward on to, fell prematurely into the water. This extra item was loudly "encored," and White scrambled back to his place and bowed his acknowledgments.

Salome, as starter, thereupon addressed the competitors.

"Ee, bless me, my men, I shall say 'Are you ready? Go!'"

His words were like a bell for silence. Upton and Fillet eyed the swimmers narrowly.

"*Are you ready? Go!*"

And then a calamity supervened. While Atwood dived with the grace of a swallow, White, well—White missed his dive; he leapt into the air, his great arms and legs appeared to hang limply down, and his body struck the water with a splash that set the whole surface in a turmoil. "Moles has gone a belly-flopper," shouted the crowd, as it wept with laughter. "Good old Moles, 'a huge, shapeless mass!'" I was too nervous to laugh, and wished that I had trousers on, for my limbs were trembling so noticeably that I felt everybody must be studying them. Johnson swore. Cully said: "Bang goes the Cup!" But White rose and started furiously to recover the lost ground, thrashing the water with his limbs. Bravely done! How the building cheered, as his long arms swung distances behind them! But he failed. Atwood, swimming with coolness, kept and increased the advantage; and, accompanied by a din from his housemates and an all-embracing smile from Upton, touched the rope beneath the diving-mat full two yards in front. Over his head dived Southwell Primus, while Johnson, in an agony, yelled to White to hurry his shapeless stumps. Moles, with a last tremendous stretch, touched the rope, and Johnson plunged splendidly to his work. I took up my position on the mat and helped White to flounder out.

"Ray," were his first words, "it's up to you now. I'm awfully sorry I muddled it, but *you'll* make it good. I know you will—you must. I shall weep if we go down."

"I'll try," I said.

Meanwhile Johnson, as is often the case with the weakest man, outstripped the most hazardous faith. To the joy of Bramhall he matched Southwell Primus with a yard for his yard. But, even so, his pace couldn't eat up the lost ground; and the Erasmus man touched home still two yards in front of the Bramhallite. In flew Lancelot, my opponent; and, with the coming of Johnson, it would be my turn. The Bramhallites, in a burst of new hope, shouted sarcastically: "Go it, Lancelot. Ray's coming. He's just coming." I got the spring in my toes, watched carefully to see Johnson touch the rope beneath me, and then, to the greatest shout of our supporters, dived into the beloved element.

They told me (but probably it was in their enthusiasm) that it was the best and longest racing-dive I had ever done; that, remaining almost parallel to the surface, I just pierced the water as a knife pierces cheese. All I know is that at the grasp of the cool water every symptom of nerves left me: and, with my face beneath the surface, and the water rushing past my ears, half shutting out a frenzied uproar, I raced confidently for the beam. The position of Lancelot I cared not to know. My one aim was to cover the sixty yards in record time; and, so doing, to pass him. On I shot, feeling that my arms were devouring the course; and, some five strokes sooner than I expected, became conscious that I was near the beam. In an overarm reach I scraped it with my finger-tips. Swinging round, I swam madly back. Extending myself to the utmost, I felt as if every stroke was swifter than its predecessor. Now my breath grew shorter and my limbs began to stiffen; but all this proved a source of speed, for, in a spirit of defiance of nature, I whipped arms and legs into even faster movement; it was my brain against my body. Then there came into view the rope, which I touched with a reach. Making no attempt to grasp it, for I seemed to be travelling too rapidly, I saw the atmosphere darken with the shadow of Cully passing over my head, and crashed head-first into the end of the baths. Not stunned, for the cold water refreshed me, I turned immediately to see if I had really got home before Lancelot. He was still in the water, three yards from the rope.

Sec.4

That moment, while many hands helped me out of the water; while the building echoed with cheers and whistles; while White, too happy to speak, beamed upon the world; while fists hammered me on the back; while Cully, splendidly swimming, made the victory sure; I experienced such a happiness as would not be outweighed by years of subsequent misery. Though my limbs were so stiff that it was pain to move them, they glowed with diffused happiness; though my heart was fluttering at an alarming pace, it beat also with the electric pulsations of joy: though my breath was too disturbed for speech, yet my mind framed the words: "I've done it, I've done it"; though my head ached with the blow it had received, it was also bursting with a delight too great to hold. I had never done anything for the house before, and now I had won for its shelf the Swimming Cup.

They helped me to my cabin, and, as I sat there, I composed the tale of success that I would send to my mother. Then I stood up to dress, and, in my excitement, put on my shirt before my vest. There was a confusion of cheers within and without the building; and Upton, Fillet, and Jerry Brisket, the judges, were to be seen in animated debate, while many others stood round and listened. Dazed, faint, and unconscious of the passage of momentous events, I took no notice of them, but drank deeply of victory. It exhilarated me to reconstruct the whole story, beginning with my early stage-fright and ending with the triumphant climax, when I crashed into the end of the baths.

I was indulging the glorious retrospect when there broke upon my reverie a sullen youth who said:

"Well, Ray, we haven't won it after all."

There was a hitch in my understanding, and I asked:

"What d'you mean?"

"You were disqualified."

"I!" It was almost a hair-whitening shock. "I! What? Why? What for?"

"They say you dived before Johnson touched the rope. Nobody believes you did."

So then; I had *lost* the cup for Bramhall. The lie! Too old to vent suffering in tears, I showed it in a panting chest, a trembling lip, and a dry, wide-eyed stare at my informant. Backed by a disorder outside, he repeated: "Nobody believes you did."

All happiness died out of my ken. Conscious only of aching limbs, a fluttering heart, uneven breath, and a bursting head, I cried:

"I didn't. I didn't. Who said so?"

"Fillet—Carpet Slippers."

"The liar! The liar!" I muttered; and, with a sudden attack of something like cramp down my left side, I fell into a sitting position, and thence into a huddled and fainting heap upon the floor.

CHAPTER X
WATERLOO CONTINUES:
THE CHARGE AT THE END OF THE DAY

Sec. 1

While I was recovering there fell the first thunderdrops of mutiny. A youth at the back of the gallery, on intercepting the flying message that Fillet had demanded my disqualification and Jerry Brisket had ended by supporting him, roared out a threatening "*No!*" Maybe, had he not done so, there would never have been the great Bramhall riot. But many other boys, catching the contagion of his defiance, cried out "*No!*" The crowd, recently so excited, was easily flushed by the new turn of events, and shouted in unison "*No!*" Isolated voices called out "Cheat!" "Liar!" Dr. Chapman, as tactless as he was kindly, declared to those about him that Fillet's judgment was at fault, and thus helped to increase the uproar. The disaffection spread to the Erasmus men, who said openly: "We don't want the beastly cup. Bramhall won it fair and square."

And then came the report that I, on receiving the news, had fainted. This, by provoking deeper sympathy with the hero and greater execration of the villain, acted like paraffin oil on the flames. Before the masters realised that anything more than disappointment was abroad, rebellion looked them in the face.

Salome saw it and knew that, if his short but brilliant record as headmaster was not to be abruptly destroyed, he must rise to prompt and statesmanlike action. His first step was to summon all the prefects in the building and say:

"Ee, bless me, my men, clear the baths."

The prefects quickly emptied the building of all boys; but outside the door they could do no more than link arms like the City Police and keep back a turbulent mob. Then Salome, accompanied by Fillet, Upton, and Radley, passed with dignity through his pupils. He was received in an ominous silence.

Now, behind this revolt there was a hidden hand; and it was the hand of Pennybet. To effect a ***coup d'etat*** and to control and move blind forces were, we know, the particular hobbies of Pennybet. Here this evening he found blind disorder and rebellion, which, if they were not to die out feebly and expose the rebels to punishment, must be guided and controlled. So he flattered himself he would take over the reins of mutiny, and hold them in such a clandestine manner that none should recognise whose was the masterhand. He would cross swords with Salome. As he said to me the following day: "*I* ran that riot, Rupert, and I never enjoyed anything so much in my life."

His method outside the baths was to keep himself in the background and to whisper to boys, at various points on the circumference of the vast and gathering mob, battle orders, which he knew would be quickly circulated. They were really his own composition, but, like a good general keeping open his means of retreat, he attributed them to some visionary people, who, in the event of failure, could bear the brunt of the insurrection.

"Some of the chaps are talking about a real organised revolt. How corking!"

"The idea seems to be that it's no good doing anything, unless it's done on a large scale. I shall stick by the others and see what they do."

"You're to pass the word, they say, to keep massed. I suppose their game is that small bodies can be dispersed, but we can't be touched if we're all caked together. You'd better pass that on and explain it."

"There are to be no dam black-legs. I've just heard that any who slink off will be mobbed."

"What are we waiting for? Can't say. Depends who's managing this shindy. You can be sure somebody's organising it, and we'll do what the others do. Toss that along."

Really, Penny didn't know what his great crowd *was* waiting for. He had not had time to formulate a plan, but had contented himself with keeping his forces together. And, while, closely compacted, they swayed about, unconscious that they were the plaything of one cool and remarkable boy, he hit upon the scheme of an offensive. He decided that it would be futile to fight here, where all the school-prefects were concentrated; it would be better to transfer the attack to the court-yard of Bramhall House, where only the Bramhall prefects would have to be reckoned with. To stay here was to attempt a frontal attack. No, he would retreat as a feint, and outflank the school-prefects by a surprise movement in the direction of Bramhall.

"Have you heard?" he said. "We're all to disperse and meet again in five minutes in Bramhall courtyard. I wonder what's in the wind."

Penny knew that not a single boy would fail to arrive at the advertised station, if only to see what *was* in the wind; and as the crowd disintegrated and the prefects strolled away, thinking the mutiny had petered out, he murmured to himself: "A crowd's an easy thing for a man to handle."

Sec. 2

So it was that there was silence everywhere when, returning to consciousness, I found myself in the empty baths with Dr. Chapman looking down upon me.

"One day we must thoroughly overhaul you, young man," he said. "There may be a weakness at your heart. How're you feeling now?"

"Oh, all right, thanks."

"Bit disappointed, I suppose?"

"Rather!"

"Frightfully so?"

I didn't answer. His words filled my throat with a lump.

"Would blub, if you could, but can't, eh?"

The question nearly brought the tears welling into my eyes. He watched them swell, and said:

"As a doctor, I should tell you to try and blub, but, as an old public-schoolboy, I should say 'Try not to.' Do which you like, old man. Both are right. I'll not stay to see."

And, without looking round, he withdrew from the building.

About ten minutes later I found myself in the deserted playing fields. Knowing nothing of any breaches of the peace, I crossed the road and passed through the gateway into the courtyard of Bramhall House. Immediately a great roar of cheers went up, I was seized by excited hands, raised on to the shoulders of several boys, and carried through a shouting multitude to the boys' entrance, where I was deposited on the steps.

Probably not a soul knew that Salome was looking down from the window of Fillet's study and watching the effect of my arrival. As soon as the theatre of hostilities had changed from the baths to Bramhall House, he, too, had crossed the road and entered unobserved by Fillet's private doorway. He knew well enough that of all the outposts in his schools' system of discipline Bramhall was the weakest held. The house was under the sway of an ineffective master with a stinging tongue; and trouble would have stirred long ago had it not been for the heavy hand of the junior house-master, Radley, whom Salome's predecessor had placed there to strengthen the position. And insubordination had been not uncommon since the accession of the too genial White to the captaincy.

In justice to White I must say that, if he had been present this evening, he would have done his best to quell the disturbance. But the decision of the judges had no sooner reached him than he had disappeared from the sight of men. As a matter of fact his great heart was breaking in the privacy of the science buildings. The only other house-prefects were, strangely enough, the redoubtable Cully and Johnson, who had sought consolation by retiring together to a cafe in the town. So, when Salome arrived at Fillet's study, there were no prefects available to disband the rebels. What was he to do? It would be quite inexpedient for a master to venture himself into the field of fire. If he suffered indignity, severe punishment would be necessary, and that might provoke further defiance. Then again, an alien prefect from another house would have little hope of success on Bramhall territory. Truly Salome was out in a storm.

Hardly had they placed me on the steps, very surprised and gratified, before Pennybet roared out:

"Was it true that you cheated, as Fillet tried to make out?"

"No!" I cried.

If I had been a nobler youth, I should have assumed that Fillet acted conscientiously from a mistake. But I believed, and wanted to believe, that his had been a piece of deliberate revenge; that, recalling my imitation of his affliction, he had determined to rob me of my triumph. So, being a vindictive young animal, I declared to the mob what I conceived to be the truth. And all of them agreed, while many began to hoot.

"Now, I've been sent by some boys at the back," said Penny, "to tell you that what you've got to do is to go up to Fillet's room and tender him a mock-apology for losing the Cup for his house. We're to cheer ironically and hoot down here, and make a hell of a noise. Then if he says 'Are those young devils cheering you or hooting me?' you're to say 'They're doing both, sir.' It's a good scheme, whoever invented it, because he can't touch you for civilly apologising and then for telling the truth when you are asked a question."

The idea fired me. Aye, it would be good to attack in a last charge and beat old Fillet, while I had all his house in fighting array behind me. It would be good that he, who had rejected my serious apology, should be obliged to hear my contemptuous one, backed by the tumult and hooting of half the school. Never had I thought that my decisive victory, for which I had waited years, would assume these splendid proportions.

Into the house I went, flushed and determined, and quite unaware that by invading Fillet's study I should walk into the arms of the head master himself. Up the stairs I rushed, but, as I set foot upon the first landing, Radley, coming out of his room, stood in the way of my further ascent.

"Come in here a minute," he said.

"Sir, I can't—"

He seized me by the right wrist and swung me almost brutally into his room. I was a muscular stripling, and he meant me to feel his strength. Suddenly disconcerted, I heard the door slam, and found that Radley was face to face with me. My breast went up and down with uncontrollable temper, while my wrist, all red and white with the marks of powerful fingers, felt as if it were broken.

"Where were you going?" he demanded, his hard mouth set.

"To Mr. Fillet's study," I snapped, purposely omitting the "sir."

"What for?"

"To apologise for losing the Swimming Cup."

"In a spirit of sincerity or one of scoffing?"

It was with no desire for veracity, but as a challenge to fight, that I replied:

"One of scoffing."

"Good." Radley's grey eyes unveiled some of their gentleness, "you can tell the truth still. Now, Ray, the shock of your disappointment has deprived you of reason, or you, of all people, would see that this tomfoolery outside is unsportsmanlike in the extreme."

"But, sir," I ventured, surprised and rather pleased to hear myself mannerly again, "every boy declares I didn't dive too soon."

"But unfortunately, Ray," replied Radley, also pleased, "every boy was not appointed a judge, and your housemaster was. Now, do you think that the judge's decision can be overruled by a mere counting of the heads that disagree with him? I put it to you; undo the damage you've done in associating yourself with this exhibition outside—at this moment you wield more influence than any other boy in the school—go out and establish order."

"Sir, I can't, sir. I'm their sort of deputy."

"Ray, there's a wave of rebellion outside, and you're nothing more important than the foam on the crest of the wave. Look here, you're a magnificent swimmer, the best in the school by a long way"—thus came the word of praise for which I had hungered so long—"well, a good swimmer will go out and breast the wave."

As he said it, he laid his hand gently upon my shoulder, and I felt, as I did once before, that in his peculiar sacramental touch there was something given by him and taken by me.

"But, sir," I said, desiring to justify myself, "I couldn't help thinking that Mr. Fillet did it on purpose to pay me out."

Radley frowned. "You mustn't say such things. But, were it so, any fool can be resentful, while it takes a big man to sacrifice himself and his petty quarrels for the good of great numbers. You will do it to save the school from hurt. I have always believed you big enough for these things."

My answer must have showed Radley how sadly I was less than his estimate of me.

"But, sir, if I turn back now they'll say I funked."

"Exactly; then go out and face their abuse. Go out and get hurt. I'm determined your life shall be big, so begin now by learning to stand buffeting. Besides, Ray, does it matter to a strong swimmer if the wave beats against him?"

I answered nothing, but gazed out of the window. And Radley shot another appeal—a less lofty one, but it flew home. Arrows pierce deeper, if they don't soar too high.

"Ray, *they'll* say you funked your master, if you don't go up to Mr. Fillet's study; *I* shall say you funked the boys, if you don't go out to them. You must choose between their contempt and mine."

I looked down at my boots.

"Which would you rather have, their contempt or mine?"

"Theirs, sir."

Radley was quite moved when I answered him thus; and it was a little while before he proceeded:

"I might have stopped your access to Mr. Fillet's study by telling you that the head master was waiting for you there. But I wanted you to stop from your own high motives, and not from fear. Come along now; we'll go together."

We ascended the stairs to the study and entered. Salome at once raised his long figure from his seat and, pointing at my tie, said:

"Ee, bless me, my man, you're very slovenly; put your tie straight."

I blushed and did so.

Then he turned to Radley.

"Did you find him in the right disposition?"

"Yes, sir."

It would not have been I if at this "Yes, sir" of Radley's my mind had not run up an irrelevant alley, in which I found myself wondering that Radley, who was always called "sir," should ever have to call anyone else "sir." Perhaps I was staring dreamily into vacancy, for Salome said:

"Bless me, I'm very glad to hear that his disposition is all right. But is the boy a fool? Why does he stand staring into vacancy like a brainless nincompoop?"

I turned redder than ever and wondered at whom to look so as to avoid vacancy, and what to do with my hands. Nervously I used the right hand to button up my coat, and then put it out of mischief in my pocket.

"Good God, man!" cried the Head. "Take that hand out of your pocket!"

I took it quickly out and unbuttoned one coat-button: then, for lack of something to do with the hand, did the button up again. I decided to keep the miserable member fingering the button. To make matters worse Salome rested his eyes like a searchlight on the hand. At last he looked distressingly straight at my face.

"Ray," he asked, "are you a perfect fool?"

"No, sir," I said, and grinned.

The Head turned to my housemaster for his testimony.

"Mr. Fillet, is the boy a fool?"

"One couldn't call him a *fool*," replied Fillet, obviously intending the conclusion: "One might, however, call him a *knave*."

The Head turned to Radley.

"Mr. Radley, is he a fool?"

"He's anything but a fool, sir; and he's still less of a knave," said Radley, angry and caring only to repudiate Fillet's innuendo.

"Ray," Salome was again staring me out of countenance. "Do you ever do any work?"

"Yes, sir," I said brightly. It was kind of him to ask questions to which I could honestly answer in the affirmative. I did occasionally do some work.

"Mr. Fillet?" queried Salome, desiring the housemaster to have his say.

"I suppose there are idler boys," announced Fillet grudgingly; and it was open to anyone to hear in his words the further meaning; "but, on the other hand, there are many more studious and more deserving." The fact is, the little man was irritated that Radley should have tried to contradict him before the Head.

"Mr. Radley?" pursued Salome, as though he were bored with the evidence, but realised that everyone must be allowed his turn to speak.

"Ray has always worked well for *me*," Radley promptly answered, and we all knew he meant it as a second stab for Fillet.

Salome once more fixed me with his disconcerting stare.

"Ray," he asked, "have you any glimmerings of moral courage?"

"I don't know, sir," said I, wondering where the conversation was leading.

The Head, apparently tired out by this catechising, contented himself with turning his face in the direction of Fillet for his endorsement or denial.

"He's as bold as they make 'em," said Fillet; and this time the double meaning was as clear as before: "the boy is utterly shameless."

The Head turned to Radley, who answered with a snap:

"Yes, he's plenty of courage; and what's better, he's easily shamed."

"Bless me, are you any good whatever at games?" continued the weary catechist.

"I can swim a bit, but I'm not much good at anything else."

"As he says, he swims a bit," corroborated Fillet. "But I don't know what else he can do."

"He's the best swimmer in the school," snapped Radley, "and will one day be the best bowler."

"Well, bless me, my man, have you any position or influence with your schoolfellows?"

"I don't know, sir."

"Hm!" sneered Fillet, whose temper was gone. "He has his *confederates*."

"Yes," said Radley, "he has a *very loyal following*."

I think it pleased the drowsy Head to see two of his masters boxing over the body of one of his boys.

"Well, well," he said, "I'm glad, Ray, to hear you give such a good account of yourself. We are satisfied, I may say, with your prowess in the baths this evening— you did your best, sir, you did your best—and we are satisfied with the attitude you have taken up in regard to this nonsensical business outside—"

"But, sir," I began, deprecatingly.

"God bless me, my man, don't interrupt! I tell you, we are satisfied. We don't sigh for the *moon*; and we're not talking of your shortcomings. We haven't *time*, bless me, we haven't *time*. We're only talking of your virtues, which won't occupy many minutes. We are satisfied that you're not altogether a fool—that you do some work—that you have some moral courage—that you're an athlete—and—what else was the matter, with him, Mr. Radley?—oh, that you have some position with your schoolfellows. We make you a house-prefect, sir, a house-prefect."

Staggered beyond measure, I suppose I showed it in my face, for Salome continued:

"Ee, my man, take off that ridiculous expression. I congratulate you, sir—con-gratulate you."

And I mechanically shook hands with him. Then Radley gripped my fingers and nearly broke the knuckle-bones. Fillet also formally proffered his hand, and I pressed it quite heartily. It was no good gloating over a man when he was down.

After this ceremony all waited for Salome to clinch proceedings, which he did as offensively as possible by saying:

"Ee, bless me, my man, don't stand there idling all day. Go out at once and establish order."

I went slowly down the stairs to the entrance, and, facing the crowd, was greeted with a fire of questions: "Did you do it?" "What did he say?" "How did he take it?" "Didn't you do it?"

"No," I said, and there was a temporary silence.

"Why not? Why not?"

"Because it wasn't the thing."

While no more eloquence came to my lips, plenty flowed from those of the boys before me. For a moment their execration seemed likely to turn upon me. At last I made myself heard.

"You see," I shouted, "only cads dispute the decision of the referee."

"Yes, but there are exceptions to every rule," said Penny's voice.

And here I sipped the sweets of authority.

"Well, there isn't going to be any exception in this case," I said.

The crowd detected something humorous in my high-handed sentence and laughed sarcastically. So, giving up all attempts to be persuasive, I said bluntly:

"Look here, Salome's upstairs, and he's made me a prefect and sent me down to establish order."

There were elements of greatness in Pennybet. He willingly acknowledged that the *coup d'etat* was not his but Salome's, and the riot must inevitably crumble away. So he made a point of leading the cheers that greeted my announcement, and, coming forward, was the first to congratulate me. His example was extensively followed, while he looked on approvingly, as though it had all been his doing, and chirruped every now and then: "This is the jolliest day I've spent at Kensingtowe."

CHAPTER XI
THE GREAT MATCH

Sec.1

The next year was 1914. It found Pennybet at Sandhurst; Doe brilliantly high in the Sixth Form, and, since he was a classical scholar and a poet, first favourite for the Horace Prize. In the cricket annals of Kensingtowe it was a remarkable year. Throughout the Summer Term victory followed victory. The M.C.C., having heard of Kensingtowe's super-batsmen, sent a strong team against us, which went under, amid cheering that lasted from 6 to 6.30 p.m. The *Sportsman* spoke of our fast bowler and captain as the "Coming Man." We called him "Honion," partly because his head, being perfectly bald, resembled that vegetable, and partly because he enjoyed the prefix "The Hon." before his name. Yes, I am speaking of the Hon. F. Lancaster, who appeared for a few moments like a new comet in the cricket heavens, just as the thundercloud of war blotted everything out. When the cloud should roll away, that new comet would be no longer there.

As the term drew to its close, and the world to the War, the cricket enthusiasm possessing Kensingtowe focussed itself on the annual fixture, "The School *v.* The Masters." For eight years the Masters, thanks to their captain, Radley, had won with ease. The previous year their task had been more difficult, for the shadow of "Honion" was already looming. This year that shadow overspread the world.

We had conquered everywhere, and this was our last fixture. We would win: we *must* win. If Radley could be eliminated from the Masters' team—if, for instance, some arsenic could be placed in his tea—our victory would be a foregone conclusion. It was a question of "Honion" *v.* Radley. The enthusiasm swelled and burst the boundaries of the school. Local papers took up the subject. London papers, in small-print paragraphs, copied them. Party feeling ran quite high outside the school: Middlesex supporters desired the triumph of the Masters, which would be the triumph of S.T. Radley, their hero; Sussex supporters backed the School, for they knew that "Honion" Lancaster was to come to them. There was no party within the school, the school being solid for "The School."

One day Radley tapped me on the shoulder.

"Why don't you try to get in the Team?" asked he. "You're the best bowler in the Second Eleven."

I grinned, and represented that such a consummation was of all earthly things impossible.

"I don't see why," said he. "The school's batting talent is great, but the bowling's weak."

Ye Gods! Had he ever heard of Honion?

"O, sir," I remonstrated, "but our strength lies in Honion—in Lancaster, I mean."

Radley smiled.

"What other bowler of any class have you?"

It was true. I mentioned Moles White as a fine slow bowler, and could think of no more "star-turns."

"Well, you come," said Radley, "and bowl at my private net every evening. Your leg-breaks are teasers. I was talking to Lancaster this morning, and he says he doesn't know who will be the last man of the Eleven. Why shouldn't it be you?"

So evening after evening I bowled to Radley, who coached me enthusiastically. I think that he was making a fascinating hobby of training his favourite pupil for the Team, much as an owner delights in running a favourite horse for the Derby. And, when one evening I uprooted his leg-stump twice in succession, he said:

"Good. Now we shall see what we shall see."

In the meantime Lancaster had buttonholed Doe.

"You used to be a great cricketer, usedn't you?"

"When I was a boy, Honion," said Doe.

"And you've slacked abominably."

"Thou sayest so, Honion."

"Well, my son, the last place in the Team is vacant. You should be too good for the Second. Practise like fury, and the situation's yours."

Sec.2

"What do you think, Doe?" said I. "Radley's making me sweat to get into the Team."

A momentary pain and jealousy overspread Doe's face. Quickly passing, it gave place to a whimsical glance, as he rejoined:

"What do you think? Honion's doing the same with me."

"Look here, then," said I, as much despairingly as generously, "I'll stand down. You'll be fifty times better than I shall."

"You won't do anything of the sort. Don't you see Radley's running you as a candidate to spite me? No, we'll fight this out, you and I. Shake on it, and good luck to your candidature!"

"You ripping old tragedy hero!" answered I. "Good luck to yours."

Now, all Kensingtowe amused itself speculating who would be the last man. Many names were mentioned, but Ray was not one of them. Bets were made, and the odds were slightly in favour of Doe. The sentiment of the school said that he ought to be played on the strength of the brilliant things he might do.

The match drew nearer, and the secret as to the last man was severely kept, if, indeed, any decision had been come to. But Doe was establishing himself as favourite. Every day a crowd surrounded the Second Eleven net, where he, with his face suffused in colour and his hair glistening with moisture, was striving to create the necessary impression. Honion, as general, surrounded by his staff-officers in their caps and colours, sometimes stood by the net and pulled his chin contemplatively. And, if Doe made a fine off-drive, all the onlookers (and Doe himself) turned and glanced at Honion, as though for a sign from Heaven. But the great man's face betrayed no emotion.

On the day before the match, which was to be a one-day game, Honion might have been seen crossing the field from the pavilion, where a council of war had just concluded. He was approaching the school-buildings, and, like the Pied Piper, had an enormous crowd of small boys at his back. In his hand was the paper which bore the list of the Team.

"Who is it? Who is it?" demanded the crowd.

"Wait and see," said Lancaster, as great captains do.

And at that moment a first spot of rain fell. Honion looked up apprehensively at a clouding sky. "I thought so," said he; and the weighty words were passed from lip to lip.

The multitude swelled as the Captain drew near the notice-boards. Rumour stalked abroad and loudly proclaimed that the lot had fallen upon Doe. That young cricketer was walking with me at the tail of the procession, very nervous but fairly confident. As for me, my heart was fluttering, and there was an emptiness within.

"Come and tell me who it is," I said to Doe. "You'll find me trembling like a frightened sparrow in the study."

With that I left him, and, going to our study, stood gazing out of the window at a sudden shower of rain. To nerve myself for any shock of disappointment I muttered monotonously some old words of Radley's: "Does it matter to a strong swimmer if the wave beats against him? Does it matter—does it matter—" Soon a roar of many voices was heard in the distance. The list was up. I could not tell whether they were cheering in triumph or groaning in dismay. Then someone ran along the corridor and burst in. I remained looking out of the window lest the expression on my friend's face should betray the secret which I longed but dreaded to hear.

"My dear old fellow," said he, "it's—"

It was coming now. What a long time he took to tell it.

"It's *you*!"

"Good Lord!"

I had swung round on him.

"And I hope you take all the wickets," said he, with a smile of generosity that he wished me to observe.

I couldn't speak, but turned again to look out of the window. The rain was beating heavily against the panes. And Doe said nothing till, being in a chastened mood, he resumed:

"I think you'll always cut me out, Rupert, because you're the solid stuff, while I'm all show. You left me nowhere in Radley's good books, and now in cricket—"

"But you leave me nowhere in brain-work," objected I, feeling that the handsome appreciation, which he had tossed to me, ought to be returned like a tennis ball.

"Oh, yes, of course, there *is* that," he assented. "And I may yet have won the Horace Prize."

Just then the kindly White, coming to express his sympathy, broke into the study and exclaimed:

"Well, we've boosted you out all right, Doe."

"Why, had I been chosen at one time, then?" asked Doe, seizing upon this little sop to his pride.

"Of course, but look at the rain. It'll be a bowlers' wicket, and the Skipper's done a daring thing. The school's never known it, but Ray's been our difficulty, ever since Radley started booming him."

Doe brought his lips firmly together, and turned on me with a bright smile.

"Radley's won this journey," he said, "but let him know I was the first to congratulate you."

Sec.3

By ten o'clock on the Great Day a huge crowd had assembled, including visitors, parents, old boys, and quite a number of Pressmen. Pennybet arrived, invested with all the sleek majesty that Sandhurst could give him: and, seeking out Doe and myself, he lent us the dignity of his presence.

At about half-past-ten Radley came to the nets for a little practice, and most of us walked up to see what sort of form he was showing. I was feeling a little shy in my Second Eleven colours and convinced that all the ladies were asking why my blazer was different from the others. Pennybet quickly saw that I was sensitive on this point, and, with his cruel humour, began emphasising the little difficulty: "Ray, how comes it that your blazer's unlike the others? It's very noticeable, isn't it?"

"Oh, shut up," urged I, blushing over face and neck and throat.

"All the ladies," continued my torturer, "will notice it and pity you, saying 'Isn't he lovely?'"

I ignored him and devoted my attention to watching Radley, as he took his place at the net, where Honion was bowling. It was clear that he did not underestimate Honion's express deliveries, for he rolled up his sleeve, displaying a massive forearm that alarmed us seriously; re-arranged his rubber bat-handle; placed his bat firmly in the block; and faced Honion.

The silence spoke of the importance of the moment; Lancaster, our captain, was measuring himself with Radley. He took his long run and bowled. Radley, with little apparent effort, drove the ball out of the net-mouth to the far end of the field, and re-commenced attending to his bat-handle.

"Oh, the full-blooded villain!" exclaimed Penny.

Someone handed Honion another ball, and he bowled. Radley hit it with great force into the net on the off side. Our spirits sank. Honion was good; he was great; but he was not great enough for Radley.

The third ball Radley tapped straight to where I was standing, and I fielded it.

"Bowl," said he.

I did not wish to do so, but it was impossible to disobey. And, as I prepared to bowl, the silence became eloquent again. The new man, the eleventh-hour bowler, was measuring himself with Radley. I realised that my first ball teased him. My second laid his leg-stump on the ground. A yell of joy showed to what a height the spirits of the crowd had risen. But mine sank in proportion: I should never bowl him out twice in one day....

The bell rang, and the field was cleared.

All over the ground there was an anticipatory silence, which made the striking of the school-clock sound wonderfully loud. Then an ovation greeted Lancaster, as he led his classic team on to the ground.

The Masters had won the toss, and the two, who were to open the batting, left the pavilion amid applause, and assumed their places at the wicket. Lancaster placed his field, bowled a lightning ball, and splintered an old Oxonian's middle stump.

Here was excitement! Delirious boys prophesied that eight years' defeats would be wiped off the slate by the school's dismissing the Masters for a handful of runs, scoring a great score, and then dismissing them again, so as to win an innings victory. But stay! Who is this coming in first-wicket-down? Not Radley? Yes, by heaven, it is! He has come to see that no rot sets in. Now, Honion, you may well spit on your hands. A laugh trembles its way round the spectators, as Lancaster places his men in the deep field. He is ready to be knocked about.

The first over closes for ten, all off Radley's bat, two fours and a two. The new bowler, White, deals in slows, and the scoring partakes of the nature of the bowling. But the outstanding fact of that over is this: that Radley hit the last ball with terrific force along the ground, and it was so brilliantly fielded and thrown in that it scattered the stumps before Radley, who had started to run, could reach the crease. Suddenly, crisply, half a thousand mouths snapped out the query: "How's that!"

"*Out.*"

With great good-humour Radley continued his run a little way, but in the direction of the pavilion. Boys stood up and clapped frantically, not a few seizing their neighbours and pummelling them with clenched fists on the back. Pennybet, sitting beside Doe, shook hands with him and with a couple of undemonstrative old gentlemen, whom he had never seen before. They seemed a little overawed, as he wrung their hands.

By one o'clock the Masters were out, having compiled the diminutive score of 99. Not once had they been asked to face my bowling. Honion and White shared the wickets between them.

Now the only question was: would the school be able to beat them by an innings, and so crown their glorious season? They had better, for the onlookers would be content with nothing less.

Everyone adjourned for lunch. The noise in the dining halls, which the masters made no attempt to check, was tremendous, since all were offering their forecasts of the result. But this fact was universally accepted: the School Eleven would play carefully till they had scored a hundred runs and so passed the Masters' total, after which they would adopt forcing tactics and lift the score over 300. Then they would declare, and bowl the Masters out for a price under the spare 200 runs. Thus the innings victory would be achieved.

Sec.4

The most effective, the most spectacular, and probably the worst innings of the School Eleven was that played by Moles White. He dragged his elephantine form to the wicket, and, looking round with his genial smile, prepared to enjoy the Masters' bowling. Again and again he lifted the ball high into the air and grinned as master after master dropped the catches. It was a method that could only have been successful in such a match as this, where the field had been taken by a team like the Masters, whose "tail" was quite out of practice and rather stiff in the joints.

Every vigorous hit of White's, even if it soared skyward, was cheered with loud cries of "Good old Moles!" Every time his unpardonable catches were dropped, the acclamations were lost in laughter. And when with a splendid stroke he lifted the score over the Masters' total and into three figures, White enjoyed the triumph of his school career.

By this time there was collected behind the railings that surround Kensingtowe a fine crowd of carters and cabmen, who had "woahed" their horses and were standing on their boxes, enjoying an excellent view. They had no idea what the match was, or who were winning, but every time they heard the boys begin to cheer, they waved their hats, brandished their whips, and cheered and whistled as well. The excellent fellows only knew that the great crowd of young gents was happy, and were benignantly pleased to share their happiness.

White made his fifty and was bowled in attempting the most abominable of blind-swipes. He returned towards the pavilion, so far forgetting himself in his pleasure as to swing about his bat like a tennis-racket. What thunderous applause he received! It was his last term, and his last match. And I am glad that the final picture, which our memory preserves of White alive, shows us the sterling oaf departing after a glorious innings, surrounded by uproarious school-fellows, and smiling as only the righteous can. Grand old boy, may we meet many more like you!

By a quarter to five the School total had reached the astonishing figure of 350. To this I had contributed 4, with which I was very satisfied, as it was four more than I expected. Lancaster declared, and the school by its applause endorsed the decision.

Now, how did the position stand? Stumps were to be drawn at 7.30. To save the innings defeat the Masters must score over 250 in two hours and a half. An impossible achievement—a hundred to one on an innings defeat! But would they all be bowled out in the little time left? With luck, and Honion in form, yes. And luck was with us, and Honion in great form this afternoon. Oh, a thousand to one on an innings defeat!

Sec.5

The School took the field without unnecessary delay, and Radley opened the Masters' innings. They were going to make a fight of it, then. But the School had set its heart on the innings victory, and the team had the moral strength derived from the concentrated determination of six hundred boys. What had the Masters to oppose this? Nothing save Radley and a handful of tarnished Blues.

It is stated that the third innings of the day opened like this: Honion started on a longer run than usual, as if to terrify this Radley fellow. The latter, so an enormous number declared, though I contend they were mistaken, started to run at the same time as the bowler, and, meeting the ball at full-pitch, smote it for six. The jubilant expectations of the crowd, always as sensitive as the Stock Exchange, fluctuated. The second ball was square-cut more quietly for four. The third was driven high over the bowler's head and travelled to the boundary-rope. Honion placed a man at the spot where the ball passed the rope, and sent down a similar delivery. Radley pulled it, as a great laugh went up, to the very spot from which the fieldsman had been removed. Eighteen in four balls! The spirits of the crowd drooped.

Penny, at his place with Doe, began to sulk, saying he was sick of it all, and wished he hadn't come.

"Oh, rot," said Doe, "they haven't put our Rupert, the dark horse, on yet. I'm afraid all that's rotten in me is wanting him to be a failure. I can't help it, and I'm *trying* to hope he'll come off. If he does, I'll bellow! Over. White's going to bowl now."

The ground apparently favoured the slow bowler, for the first wicket fell to White's second ball. But the victim, sad to tell, was not Radley.

Hush—oh, hush. The head master was coming out to partner Radley! And, considering the silence of respect with which he was greeted, I think Salome scarcely behaved becomingly. He hit an undignified boundary for four.

"Ee, bless me, my man!" whispered the wits.

But Salome, ignorant of this mild flippancy, actually undertook to run a vulgar five for an overthrow: and by like methods succeeded in amassing a score of runs in a dozen minutes.

Meanwhile, Radley, who from the beginning had taken his life in his hands, was flogging the bowling. He and Salome quickly added fifty to the Masters' total.

But Salome's bright young life was destined to be curtailed. A straight, swift ball from Honion he stopped with his instep, and promptly obeyed two laws which operate in such circumstances: the one compelling him to execute a pleasing dance and rub the injured bone; and the other involving his return to the pavilion (l.b.w.) in favour of the succeeding batsman.

At this interesting development Penny bobbed up and down in his seat with glee. "Ee, bless me! Ee, hang me! Ee, curse me!" he chirruped. "He's bust the bone. He'll never walk again. Probably mortification will set in, and he'll have his foot off. Next man in, please. Oh, I never enjoyed anything so much in my life."

The following two wickets were shared by Honion and White, and the score stood at 90 for four, when the school chaplain approached the wicket. This reverend gentleman walked to his place with zealous rapidity, and proceeded to propagate the gospel with some excellent hits to leg. Three such yielded him nine runs, and at the end of the over he found himself facing Honion's bowling. The temporary dismay of the crowd disappeared. Honion, it was conjectured, would soon send the parson indoors to evensong. But the conjecture was faulty. Honion instead was sent for a two, a boundary, and a single.

"Curse me!" grumbled Penny. "It's not in the best taste for the learned divine to play like any godless layman. Has he nothing better to do? Are there no souls to save?"

"No, but there's a match to save," suggested Doe.

There was perhaps some justification for Penny's indignation, when this indecent ecclesiastic scored two fours in succession, and by his beaming face and intermittent giggle showed that he was feeling a very carnal satisfaction in sending ten members of his congregation, one after another, in search of the ball. Ultimately he was caught low down in the slips, having compiled an excellent thirty; and he walked off, hardly concealing a smile.

As he ran up the steps of the pavilion, Upton came down, drawing on his gloves and ready to prove that Erasmus could exhibit very creditable pedagogues, as well as Bramhall. This slender, grey-haired master with the ruddy countenance was much favoured by the ladies. He looked a young and blooming veteran. The boys of Erasmus gave him a cheer (for he was a good man) and prayed that he might not survive the first ball. He did, however, and held his end up in dogged fashion, leaving Radley to develop the score, and only occasionally taking a modest four for himself.

It was about this time that Radley got under a ball and sent a chance whizzing towards me. It flew high, and I shot up my left hand for it. The ball hit me right in the centre of the palm with such force that it stung most painfully, and I had not the least hesitation in dropping it. There were groans of disappointment from the males, execrations from Penny, and murmurs of sympathy and love from the female portion of the crowd. But my sensations were again the opposite to the crowd's. The pain in my hand was exactly the same as when Radley caned me years before on the left hand: and I was reminded of the scene. "Put up your left hand," he had said sarcastically. "You'll need the other for writing your lines." Now I had accidentally put up my left. It was surely because I should need the other for bowling him out. Such strange alleys do my thoughts run along when I am woolgathering in the field.

It must be admitted that Honion was by this time a failure. Radley was doing what he liked with the bowling. By six-thirty the score stood at 180, and the Masters only required 70 to save them from the innings defeat. There was an hour before them, and they had five wickets in hand. But the light was not so good. We might do it yet.

Thirty minutes of that last hour passed, and in them forty runs were scored at a cost of three wickets. So there was half an hour left to play, two wickets in hand, and thirty runs to get.

The ninth man failed at a quarter past seven, leaving the score at 225. It rested, then, with Radley and the last man to make 25 in fifteen minutes and a bad light.

The schoolboy crowd was suffering; and, when Radley smote Honion for a six, the suffering became agony. Some drastic step must be taken.

Suddenly a shrill-voiced boy sang out:

"Put Ray on. Give Ray a chance."

The crowd took it up and roared out its instructions to put Ray on. Bad form, I grant you, but then they scarcely knew what they were doing, for they were in an ecstasy of suspense and excitement. The cry became formidable. "Put Ray on." My face felt as if it had been scorched at the fire. One boy roared out: "Hoo- *Ray*, hoo-***Ray***, hoo-blooming-***Ray***!"

The crowd laughed, and, while many inquired of one another: "What did he say? Do tell me," the majority adopted the cry as a slogan.

"Hoo-***Ray***, hoo-***Ray***, hoo-blooming-***Ray***!"

Our captain deferred to the voice of public opinion.

"Take next over this end, Ray," he said.

The permission was belated enough. When amid terrific applause I faced Radley, there were only fourteen runs to be made and ten minutes to play.

But, then, I had only one wicket to take. The pulsations of my heart were rapid—but dull, deliberate, and heavy as a strong man's fist. I felt as though I had not eaten anything for weeks, nor was ever likely to eat again. Honion shook his head; he saw that I was trembling. Radley smiled encouragingly. White said: "For God's sake, Ray, pull it off." And I murmured: "Right. I'll try." I was surprised at the way my voice shook.

I took a quiet run (though my feet sounded noisily on the turf, owing to the breathless silence) and bowled.

"Wide!"

The crowd laughed, but it was the laugh of despair. My second ball Radley hit for four. My third followed it to the boundary.

"This'll be Ray's last over," said the witty critics. It was. There were only five more runs to be made. The ladies, preparing for departure, drew on their gloves. Sedate gentlemen, who had removed top-hats from perspiring brows, brushed the silk with their sleeves. Within a few minutes the innings victory would be won or lost.

Despair cured me of nerves. I bowled my fourth ball without any excitement. Radley fumbled and missed it. He smiled grimly, twisted his bat round, adjusted the handle, and resumed his position at the block.

Murmurs of "Well bowled" reached me: and so silent was the crowd and so still the evening, that I heard a voice saying to someone: "That was a good ball, wasn't it? Absolutely beat him. In a light like this—"

Now I was trembling, if you like. But it was not nerves. It was confidence that the supreme moment of my schooldays was upon me. I picked up the ball, muttering repeatedly but unconsciously: "O God, make me do it." I turned and faced

Radley. As I took my short run, I felt perfectly certain that I should bowl him. And the next thing I remember was seeing my master's leg-bail fall to the ground.

All together, none before and none after the other, every male in the crowd bellowed forth the accumulated excitement of the day:

"OUT!"

Sec.6

Not for half an hour that evening did the cheering cease or the mass of boys begin to disperse. Even then there were little outbreaks of fresh cheering coming from separate groups. A line of day-boys, who had linked arms as, homeward bound, they left the field, droned merrily:

> "Now the day is over,
>   Night is drawing nigh,
> Shadows of the evening
>   Steal across the sky."

And among the dissolving cheers from the distance could occasionally be heard the refrain of "Hoo-*Ray*, hoo-*Ray*, hoo-blooming-*Ray*!"

CHAPTER XII
CASTLES AND BRICK-DUST

Sec.1

It was on the day when those two pistol shots were fired at an Austrian Arch-duke in the streets of Serajevo that the Masters' match was played out at Kensingtowe. By the early evening the reverberation of the revolver reports had been felt like an earthquake-shock in all the capitals of Europe; and in a failing light the last wicket had fallen at Kensingtowe. So it happened that, while the Emperors of Central Europe were whispering that the Day had come and the slaughter of the youth of Christendom might begin, there was a gathering in Radley's room of those insignificant people whose little doings you have watched at Kensingtowe. They were assembled to drink tea and discuss the match. There were Radley as host; Pennybet, to represent the Old Boys; Doe and I, in fine fettle for the School; and Dr. Chappy, who, having sworn that he was a busy man and couldn't spare the time, sat spilling cigar-ash in the best armchair, and looked like remaining for the rest of the evening.

"Stop quarrelling about the match," said Radley, as he stood with his back to the mantelpiece, "and listen to me. It's a great day, this—a day of triumph. Ray has won the innings victory for the School, and Doe—"

Doe pricked up his ears.

"It's just out—Doe has won the Horace Prize."

At this news there were great congratulations of the poet, who went red with pleasure.

"When you've all finished," said Radley, "I'll read the Prize Poem."

So Radley began faithfully from a manuscript:

"Horace, Odes I, 9. ***Vides ut Alta Stet.***

"White is the mountain, fleeced in snows,
And the pale trees depress their weighted boughs—"

"Oh, spare us!" interrupted Chappy.

"Not a bit," said Radley. "Hark to this:

"Bring out the mellow wine, the best,
The sweet convivial wine, and test
  Its four-year-old maturity:
To Jove commit the rest,
Nor question his divine intents
For, when he stays the battling elements,
  The wind shall brood o'er prostrate seas
And fail to move the ash's crest
  Or stir the stilly cypress trees.
Be no forecaster of the dawn;
  Deem it an asset, and be gay—
Come, merge to-morrow's misty morn
  In the resplendence of to-day.

"Youth is the day the field to scour,
  The time of conquests won,
The pause, wherein to hark at trysting hour
  To the whispered word
  That is gently heard
In the wake of the passing sun—"

"What's it all about?" grumbled Chappy. "And I'm sure 'morn' doesn't rhyme with 'dawn.'" at which Doe went white with pain, and numbered the doctor among the Philistines.

"It's a very distinguished attempt to catch the spirit of Horace's fine ode," answered Radley, and Doe turned red again with pleasure, forgiving Radley all the unkindness he had ever perpetrated, and enrolling him among the Elect.

Now Pennybet liked to be the centre of attraction at friendly little gatherings like this, and had little inclination to sit and listen to people praising those who recently had been nothing but his satellites. So he lit a cigarette and said:

"It's entirely the result of my training that these young people have turned out so well."

"Pennybet," explained Radley, "you're a purblind egotist and will come to a bad end."

"Oh, I don't think so, sir," said Penny, crossing his legs that he might the more comfortably discuss his end with Radley. "I've always managed to do what I've wanted and to come out of it all right."

"Oh, you have, have you?" sneered Chappy.

"Always," answered Penny, unabashed. "It's a favourite saying of my mother's that 'adverse conditions will never conquer her wilful son.'"

"Good God!" cried the doctor, rightly appalled.

"Yes," continued the speaker, delighted to tease the doctor, "for instance, I made up my mind all the time I was here to stick in a low form. It was an easier life, and fun to boss kids like Edgar Doe and Rupert Ray. And I pulled all the strings of the famous Bramhall Riot, as Ray knows. And I just did sufficient work to pass into Sandhurst. And I shall be just satisfactory enough to get my commission. Then I shall do all in my power to provoke a European War, so that there will be a good chance of promotion—"

"There's a type of man," interrupted Radley, "who'd start a prairie fire, if it were the only way to light his pipe."

"Exactly. And I am he."

"Good God!" repeated Chappy.

"And, after peace is declared, I shall settle down to a comfortable life at the club."

"It's a relief," smiled Radley, "that you won't lead a revolution and usurp the throne."

"Too much trouble. I may go into Parliament, which is a comfortable job. On the Tory side, of course, because there you don't have to think."

"You've about fifty years of life," suggested Radley. "And don't you want to do anything constructive in that time?"

"Not in these trousers! I know that, if I were sincere and constructive in my politics, I should be a Socialist. It stands to reason that it can't be right for all the wealth to be in the pockets of the few, and for there to be a distinct and cocky governing class. But, as I want to amass wealth and enjoy the position of the ruling class, I shall be careful not to think out my politics, lest I develop a pernicious Socialism."

"Oh, Lord!" groaned the doctor.

"I think *I*'m a Socialist," suddenly put in Doe, and Chappy turned to him, dumbfounded to witness the eruption of a second youth. "I've long thought that, when I find my feet in politics, I shall be in the Socialist camp. They may be visionary, but they are idealists. And I think it's up to us public-schoolboys to lead the great mass of uneducated people, who can't articulate their needs. I'd love to be their leader."

"What you're going to be," said Radley, "is an intellectual rebel. When you go up to Oxford in a year or so, you'll pose as most painfully intellectual. You'll be a Socialist in Politics, a Futurist in Art, and a Modernist or Ultramontane in Religion—anything that's a rebellion against the established order. At all costs let us be original and outrageous."

"Hear, hear," whispered Penny.

"Ray has been the strong, silent man so far," said Radley. "Let's hear his Castle in the Air."

"For God's sake—" began Chappy.

"Speech! Speech!" demanded Pennybet.

"Oh, I don't know," demurred I. "I've not many ideas. I generally think I'd like to be a country squire, very popular among the tenants, who'd have my photo on their dressers. And I'd send them all hares and pheasants at Christmas and be interested in their drains—"

I was elaborating this picture, when Penny, feeling that he had made his speech and was not particularly interested in anyone else's, glanced at a gold wrist-watch, and decided that it was time for him to go. He made a peculiarly effective exit, his hat tilted at what he called a "damn-your-eyes" angle. Never again did Doe or I see him, though we heard of his doings. God speed to him, our cocksure Pennybet. Let us always think the best of him.

No sooner had the door clicked than Chappy exploded.

"That high youth ought to have his trousers taken down and be birched. What are we coming to, when boys like him lecture their elders on how to run the world?"

"That question," Radley retorted, "Adam probably asked Eve, when Cain and Abel decided to be Socialists."

"I tell you, these self-opinionated boys want whipping, and so do you, Master Doe, with your damned Fabianism."

"Oh, come, come," objected Radley. "I like them to be gloriously self-confident. Young blood is heady stuff. And there'd be something wrong, if a body full of young blood didn't have a head full of glittering illusions."

"Rot!" proclaimed Chappy.

"I like them to be Socialists and Futurists and everything. If *they* don't want to put the world to rights, who will?"

"Damned rot!"

"It's nothing of the sort," rejoined Radley, getting annoyed. "They ought to break out at this time. You can't bind up a bud to prevent it bursting into flower."

"If I'd children who burst like that, I'd bind them for you!"

"No, you wouldn't," contradicted Radley, softening again. "You'd expect them to be intolerant of you as old fashioned. You'd withdraw behind your cigar-smoke and your old-fashioned ideas, and leave *them* to put the world to rights. After all, it's their world."

Sec.2

Now, though you may think this a very uninteresting chapter—a mere dialogue over the tea-cups, I take leave to present it to you as quite the most dramatic and most central of our humble tale. The events that lend it this distinguished character were happening hundreds of miles from Radley's room, in places where more powerful people than Penny or Doe or I were building Castles in the Air. An Emperor was dreaming of a towering, feudal Castle, broad-based upon a conquered Europe and a servile East. Nay, more, he had finished with dreaming. All the materials of this master-mason were ready to the last stone. And, if the two pistol-shots meant anything, they meant that the Emperor had begun to build.

And, since building was the order of the day, there were wise men in the councils of the Free Nations who saw that they must destroy the Emperor's handiwork and build instead a Castle of their own, where Liberty, International Honour, and many other lovely things might find a home. So for all of us self-opinionated boys, it was a matter of hours this summer evening before we should be told to tumble our petty Castles down, and shape from their ruins a brick or two for the Castle of the Free Peoples. Well, we tumbled them down. And the rest of this story, I think, is the story of the bricks that were made from their dust.

Sec.3

Doe and I left Radley and the doctor to their dispute, and retired to our study. It was then that Doe began to blush and say:

"Funny the subject of our ambitions cropped up. Only a few days ago I tried to write a poem about it."

I pleaded for permission to read it.

"You can, if you like," he said, getting very crimson. With trembling hands he extracted a notebook from his pocket and indicated the poem to me. From that moment I saw that he was waiting in an agony of suspense for my approval.

I took it to the window, and, by the half-light of evening, read:

> If God were pleased to satisfy
>   My every whim,
> I'd tell you just the little things
>   I'd ask of Him:
> A little love—a little love, and that comes first of all,
> And then a chance, and more than one, to raise up them that fall;
>   Enough, not overmuch, to spend;
> And discourse that would charm me
>   With one familiar friend;
> A little music, and, perhaps, a song or two to sing;

And I would ask of God above to grant one other thing:
　Before old Death can grimly smile
　　And take me unawares,
　A little time to rest awhile,
　　To think, and say my prayers.

"Gad!" I said. "You're a poet."

I liked the little trifle, not least because I suspected that the "one familiar friend" was myself. Everyone likes to be mentioned in a poem.

Doe beamed with pleasure that I had not spoken harshly of his off-spring.

"Glad you like it," he said.

"There's this," I suggested, "you talk about only wanting 'these little things' out of life. But it seems to me that you want quite a lot."

"A lot! By Jove, Ray," cried Doe excitedly, "it's only when I'm in my unworldly moods that I want so little as that. In my worse moments—that's nine-tenths of the day—I want yards more: Fame and Flattery and Power."

"Funny. Once, outside the baths, I had a sort of longing to—"

"Ray, I only tell *you* these things," interrupted Doe, now worked up, "but often I feel I've something in me that must come out—something strong—something forceful."

"I don't think I ever felt quite like that," said I, ruminating. "But I did once feel outside the baths—"

"The trouble is," Doe carried on, "that this something in me isn't pure. It's mixed up with the desire for glory. When I told Radley I'd like to be a leader of the people, I knew that one-third was a real desire for their good, and two-thirds a desire for my own glory."

"Yes, but I was going to tell you that once—"

"And I wish it were a pure force. I'd love to pursue an Ideal for its own sake, and without any thought for my own glory. I wonder if I shall ever do a really perfect thing."

"I was going to tell you," I persisted; and, though I knew he measured my temperament as far inferior to Edgar Doe's artistic soul, and would rather have continued his own revelations, yet must I interrupt by telling him of my one moment of aspiration and yearning. Perhaps, I, too, wanted to pour out my mind's little adventures. We're all the same, and like a heart-to-heart talk, so long as it is about ourselves.

I told him, accordingly, of that strange evening outside the baths, when I had felt so overpowering an aspiration towards a vague ideal—an ideal that could not be grasped or seen, but was somehow both great and good.

Sec.4

The last evening of that summer term there was a noisy breaking-up banquet at Bramhall House. And in the morning I went to Radley's room to say a separate good-bye. I was exultant. Next term seemed worlds away: and, meanwhile, eight sunny weeks of holiday stretched before me. My mother and I were off for Switzerland, to whose white heights and blue Genevan lake she loved to take me, for it was my birthplace, and, in her fond way, she would call me her "mountain boy," and tell an old story of a Colonel who had gazed into his grandson's eyes, and said: "*Il a dans les yeux un coin du lac.*" I was dreaming, then, of the Swiss mountain air, and of twin white sails on a lovely lake; and I was visualising, let me admit it, a new well-tailored suit, grey spats, socks of a mauve variety, and other holiday eruptions. So there was no space in my parochial mind for international issues and rumours of wars. Rather I was ridiculously flushed and shining, as I came upon Radley and wished him a happy holiday.

Radley seemed strained, as though he had something ominous to break, and said with a dull and meaning laugh: "I'm sure I hope you have one too."

Observing that he was in one of his harder moods, I at once became awkwardly dumb; and there was a difficult silence, till he asked:

"Have you heard about Herr Reinhardt?"

"Mr. Caesar? No, sir."

"Well, he left to-day for Germany."

"What on earth for?"

"Why, to shoulder a rifle, of course, and fight in the German ranks. Don't you know Germany is mobilising and will be at war with France in about thirty hours?"

"Oh, I read something about it. But what fun!"

Radley looked irritated. In trying to break some strange news he had walked up a blind alley and been met by my blank wall of density. So he took another path.

"Pennybet is in luck, according to his ideas. All Europe plays into his hands. He's got the war he wanted to give him rapid promotion."

"Why, sir, how will Germany affect him?"

"Only in this way," Radley announced, desperately trying to get through my blank wall by exploding a surprise, "that England will be at war with Germany in about three days."

"Oh, what fun! We'll give 'em no end of a thrashing. I hate Germans. Excepting Herr Reinhardt. I hope *he* has a decent time."

"And White and Lancaster, and all who leave this term, and perhaps even— perhaps others will get commissions at once."

"Why, sir? They're not going to Sandhurst."

"No," sighed Radley, "but they give commissions to all old public-schoolboys, if there's a big war. White and Lancaster will be in the fight before many months."

"Lucky beggars!"

It was this fatuous remark which showed Radley that I had no idea of my own relation to the coming conflict. So he forbore to spring upon me the greatest surprise of all. He just said with a sadness and a strange emphasis:

"Well, good-bye, ***and the best of luck***. Make the most of your holiday. There are great times in front of you."

All the while he said it, he held my hand in a demonstrative way, very unlike the normal Radley. Then he dropped it abruptly and turned away. And I went exuberantly out—so exuberantly that I left my hat upon his table, and was obliged to hasten back for it. When I entered the room again, he was staring out of the window over the empty cricket fields. Though he heard me come, he never once turned round, as I picked up my hat and went out through the door.

And because of that I dared to wonder whether his grey eyes, where the gentleness lay, were not inquiring of the deserted fields: "Have I allowed myself to grow too fond?" He seemed as if braced for suffering.

Farewell, Radley, farewell. After all, does it matter to a strong swimmer if the wave beats against him?

Now Thames is long and winds its changing way
  Through wooded reach to dusky ports and gray,
  Till, wearily, it strikes the Flats of Leigh,
  An old life, tidal with Eternity.

But Fal is short, full, deep, and very wide,
Nor old, nor sleepy, when it meets the tide;
Through hills and groves where birds and branches sing
It runs its course of sunny wandering,
And passes, careless that it soon shall be
Lost in the old, gray mists that hide the sea.

  Ah, they were good, those up-stream reaches when
  Ourselves were young and dreamed of being men,
  But Fal! the tide had touched us even then!
  One tribal God, we bow to, thou and we,
  And praise Him, Who ordained our lives should be
  So early tidal with Eternity.

BOOK II AND THE REST—WAR

Part I: "Rangoon" Nights

CHAPTER I
THE ETERNAL WATERWAY

Sec.1

The most clearly marked moment of my life was when I passed the fat policeman who was standing just inside the great gateway of Devonport Dockyard. I was to embark that morning on a troopship bound for the Dardanelles. As I stepped out of the public thoroughfare, and walking through the gate, saw the fat policeman. I passed out of one period of my life and entered upon another.

The first period that remained outside the tall walls of the dockyard was made up of chapters of boyhood and schooldays; and a gallant last chapter of playing at soldiers. Ah! this last chapter—it had tennis and theatres and girls and kisses: a great patch of life! And I left it all outside the docks.

The second period, on to which I now abruptly set foot, was to be intense, highly-coloured, and scented; a rush of rapidly moving pictures of the blue waters of the Mediterranean, the bleak hills of Mudros, and the exploding shells on the peninsula of Gallipoli.

The fat policeman had a revolver slung over his shoulder, and his businesslike weapon expressed better than anything else that England was at war and taking no risks. He suitably challenged me:

"Your authority to go through, sir?" demanded he.

"That's where I've got you by the winter garments," said I vulgarly; and, diving my hand into my pocket, I drew out my Embarkation Orders. They were heavily marked in red "SECRET," but I judged the policeman to be "in the know," and showed them to him. Properly impressed with the historic document, he turned to a fair-haired young officer who was with me, and asked:

"You the same, sir?"

"Surely," answered my companion, which was a new way he had acquired of saying "yes."

"Right y'are, sir," said the policeman, and we crossed the line.

My fair-haired companion was, of course, Second Lieutenant Edgar Gray Doe; and it was in keeping with the destiny that entwined our lives that we should pass the fat policeman together. And now I had better tell you how it happened.

Sec.2

On August 3, 1914, eleven months before my solemn admission into Devonport Dockyard, I was a young schoolboy on my holidays, playing tennis in a set of mixed doubles. About five o'clock a paper-boy entered the tennis-club grounds with the *Evening News*. My male opponent, although he was serving, stopped his game for a minute and bought a paper.

"Hang the paper!" called I, indifferent to the fact that the Old World was falling about our ears and England's last day of peace was going down with the afternoon sun. "Your service. Love—fifteen."

"By Jove," he cried, after scanning the paper, "we're in!"

"What do you mean," cried the girls, "have the Germans declared war on us?"

"No. But we've sent an ultimatum to Germany which expires at twelve tonight. That means Britain will be in a state of war with Germany as from midnight." The hand that held the paper trembled with excitement.

"How frightfully thrilling!" said one girl.

"How awful!" whispered the other.

"How ripping!" corrected I. "Crash on with the game. Your service.

Love—fifteen."

Five days later it was decided that I should not return to school, but should go at once into the army. So it was that I never finished up in the correct style at Kensingtowe with an emotional last chapel, endless good wishes and a lump in my throat. I just didn't go back.

Instead, an influential friend, who knew the old Colonel of the 2nd Tenth East Cheshires, a territorial battalion of my grandfather's regiment, secured for me and, at my request, for Doe commissions in that unit. His Majesty the King (whom, and whose dominions, might God preserve in this grand moment of peril) had, it seemed, great faith in the loyalty and gallantry of "Our trusty and well-beloved Rupert Ray," as also of "Our trusty and well-beloved Edgar Gray Doe," and was pleased to accept our swords in the defence of his realm.

So one day we two trusty and well-beloved subjects, flushed, very nervous, and clad in the most expensive khaki uniforms that London could provide, took train for the North to interview the Colonel of the 2nd Tenth. He was sitting at a littered writing-table, when we were shown in by a smart orderly. We saw a plump old territorial Colonel, grey-haired, grey-moustached, and kindly in face. His khaki jacket was brightened by the two South African medal ribbons; and we were so sadly fresh to things military as to wonder whether either was the V.C. We saluted with great smartness, and hoped we had made the movement correctly: for really, we knew very little about it. I wasn't sure whether we ought to salute indoors; and Doe, having politely bared his fair head on entering the office, saluted without a cap. I blushed at my bad manners and surreptitiously removed mine. Not knowing what to do with my hands, I put them in my pockets. I knew that, if something didn't happen quickly, I should start giggling. Here in the presence of our new commanding officer I felt as I used to when I stood before the head master.

"Sit down," beamed the C.O.

We sat down, crossed our legs, and tried to appear at our ease, and languid; as became officers.

"How old are you?" the Colonel asked Doe.

Doe hesitated, wondering whether to perjure himself and say "Twenty."

"Eighteen, sir," he admitted, obviously ashamed.

"And you, Ray?"

"Eighteen, sir," said I, feeling Doe's companion in guilt.

"Splendid, perfectly splendid!" replied the Colonel. "Eighteen, by Jove! You've timed your lives wonderfully, my boys. To be eighteen in 1914 is to be the best thing in England. England's wealth used to consist in other things. Nowadays you boys are the richest thing she's got. She's solvent with you, and bankrupt without you. Eighteen, confound it! It's a virtue to be your age, just as it's a crime to be mine. Now, look here"—the Colonel drew up his chair, as if he were going to get to business—"look here. Eighteen years ago you were born for this day. Through the last eighteen years you've been educated for it. Your birth and breeding were given you that you might officer England's youth in this hour. And now you enter upon your inheritance. Just as this is *the* day in the history of the world so yours is *the* generation. No other generation has been called to such grand things, and to such crowded, glorious living. Any other generation at your age would be footling around, living a shallow existence in the valleys, or just beginning to climb a slope to higher things. But you"—here the Colonel tapped the writing-table with his forefinger—"you, just because you've timed your lives aright, are going to be transferred straight to the mountain-tops. Well, I'm damned. Eighteen!"

I remember how his enthusiasm radiated from him and kindled a responsive excitement in me. I had entered his room a silly boy with no nobler thought than a thrill in the new adventure on which I had so suddenly embarked. But, as this fatherly old poet, touched by England's need and by the sight of two boys entering his room, so fresh and strong and ready for anything, broke into eloquence, I saw dimly the great ideas he was striving to express. I felt the brilliance of being alive in this big moment; the pride of youth and strength. I felt Aspiration surging in me and speeding up the action of my heart. I think I half hoped it would be my high lot to die on the battlefield. It was just the same glowing sensation that pervaded me one strange evening when, standing outside the baths at Kensingtowe, I first awoke to the joy of conscious life.

"D'you see what I'm driving at?" asked the old Colonel.

"Rather!" answered Doe, with eagerness. Turning towards him as he spoke, I saw by the shining in his brown eyes that the poet in him had answered to the call of the old officer's words. His aspiration as well as mine was inflamed. Doe was feeling great. He was picturing himself, no doubt, leading a forlorn hope into triumph, or fighting a rearguard action and saving the British line. The heroic creature was going to be equal to the great moment and save England dramatically.

Pleased with Doe's ready understanding—my friend always captivated people in the first few minutes—our C.O. warmed still more to his subject. Having put his hands in his pockets and leant back in his chair to survey us the better, he continued:

"What I mean is—had you been eighteen a generation earlier, the British Empire could have treated you as very insignificant fry, whereas to-day she is obliged to come to you boys and say 'You take top place in my aristocracy. You're on top because I must place the whole weight of everything I have upon your shoulders. You're on top because you are the Capitalists, possessing an enormous capital of youth and strength and boldness and endurance. You must give it all to me—to gamble with—for my life. I've nothing to give you in return, except suffering and—'"

The Colonel paused, feeling he had said enough—or too much. We made no murmur of agreement. It would have seemed like applauding in church. Then he proceeded:

"Well, you're coming to my battalion, aren't you?"

"Yes, rather, sir," said Doe.

"Right. You're just the sort of boys that I want. If you're young and bold, your men will follow you anywhere. In this fight it's going to be better to be a young officer, followed and loved because of his youth, than to be an old one, followed and trusted because of his knowledge. Dammit! I wish I could make you see it. But, for God's sake, be enthusiastic. Be enthusiastic over the great crisis, over the responsibility, over your amazingly high calling."

He stopped, and began playing with a pencil; and it was some while before he added, speaking uncomfortably and keeping his eyes upon the pencil:

"Take a pride in your bodies, and hold them in condition. You'll want 'em. There are more ways than one of getting them tainted in the life of temptations you're going to face. I expect you—you grasp my meaning.... But, if only you'll light up your enthusiasm, everything else will be all right."

He raised his eyes and looked at us again, saying:

"Well, good-bye for the present."

We shook hands, saluted, and went out. And, as I shut the door, I heard the old enthusiast call out to someone who must have been in an inner room: "I've two gems of boys there—straight from school. Bless my soul, England'll win through."

Sec.3

But, lack-a-day, here's the trouble with me. My moments of exaltation have always been fleeting. Just as in the old school-days I would leave Radley's room, brimful of lofty resolutions, and fall away almost immediately into littleness again, so now I soon allowed the lamp of enthusiasm, lit by the Colonel, to grow very dim.

It was ridicule of the fine old visionary that destroyed his power. "Hallo, here come two more of the Colonel's blue-eyed boys," laughed the officers of our new battalion the first time we came into their view. And "The old man's mounted his hobby again," said they, after any lecture in which he alluded to Youth and Enthusiasm.

Yet the Colonel was right, and the scoffers wrong. The Colonel was a poet who could listen and hear how the heart of the world was beating; the scoffers were prosaic cattle who scarcely knew that the world had a heart at all. He turned us, if only for a moment, into young knights of high ideals, while they made us sorry, conceited young knaves.

You shall know what knaves we were.

So far from being enthusiastic over parades and field days, we found them most detestably dull and longed for the pleasures that followed the order to dismiss. And after the Dismiss we were utterly happy.

It was happiness to walk the streets in our new uniforms, and to take the salutes of the Tommies, the important boy-scouts, and the military-minded gutter urchins. I longed to go home on leave, so that in company with my mother I could walk through the world saluted at every twenty paces, and thus she should see me in all my glory. And when one day I strolled with her past a Hussar sentry who brought his sword flashing in the sun to the salute, I felt I had seldom experienced anything so satisfying.

I was secretly elated, too, in possessing a soldier servant to wait on me hand

and foot—almost to bath me. I spoke with a concealed relish of "my agents," and loved to draw cheques on Cox and Co. I looked forward to Sunday Church Parade, for there I could wear my sword. It was my grandfather's sword, and I'm afraid I thought less of the romance of bearing it in defence of the Britain that he loved and the France where he lay buried than of its flashy appearance and the fine finish it gave to my uniform. I was a strange mixture, for, when the preacher, looking down the old Gothic arches, said: "This historic church has often before filled with armed men," I shivered with the poetry of it; and yet, no sooner had I come out into the modern sunlight and seen the congregation waiting for the soldiers to be marched off, than I must needs be occupied again with the peculiarly dashing figure I was cutting.

Once Doe and I went on a visit to Kensingtowe, partly out of loyalty to the old school, and partly to display ourselves in our new greatness. We wore our field-service caps at the jaunty angle of all right-minded subalterns. Though only un-mounted officers, we were dressed in yellow riding-breeches with white leather strappings. Fixed to our heels were the spurs that we had long possessed in secret. They jingled with every step, and the only thing that marred the music of their tinkle was the anxiety lest some officer of the 2nd Tenth should see us thus arrayed. Doe was in field boots, but his pleasure in being seen in this cavalry kit was quite spoiled by his fear of being ridiculed for "swank." Both of us would have liked to take our batmen with us and to say: "Don't trouble, my man will do that for you."

We created a gratifying sensation at Kensingtowe. It was exhilarating to have a friend come up to me and exclaim: "By Jove, Ray, you're no end of a dog now," and to notice that he didn't heed my self-depreciatory answer because he was busy looking into every detail of my uniform. "What devilish fine fellows we are, eh what?" cried our admirers, and we blushed and said "Oh, shut up." We met old Dr. Chappy, who looked us up and down, roared with laughter, and said "Well, I'll be damned!" We were welcomed into Radley's room, and were boys enough to address him as "sir" as though we were still his pupils. He examined our appearance like a big brother proud of two young ones, and said after a silence:

"So this is what it has all come to."

I took a lot of my cronies out to tea in the town, and, as we walked to the shops, stared down the road to see if any Tommies were coming who would salute me in front of my guests. Luck was kind to me. For a large party, marching under an N.C.O., approached us; and the N.C.O. in a voice like the crack of doom cried "Party—eyes RIGHT!" Heads and eyes swung towards me, the N.C.O. saluted briskly, and, when the party had passed us, yelled "Eyes FRONT!" It was one of the most triumphant moments of my career.

Scarcely, however, had this pride-tickling honour been paid to me before there happened as distressing a thing as—oh, it was dreadful! I passed one of your full-blooded regular-army sergeants, and, since he raised his hand towards his face, I apprehended he was about to salute me. Promptly I acknowledged the expected salute, only to discover that the sergeant had raised his hand for no other purpose than to blow his nose with his naked fingers. Believe me, even now, when I think of this blunder, I catch my breath with shame.

What young bucks we were, Doe and I! We bought motor-bicycles and raced over the country-side, Doe, ever a preacher of Life, calling out "This is Life, isn't it?" I remember our bowling along a deserted country road and shouting for a lark: "Sing of joy, sing of bliss, it was never like this, Yip-i-addy-i-ay!" I remember our scorching recklessly down white English highways, with a laugh for every bone-shaking bump, and a heart-thrill for every time we risked our lives tearing through a narrow passage between two War Department motor lorries. I see the figure of Doe standing breathless by his bicycle after a break-neck run, his hair blown into disorder by the wind, and the white dust of England round his eyes and on his cheeks, and saying: "My godfathers, this is Life!" Oh, yes, it was a rosy patch of life and freedom.

Sec.4

But, in our abandonment, we tumbled into more sinister things. It was disillusionment that bowled us down. The evil that we saw in the world and the army smashed our allegiance to the old moral codes. We suddenly lost the old anchors and blew adrift, strange new theories filling our sails. We ceased to think there was any harm in being occasionally "blotto" at night, or in employing the picturesque army word "bloody." Worse than that, we began to believe that vicious things, which in our boyhood had been very secret sins, were universally committed and bragged about.

"It's so, Rupert," said Doe, in a corner of the Officers' ante-room one night before dinner, "I'm an Epicurean. Surely the Body doesn't prompt to pleasure only to be throttled? There's something in what they were saying at Mess yesterday that these things are normal and natural. I mean, human nature is human nature, and you can't alter it. I don't think any man is, or can be, what they call 'pure.' I s'pose every man has done these things, don't you?"

"No, I don't," I answered, conscious of hot cheeks. " **We** may do them, but there are people I can't imagine it of."

"But, again, there's the question whether War doesn't mean the suspension of all ordinary moral laws. The law that you shan't kill is in abeyance. The instinct of self-preservation has to be suppressed. There's some justification for being an Epicurean for the duration of the war."

"Perhaps so," acknowledged I. "I don't know."

As we left the ante-room and sat down to Mess, Doe announced:

"I've every intention of getting tight to-night."

" *Pourquoi pas?* " said I. " *C'est la guerre!* "

"Before I die," continued Doe, who was already flushed with gin and vermouth, "I want to have lived. I want to have touched all the joys and experiences of life. Pass the Chablis. Here's to you, Rupert. Cheerioh!"

"Cheerioh!" toasted I, raising my glass. "Happy days!"

"I'm determined to be able to say, Rupert, whatever happens: 'Never mind, I had a good time while it lasted!'"

"I'm with you," said I, who was now nearly as flushed as he. "Let's be in everything up to the neck."

"Surely," Doe endorsed. " *C'est la guerre!* "

So with the meat and sweets went the wines of France; with the nuts the sparkling "bubbly"; and in the ante-room Martinis, Benedictines, and Whisky-Macdonalds. Soon the night became noisy, and Doe, encouraged by riotous subalterns, jumped on a table and declaimed a little thickly his prize Horatian Ode:

"Bring out the mellow wine, the best,
The sweet, convivial wine, and test

Its four-year-old maturity;
To Jove commit the rest:
Nor question his divine intents,
For, when he stays the battling elements
   The wind shall brood o'er prostrate sea
And fail to move the ash's crest
   Or stir the stilly cypress trees.
Be no forecaster of the dawn;
   Deem it an asset, and be gay—
Come, merge to-morrow's misty morn
   In the resplendence of to-day."

And, after all this, it was an easy step, lightly taken, to the things of night. We set out for the strange streets; and there, in the night air, the precocious young pedant, Edgar Doe, became, despite all the new theories, the shy, simple boy he really was. We would both become shy—shy of each other, and shy of the shameful doorway.

And then the misery of the morning, to be quickly forgotten in the joy of life!

Sec.5

It was now that the Battle of Neuve Chapelle quenched Pennybet. Archibald Pennybet, the boy who left school, determined to conquer the world, and coolly confident of his power to mould circumstances to his own ends, was crushed like an insect beneath the heavy foot of war. He was just put out by a high-explosive shell. It didn't kill him outright, but whipped forty jagged splinters into his body. He was taken to an Advanced Dressing Station, where a chaplain, who told us about his last minutes, found him, swathed in bandages from his head to his heel. On a stretcher that rested on trestles he was lying, conscious, though a little confused by morphia. He saw the chaplain approaching him, and murmured, "Hallo, padre." So numerous were his bandages that the chaplain saw nothing of the boy who was speaking save the lazy Arab eyes and the mouth that had framed impudence for twenty years.

"Hallo, what have you been doing to yourself?" asked the chaplain.

"Oh, only trying conclusions with an H.E., padre." The mouth smiled at the corners.

"What about a cup of tea, now? Could you drink it?"

"I'll—try, padre." The eyes twinkled a little.

So the chaplain brought a mug of stewed tea, and Penny, laughing weakly, said:

"You'll—have to pour it down—for me, padre. I can't move a muscle. These bloody bandages—sorry, padre—these bandages. O God—"

"In pain?" gently inquired the chaplain.

"No. Only a prisoner. I can't move. Pour the tea down."

He gulped a little of the drink, and, dropping the heavily-fringed eyelids, so that he appeared to be asleep, muttered:

"I suppose—I haven't a dog's chance. Find out if—I'm done for. Find out for me, please."

"I asked the doctor before I came to you, old chap."

On hearing this, Penny opened and shut his eyes, and remained so long just breathing that the chaplain wondered if he had lost consciousness. But the eyes unclosed again, and the lips asked:

"Aren't you going to tell me, padre?"

"Yes, I—you won't be a prisoner much longer, old chap."

Not a word said Penny, but stared in wonder at his informant. It was clear that he wanted to live, and to mould the world to his will. There was a long silence, and then he murmured:

"Well, there are lots of others—who've gone through it—and lots more who'll—have to go." And he shut his eyes in weary submission.

The chaplain suggested a prayer with him, and Penny agreed in the half-jesting words: "But you'll—have to do it all for me, just as you poured the tea down. I'm no good at that sort of thing."

And, when the prayer was over, he said with his old haughtiness:

"You know, padre—I was thinking—while you prayed. I suppose I've led a selfish life—seeking my own ends—but, by Jove, I've had my good time—and am ready to pay for it—if I must." His eyes flashed defiantly. "If God puts me through it, *I* shan't whine."

As the end drew nearer, he turned more and more into a child. After all, he had never come of age. He spoke about his mother, sending her his love, and saying: "I'm afraid, padre, that I led her a life—but I'll bet she'd rather have had me and my plagues than not. Don't you think so?"

He mentioned us with affection as "those two kids," and sent the message that he hoped we at least should come through all right.

And then the lazy eyes closed in their last weariness, the impudent lips parted, and Penny was dead. The War had beaten him. It was too big a circumstance for him to tame.

Sec.6

The night we heard of it, Doe threw himself into a chair and said:

"I'm miserable to-night, Rupert."

"So'm I," said I, looking out of the window over a moonlit sea. "Poor old Penny. I don't know why it makes one feel a cur, but it does, doesn't it?"

"Surely," answered Doe.

For a time we smoked our pipes in silence. I gazed at the long silver pathway that the light of the moon had laid on the sea. Right on the horizon, where the pathway met the sky, a boat with a tall sail stood black against the light. Fancifully I imagined that its dark shape resembled the outline of a man—say, perhaps, the figure of Destiny—walking down the sparkling pathway towards us. I was in the mood to fancy such things. Then Doe from his chair said:

"Old Penny always took the lead with us, didn't he? He's taken it again."

"I don't see what you mean," answered I.

"Oh, it doesn't matter what I mean. I'm depressed to-night."

We spoke of it with the Colonel the next afternoon, when we were having tea in his private room.

"It doesn't seem fair," complained Doe. "He could have done anything with his life," and he added rather tritely: "Penny's story which might have been monumental is now only a sort of broken pillar over a churchyard grave."

"Nonsense," snapped the Colonel. "It was splendid, perfectly splendid." And he arose from his chair and took down from a shelf a little blue volume bearing the title "1914." With a pencil he underlined certain phrases in a sonnet, and handed the book to us. Doe brought his head close to mine, and we leant over the marked page and read the lines together:

> "These laid the world away, poured out the red
> Sweet wine of youth, gave up the years to be
> Of hope and joy—
>
> Blow, bugles, blow—
> Nobleness walks in our ways again—"

The Colonel—how like him!—saw the story of Pennybet, not as a broken pillar, but as a graceful, upright column, with a richly foliated capital.

Sec.7

The march of History in these wonderful months brought with it an event that stirred the world. This was the first great landing of the British Forces on the toe of the Gallipoli Peninsula, in their attempt to win a way for the Allied Navy through the Straits of the Dardanelles. On April 25th, 1915, as all the world knows, the men of the 29th Division came up like a sea-breeze out of the sea, and, driving the Turks and Germans from their coastal defences, swept clear for themselves a small tract of breathing room across that extremity of Turkey. Leaping out of their boats, and crashing through a murderous fire, they won a footing on Cape Helles, and planted their feet firmly on the invaded territory.

Three Kensingtonians known to us fell dead in that costly battle. Stanley, who tried me in the Prefects' Room, took seven machine-gun bullets in his body, and died in a lighter as it approached the beach. Lancaster, who in less grand years would undoubtedly have bowled for Oxford and England, lay down on W. Beach and died. And White, the gentle giant—Moles White, who swam so bravely in the Bramhall-Erasmus Race, was knocked out somewhere on the high ground inland.

And, almost immediately after that distant battle of the Helles beaches, in the early days of May, when England was all blossom and bud, our First Line of the

Cheshires was landed on Gallipoli to support the 29th Division. The news was all over the regiment in no time. The First Line had gone to the Dardanelles! Had we heard the latest? The First Line were actually on Gallipoli!

Consider what it meant to us. We were the Second Line, whose object was to supply reinforcing drafts to the First Line in whatever country it might be ordered to fight. The First Line—we were proud of the fact—had been the first territorial division to leave England. In September, 1914, it had sailed away, in an imposing convoy of transports escorted by cruisers and destroyers, under orders to garrison Egypt. There it had acted as the Army of Occupation till that April day when the 29th Division laughed at the prophecies of the German experts and stormed from the AEgean Sea the beaches of Cape Helles. Scarcely had the news electrified Egypt before the First Line received its orders to embark for Overseas. And every man of them knew what *that* meant.

So all we of the 2nd Tenth seemed marked down like branded sheep for the Gallipoli front. The Colonel was full of it. With his elect mind that saw right into the heart of things, he quickly unveiled the poetry and romance of Britain's great enterprise at Gallipoli. He crowded all his young officers into his private room for a lecture on the campaign that was calling them. Having placed them on chairs, on the carpet, on the hearth-rug, and on the fender, he seated himself at his writing-table, like a hen in the midst of its chickens, and began:

"For epic and dramatic interest this Dardanelles business is easily top."

To the Colonel everything that he was enthusiastic about was epic and dramatic and "on top." Just as he told us that our day was *the* day and our generation *the* generation, so now he set out to assure us that Gallipoli was *the* front.

"If you'll only get at the IDEAS behind what's going on at the Helles beaches," he declared, with a rap on the table, "you'll be thrilled, boys."

Then he reminded us that the Dardanelles Straits were the Hellespont of the Ancient world, and the neighbouring AEgean Sea the most mystic of the "wine-dark seas of Greece": he retold stories of Jason and the Argonauts; of "Burning Sappho" in Lesbos; of Achilles in Scyros; of Poseidon sitting upon Samothrace to watch the fight at Troy; and of St. John the Divine at Patmos gazing up into the Heavenly Jerusalem.

As he spoke, we were schoolboys again and listened with wide-open, wistful eyes. From the fender and the hearth-rug, we saw Leander swimming to Hero across the Dardanelles; we saw Darius, the Persian, throwing his bridge over the same narrow passage, only to be defeated at Marathon; and Xerxes, too, bridging the famous straits to carry victory into Greece, till at last his navy went under at Salamis. We saw the pathetic figure of Byron swimming where Leander swam; and, in all, such an array of visions that the lure of the Eternal Waterway gripped us, and we were a-fidget to be there.

"Have eyes to see this idea also," said the Colonel, who was a Tory of Tories. "England dominates Gibraltar and Suez, the doors of the Mediterranean; let her complete her constellation by winning from the Turk the lost star of the Dardanelles, the only other entrance to the Great Sea."

This roused the jingo devil in us, and we burst into applause.

Knowing thereby that he had won his audience, the Colonel beamed with inspiration. He rose, as though so enthralling a subject could only be dealt with standing, and cried:

"See this greater idea. For 500 years the Turk, by occupying Constantinople, has blocked the old Royal Road to India and the East. He is astride the very centre of the highways that should link up the continents. He oppresses and destroys the Arab world, which should be the natural junction of the great trunk railways that, to-morrow, shall join Asia, Africa, and Europe in one splendid spider's web. You are going to move the block from the line, and to join the hands of the continents. Understand, and be enthusiastic. I tell you, this joining of the continents is an unborn babe of history that leapt in the womb the moment the British battleships appeared off Cape Helles."

"By Jove, the Colonel's great!" thought I, as my heart jumped at his magnificent words. "Where are his scoffers to-day? He's come into his own." Lord, how small my little vanities seemed now! A fig for them all! I was going out to build history. The Colonel had one at least who was with him to the death.

"So much for secular interest," continued the Colonel, dropping his voice. "Now, boys, follow me through this. You're not over-religious, I expect, but you're Christians before you're Moslems, and your hands should fly to your swords when I say the Gallipoli campaign is a New Crusade. You're going out to force a passage through the Dardanelles to Constantinople. And Constantinople is a sacred city. It's the only ancient city purely Christian in its origin, having been built by the first Christian Emperor in honour of the Blessed Virgin. Which brings us to the noblest idea of all. In their fight to wrest this city from the Turk, the three great divisions of the Church are united once more. The great Roman branch is represented by the soldiers and ships of France: the great Eastern Orthodox branch by the Russians, who are behind the fight: the great Anglican branch by the British, who can be proud to have started the movement, and to be leading it. Thus Christendom United fights for Constantinople, under the leadership of the British, whose flag is made up of the crosses of the saints. The army opposing the Christians fights under the crescent of Islam.

"It's the Cross against the Crescent again, my lads. By Jove, it's splendid, perfectly splendid! And an English cross, too!

"Thank you, gentlemen; that's all; thank you."

Sec.8

The blossom and buds of our English May became the fruit and flowers of July, and Doe and I, maturing too, entered upon the age for Active Service. There came a day when we were ordered to report for a doctor's examination to see if we were fit for the front.

I shan't forget that testing. All thought we had little to fear from the doctor. The drills and route-marches in sun, wind and rain had tanned our flesh to pink and brown, and lit the lamps of health in our eyes. And the whites of those eyes were blue-white.

But the doctor, a curt major, said "Strip," and took Doe first.

Now, a glance at Doe, when stripped, ought to have satisfied a doctor. His figure, small in the hips, widened to a chest like a Greek statue's; his limbs were slender and rounded; his skin was a baby's. But no, the stolid old doctor carried on, as though Doe were nothing to sing songs about. He tested his eyes, surveyed his teeth, tried his chest, tapping him before and behind, and telling him to say "99" and to cough. All these liberties so amused Doe that he could scarcely manage the "99" or the cough for giggling. And I was doing my best to increase his difficulty by pretending to be in convulsions of smothered laughter.

Then the doctor sounded Doe's heart, and, as he did it, all the laughter went out of my life. I suddenly remembered a scene, wherein I lay in the baths at Kensingtowe, recovering from a faint, and Dr. Chappy looked down upon me and said: "There may be a weakness at your heart." As I remembered it, the first time for years, my heart missed its beats. I saw rapidly succeeding visions of my rejection by the doctor; my farewell to Doe, as he left for romantic Gallipoli; and my return to the undistinguished career of the Medically Unfit. I found myself repeating, after the fashion of younger days (though at this wild-colt period I had done with God): "O God, make him pass me. O God, make him pass me."

"All right, get dressed," the doctor commanded Doe.

"Come here, you," he said to me, brutally.

My eyes, teeth, and chest satisfied him; and then, like a loathly eavesdropper, he listened at my heart. I was afraid my nervousness would cause some irregular action of the detestable organ that would finally down me in his eyes.

"All right, get dressed," he said; and, having put his stethoscope away, he wrote something on two printed Army Forms and sealed them.

"Are we fit, sir?" asked I, in suspense.

"I've written my verdict," he said snappily, looking at me as much as to say: "You aren't asked to converse. This isn't a conversazione"; but, when he caught my gaze, he seemed, to repent of his harshness, and answered gruffly:

"Both perfect."

"Oh, thanks, sir," said I. I could have kissed the old churl.

And so, before July was out, when Doe and I were at our separate homes on a last leave, we received from the Director-General of Movements our Embarkation Orders. Marked "SECRET," the documents informed us that we were to report at Devonport "in service dress uniform," with a view to proceeding to "the Mediterranean." Seemingly we were to take no drafts of men, but travel independently as reinforcements to the First Line at Cape Helles.

My mother turned very white when I showed her the letter. She had heard ugly things about the Gallipoli Peninsula. People were saying that the life of a junior subaltern on Helles was working out to an average of fourteen days; and that, in the heat, the flies and dust were scattering broadcast the germs of dysentery and enteric. And I believe my restless excitement hurt her. But she only said: "I'm so proud of it all," and kissed me.

The last night, however, as she sat in her chair, and I, after walking excitedly about, stood in front of her, she took both my hands and drew me, facing her, against her knees. I know she found it sweet and poignant to have me in that position, for, when I was a very small boy, it had been thus that she had drawn me to tell me stories of my grandfather, Colonel Ray. She had dropped the habit, when I was a shy and undemonstrative schoolboy, but had resumed it happily during the last two years, for, by then, I had learnt in my growing mannishness to delight in half-protectingly, half-childishly stroking and embracing her.

She drew me, then, this last night against her knees and looked lovingly at me. Her yearning heart was in her eyes. Her hands, clasping mine, involuntarily gripped them very tight, as though she were thinking: "I cannot give him up; I cannot let him go."

I smiled down at her, and, as I saw the moisture veil her eyes, I felt that I, too, would like to cry. At last she said:

"If I'm never to see you again, Rupert, I shall yet always be thankful for the nineteen years' happiness you've given me."

"Oh, mother," I said. No more words could I utter, for my eyes were smarting worse than ever. I felt about eight years old.

"If all the rest of my life had to be sorrow," she whispered, no longer concealing the fact that she was breaking down, "the last nineteen years of you, Rupert, have made it all so well worth living. I shall have had more happiness out of it than sorrow. Thank you—for all you've given me."

She let go of my left hand, so as to free her own, with which she might wipe her overflowing eyes. Then she dropped the cambric handkerchief into her lap, and grasped my hand again. As for me, I kept silence, for my mother's thanks were making my breath come in those short, quick gasps, which a man must control if he would prevent them breaking into sobs.

"You see," she explained, "you had *his* eyes. Your grandfather used to say of you, 'he has that Rupert's eyes.'"

"Mother!" I ejaculated. Only in that last moment did I, thoughtless boy that I was, enter into an understanding of my mother's love for the father I had never seen. In the last evening of nineteen years there was revealed to me all that my mother's young widowhood had meant to her.

"I didn't want to break down," she apologised, drawing me even closer to her, as though appealing for my forgiveness, "but, oh! I couldn't help it. I've never loved you so desperately as I do at this moment."

"Mother," I stuttered, "I've been rotten—more rotten than you know."

"No, my big boy, you've been perfect. I wouldn't have had you different in any way. Everything about you pleased me. And how—how can I give you up?"

"I'll come back to you, mother. I swear I will."

"Oh, but you mustn't allow any thought of me to unnerve you out there, Rupert," she said, quickly releasing my hands, lest it were traitorous to hold me back. "Do everything you are called to do—however dangerous—" The word caused her to sob. "Don't think of me when you've got to fight. No, I don't mean that—" Mother was torn between her emotions. "Rather think of me, and do the—dangerous thing—if it's right—yes, do it—because I want you to, but oh!" she sobbed, "come back to me—come back—come back."

I leant over and, lifting her face up gently with both my hands, kissed her and said:

"Yes, mother."

And then by a sudden effort of her will she seemed to recover. She said smilingly and almost calmly:

"I'm so proud. I think it's wonderful your going out there."

Sec.9

What more is there to tell of that old first period of my life which ended at the gates of Devonport Dockyard? There was a long railway journey with Doe, where half the best of green England, clad in summer dress, swept in panorama past our carriage windows. Perhaps we both watched it pass a little wistfully. Perhaps we thought of bygone holiday-runs, when we had watched the same telegraph lines switchbacking to Falmouth. There was a one-night stay at the Royal Hotel, Devonport; and a walk together in the fresh morning down to the Docks. There was a woman who touched Doe's sleeve and said: "You poor dear lamb," and annoyed him grievously. There was the fat policeman's challenge at the gates. And then we were through.

We had walked a little way, when a boy from the Royal Hotel, whom the policeman suffered to pass, ran up to us like a messenger from a world we had left behind.

"Lieutenant Ray, sir," he called.

I turned round and said "Yes?" inquiringly.

"Here's a telegram, sir, that arrived just after you left."

I took it undismayed, knowing it to be yet another telegram of good wishes. "I'll bet you, you poor dear lamb," I said to Doe, "the words are either 'Good-bye and God-speed,' or 'Cheerioh and a safe return.'"

"Not taking the bet," said Doe. "How else could it be phrased?"

"Well, we'll see," said I, and opened the envelope. The words were:

"I am with you every moment—MOTHER."

CHAPTER II
PADRE MONTY AND MAJOR HARDY
COME ABOARD

Sec.1

Doe and I have often looked back on our first glimpse of Padre Monty and wondered why nothing foreshadowed all that he was going to be to us. We had entered the Transport Office on one of the Devonport Quays, to report according to orders. Several other officers were before us, handing in their papers to a Staff Officer. The one in a chaplain's uniform, bearing on his back a weighty Tommy's pack, that made him look like a campaigner from France, was Padre Monty. We could only see his back, but it seemed the back of a young man, spare, lean, and vigorous. His colloquy with the Staff Officer was creating some amusement in his audience.

"Well, padre," the Staff Officer was saying, as he handed back Monty's papers, "I'm at a loss what to do with you."

"The Army always is at a loss what to do with padres," rejoined Monty pleasantly, as he took the papers and placed them in a pocket. "However, you needn't worry, because, having got so far, I'm going on this blooming boat."

"But I've no official intimation of your embarking on the *Rangoon*."

Padre Monty picked up a square leather case and, moving to the door, said:

"No, but you've ocular demonstration of it."

And he was gone.

When our turn came, the Staff Officer consulted a list of names before him and said:

"The *Rangoon*. She's at the quay opposite the Great Crane."

The *Rangoon*, as we drew near, showed herself to be a splendid liner, painted from funnel to keel the uniform dull-black of a transport. All over and about this great black thing scurried and swarmed khaki figures, busy in the work of embarkation. We rushed up the long gangway, and pleaded with the Embarkation Officer for a two-berth cabin to ourselves. The gentleman damned us most heartily, and said: "Take No. 54." We hurried away to the State Rooms and flung our kit triumphantly on to the bunks of Cabin 54.

It was at this moment that a mysterious occupant of Cabin 55, next door, who had been singing "A Life on the Ocean Wave," came to the end of his song and roared: "Steward!"; after which he commenced to whistle "The Death of Nelson." We heard the steps of the steward pass along the alley-way and enter 55.

"Yes, sir?" his voice inquired.

But our neighbour was not to be interrupted in his tune. He whistled it to its last note, and then said:

"I say, steward, I'm sure you're not at all a damnable fellow, so I want you to understand early that you'll get into awful trouble if I'm not looked after properly—*-what*. There'll be the most deplorable row if I'm not looked after properly."

"Well, I'm hanged!" whispered Doe. "I'm going to see who the merchant is." He disappeared; and was back in ten seconds, muttering, "Good Lord, Rupert, it's a middle-aged major with a monocle; and its kit's marked 'Hardy.'"

And, while we were wondering at such spirits in a major, and in one who was both middle-aged and monocled, two bells sounded from the bows, two more answered like an echo from the boat-deck above, and Major Hardy was heard departing with unbecoming haste down the alley-way.

"What's that mean?" asked Doe.

"Luncheon bell, I s'pose," replied I. "Come along."

We found our way down to the huge dining saloon, which was furnished with thirty separate tables. Looking for a place where we could lunch together, we saw two seats next the padre, whose conversation in the Transport Office had entertained us. We picked a route through the other tables towards him.

"Are these two seats reserved, sir?" I asked.

Padre Monty turned a lean face towards Doe and me, and looked us up and down.

"Yes," he said. "Reserved for you."

I smiled at so flattering a way of putting it, and, sitting down, mumbled: "Thanks awfully."

There were two other people already at the table. One was a long and languid young subaltern, named Jimmy Doon, who declared that he had lost his draft of men (about eighty of them) and felt much happier without them. He thought they were perhaps on another boat.

"Are they *officially* on board the *Rangoon*?" asked Padre Monty.

"Officially they are," sighed Jimmy Doon, "but that's all. However, I expect it's enough."

"Well, your draft is better off than I am," said Monty. "It at least exists officially, whereas I'm *missing*. I haven't officially arrived at Devonport. The War Office will probably spend months and reams of paper (which is getting scarce) in looking for me. But I don't suppose it matters."

"Oh, what does anything matter?" grumbled Jimmy Doon. "We shall all be dead in a month—all my draft and you and I; and that'll save the War Office a lot of trouble and a lot of paper." He trifled with a piece of bread, and concluded wearily: "Besides this unseemly war will be over in six months. The Germans will have us beaten by then."

At this point the other passenger at the table gave us a shock by suddenly disclosing his identity. He put a monocle in his eye, summoned a steward, and explained:

"This is my seat at meals— *what*. Do you see, steward? And understand, there'll be the most awful bloody row, if I'm not looked after properly."

Major Hardy dropped the monocle on his chest and apologised to Monty: "Sorry, padre." Then he took the menu from the steward, and, having replaced his monocle and read down a list of no less than fourteen courses, announced:

"Straight through, steward— *what*."

The steward seemed a trifle taken aback, but concealed his emotion and passed the menu to Jimmy Doon. Mr. Doon, it was clear, found in this choosing of a dish an intellectual crisis of the first order.

"Oh, I don't know, steward, damn you," he sighed. "I'll have a tedious lemon sole. No—as you were—I'll, have a grilled chop." And, quite spent with this effort, he fell to making balls out of pellets of bread and playing clock golf with a spoon.

During the meal Major Hardy and Padre Monty talked "France," as veterans from the Western Front will continue to do till their generation has passed away.

"I was wounded at Neuve Chapelle—*what*," explained the Major. "Sent to a convalescent home in Blighty. Discharged as fit for duty the day we heard of the landing at Cape Helles. Moved Heaven and earth, and ultimately the War Office, to be allowed to go to Gallipoli."

(Major Hardy might have said more. He might have told us that he had been recommended once for a D.S.O., and twice for a court-martial, because he persisted in devoting his playtime to sharpshooting and sniping in No Man's Land, and to leading unauthorised patrols on to the enemy's wire. But it was not till later that we were to learn why he had been known throughout his Army Corps as Major Fool-hardy.)

Padre Monty had not been wounded, it seemed, but only buried alive.

"The doctor and I had been taking cover in a shell-hole," he explained, between the sweet and the dessert, "when a high-explosive hurled the whole of our shelter on top of us, leaving only our heads free. We were two heads sticking out of the ground like two turnips. After about five hours the C.O. sent a runner to find the padre and the M.O., alive or dead. The fellow traced us to our shell-hole, and when he saw our heads, he actually came to attention and saluted. 'The C.O. would like to see you in the Mess, sir,' said he to me. 'And I should dearly like to see him in the Mess,' said I. 'However, stand at ease.' 'Stand at the devil,' said the doctor. 'Go and get spades and dig us out.'"

"Hum," commented Major Hardy, "if you weren't a padre, I should believe that story. But all padre are liars, *what*."

Monty bowed acknowledgments.

"And then," suggested the Major, "you felt the pull of the Dardanelles."

"Exactly, who could resist it? I wasn't going to miss the most romantic fight of all. The whole world's off to the Dardanelles. I knew the East Cheshire's chaplain was coming home, time expired, so I applied—"

"How ripping! That's our brigade," interrupted I, unconsciously returning his previous flattery.

"Is that so?" said he. "Well, let's go above and get to know one another."

We went on deck, he, Doe, and I, and watched the new arrivals. Troop-trains were rolling right up to the quay and disgorging hundreds of men, spruce in their tropical kit of new yellow drill and pith helmets. Unattached officers arrived singly or in pairs; in carriages or on foot. Many of them were doctors, who were being drafted to the East in large numbers. A still greater proportion consisted of young Second Lieutenants, who, like ourselves, were being sent out to replace the terrible losses in subalterns.

"The world looks East this summer," mused Monty. Then he turned to me in a sudden, emphatic way that he had when he was going to hold forth. "But there's a thrill about it all, my lads. It means great developments where we're going to. Six new divisions are being quietly shipped to the Mediterranean. You and I are only atoms in a landslide towards Gallipoli. There's some secret move to force the gates of the Dardanelles in a month, and enter Constantinople before Christmas. Big things afoot! Big things afoot!"

"Jove! I hope so," said I, caught by his keenness.

"Just look round," pursued Monty, switching off in his own style to a new subject, "isn't our Tommy the most lovable creature in the world?"

I followed his glance, and saw that the decks were littered with recumbent Tommies, who, considering themselves to have embarked, had cast off their equipment and lain down to get cool and rested.

"Look at them!" spouted Monty, and by his suddenness I knew he was about to hold forth at some length. "You'll learn that the Army, when on active service, does an astonishing amount of waiting; and Tommy does an astonishing amount of reclining. Lying down, while you wait to get started, is two-thirds of the Army's work. Directly the Army begins to wait, Tommy relieves his aching back and shoulders of equipment, and reclines. Quite right, too. There's no other profession in the world, where, with perfect dutifulness, you can spend so much time on your back. Active Service is two-parts Inaction—"

What more of his views Monty would have expounded I can't say, for a voice yelled from the promenade-deck above us:

"You there! What's your rank?"

I jumped out of my skin, and Doe out of his, for we thought the voice was addressing us, Monty turned without agitation and looked up at the speaker. It was Major Hardy. He was leaning against the deck-rail, and had fixed with his monocle the nearest recumbent soldier. This soldier was just the other side of us, so the Major was obliged to shout over our heads.

"What's your rank?" he repeated. "Come along, my man. Get a move on. Jump to it. What's your rank?"

The Tommy, flurried by this surprise attack, climbed on to his feet, came to attention, and said:

"Inniskillings, sir."

"Damn the man—*what*," cried the Major. "What's your *rank*? I said."

"What, sir?" respectfully inquired the Tommy, whose powers of apprehension had been disorganised by so sudden a raid.

The Major adopted two methods calculated to penetrate the soldier's intelligence: he leant over the rail, and he spoke very slowly.

"What's—your—bloody—rank? Are you a general, or a private?"

"No, sir," answered the bewildered Tommy.

"Oh, God damn you to hell! What's your *rank*?"

"Oh, private, sir."

"Then, for Christ's sake, go and do some work. What are privates for? Get that kit of mine from the quay."

The Major dropped his monocle on his chest, and looked down at us.

"Sorry, padre," he said, and walked away.

I watched till he was out of sight, and then said indignantly:

"So he jolly well ought to have apologised."

"And he *did*," retorted Monty. "Be just to him. It took me six months—"

"He's off," thought I.

"—to get the Army's bad language into proportion. At first I opened on it with my heavies in sermon after sermon. Then I saw proportion, and decided on a tariff, allowing an officer a 'damn' and a man a 'bloody.' Winter and Neuve Chapelle taught me the rock-bottom level on which we are fighting this war, and I spiked my guns. No one has a right to condemn them, who hasn't floundered in mud under shell-fire."

I think that, after this, we dropped into silence, and watched the quay emptying itself of men, and the **Rangoon's** decks becoming more and more crowded, as the day declined. The Embarkation was practically complete. The Devonport Staff Officers wished us "a good voyage," and went home to their teas in Plymouth. And, just before dinner, the gangway was hauled on to the quay. This was the final act, for, though the ship was not yet moving, we had broken communication with England.

Sec.2

At dinner, it being the first night afloat, the champagne corks began to pop, and the conversation to grow noisier and noisier. By the time the nutcrackers were busy, the more riotous subalterns had reached that state of merriness, in which they found every distant pop of a cork the excuse for a fresh cheer and cries of "Take cover!"

Major Hardy, too, was beaming. He had sipped the best part of three bottles of champagne, and was feeling himself, multiplied by three. He assured Monty that the padres had been the most magnificent people of the war. He told three times the story of one who had died going over the top with his men. That padre was a man. The men would have followed him anywhere. For he was a man every inch of him. But, of course, the victim and hero of the war, said Major Hardy, looking at Doe, myself, and the weary Jimmy Doon, was the junior subaltern. Everybody was prepared to take off his hat to the junior subaltern. He had died in greater numbers than any other rank. He had only just left school, and yet he had led his men from in front. The Major, if he had fifty hats, would take them all off to the junior subaltern. His heart beat at one with the heart of the junior subaltern. And, steward, confound it, where was the drink-steward? There would be the most awful bloody row, if he weren't looked after properly.

Dinner over, the riotous juniors rushed upstairs to the Officers' Lounge, a large room with a bar at one end, and a piano at the other. Some congregated near the bar to order liqueurs, while others surrounded the piano to roar rag-time choruses that one of their number was playing. This artist had a whole manual of rag-time tunes, and seemed to have begun at Number One and decided to work through the collection. Each air was caught up and sung with more enthusiasm than the last.

And see, there was Major Hardy, leaning over the pianist that he might read the words through his monocle, and singing with the best of them: "Everybody's doing it—doing it—doing it," and "Hitchy-koo, hitchy-koo, hitchy-koo."

The Spirit of Riot was aboard to-night. The wines of Heidsieck and Veuve Pommery glowed in the cheeks of the subalterns. It was the last night in an English harbour, and what ho! for a rag. It was the first night afloat, and what ho! for a rough-house. And there was Elation in the air at the sight of Britain embarking for the Dardanelles to teach the Turk what the Empire meant. So shout, my lads. "Hitchy-koo, hitchy-koo, hitchy-koo."

Major Hardy was equal to any of them. He was the Master of the Revels. He had a big space cleared at one end of the lounge, and organised a Rugby scrum. He arranged the sides, interlocked the subalterns in the three-two-three formation, forced their heads down like a master coaching boys, and, when he had given the word "Shove like hell," ran round to the back of the scrum, got into it with his head well down, and pushed to such purpose that the whole of the opposite side was rushed off its feet, and the scrum sent hurtling across the lounge. A few chairs were broken, as the scrimmagers swept like an avalanche over the room. Major Hardy was hot with success. "A walk over! Absolutely ran them off their feet! Come and shove for them, you slackers," he shouted to those, who so far had only looked on and laughed. A score of fellows rushed to add their weight to the defeated side, and another score to swell the pack of the victors. "That's the style," cried the Major. "There are only about sixty of us in this scrum. Pack well down, boys. Not more than twenty in the front row. Ball's in! Shove like blazes!" Into it he got himself, and shoved—shoved till the scrum was rolled back across the lounge; shoved till the side, which was being run off its feet, broke up in laughter, and was at once knocked down like ninepins by the rush of the winning forwards; shoved till his own crowd fell over the prostrate forms of their victims, and collapsed into a heap of humanity on to the floor.

Wiping his brow and whistling, he organised musical chairs; and, after musical chairs, cock-fighting. Already he was limping on one knee, and his left eye was red and swollen. But he was enjoying himself so much that his enjoyment was infectious. To see him was to feel that Life was a riotous adventure, and this planet of ours the liveliest of lively worlds. And really, in spite of all, I'm not sure that it isn't.

Doe and I with our hands in our pockets had contented ourselves with being onlookers. The high spirits of Major Hardy's disorderly mob were radiating too much like electric waves through the room for us not to be caught by an artificial spell of happiness. But neither of us felt rowdy to-night. Monty, too, as he stood between us, looked on and moralised.

"It's three parts Wine and seven parts Youth," he ruled (he was always giving a ruling on something), "so I'm three parts shocked and seven parts braced. But I say, Doe, we're a race to rejoice in. Look at these officers. Aren't they a bonny crowd? The horrible, pink Huns, with their round heads, cropped hair, and large necks, may have officers better versed in the drill-book. But no army in the world is officered by such a lot of fresh sportsmen as ours. Come on deck."

When we got out into the warm air of a July evening, we found that the quay, which before dinner had been alongside the ship, was floating away from our port-quarter. Clearer thinking showed us that it was the ship which was veering round, and not the shore. We were really moving. The *Rangoon* was off for the Dardanelles. There was no crowd to cheer us and wave white handkerchiefs; nothing but a silent, deserted dockyard—because of that policeman at the gate. It was only as we crept past a great cruiser, whose rails were crowded with Jack Tars, that cheers and banter greeted us.

"The Navy gives a send-off to the Army," said Doe; and the voice of one of our Tommies shouted from the stern of the *Rangoon*:

"Bye-bye, Jack. We'll make a passage for you through them Dardanelles."

"We will," whispered Monty.

"We will," echoed I.

Soon the *Rangoon* was past the cruiser and abreast of the sinister low hulls of the destroyers that were going to escort us out to sea. But here, to our surprise, the noise of an anchor's cable rattling and racing away grated on our ears.

"She's dropping anchor till the morning," said Monty. "All right, then we'll sit down."

We placed hammock-chairs on a lonely part of the boat-deck. I reclined on the right of Monty, and Doe took his chair and placed it on his left. Just as, in the old world behind the dockyard gates, he would not have been satisfied unless he had been next to Radley, so now he must contrive to have no one between himself and Monty. Meantime down in the lounge they seemed to have abandoned cock-fighting for music. A man was singing "Come to me, Thora," and his voice modified by distance could be heard all over the ship. The refrain was taken up by a hundred voices: "Come—come—come to me, Thora"; and, when the last note had been finished, the hundred performers were so pleased with their effort that they burst into cheers and whistling and catcalls. It sounded like a distant jackal chorus.

Now that we were on deck, the spell, which the electric waves of enjoyment had played on me in the lounge, was removed. Rather, an emptiness and a loneliness began to oppress me, only increased by the rowdyism below.

"It's going to degenerate into a drunken brawl," I complained.

Monty turned and slapped me merrily on the knee. "Don't be so ready to think the worst of things," he said.

Something in the gathering darkness and the gathering sadness of this farewell evening made me communicative. I wanted to speak of things that were near my heart.

"I s'pose just nowadays I *am* thinking the worst of people. I've seen so much evil since I've been in the army that my opinion of mankind has sunk to zero."

"So's mine," murmured Doe.

"And mine has gone up and up and up with all that I've seen in the army," said Monty, speaking with some solemnity. "I never knew till I joined the army that there were so many fine people in the world. I never knew there was so much kindliness and unselfishness in the world. I never knew men could suffer so cheerfully. I never knew humanity could reach such heights."

We remained silent and thinking.

"Good heavens!" continued Monty. "There's beauty in what's going on in the lounge. Can't you see it? These boys, a third of them, have only a month or more in which to sing. Some of them will never see England again. And all know it, and none thinks about it. Granted that a few of them are flushed with wine, but, before God, I've learnt to forgive the junior subaltern everything—

"Everything," he added, with passionate conviction.

Doe turned in his seat towards Monty. I knew what my friend was feeling, because I was feeling the same. These words had a personal application and were striking home.

"What do you mean by 'everything'?" asked Doe, after looking round to see that the deck was deserted. "Just getting tight?"

"I said 'everything,'" answered Monty deliberately. "I learnt to do it out in France. What's the position of the junior subaltern out there? Under sentence of death, and lucky if he gets a reprieve. The temptation to experience everything while they can must be pretty subtle. I don't say it's right—" Monty furrowed his forehead, as a man does who is trying to think things out—"To say I would forgive it is to admit that it's wrong, but ah! the boy-officer's been so grand, and so boyishly unconscious of his grandeur all the time. I remember one flighty youth, who sat down on the firing-step the night before he had to go over the top, and wrote a simple letter to everybody he'd cared for. He wrote to his father, saying: 'If there's anything in my bank, I'd like my brother to have it. But, if there's a deficit, I'm beastly sorry.' Think of him putting his tin-pot house in order like that. He was—he was blown to pieces in the morning....

"They found he had L60 to his credit. It wouldn't have been there a week, if the young spendthrift had known."

It was now dark enough for the stars and the lights of England and the glow in our pipe-bowls to be the most visible things.

"Go on," said Doe. "You're thrilling me."

"I remember another coming to me just before the assault, and handing me a sealed letter addressed to his mother. What he said was a lyric poem, but, as usual, he didn't know it. He just muttered: 'Padre, you might look after this: I may not get an opportunity of posting it.' So English that! A Frenchman would have put his hand on his heart and exclaimed: 'I die for France and humanity.' This reserved English child said: 'I may not get an opportunity of posting it.' My God, they're wonderful!"

Monty stared across the stream at the thousand lights of Devonport and Plymouth. He was listening to the voices in the lounge singing: "When you come to the end of a perfect day"; and he waited to hear the song through, before he pursued:

"There was one youngster who, the morning of an attack, gave me a long envelope. He said: 'I'll leave this with you, padre. It's my—it's my—' And he laughed. Laughed, mind you. You see, he was shy of the word 'will'; it seemed so silly...."

Monty stopped; and finally added:

"Neither did that boy know he was a Poem."

"Go on," said Doe, "I could listen all night."

"It's a lovely night, isn't it?" admitted Monty. "Inspires one to see only the Beauty there is in everything. Isn't there Beauty in Major Hardy's black eye?"

"It's a Poem—*what*," laughed Doe.

"You may laugh, but that's just what it is. He said that his heart beat at one with the heart of a junior subaltern; and it does that because it's the heart of a boy. And the heart of a boy is matter for a poem."

"By Jove," said Doe, "you seem to be in love with all the world."

"So I am," Monty conceded, pleased with Doe's poetic phrase; "and with the young world in particular."

"I think I could be that too," began Doe—

Doe was carrying on the conversation with ease. I left it to him, for these words were winning eternity in my memory: "I could forgive them everything." With a sense of loneliness, and that I had lost my anchor in those last days of the old world, I felt that one day I would unburden myself to Monty. I would like an anchor again, I thought. The same idea must have been possessing Doe, for he was saying:

"Somehow I could forgive everything to those fellows you've been telling us about, but I'm blowed if I can forgive myself everything."

And here Monty, with the utmost naturalness, as though so deep a question flowed necessarily from what had gone before, asked:

"Have you *everything* to be forgiven?"

It is wonderful the questions that will be asked and the answers that will be given under the stars.

Doe looked out over the water, and moved his right foot to and fro. Then he drew his knee up and clasped it with both hands.

"Everything," he said, rather softly.

And, when I heard him say that, I felt I was letting him take blame that I ought to share with him. So I added simply:

"It's the same with both of us."

Monty held his peace, but his eyes glistened in the starlight. I think he was happy that we two boys had been drawn to him, as inevitably as needles to a magnet.

At last he said:

"I suppose we ought to turn in now. But promise me you'll continue this talk to-morrow, if it's another lovely night like this."

"Surely," assented Doe, as we arose and folded up the chairs.

"I hope when we wake we shan't be out at sea," suggested I, "for I want to watch old England receding into the distance."

Monty looked at me and smiled.

"Rupert," he said, and it was like him to use my Christian name without as much as a "by your leave" within the first dozen hours of our acquaintance, "you're one of them."

"One of whom?"

"One of those to whom I could forgive everything. You both are. Good night, Rupert. Good night, Edgar."

CHAPTER III
"C. OF E., NOW AND ALWAYS"

Sec.1

Awaking at 5.30 the next morning, I heard a noise as of the anchor's cable being hauled in. The engines, too, were throbbing, and overhead there were rattling and movement. I tumbled Doe out of his top bunk, telling him to get up and see the last of England. Slipping a British warm over my blue silk pyjamas—mother always made me wear pale blue—I went on deck. Doe covered his pink-striped pyjamas with a grey silk kimono embroidered with flowers—the chance of wearing which garment reconciled him to this cold and early rising—and followed me sleepily. In a minute we were leaning over the deck-rails, and watching the sea, as it raced past the ship's hull.

Our *Rangoon* was really off now. As we left Devonport, two devilish little destroyers gave us fifty in the hundred, caught us up, and passed us, before we were in the open sea. Then they waited for us like dogs who have run ahead of their master, and finally took up positions one on either side of us. We felt it was now a poor look out for all enemy submarines.

"Well, ta-ta, England," said Doe, looking towards a long strip of Devon and Cornwall. "See, there, Rupert? Falmouth's there somewhere. In a year's time I'll be back, with you as my guest. We'll have the great times over again. We'll go mackerel-fishing, when the wind is fresh. We'll put a sail on the *Lady Fal*, and blow down the breeze on the estuary. We'll—"

"And when's all this to be?" broke in a languid voice. We turned and saw our exhausted young table companion, Jimmy Doon, who had arrived on deck, yawning, to assume the duties of Officer on Submarine Watch.

"After the war, sure," answered Doe.

Mr. Doon looked pained at such folly.

"My tedious lad," he said, "do I gather that you are in the cavalry?"

"You do not, Jimmy," said Doe.

"Nor yet in the artillery?"

"No, Jimmy."

"Then I conceive you to be in the infantry."

"You conceive aright, Jimmy."

"Well, then, don't be an unseemly ass. There'll be no 'after the war' for the infantry."

"In that case," laughed Doe, who had been offensively classical, ever since he won the Horace Prize, "***Ave, atque vale***, England."

After gazing down the wake of the ***Rangoon*** a little longer, we decided that England was finished with, and returned to our cabins to dress in silence. And then, having read through twice the directions provided with Mothersill's Sea-sick Remedy, we went down to breakfast.

At this meal the chief entertainment was the arrival of Major Hardy, limping from injuries sustained the previous night, and with an eye the colour of a Victoria plum. "The old sport!" whispered the subalterns. And that's just what he was; for he was a major, who could run amok like any second lieutenant, and he was forty, if a day.

In the afternoon, when the sea was very lonely, the destroyers left us, which we thought amazingly thin of them. So we searched out Jimmy Doon, and told him that, as Officer on Submarine Watch, he ought to swim alongside in their place.

Jimmy was much aggrieved, it appeared, at being detailed for the tiresome duty of looking for submarines. It was the unseemly limit, he said, to watch all day for a periscope, and it would be the very devil suddenly to see one. Besides, he had hoped that by losing his draft of men he would be freed from all duties, and a passenger for a fortnight. He would have just sat down, and drawn his pay. As it was, he assured us, he hadn't the faintest idea what to do if he should sight a submarine—whether to shoot it, or tell the skipper. He was nervous lest in his excitement he should shoot the skipper. At any rate, he had a firing-party of twenty in the bows, and was determined to shoot someone, if he spotted a periscope. And, moreover, the whole thing made him tediously homesick, and he wanted his mother.

He was mouching off quite sad and sulky about it all, when the ship's clock pointed to 4 p.m. (and no one ever argues with a ship's clock), eight bells rang out, and all the junior officers were impressed into a lecture on Turkey—even including Jimmy Doon, who thought that his important duties ought to have secured him exemption from such an ordeal. The lecturer was Major Hardy, who, being a man of the wanderlust, had planted in Assam, done some shady gun-running in Mexico, fought for one, or both, or all sides in the late Balkan War, and sauntered, with a hammock to hang under the trees, in all parts of Turkey, Anatolia, and the Ottoman world. He limped to the lecturer's table, in the lounge, and, holding his monocle in his hand from the first word to the last, delivered a discourse of which this was the gist:

Before Christmas we should be in Constantinople—*what*. (Laughter, rather at the *what* than at the substance of the sentence.) He was confident the Dardanelles would be conquered any day now, and wished the ship would go a bit faster, so that we should not be too late to miss all the fun. (Hear, hear.) The only thing that was holding up our army at Cape Helles was the hill of Achi Baba. Now he had stood on Achi Baba and looked down upon the Straits at that point where they became the silver Narrows: and he knew that old Achi was a wee pimple, which he could capture before breakfast, given a fighting crowd of blaspheming heathens, like those he saw before him. (Loud cheers.) When we penetrated Turkey, we were to understand that the Turk with a beard was a teetotaller, like himself, Major Hardy. (Cheers.) We were never to kick a dog in Turkey—*what* (laughter), and, above all, never to raise our eyes to a Turkish woman, whether veiled or not, if we would keep our lives worth the value of a tram ticket. "One thinks," he concluded, "of the crowd of susceptible Tommies reclining on the decks outside, and fears the worst." (Loud laughter, cheers, and Jimmy Doon's weary voice: "Good-bye-ee.")

Sec.2

So the first afternoon at sea declined into evening. I had been looking forward all day to the starlight night, in which we should discuss again with Monty the things that had crept into our conversation the night before. I had gone to bed, happy in the thought that the breastworks had been broken down, and the way made easier for further unburdening. I had fallen asleep, contented in the conviction that

Monty had been sent into my life to help me to put things straight. In my simple theology, I was pleased to imagine I saw how God was working. Somewhere in that old world behind the dockyard lay my shattered ideals, shattered morals, shattered religion. Monty was to rebuild my faith in humanity and in God. Some where in that rosy year which was past lay the anchor that I had cast away. Monty was to find me drifting to the Dardanelles with no anchor aboard, and to give me one that would hold. Yes, I saw a ruling Hand. Radley had been the great influence of my schooldays; and, now that he was fast fading into the memories of a remote past, Monty, this lean and whimsical priest, had stepped in to fill the stage. The story of our spiritual development must ever be the story of other people's influence over us. I could see it all, and went to sleep lonely but happy.

It is difficult to say why I wanted to set my life aright. The thought of my mother; the peaceful movement of the ship away from England; Monty's stories of his lovable boy officers; and the beauty of the seascape—all had something to do with it. At any rate, I found myself longing for the time when, after dinner, Doe and I, with Monty between us, should recline in deck-chairs under the stars, and speak of intimate things.

When the time came, it was very dark, for deck-lamps were not allowed, and every port-hole was obscured, so that no chink of light should betray our where-abouts to a prowling submarine. We began by star-gazing. Then we brought eyes and faces downwards, and watched the wide, rippling sea. Monty, having refilled his pipe on his knees, lit it with some difficulty in the gentle wind, before he re-membered that, after dark, smoking was forbidden on deck. The match flared up, and illuminated the world alarmingly.... We listened for the torpedo.

Nothing evil coming from the darkness, Monty knocked out the forbidden to-bacco, and placed an empty pipe between his teeth.

"I suppose you fellows know," he said, "that we've got a daily Mass on board."

"What's that?" asked Doe.

Monty removed his pipe and gazed with affected horror at his questioner. Certainly he would hold forth now.

"Bah!" he began, but he changed it with quick generosity to "Ah well, ah well, ah well! I know the sort of religion you've enjoyed—and, for that matter, adorned. It's a wonderful creed! Have a bath every morning, and go to church with your people. It saves you from bad form, but can't save you from vice."

Doe moved slightly in his chair, as one does when a dentist touches a nerve. Monty stopped, and then added:

"'A daily Mass' is my short way of saying 'A daily celebration of the Holy Communion.'"

"Heavens!" thought I. "He's an R.C."

I felt as though I had lost a friend. Doe, however, was quicker in appraising the terrible facts.

"I s'pose you're a High Churchman," he said; and I've little doubt that he there-upon made up his mind to be a High Churchman too. Monty groaned. He placed in front of Doe his left wrist on which was clasped a bracelet identity disc. He switched on to the disc a shaft of light from an electric torch, and we saw engraved on it his name and the letters "C.E."

"That's what I am, Gazelle," said he, as the light went out, "C. of E., now and always."

("Gazelle" was ostensibly a silly play on my friend's name, but, doubtless, Doe's sleek figure and brown eyes, which had made the name of "The Grey Doe" so appropriate, inspired Monty to style him "Gazelle.")

"C. of E.," muttered I, audibly. "What a relief!"

"You beastly, little, supercilious snob!" exclaimed Monty, who was easily the rudest man I have ever met.

I didn't mind him calling me "little," for he so overtopped me intellectually that in his presence I never realised that I had grown tall. I felt about fourteen.

"You beastly, little, intolerant, mediaeval humbug. I suppose you think 'C. of E.' is the only respectable thing to be. And yet your C. of E.-ism hasn't—" He stopped abruptly, as if he had just arrested himself in a tactless remark.

"Go on," I said.

"And yet your religion," he continued gently, "hasn't proved much of a vital force in your life, has it? Didn't it go to pieces at the first assault of the world?"

"I s'pose it did," I confessed humbly.

"Shall I tell you the outstanding religious fact of the war?" asked he. "Let me recover my breath which your unspeakable friend here put out by calling me a 'High Churchman,' and then I'll begin. It begins eighty years ago."

So Monty began the great story of the Catholic movement in the Church of England. He told us of Keble and Pusey; he made heroes for us of Father Mackonochie dying amongst his dogs in the Scotch snows, and of Father Stanton, whose coffin was drawn through London on a barrow. He knew how to capture the interest and sympathy of boy minds. At the end of his stories about the heroes and martyrs of the Catholic movement, though we hadn't grasped the theology of it, yet we knew we were on the side of Keble and Pusey, Mackonochie and Stanton. We would have liked to be sent to prison for wearing vestments.

"But hang the vestments!" cried Monty in his vigorous way. "Hang the cottas, the candles, and the incense! What the Catholic movement really meant was the recovery for our Church of England—God bless her—of the old exalted ideas of the Mass and of the great practice of private confession. 'What we want,' said the Catholic movement, 'is the faith of St. Augustine of Canterbury, and of St. Aidan of the North; the faith of the saints who built the Church of England, and not the faith of Queen Elizabeth, nor even of the Pope of Rome.'"

We thought this very fine, and Doe, who generally carried on these conversations while I was silent, inquired what exactly this faith might be, which was neither Protestantism nor Romanism.

"Rehearse the articles of my belief, eh?" laughed Monty. "Well, I believe in the Mass, and I believe in confession, and I believe that where you've those, you've everything else."

"And what's the outstanding fact of the war?" asked Doe.

"The outstanding fact of my experience at least, Gazelle, has been the astonishing loyalty to his chaplains and his church of that awful phenomenon, the young High Church fop, the ecclesiastical youth. He has known what his chaplains are for, and what they can give him; he hasn't needed to be looked up and persuaded to do his religious duties, but has rather looked up his chaplains and persuaded them to do theirs—confound his impudence! He has got up early and walked a mile for his Mass. His faith, for all its foppery, has stood four-square."

Monty started to relight his pipe, forgetting again in his enthusiasm all routine orders. He tossed the match away, and added:

"Yes: and there's another whose religion is vital—the extreme Protestant. He's a gem! I disagree with him on every point, and I love him."

Monty held the floor. We were content to wait in silence for him to continue. He looked at a bright star and murmured, as if thinking aloud:

"Out there—out there the spike has come into his own."

"What's a spike?" interrupted Doe, intent on learning his part.

"They called those High Church boys who before the war could talk of nothing but cottas and candles, 'spikes.' They were a bit insufferable. But, by Jove, they've had to do without all those pretty ornaments out there, and they've proved that they had the real thing. My altar has generally been two ration boxes, marked 'Unsweetened Milk,' but the spike has surrounded it. And, look here, Gazelle, the spike knows how to die. He just asks for his absolution and his last sacrament, and—and dies."

There was silence again. All we heard was the ship chopping along through the dark sea, and distant voices in the saloons below. And we thought of the passing of the spike, shriven, and with food for his journey.

"And what are we to believe about the Mass?" asked Doe, who, deeply interested, had turned in his chair towards Monty.

Monty told us. He told us things strange for us to hear. We were to believe that the bread and wine, after consecration, were the same Holy Thing as the Babe of Bethlehem; and we could come to Mass, not to partake, but to worship like the shepherds and the magi; and there, and there only, should we learn how to worship. He told us that the Mass was the most dramatic service in the world, for it was the acting before God of Calvary's ancient sacrifice; and under the shadow of that sacrifice we could pray out all our longings and all our loneliness.

"Now, come along to daily Mass," he pleaded. "Just come and see how they work out, these ideas of worshipping like the shepherds and of kneeling beneath the shadow of a sacrifice. You'll find the early half-hour before the altar the happiest half-hour of the day. You'll find your spiritual recovery there. It'll be your healing spring."

Turning with the Monty suddenness to Doe, he proved by his next words how quickly he had read my friend's character.

"You boys are born hero-worshippers," he said. "And there's nothing that warm young blood likes better than to do homage to its hero, and mould itself on its hero's lines. In the Mass you simply bow the knee to your Hero, and say: 'I swear fealty.

I'm going to mould myself on you.'"

He had not known Edgar Doe forty-eight hours, but he had his measure.

"All right," said Doe, "I'll come."

"Tell us about the other thing, confession," I suggested.

"Not now, Rupert. 'Ye are babes,' and I've fed you with milk. Confession'll come, but it's strong meat for you yet."

"I don't know," demurred I.

Monty's face brightened, as the fact of one who sees the dawn of victory. But Doe, though his whole nature moved him to be a picturesque High Churchman, yet, because he wanted Monty to think well of him, drew up abruptly at the prospect of a detailed confession.

"You'll never get me to come to confession," he laughed, "never—never —never."

"My dear Gazelle, don't be silly," rejoined Monty. "I'll have you within the week."

"You won't!"

"I will! Oh, I admit I'm out to win you two. I want to prove that the old Church of England has everything you public schoolboys need, and capture you and hold you. I want all the young blood for her. I want to prove that you can be the pride of the Church of England. And I'll prove it. I'll prove it on this ship."

Whether he proved it, I can't say. I am only telling a tale of what happened. I dare say that, if instead of Monty, the Catholic, some militant Protestant had stepped at this critical moment into our lives, full of enthusiasm for his cause and of tales of the Protestant martyrs, he would have won us to his side, and provided a different means of spiritual recovery. I don't know.

For the tale I'm telling is simply this: that in these moments, when every turn of the ship's screw brought us nearer Gibraltar, the gate of the Great Sea, and God alone knew what awaited us in the Gallipoli corner of that Mediterranean arena, came Padre Monty, crashing up to us with his Gospel of the saints. It was the ideal moment for a priest to do his priestly work, and bring our Mother Church to our side. And Monty failed neither her nor us.

CHAPTER IV
THE VIGIL

Sec.1

Night or day, the ship ploughed remorselessly on. It was steered a bewildering zigzag course to outwit the submarines. The second day of the voyage saw us in the Bay of Biscay, a hundred miles off Cape Finisterre. The sun got steadily hotter, and the sea bluer.

And the subalterns blessed the sun, because it gave them an excuse for putting on the white tennis-flannels which they had brought for deck wear. All honest boys, we know, fancy themselves in their whites. And the mention of their deck-flannels reminds me, strangely enough, of Monty's daily masses. It was evident from the attendance at these quiet little services that he had been busy persuading other young officers to see "how it worked."

Every morning the smoking room was equipped with a little altar that supported two lighted candles. And to this chapel there wandered, morning after morning, stray and rather shy young subalterns, who knelt "beneath the shadow," occupied with their own thoughts, while Calvary's ancient sacrifice was acted before God.

Monty had formed a dozen subalterns into a guild of servers. And on these sun-baked mornings he would insist that his servers should kneel at their place beside the altar in their white sporting attire. "*His* Mass," said he, "was meant to be mixed up with the week-day play."

It was all quiet—in fact, ever so quiet. Outside on the deck there would be noises, and in the alley-way there would be bangings of cabin-doors, and voices calling for the bath steward. But these things only intensified the quiet of the smoking room. Monty would keep his voice very low, loud enough to be heard by those who wished to follow him, and soft enough not to interrupt those who preferred to pursue their private devotions.

Whether he was right in all that he did and taught, or was only a joyous rebel, better theologians than I must determine. He was at least right in this: the attraction of that early morning service was irresistible. I began to look forward to it. I enjoyed it. When my comfortable bunk pulled strongly, and I was too lazy to get up, I would feel all day a sense of having missed something. I had never been able to pray anywhere else so easily as I prayed there. I had never before understood the satisfaction of worship.

Monty soon found that the only enemy who could beat him and prevent a swelling attendance of Youth at the Mass, was Cosy Bed. C.B., as he contemptuously called him, was most powerful at 7.0 in the morning. Padre Monty would not have been Padre Monty, had he failed to declare war on the foe at once. He drew up a "Waking List" of his family (for he had adopted everybody on the ship under 25), and each morning went his rounds, visiting a score of cabins, where the "children" slept. He burst upon them unceremoniously, and threw open the darkened port-holes to let the sunlight in. For the sunlight, like all bright things, was on the side of the Mass.

Of course it was only a minority, at best, who thus bowed their young heads to the Mass. The rest remained gentiles without the Law. And Monty's undismayed comment was characteristic of him. "I say, Rupert," he said, coolly assuming that I was his partner in the work, "We've only a few at present, our apostolic few. But don't you love these big, handsome boys, who *will not* come to church?"

One immortal Friday fully forty wandered in to Mass. Monty was radiant. Immediately after the service he said to me: "Come on deck, and have a game of quoits-tennis before breakfast. Mass first, then tennis—that's as it should be." We went on deck, and, having fixed the rope that acted as a net, played a hard game. And, when the first game was finished, Monty, still flushed with his victory down in the smoking room, came and looked at me over the high intervening rope, much as a horse looks over a wall, and proceeded to hold forth:

"D'you remember that picture, 'The Vigil,' Rupert, where a knight is kneeling with his sword before the altar, being consecrated for the work he has in hand? Well, this voyage is the vigil for these fellows. Before they step ashore, they shall kneel in front of the same altar, and seek a blessing on their swords. Hang it! aren't they young knights setting out on perilous work? And I'll prove we have a Church still, and an Altar, and a Vigil."

Then he asked me what I was stopping for and talking about, and why I didn't get on with the game. His spirits were irrepressible.

Sec.2

After tea, on the fourth day, everyone hurried to the boat-deck, for land was on our port side. There to our left, looking like a long, riftless cloud bank, lay a pale-washed impression of the coast of Spain. A little town, of which every building seemed a dead white, could be distinguished on the slope of a lofty hill. There was a long undulation of mountainous country, and a promontory that we were told was Cape Trafalgar.

I should have kept my eyes fixed on this, my first view of Sunny Spain, if there had not been excited talk of another land looming on the starboard side. Looking quickly that way, I made out the grey wraith of a continent, and realised that, for the first time, Dark Africa had crept, with becomingly mysterious silence, into my range of vision.

Doe let his field-glasses drop, and stared dreamily at the beautiful picture, which was being given us, as we approached in the fall of a summer day towards the famous Straits of Gibraltar. Not long, however, could his reverie last, for Jimmy Doon poked him in the ribs and said:

"Wake up. Do you grasp the fact that you are just about to go through the gate of the Mediterranean, and you'll be damned lucky if you ever come out through it again? It's like going through the entrance of the Colosseum to the lions. It's both tedious and unseemly."

"Oh, get away, Jimmy," retorted Doe, "you spoil the view. Look, Rupert—don't look out of the bows all the time; turn round and look astern, if you want to see a glorious sunset."

I turned. We were steering due east, so the disc of the sun, this still evening, was going down behind our stern. The sea maintained a hue of sparkling indigo, while the sun encircled itself with widening haloes of gold and orange. The vision was so gorgeous that I turned again to see its happy effect upon the coast of Spain, and found that the long strip of land had become apple pink. Meanwhile I was aware that my hands and all my exposed flesh had a covering of sticky moisture, the outcome of a damp wind blowing from grey and melancholy Africa.

"The sirocco," said someone, and foretold a heavy mist with the night.

It happened so. The darkness had scarcely succeeded the highly coloured sunset before the raucous booming of the fog-horn sounded from the ship's funnel, and the whole vessel was surrounded with a thick mist—African breath again—which, laden with damp, left everything superficially wet. The mist continued, and the darkness deepened, as we went through the Straits. The siren boomed intermittently, and Gibraltar, invisible, flashed Morse messages in long and short shafts of light on the thick, moist atmosphere. To add to the eerie effect of it all, a ship's light was hung upon the mast, and cast yellow rays over the fog-damp.

"Beastly shame," grumbled Doe, looking into the opaque darkness, "we shan't see the Rock this trip through. Never mind, we'll see it on the homeward route."

"*Per*-haps," corrected Jimmy Doon.

Thus we went through the gate into the Mediterranean theatre, where the big battle for those other Straits was being fought. We left the fog behind us, as we got into wider seas, and steamed into a hot Mediterranean night.

Sec.3

Oh, it was torrid. Ere we came on deck for our talk with Monty under the stars, we had changed into our coolest things. And now, awaiting his arrival, I lolled in my deck-chair, clothed in my Cambridge blue sleeping-suit, and Doe lay with his pink stripes peeping from beneath the grey embroidered kimono.

It had become a regular practice, our nightly talk with Monty on what he called "Big Things." Certainly he did most of the talking. But his ideas were so new and illuminating, and he opened up such undreamed-of vistas of thought, that we were pleased to lie lazily and listen.

"What's it to be to-night?" he began, as he walked up to us; but he suddenly saw our pyjama outfit, and was very rude about it, calling us "popinjays," and "degenerate aesthetes." "My poor boys," he summed up, as he dropped into the chair, which we had thoughtfully placed between us for his judgment throne, "you can't help it, but you're a public nuisance and an offence against society. What's it to be to-night?"

"Tell us about confession," I said, and curled myself up to listen.

"Right," agreed Monty.

"But wait," warned Doe. "You're not going to get me to come to confession. I value your good opinion too highly."

"My dear Gazelle, don't be absurd. I'll have your promise to-night."

"You won't!"

"I will! Here goes."

And Monty opened with a preliminary bombardment in which, in his shattering style, he fired at us every argument that ever has been adduced for private confession—"the Sacrament of Penance," as he startled us by calling it. The Bible was poured out upon us. The doctrine and practice of the Church came hurtling after. Then suddenly he threw away theological weapons, and launched a specialised attack on each of us in turn, obviously suiting his words to his reading of our separate characters. He turned on me, and said:

"You see, Rupert. Confession is simply the consecration of your own natural instinct—the instinct to unburden yourself to one who waits with love and a gift of forgiveness—the instinct to have someone in the world who knows exactly all that you are. You realise that you are utterly lonely, as long as you are acting a part before all the world. But your loneliness goes when you know of at least one to whom you stand revealed."

As he said it, my whole soul seemed to answer "Yes."

"It's so," he continued. "Christianity from beginning to end is the consecration of human instincts."

So warmed up was he to his subject that he brought out his next arguments like an exultant player leading honour after honour from a hand of trumps. He slapped me triumphantly on the knee, and brought out his ace:

"The Christ-idea is the consecration of the instinct to have a visible, tangible hero for a god."

Again he slapped me on the knee, and said:

"The Mass is the consecration of the instinct to have a place and a time and an

Objective Presence, where one can touch the hem of His garment and worship."

That was his king. He emphasised his final argument on my knee more triumphantly than ever.

"And confession is the consecration of the instinct to unburden your soul; to know that you are not alone in your knowledge of yourself; to know that at a given moment, by a definite sacrament, your sins are blotted away, as though they had never been."

His victorious contention, by its very impulse, carried its colours into my heart. I yielded to his conviction that Catholic Christianity held all the honours. But I fancy I had wanted to capitulate, before ever the attack began.

"By Jove," I said. "I never saw things like that before."

"Of course you didn't," he snapped.

Having broken through my front, he was re-marshalling his arguments into a new formation, ready to bear down upon Doe, when that spirited youth, who alone did any counter-attacking, assumed the initiative, and assaulted Monty with the words:

"It's no good. If I made my confession to a priest who'd been my friend, I'd never want to see him again for shame. I'd run round the corner, if he appeared in the street."

"On the contrary," said Monty, "you'd run to meet him. You'd know that you were dearer to him than you could possibly have been, if you had never gone to him in confession. You'd know that your relations after the sacred moment of confession were more intimate than ever before."

I saw Doe's defence crumbling beneath this attack. I knew he would instantly want these intimate relations to exist between Monty and himself. Monty, subtly enough, had borne down on that part of Doe's make-up which was most certain to give way—his yielding affectionateness.

And, while Doe remained silent and thoughtful, Monty attacked with a new weight of argument at a fresh point—Doe's love of the heroic.

"Don't you think," he asked, "that, if you've gone the whole way with your sins, it's up to a sportsman to go the whole way with his confession. And anybody knows that it's much more difficult to confess to God through a priest than in the privacy of one's own room. It's difficult, but it's the grand thing; and so it appeals to an heroic nature more."

"Yes, I see that," assented Doe.

Monty said nothing further for awhile, as if hoping we would declare our decision without any prompting from him. But we were shy and silent; and at last he asked:

"Well, what's the decision?"

"I'll come to you," I said, "if you'll show me how to do it all."

He replied nothing. I believe he was too happy to speak. Then he turned to Doe.

"Gazelle, what about you?"

And Doe said one of those engaging things that only he could utter:

"I imagine I ought to do it for love of Our Lord. But s'posing I know that isn't the real motive—s'posing I feel that someone has been sent into my life to put it right, and I do it rather for—for him?"

There Monty was beaten. Doe's meaning was too plain; and the rich prize it threw at Monty's feet too overwhelming. The only answer he could give was: "You must try and link it to love for the Higher One."

"All right," said Doe, simply. "I'll try."

A silence of unusual length followed. The noise of the ship going through the water, and the beat of the engines, assumed the monopoly of sound. Doe and I were thinking of the thorny and troublesome path of confession, which in a few days we must traverse. And Monty indicated what his thoughts were by the remark with which he prepared to close that night's conversation under the stars.

"The two cardinal dogmas of my faith are—"

"The Mass and confession," I volunteered, in a flash of impudence.

"Don't interrupt, you rude little cub. They are these. Just as there is more beauty in nature than ugliness, so there is more goodness in humanity than evil, and more happiness in the world than sorrow...."

"Now and then one is allowed a joy that would outweigh years of disappointment. You two pups have given me one of those joys to-night. It's my task to make this voyage your Vigil; and a perfect Vigil. It's all inexpressibly dear to me. I'm going to send you down the gangway when you go ashore to this crusade—properly absolved by your Church. I'm going to send you into the fight—*white*."

CHAPTER V
PENANCE

Sec. 1

Upon the rail leaned Doe and I watching the waves break away from the ship. It was morning, and we were troubled—troubled over the awful difficulty of making our life confession on the morrow. Monty had given much pains to preparing us. He had sat with each under the awning on sunny days, and told him how to do it. We were to divide our lives into periods: our childhood, our schooldays, and our life in the army. We were to search each period carefully, and note down on a single sheet of writing-paper the sins that we must confess. But, wanting to do it thoroughly, I had already reached my ninth sheet. And I was still only at the beginning of my schooldays. I had acknowledged this to Monty, who smiled kindly, and said: "It is a **Via Dolorosa**, isn't it? But carry on. For the joy that is set before you, endure the cross."

"It was easy enough," complained Doe, "to say frankly 'everything' when he asked us what we had to confess; but, when you've got to go into details, it's the limit. I wish I were dead. Monty gave me a long list of questions for self-examination, and I had to go back and ask him for more. They didn't nearly cover all *I*'d done."

I couldn't help smiling.

"Yes," proceeded Doe, "Monty laughed too, and said: 'Don't get rattled. You're one of the best, and proving it every moment.' And that brings me to my other difficulty. Rupert, all my life I've done things for my own glory; and I did want to make this confession a perfect thing, free from wrong motives like that. But you've no idea how self-glorification has eaten into me. I find myself hoping Monty will say mine is the best life confession he has ever heard. Isn't it awful?" He sighed and murmured: "I wonder if I shall ever do an ***absolutely perfect*** thing."

Such a character as Doe's must ever love to unrobe itself before a friend; and he continued:

"No, I know my motives are mixed with wrong. For example, I don't believe I should do this, if some other chaplain, instead of Monty, had asked me to do it. And your saying you'd do it had much too much to do with my consenting. But I ***am*** trying to do it properly. And, after turning my life inside out, I've come to the conclusion that I'm a bundle of sentiment and self-glorification. The only good thing that I can see in myself is that where I love I give myself utterly. It's awful."

So, you see, in these words did Doe admit that the dog-like devotion, which he had once given to Radley, was transferred to Monty. In my own less intense way I felt the same thing. Radley had become remote, and ceased to be a force in our lives; Monty reigned in his stead. We were boys; and what's the use of pretending? A boy's affection is not eternal.

Of Doe's confession I can relate no more. It withdraws itself into a privacy. I can but tell you the tale of my own experience.

Sec.2

Monty's cabin was to be his confessional. I was to go to him early the next morning, as I had been detailed for Submarine Watch for the remainder of the day.

I approached his door, stimulating myself for the ordeal by saying "In half an hour I shall have told all, and the thing will be done." A certain happiness fought in my mind against my shrinking from self-humiliation. Two moods wrestled in me; the one said: "The long-dreaded moment is on you"; the other said: "The eagerly awaited moment has come."

I found Monty ready for me, robed in a surplice and violet stole. In front of the place where I was to kneel was a crucifix.

"Kneel there," said Monty, "and, if necessary, look at that. ***He*** was so much a man like us that He kept the glory that was set before Him as a motive for enduring the cross."

I knelt down. Nervousness suddenly possessed me, and my voice trembled, as I read the printed words:

"Father, give me thy blessing, for I have sinned."

Then nervousness left me. The scene became very calm. It seemed to be taking place somewhere out of the world. The worldly relations of the two taking part in it changed as in a transfiguration. I ceased to think of Monty as a lively friend. He had become a stately priest, and I a penitent. He had become a father, and I a child.

With a quiet deliberateness that surprised me, I said the "Confiteor," and accused myself of the long catalogue of sins that I had prepared. It was almost mechanical. Such merit as there may have been in my exhaustive confession must have lain in what conquering of obstacles I achieved before I came to my knees in Monty's presence, because I was conscious of no meritorious effort then. It was as if I had battled against a running current, and had at last got into the stream; for now, as I spoke in the confessional, I was just floating without exertion down the current.

When I had finished, Monty sat without saying a word. I kept my face in my hands, and waited for the counsel that he would offer.

He gave me the very thing that my opening manhood was craving; one clear and lofty ideal. I had felt blindly for it that far-off time when, as a small boy, the recollection of my grandfather's words: "That Rupert, the best of the lot," had lifted me out of cheating and lies. I had aspired towards it, but had not seen it, that evening outside Kensingtowe's baths. I had seen it hazily that day the old Colonel spoke of our Youth and our High Calling.

And now Monty set the vision in front of me. I was to see three ideals, Goodness, Truth, and Beauty, and merge them all in one vision—Beauty. For Goodness was only beauty in morals, and Truth was only beauty in knowledge. And I was to overcome my sins, not by negatively fighting against them when they were hard upon me, but by positively pursuing in the long days free from temptation my goal of Beauty. Then the things which I had confessed would gradually drop out of my life, as things which did not fit in with my ideal. For they were not good, nor true, nor beautiful.

"Pursue Beauty," he said, "like the Holy Grail."

With my head still bowed in my hands, I felt that happiness which comes upon men when they grasp a great idea. I felt lofty resolution and serene confidence flowing into me like wine.

"And, finally," said this masterly priest, "know how certain you can be that the absolution which I am going to pronounce is full and final. God only asks a true penitence, and you can offer Him no fairer fruits of penitence than those you have brought this morning. Know, then, that there will be no whiter soul in all God's church than yours, when you leave this room. For you will be as white as when you left the baptismal font. Now listen. You shall hear what was worked for you on Calvary."

I listened, and heard him speak with studied solemnity the words of absolution. And if a feeling can be said to grow up and get older, then there came upon me at that moment the feeling of a child released to play in the sunlight; only it was that feeling grown to a man's estate.

I rose from my knees to find that I was standing again in the world. I saw a ship's cabin, and a man removing a violet stole from a white surplice. It didn't seem a time in which to talk, so I turned the handle of the cabin door, and went out quietly.

I went straight to my Submarine Watch on the deck. There was a glow pervading me, as of something pleasant which had just occurred. Forgive me if it be weak to have these fleeting moments of exaltation, but I was seeing goodness, truth, and beauty in everything. The bright sunlight was beauty; of course it was; the blue sea was beauty. And it all had something to do with beauty of character and beauty of life.

Imagine me this rare day, lost in my thoughts, as I watched the sea running by, or the new world coming to meet the bows. Sometimes I watched it with my naked eyes. Sometimes I hastened the approach of the new things by bringing my field glasses to bear upon them. And, all the time, I had a sense of satisfaction, as of something pleasant which had just occurred.

At first the broad blue floor of the sea stretched right away on every side without a sail anywhere to suggest that it was a medium of traffic. The sky, a far paler blue, met the horizon all round. It was only a slight restlessness over the surface that made the Mediterranean distinguishable from a vast and still inland lake. The ship plied steadily onward in the opposite direction to the sun, which looked down upon the scene with its hot glance unmodified by cloud or haze.

With my glasses I swept the empty waters. At last I saw, sketched over there with palest touch, a line of mountains—just such a range as a child would draw, one peak having a narrow point, another a rounded summit. This land lay at so great a distance that it was shadowless, and looked like a long bit of broken slate with its jagged ends uppermost. I cast in my mind whether Gallipoli loomed like this: and Gallipoli, somehow, seemed more peaceful since that satisfying event of the morning.

I dropped my glasses. For the first time I realised that I was setting out to do something difficult for England. Actually I! I glowed in the thought, for to-day, if ever, I was in an heroic mood. I touched for a moment the perfect patriotism. Yes, if Beauty demanded it, I could give all for England—all.

As the day went by, we seemed to be rounding that mountainous island, for it lingered on our port, always changing its aspect, but always remaining beautiful.

The whole scene was Beauty. And this Beauty, urged the voice of the priest, was to have something to say in moments when I must choose between this bad deed and that good one. Of the two, I was to do the one that was the more like the Mediterranean on a summer day.

Oh, I had a clear enough ideal now. And why had I never seen before, as Monty had seen, that, just as there was far more beauty in seas and hills than ugliness, so on the whole there was more goodness in human characters than evil, and, assuredly, more happiness in life than pain. And the old Colonel, too, had seen beauty in youth and strength; he had seen it triumphing in Penny's death and in all this sanguinary Dardanelles campaign.

Yes, I had closed on the idea. Even the lively excesses of Major Hardy's mob, even Jimmy Doon's cynical humour at the prospect of death had much in them like the Mediterranean on a summer day.

Or, say, on a summer night like this. For, as the evening wore on, we were still passing this long island; and a pale mist had risen in a narrow ribbon from the sea-line, and hidden a lower belt of its hills from my view, so that the peaks towered like Mount Ararats above a rising flood of fog-damp; and, as this bank of mist rose upward, the sun sank downward, a disc of gold fire.

I followed it with my glasses; and so rapid was its descent that, before I could count a hundred, it had dipped beneath the water-line—become a flaming semicircle—then only a glowing rim—and disappeared. It left a few minutes' afterglow, with the sky every shade from crimson at the horizon to blue at the zenith.

The world got darker, and the waves, breaking from the ship's bows, began to spill a luminous phosphorescence on the sea. I watched a little longer; and then the stars and the phosphorescent wave-crests glistened in a Mediterranean night.

CHAPTER VI
MAJOR HARDY AND PADRE MONTY
FINISH THE VOYAGE

Sec.1

B ut I must hurry on. Here am I dawdling over what happened indoors in the minds of two boys, while out of doors nations were battling against nations, and the whole world was in upheaval. Here am I happily describing so local a thing as the effort of a big-hearted priest to rebuild our spiritual lives on the quiet moments of the Mass and the strange glorious mystery of penance, while the great Division which captured the beaches of Cape Helles had been brought to a standstill by the impregnable hill of Achi Baba, and uncounted troopships like our own were pouring through the Mediterranean to retrieve the fight.

On with the war, then. One morning I was wakened by much talking and movement all over the boat, and by Doe's leaping out of his top bunk, kicking me in passing, and disappearing through the cabin door. Back he came in a minute, crying: "You must come out and see this lovely, white dream-city. We're outside Malta."

I rushed out to find Valetta, the grand harbour of Malta, on three sides of us. We were anchored; and the hull of the **Rangoon**, which looked very huge now, was surrounded by Maltese bumboats.

Shore leave was granted us. And, ashore, we hurried through the blazing heat to visit the hospitals and learn from the crowds of Gallipoli sick and wounded something about the fighting at Helles. These cheery patients shocked our optimism by telling us that it was hopeless to expect the capture of the hill of Achi Baba by frontal assault and that any further advance at Cape Helles was scratched off the programme. The hosts of troops that were passing through Malta must, they surprised us by declaring, be destined for some secret move elsewhere than at Helles, for there was no room for them on the narrow tongue of land beneath Achi Baba.

"We're wild to know what's in the wind," said a sister. "The stream of transports has never stopped for the last few days."

That we could well believe. There were two huge liners crammed with khaki figures in the harbour that morning.

"We are going to win, I imagine?" asked Monty, with a note of doubt.

"O lord, yes," replied a superbly bonny youngster, without a right arm. "But I don't envy you going to the Peninsula. It's heat, dust, flies, and dysentery. And Mudros is ten times worse."

"What's Mudros?" asked I.

"Mudros," broke in Doe, blushing, as he aired his classical learning, "is a harbour in the Isle of Lemnos famous in classical—"

"Mudros," interrupted the one-armed man, proud of his experience, "is a harbour in the Island of Lemnos, and the filthiest hole—"

"Mudros," continued Doe, refusing to be beaten, "is a harbour in the Isle of Lemnos, which is the island where Jason and the Argonauts landed, and found Hypsipele and the women who had murdered their husbands. Jupiter hurled Vulcan from Heaven, and he fell upon Lemnos. And it's sad to relate that Achilles and Agamemnon had a bit of a dust-up there."

"Well, that may be," said the one-armed hero, rather crushed by Doe's weighty lecture. "But you're going to Mudros first in your transport, and you'll probably die of dysentery there."

"Good Lord," said I.

We selected the ward where we would have our beds when we came down wounded, and the particular pretty sister who should nurse us; and went out into the dazzling sun. Having climbed to a high level that overlooked the harbour, we leaned against a stone parapet, and examined the French warships that slept, with one eye open, up a narrow blue waterway. For Malta in 1915 was a French naval base.

"Sad to see them there, sir," said a convalescent Tommy, pointing to the grey cruisers flying the tricolour. "They've been bottled up there, since the submarines appeared off Helles and sank the *Majestic* and t'other boats. There's only destroyers loafing around Cape Helles now, sir."

"Great Scott, is that so?" asked Monty. "But I suppose we're going to win?"

"O lord, yes," said the Tommy.

We got back to the *Rangoon* just before sundown. And, when the sun began to soften and to bathe the white buildings of Valetta in ruddy hues, our siren boomed out its farewell, and two English girls in a small boat waved an incessant good-bye. Crowds gathered to brandish handkerchiefs, as our transport crept away, with the boys singing: "Roaming in the gloaming on the banks of the Dardanelles," and yelling: "Are we downhearted? NO! Are we going to win? YES!"

"Well, that's the last of Malta," murmured Jimmy Doon. "Another landmark in our lives gone."

Sec. 2

Two days' run brought us outside Alexandria. And the confoundedly learned Doe, pointing out to me the pink and yellow town upon the African sands, among its palms and its shipping, said: "Behold the city of Alexander the Great, of Julius Caesar and Cleopatra; the home of the Greek scriptures; and the see of the great saints, Clement, Athanasius, and Cyril."

So I did what he wanted. I called him a Classical Encyclopaedia, at which he looked uncomfortable and pleased.

It was Alexandria right enough. We had reached at last the base of the Dardanelles fight, and entered the outskirts of that ancient imperial world, which the old Colonel had told us was the theatre of the campaign.

Travelling very slowly, we steamed into the huge harbour. And soon we were moored against one of its forty quays, and being addressed in an infernal jangle of tongues by hundreds of begging Arabs who came rushing through the guns, limbers and field kitchens arrayed on the quay.

More anxious than ever for news of the fight, we applied for shore leave, and, after lunch, went down the gangway, and trod the soil of Africa for the first time.

At once, like an overpowering personality, the East rose up to greet us, oppressing us with its merciless Egyptian sun and its pungent smell of dark humanity. Heady with the sun, and sick with the smell, we found ourselves in one of the worst streets of Alexandria, the "Rue des Soeurs," a filthy thoroughfare of brothels masquerading as shops, and of taverns, which, like the rest of the world, had gone into military dress and called themselves: "The Army and Navy Bar," "The Lord Kitchener Bar," and "The Victory Bar."

Phew! the sweat and the stench! The East was a vapour bath. What a climate for a white man to make war in! And yet everywhere in this city of Alexander and Athanasius, British and Australian soldiers sauntered on foot or drove government waggons through the streets. Sick and wounded, too, roamed abroad in their blue hospital uniforms. Only too pleased to display before three eager novices their superior acquaintance with Gallipoli, they told us the story we had heard at Malta: the Helles army, firmly stopped by the hill of Achi Baba, was melting away in the atrocious heat; but some startling new venture was expected, for the forty quays of Alexandria had been scarcely sufficient to cater for the troops and stores that had put in there; and all the hospitals in Egypt had been emptied to admit twenty thousand casualties.

We hired a buggy, and drove back through the same odorous street to the dockyard, and, having given the thief of an Arab driver a third of his demands, went straight to our cabins to rinse our mouths out.

Next day at sundown, the siren boomed good-bye. Perhaps there was a military reason for it, but we always left these ports at sunset. It was sunset, as we steamed out of Malta; and now, with the sky flushed and the air rose-tinted, we began to slip gently out of the harbour, amid cheers and handwavings from every ship that we passed. We were picking our course between the ships, when Monty plucked my sleeve, and, pointing to a home-bound liner, murmured:

"Beauty, Rupert."

I looked, and saw what he meant. For in the big liner's bows two tiny English children clad in white, a little boy and girl, waved mechanically under the instructions of their sweet-faced English mother, who, though a young one, looked with a mother's eyes at our yellow rows of helmeted lads, and waved the more energetically (I doubt not) as she strove to keep back her tears. In the sad eyes of that youthful mother I saw looking out at us the maternal love of her sex for all the sons of woman. She was the last Englishwoman that many of these boys ever saw.

As we drew near the entrance of the harbour, a cheery Englishman was swept past in a white-sailed craft, and called out, as the wind bore him away: "Good-bye, lads. Do your duty, lads. Give 'em hell ev'ry time." Almost the next minute he was a white speck among the shipping of the harbour, and we were out in the open sea.

Sec.3

The ***Rangoon*** had taken aboard at Alexandria a number of new officers who, after being wounded on Gallipoli and treated in Egypt, were now returning as fit for duty. One showed a long, white scar across his scalp, where a bullet had just missed his brain. Another, who had still two bullets in his body, had been with our school-fellow Moles White in the ***River Clyde*** on the great April morning. These were people to be stared at and admired. They occupied exactly the same position to us as the bloods did when we were at school. They spoke with ease and grace of Mudros Harbour, of the great April landing at Helles, of the ***Eski Line***, the ***River Clyde***, the ***Gully Ravine***, and ***Asiatic Annie***. We felt very near the trenches, when they thus tossed fabled names about in commonplace conversations. They never used the name "Gallipoli," but always "The Peninsula." We made a mental note of this.

And they affected very shrewd ideas about the surprise push that was coming off; but since they only nodded their heads wisely and refused to be drawn, we suspected that they knew no more about it than we did. They would point, with the pride of previous knowledge, to the purple-hilled islands of the AEgean that we were passing all day: Rhodes, and Patmos, and Mitylene. They laughed with damnable superiority at our extensive kit, declaring that for their part they had left everything at the base, and were carrying only a few pounds of necessaries to the Peninsula. Some of them walked the deck in private's uniform, maintaining that it was suicide to go to the Peninsula trenches in the distinctive dress of an officer. They were quite modest, simple folk, no doubt, but they certainly thought they were the only people who realised that there was a war on.

Jimmy Doon, who had heard nothing of his lost draft at Alexandria, and was much relieved thereby, became incorrigible when he smelt the whiff of the trenches brought by these heroes. He would invite our subscriptions to the daily sweepstake with the words: "Come along, fork out. Last few sweeps of your life." And he would take me aside and say: "I suppose I shall be daisy-pushing soon. Tedious, isn't it?"

Late one afternoon, when we were only an hour's run from Mudros, there came by wireless the inspiring news that solved the riddle of the chain of transports in the Mediterranean and the empty hospitals in Alexandria. The simple typed message that was pinned on the notice-board, and could scarcely be read for the crowds surrounding it, ran: " ***We have landed in strong force at Suvla Bay and penetrated seven miles inland. Ends.***"

A new landing, hurrah! April 25th over again! The miracle of Helles repeated at Suvla! Out with the maps to study the strategy of the move! The map showed us Suvla Bay far up the coast of the Peninsula, a long way behind Achi Baba. We measured seven miles, and decided that the Turks' communications with Achi Baba must have been cut. "Curse it," said an enthusiast, "we're just too late." We had visions of the Turkish Army flying from the Helles front in frantic efforts to escape the surrounding threatened by this landing in their rear. We saw them abandoning their impregnable positions at Achi Baba, abandoning the forts of the Narrows, and retreating, if they could elude destruction, upon Constantinople.

And while the strategists on deck were getting delirious in their prophecies, the ship steered a path round two outlying islets, and entered the deep indentation in Lemnos Island, which is the mighty, hill-locked harbour of Mudros. A little French destroyer, pearl-grey in the evening light, steamed past us, and the French sailors waved their arms, and danced a welcome to this troopship of their allies. The ***Rangoon*** yelled at them: "What price Suvla?" Some English sailors, towed past in coal barges, asked us whether we were downhearted, and we called back: "NO! What—price—SUVLA! Are we going to win? YES!"

Now, I ask you, have the subalterns an excuse, or have they not, for a rough-house this night? It's their last night aboard, for to-morrow morning the smaller boats will come and carry them to the deadly Peninsula: and it's the evening that has brought the news of the Suvla landing. Excuse or not, they fetch the money out of their pockets at dinner, and order the champagne before the soup is off the table. Jimmy Doon, whipping the golden cap off his magnum of "bubbly wine," says: "I've the horrible feeling I shall be dead this time to-morrow. Pass your glasses, damn you. Cheerioh! Many 'appy returns from the Great War—some day." "Cheerioh, Jimmy," we acknowledge. "'Appy days!"

And, when the hundred subalterns, who form the first sitting at dinner, vacate their places at the tables to make room for the seniors, who come in state to the second sitting, anyone who sees them rushing upstairs to the lounge, the bar, and the piano, knows that there will be noise before the clock is an hour older. It begins in the lounge: but the impulse of the spirit of riot is too strong for the rough-house to be localised there. It's the end of the voyage, and they must forthwith go and cheer the General. They must cheer the Captain. Above all they must cheer Major Hardy, the old sport! The mass of subalterns flows down the first flight of stairs to the square gallery which overlooks the dining saloon, like railings looking down into a bear-pit. And, like the bears, the seniors were feeding in the bottom of the saloon. They look up from their nuts and wine to see a hundred flushed young faces staring from the gallery at their meal.

"Three cheers for the General!" cries a voice in the gallery.

Three of the noisiest fill the ship. And, when a hundred British officers have yelled three cheers, it's in the nature of them to go on and sing: "For he's a jolly good fellow," and to finish up with a final cheer that leaves its forerunners nowhere. It's a way they have in the Army.

"Speech! Speech!" demand exalted voices.

The General rises: and that's an excuse, heaven help us, for more cheers, and "He's a jolly good fellow" all over again. The seniors are young enough to beat time on the tables by hammering with their spoons till the plates dance; and by tinkling their glasses like tubular bells. In the last cheer one major so far forgets himself—his name is Hardy—as to let go with a cat-call, after which he immediately retires into his monocle, and pretends he hasn't.

The General, who is a kindly old brigadier with twinkling eyes, says: "I can't make a speech, but I'll sing you a song." He raises his glass to the gallery, and to the hundred faces looking down, and starts in a wheezy tenor: "For *they* are jolly good fellows." He gets no further, but takes advantage of the tumult of cheering to resume his seat.

The Captain, a naval hero of the Helles landing, is put through it. And in his speech he says: "If the Navy is really the father and mother of the Army in this

Gallipoli stunt, then I say—father and mother are proud of their children"—(cheers from the ship's officers). "The ships came as close in shore as possible—and always will, gentlemen, as long as you're on that plagued Peninsula—but, by God! it was the Army that left the shelter of the ships, and went through the blizzard of bullets on to the beaches of Cape Helles."

Can such a compliment be acknowledged otherwise than uproariously? Close your ears, if you can't stand a noise.

The Chief Officer is put through it. And by way of a speech he says: "Suppose, instead of cheering me, you cheer the fellows who have landed at Suvla?"

"Highland Honours!" yells a voice. And the seniors rise, stand upon their chairs, put one foot on the table amongst the plates, and, raising their glasses, join in the musical honours given to the new army at Suvla.

Major Hardy is called, and a speech demanded from him. Loudly applauded, he limps to the middle of the saloon, puts his monocle in his eye, and says one sentence: "I never heard such bloody nonsense in all my life." Releasing his monocle so that it falls on his chest, he limps back to his seat, and apologises to Monty.

The seniors having been thus sporting, it occurs to some bright young devil that it would be a graceful thing to sing "Home, sweet Home" to them, as they finish their meal. And "Home, sweet Home" leads naturally to "Auld Lang Syne," sung with linked arms and swaying bodies.

And then the crowd of subalterns, worked up by the licence allowed it, like a horse excited by a head-free gallop, returns in force to the lounge. The pianist strikes up "The Old Folks at Home." A Scotsman breaks in with the proclamation that It's oh! but he's longing for his ain folk; Though he's far across the sea, Yet his heart will ever be Away in dear old Scotland with his ain folk. And an Irishman, feeling that there's too much of Scotland about these songs, begins to publish the attractions of the hills of Donegal:

> "And, please God, if He so wills,
> Soon I'll see my Irish hills,
> The hills of Donegal, so dear to me."

Then the piano rings out with ancient dance-tunes, and Harry Fenwick, prince of dancers, seizes Edgar Doe round the waist, and, clasping the slim youth to him, leads the boy (who's as graceful as a girl and as sinuous as a serpent) through the voluptuous movements of the latest dance. Up and down go their outstretched arms like a pump handle, but oh! so sweetly; round and round with eyes half-closed swirl their bodies; and, just as you think they are going round again, they surprise you by teasingly stepping out the music in a straight line across the lounge; and, when you least expect it, they are retracing dainty steps along the same straight line—always seductive, tantalising, enticing.

But stop the dance. Here arrives Major Hardy to a din of welcome. And under his instructions they burn the champagne corks, and therewith decorate their faces. One is ornamented with a pointed beard and the devil's horns, and turned into Mephistopheles. One is given an unshaven chin, and made to represent Moses Ikeystein. Another is a White-eyed Kaffir. And don't think Major Hardy omits himself. Not he. He is Hindenburg.

Jimmy Doon, I regret to say, is undoubtedly drunk. He is walking about seeking someone to fight. To my discomfiture he approaches me as his best friend, and therefore the one most likely to fight him.

"Will you fight?" says he. "There's a decent shap."

I try with a sickly laugh to appear at my ease, and answer: "No, damned if I will," blushing to the roots of my hair, and wishing the painful person would go away.

"And you call yourself a Christian!" retorts Jimmy; which provokes the rest of the subalterns to hold a court-martial on James Doon for being tight. And they court-martial Fishy Fielding, an ugly fellow, whose eyes are like a cod's. What for, you seek to know. Well, they court-martial him because of his face. Both culprits are found guilty.

At 1 a.m. Jimmy staggers to his cabin to rest a swimming head. But he doesn't go to sleep till he has summoned his steward, and instructed him to call him early in the morning—call him early—call him early, for he's to be Queen of the May.

Sec.4

The riot had been still young when Doe entered the lounge from the deck, and, walking up to me, said:

"Come outside a minute."

He moved and spoke with the slight excitement and mysteriousness of one who had discovered something. I followed him out from the noise of the lounge into the silence of the deck.

"Come where it's quiet," he whispered.

We walked to the deserted bows.

"Now listen. Do you hear anything?"

"No," I answered, after awhile.

"Listen again. You won't catch it first go."

I strained my ears, while Doe stared at me.

"Yes, I hear it," I proclaimed at last. "Is it Helles, do you think, or Suvla?"

"I expect some of it is the old Turk trying to resist the invasion of Suvla."

For I had heard a distant throb in the air—no more—like a heart beating miles away. At times the throb became a rumble which could be felt rather than heard. Something in me jumped at the sound. The startled feeling was rather pleasing than otherwise. It was not a small thing to hear for the first time the guns of Gallipoli, to whose mouths our lives had been slowly drawing us during nineteen years.

Sec.5

Padre Monty finished the voyage in his own style. Early the next morning he had a corporate farewell Mass for all his servers and his family. And this is the true story how Major Hardy chanced to limp to the service.

He retired early from the revels of the previous night, and, as Doe and I were getting into our bunks, we heard him in his cabin next door whistling "Home, sweet Home," while he disrobed. We heard the steward ask him:

"What time will you be called in the morning, sir?"

"What time?" answered the Major's voice, when he had finished the tune. "What time? Let's see. I say, Ray," he inquired through the wall, "this padre-fellow's got a service or something in the morning—*what*?"

"Yes, sir," shouted I.

"Some unearthly hour, seven or what?"

"Seven-thirty, sir."

"Ah yes," said the Major's voice, soft again, to the steward, "call me six-thirty."

"Yes, sir. Will you have shaving water then, sir?"

"Shaving water—*what*? Yes, surely." And the Major shouted through the wall: "We shave, don't we, Ray?"

"Well, yes, sir," agreed I.

"Of course," continued the Major, reproachfully, to the steward. "Bring shaving water. And there'll be the most deplorable row if it's not hot."

"Will you have a cup of tea to get up with, sir?" asked the steward.

"Tea? What? No, I don't think so. No, surely not." Once more he sought enlightenment through the wall. "We don't have tea, do we, Ray?"

"Well, no, sir. That's as you please."

"No. No tea, steward. Of course not. What nonsense!"

"Very good, sir. Good night, sir."

"Good night, steward.... You see, Ray," shouted Major Hardy, "I am a bit out of this church business. Must get into it again—*what*. And the padre's a good fellow."

In such wise Major Hardy half apologised to two boys for being present, and limped to the service.

Half a hundred others crowded the smoking room. This last Mass being what Monty called his "prize effort," he insisted on having two servers, and selected Doe and myself, whom he chose to regard as his "prize products." On either side of the altar we took our places, not now clad in white flannels, but uniformed and booted for going ashore. Monty, as he approached the altar, gave one quick, involuntary glance at his packed congregation, ready dressed for war, and slightly sparkled and flushed with pleasure.

After the Creed had been said, Monty turned to deliver a little farewell address. Very simply he told his hearers that, when in a few hours' time the boats came to take them to the Peninsula Beaches, they were to know that they were doing the right thing. There was a tense stillness, as he said with suggestive slowness: "I am only the lips of your Church. She has been with you on this ship, and striven not to fail you. And now to God's mercy and protection she commits you. The Lord bless you and keep you. The Lord give you His peace this day and evermore."

If Monty desired to fill the room with an unworldly atmosphere, and to raise the cloud "Shechinah" around his little altar, he knew by the solemn hush, as he turned to continue the Mass, that he had succeeded. And at the end of it all he added a farewell hymn, which the congregation rose from their knees to sing. Sung to the tune of "Home, sweet Home," like an echo from the purer parts of the previous night, its words were designed by Monty to linger for many a day in the minds of his soldier-servers.

> "Dismiss me not Thy service, Lord,
>   But train me for Thy will:
> For even I in fields so broad
>   Some duties may fulfil:
> And I would ask for no reward
>   Except to serve Thee still."

So they sang: and they went out on to the sunlit deck trailing clouds of glory.

Sec.6

It really did seem the end of the voyage, and the beginning of something utterly new—and something so dangerous withal that our pulse-rate quickened with suspense—when the Military Landing Officer came aboard, laden with papers, and, sitting at a table in the lounge, gave into the hands of boys, who yesterday were playing quoits-tennis, written orders to proceed at once to such places as W. Beach on Helles or the new front at Suvla.

"Here we take our tickets for the tumbrils," murmured Jimmy Doon, as we stood awaiting our turn. "Third single for La Guillotine."

And yet it was with a jar of disappointment that we heard the M.L.O. say to Doe, after consulting his papers:

"Stop at Mudros. Report to Rest Camp, Mudros East."

"Why, sir, am I not going to—" began Doe.

"Next, please. What name?" interrupted the M.L.O. There was war forty miles away, and no time to argue with a young subaltern. "What name, you?"

"Ray, sir. East Cheshires."

"Rest Camp, Mudros."

"But is it for long, sir?" ventured I.

"Next, please. What name, padre?"

"Monty," answered our friend. "East Cheshires."

"Report Rest Camp," promptly said the M.L.O., and, raising his voice, called to the waiting crowd: "All East Cheshire Details detained at Mudros."

"But I have to relieve—" began Monty.

"Next, please. What name?" the M.L.O. burst in, looking up into Jimmy Doon's face.

"Jimmy—I mean, Lieutenant Doon, Fifth East Lancs."

"Held up, Mudros. Report—"

"But my draft, sir, has—"

"Next, please."

And Jimmy came away, hoping he had heard the last of his draft. He joined our Cheshire group, which was discussing the latest thunderbolt.

"Lord, isn't it enormously unseemly?" he grumbled. "I'm left out, too. Why, I've been a year in the Army, and not yet seen a man killed. I hoped I was certain to see one now."

"You detestably gruesome little cad," said Monty.

"I wonder if it's for long," murmured Doe. "I'd take the risk of being killed rather than not be able to say I'd seen the great Cape Helles, or, failing Helles, this new Suvla front."

"As it is," grunted Jimmy, "we shall probably be at Mudros till the end of the world."

The M.L.O. had not been gone an hour before the Navy sent its pinnaces with large lighters in tow for conveying the first drafts to the Peninsula ferry-boats. Each pinnace was in command of a midshipman, generally a fair-haired English boy looking about fifteen. These baby officers, who gave their orders to wide-chested and bronzed Tars, old enough to be their fathers, were stared at by us with romantic interest. For there had been stories in England of the deeds of the middies in the famous First Landing at Helles, when they remained in the bows of the boats they commanded, scorning cover of any kind, as became British officers in charge of men.

After the lighters, the *Snaefell*, an old Isle of Man steamer, came alongside, and, having taken some hundreds of men aboard, edged away from us, while Major Hardy, his heart ever overthrowing his dignity, said wrathfully:

"Give 'em a cheer or something, damn you."

We raised a cheer. The men responded, though not very effectively, and cheered and waved as the *Snaefell* carried them away.

"They know what they're going to, poor lads," mumbled Major Hardy.

Next came the *Redbreast*, whose decks were soon as crowded as the *Snaefell's* had been. Major Hardy scanned them through his eyeglass, and then turned snuffily upon us and said:

"Damn your English reticence! Damn your unimaginative silence! Why don't you study the psychology of these boys and this moment?"

Leaning over the rail, he cried at the crowd on the *Redbreast*:

"Good-bye, lads. Let fly! Three cheers for the king! Let 'em go!"

The boys caught his enthusiasm, as boys always will, and followed his lead, cheering the king and singing: "For he's a jolly good fellow.... And so say all of us. With a hip-hip-hip-hurrah!"

And with them cheering and singing thus, the *Redbreast* slipped quietly away.

Major Hardy dropped his monocle on his chest. A good voyage—a jolly voyage—was over.

And now a little motor-launch puffed alongside to collect the Mudros Details: and we went down the *Rangoon's* hull to be ferried ashore. We were ferried, as you shall see, out of our dazzling news of the campaign into the darkness of collapsing things.

Part II: The White Heights

CHAPTER VII
MUDROS, IN THE ISLE OF LEMNOS

Sec.1

The motor-launch beat away from the **Rangoon**. Monty, standing in the stern, lit a pipe, and stared over the match-flame at the empty troopship. Jimmy Doon, sitting in the bows, surveyed the hill-locked harbour, and said to me:

"Well, there's one comfort: we shan't be killed on Gallipoli."

"Why not?"

"Because we shall certainly die at Mudros."

Doe was brooding over the ships of the Navy on the water, and over the white camps of the Army on the dull, bleak hill-slopes.

"I didn't know there were so many ships in the world," he said.

It was a wonderful revelation of sea power. There were battleships, heavy and squat; cruisers, more slender and graceful; low-lying destroyers, coal black or silver grey; and hospital ships, which, in their glistening white paint, were as much more lovely than the men-of-war as ruth is more lovely than ruthlessness. Our little launch was passing heavy-gunned monitors; skirting round submarines that lay above the surface like the backs of whales; and panting along beneath the enormous **Aquitania**, whose funnels appeared to reach a higher sky than the surrounding hills. Flags flew everywhere: the white ensign from the masts of the Navy, the red ensign from the troopers, and the martial tricolour from the vessels of the Frenchmen.

Jimmy Doon sighed and pointed ashore. "Look at the unseemly hospitals," he said.

As he spoke, we were steering towards a little landing-jetty, called the "Egyptian Pier," and could see the Red Cross floating over the camps.

"Hospitals at Malta," groaned Jimmy, "hospitals at Alexandria, hospital ships all over the Mediterranean and the AEgean—Ray, it's dangerous: we'll go home."

But, instead, we stepped ashore. At once the reflected coolness of the water deserted us; the heady heat off the dusty land hit our flesh like the hot air from an oven; and a glare from the white, trampled dust and the white canvas tents troubled our eyes and set our temples aching. And the rolling hills, empty of growth, except grass burnt brown and thistles burnt yellow, gave us a shock of depression.

"Damn, oh damn," said Jimmy.

"Precisely," agreed Monty.

We walked on, till we reached an array of square tents that formed No. 16 Stationary Hospital. Here pale and emaciated men were wandering in pyjamas between tents marked "Dysentery," "Enteric," and "Infectious Wards."

"Damn," repeated Jimmy.

Then we came upon a barbed-wire compound, and, caught by the morbid fascination of all prisons, looked in. It was full of sick and wounded Turks, who lay on stretchers in bell-tents, and, by a miserable pantomime of raising two fingers to their lips and blowing into the air, besought of our charity a cigarette. We went in, and handed Abdullas among them. And that—now I come to think of it—was our first encounter with the enemy we had been sent to fight.

At the Rest Camp Doe and I were pushed into a tent that, insufficiently supplied with pegs, was flapping irritatingly in a rising wind. Sighing for the cosy cabins of the *Rangoon*, we tossed off our equipment on to the earthy floor and lounged into the mess for lunch. In the mess tent we sat down to trestle-tables, laid with coarse enamelled plates and mugs.

Monty turned to Jimmy, and asked: "What was that remark you made just now, James Doon?"

"Damn," answered Jimmy with great readiness.

"Thanks," said Monty.

After lunch there came to Doe and myself the only pleasing thing in a day of gloom. That was the joy of dressing up in the true tropical kit worn at Mudros; brown brogue shoes; pale brown stockings, turned down at the calves; khaki drill shorts, displaying bare knees; khaki shirts open at the throats, and with sleeves rolled up above white elbows; our topees, and no more. And, since we were sure we looked very nice, we decided to walk abroad among men. Besides, the shameful whiteness of our knees and forearms must be browned at once by a walk in the toasting sun.

We set off for the village of Mudros East. It proved to be a collection of ramshackle dwellings, as little habitable as English cowhouses; of stores, where thieving Greeks sold groceries to the soldiers; and of taverns, whose vines hung heavily clustered over porch and window. There was an ornate and lofty Greek Orthodox Church, and a little, unconsidered cemetery, where the bones of the dead were working their way above the ground.

In the streets of this tumble-down town walked every type of Gallipoli campaigner: British Tommies, grousing and cheerful; Australians, remarkable for their physique; deep-brown Maoris; bearded Frenchmen in baggy trousers; shining and grinning African negroes from French colonies; stately Sikhs; charming little Gurkhas, looking like chocolate Japanese; British Tars in their white drill; and similarly clad sailors of Russia, France and Greece.

It was while strolling through this fancy-dress fair that we suddenly came upon the camp of the French, and were briskly saluted by a French sentry. We returned a thrilling acknowledgment. For it was the first time that our great Ally had greeted our advent into the area of war.

Lord! how the wind was rising! And with it the dust! The grey motor ambulances, as they purred past with their sick, raised dust storms, that blew away over the roofs in clouds as high again as the houses. The ships and the harbour, though it was a sunny, cloudless day, could only be seen through a flying veil of dust. Quickly the vines, overhanging the porches, became white with dust; our teeth and palates coated with it. We hastened home to the sorry shelter of the mess that we might wash the dust down our throats with tea.

But bah! we went out of the dust into the flies. The mess was buzzing with them; and they were accompanied in their attacks upon our persons by bees, who hummed about like air-ships among aeroplanes. I dropped upon the table a speck of Sir Joseph Paxton's excellent jam, now peppered and gritty with dust, and in a few seconds it was hidden by a scrimmage of black flies, fighting over it and over one another. Other flies fell into my tea, and did the breast-stroke for the side of the mug. I pushed the mug along to Jimmy Doon, and pointed out to him, with the conceit of the expert, that they were making the mistake of all novices at swimming; they were moving their arms and legs too fast, and getting no motive power out of their leg-drive.

"Don't talk to me about 'em," said Jimmy. "I'm fast going mad. I'm not knocking 'em off my jam, but swallowing the little devils as they sit there. If I didn't do that, they'd commit suicide down my throat. Every time so far that I've opened my mouth to inhale the breeze, I've taken down a fly. It's tedious."

Ah! this wit was all forced gaiety, and the more depressing for that. It generated melancholy, as a damp fire generates smoke. I felt there was something wrong around me this afternoon—a shadow of evil. The conversation died: only the flies buzzed monotonously over us, as though we were offal or carrion; and the wind blew the dust in hail-storms against the canvas walls of the tent. And then it came— the terribly evil thing. The O.C. Rest Camp entered the mess, and announced with cynical cheerfulness:

" *Well, we've lost this campaign.* The great new landing at Suvla has failed."

There was a ghastly silence, and a voice muttered, "God!"

"Yes, and had it succeeded we'd have won. But the Turks have got us held at Suvla beneath Sari Bair, same as they've got us held at Helles beneath Achi Baba. The news is just filtering through."

With horror I listened to the cold-blooded statement. The shock of it produced a beating in the head, and a sickness. And I felt foolish, as though I might do something lunatic, like giving a witless shout, or running amok with a table-knife. I touched Doe, and whispered: "I'm going to get out of this. The old fool doesn't know what he's talking about."

I went away, and flung myself down on my valise in my flapping tent. I lay on my back, my hands clasped behind my head, and gazed up into the tent-roof loud with flies. Suvla had failed! It was a lie—an alarmist lie! Why, only yesterday we had exulted in it as the winning move, declaring that the game was over bar shouting, and regretting that we could not be in at the death. What was it reminding me of—this sudden "black-out," just as the lights had been brightest? Ah, I had it: that moment, when, in the flush of winning the Swimming Cup for Bramhall, I learned that I had lost it. How similar this was! Then the prize had been a silver cup, which had been fought for by a parcel of schoolboys. Now the grander trophy was that silver strip of the Dardanelles which men called "the Narrows," and the combatants were a pack of nations.

Suvla had failed! Why was I identifying my tiny self with a huge thing like Britain, and feeling that, because she had failed in her great fight for the Dardanelles, so I would fail, and purposely, in my little struggle after moral beauty? What a fool I was—but that was how it was working out. Beauty be hanged! Monty was badly wrong in proclaiming that nature was chiefly beautiful, and life on the whole was good. And, if he were wrong, why, then there was no further need to toil after a beauty of character to match the beauty of seas and hills. Good heavens! Beauty in the Mudros Hills! They were but homes of thirsty grass and dying thistles, dust and torturing flies. These ideals of Monty's were vapoury. Why not throw them up—throw up moral effort? I would. There was *not* more beauty—

It was at this moment that Monty himself stood in the tent door.

"Down, Rupert?" he asked. "What's the matter?"

I looked up into his eyes, and saw in them that inquiring sympathy which could so quickly transfigure him from a lively friend into a gentle priest.

"Oh, nothing," I said. I was in no mood just now to tell him anything. "Bored, that's all."

And then I looked round, and noticed that the tent was full of a violet light. It was as if limelight had been turned on from behind a violet glass.

"Good Lord!" I exclaimed. "The air's all coloured!"

"Yes," said he, "I was coming to tell you to look at the sunset. It's bad old Mudros's one good deed."

Out to the tent door I went, and looked over the harbour to the western shores. And there, very rapidly, the ball of the sun was going down behind the hills with an affair of gold and crimson lights, while all the hills were violet. The colour was so strong that it came out and flushed with violet the black hulls of the ships. And they, strangely motionless, lay mirrored in a water of white and gold.

"Listen!" said Monty.

For from all the camps the British bugles were singing the sad call of "Retreat"; the French trumpets wailing "Sun-down," and their rifles firing a rapid fusillade to speed the departing day. Meanwhile the heat had died into a refreshing coolness; the wind had dropped, leaving the dust undisturbed on the ground; and the flies were roosting in the tops of the tents.

Very soon it was quite dark. Then everything lit up: first, the camps on the hills, their innumerable hurricane-lamps resembling the lights of great cities; then, the vessels in the bay—and, in the quiet of the windless evening, their bells, telling the hour, came clearly over the water. The long hulls of the hospital ships marked themselves off by rows of green lights and large, luminous red crosses. Reflected in the still water, they gave to the basin the appearance of a pleasure lake, gay with red and green fairy lamps. The battleships hid their bellicose features in the darkness, and, since one or two of them had their bands playing, might have been pleasure steamers. And from an Indian encampment behind us came a weird incantation and the steady beat of the tom-tom.

Somehow, in the beauty of the Mudros night, I felt a spring of new hope in our campaign. We would win in the end. And with this re-born confidence went nobler resolutions for myself. To-morrow I would resume moral effort. To-morrow I would begin again.

CHAPTER VIII
THE GREEN ROOM

Sec. 1

The story of our two-months' delay at Mudros is largely the story of Monty's eccentricities. As for Doe and myself, we just watched with growing pride our knees burning in the sun to a Maori brown. When we bathed in the bay and saw that, while our bodies as a whole were a pale English pink, our elbows, knees and necks, that were daily exposed to the sun, were turning to this beautiful tint, we would place our limbs side by side to see which of us achieved the greater depth of colour. For this we drew our pay.

Jimmy Doon received early his orders to join his regiment on the Peninsula. He left us, declaring that he only contemplated paying a flying visit to the front, as the very sound of the guns convinced him that he was a civilian at heart. He would be back soon, he said.

Monty appointed himself Chaplain to No. 16 Stationary Hospital, and set to work. And during this period at Mudros he was just about as regrettable and impossible in his behaviour as I have ever known him. He procured a gramophone, and, touring the tents, in which the sick men lay, would set the atrocious instrument playing, "Kitty, Kitty, isn't it a pity in the city you work so hard?" The invalids loved the jingling refrain, and added to the plagues of Mudros by roaring its chorus. Then Monty would return in the worst of tempers to our tent, and, putting the instrument roughly away, sit down and look miserable. If Doe asked permission to feel his pulse or see his tongue, he would shut him up with the words, "Oh, stuff!" But once he laughed sarcastically and burst, with all the Monty enthusiasm and emphasis, into a diatribe against Broad Churchmanship, the ignorance of laymen, the timidity of the clergy, wishy-washy sermons—in short, the criminal lack of dogmatic teaching. Not seeing any connexion between dogmatic teaching and a gramophone, Doe looked so amazed that Monty laughed, and grumbled:

"It's fine priestly work I'm doing for these lads, isn't it? Work any hospital orderly could do. I ought to be hearing their confessions, and saying Mass for them. Instead I play them 'Kitty, Kitty, isn't it a pity—?' But they don't understand—they don't understand."

"But, gracious heavens," said Doe, "you can't be always doing priestly work. And we know to our sorrow that you do have sing-song services sometimes. Why, last night you had at least a couple of hundred bawling hymns at the tops of their voices, and making the night hideous. Wasn't that priestly enough?"

"No," he snapped. "It was a service any layman or hot-gospeller could hold. There they were—a mass of bonny lads, all calling themselves 'C. of E.,' and none of them knowing anything about the Mass or confession. Ah, they don't understand. It breaks my heart, Rupert. All sons of the Church; and they don't know the lines of their mother's face!"

"Well, why on earth," said Doe, impatiently, "do you run your beastly gramophone and your rousing services, if they're not your proper work?"

"Why, don't you see?" murmured Monty, turning away to watch the sun setting behind a sweep of violet hills, "I *must* pull my weight. I can feel patriotic at times. And, if I can't be a priest to the big majority, I can at least be their pal. That's how a padre's work pans out: a priest to the tiny few, and a pal to the big majority. I suppose it's something. Perhaps it's something."

Sec.2

It was Monty who first called Mudros, "The Green Room." The name was happily chosen, for here at Mudros the actors either prepared for their entry on the Gallipoli stage, or returned for a breather, till the call-boy should summon them again. In it, after the manner of green rooms, we discussed how the show in the limelight was going. We saw much that made us gossip.

We saw the huge black transports bear into Mudros Bay. Many were ships that were the pride of this watery planet. Like a duchess sailing into a ball-room came

the *Mauretania*, making the mere professional warships and the common mer-
chantmen look very small indeed. But even she, haughty lady, was put in the shade,
when her young but gargantuan sister, the *Aquitania*, floating leisurely between
the booms, claimed the attention of the harbour, and reduced us all to a state of
grovelling homage. And then the *Olympic*, not to be outdone by these overrated
Cunarders, would join the company with her nose in the air.

They were packed with yellow-clad and helmeted soldiers, who were as noisy
about their entrance as the great ships were silent. Tommy, coming into harbour
at the end of a voyage, had a habit of announcing his approach. So, when we on
the land heard over the water shouting, singing, genial oaths, "How-d'ye-do's," and
"What-ho's"; and such advices as "Cheerioh! The Cheshires are here!" "We'll open
them Narrows for you"; "Here we are, here we are, here we are again," or the simple
statement "We've coom!" we left our tents, and just went into our field-glasses, as
one goes into a theatre.

The men in the transports were delayed a night in the harbour, and on the
following day disgorged into the floating omnibuses that plied nightly to Suvla or
Helles. These omnibuses were old Isle of Man passenger steamers, jolly old tubs, doing their bit like papa and uncle and grandad in the National Guard at home. Being
due to arrive with their crowds of fighting men at the Peninsula in the darkness of
midnight, they would get under way just before dusk. They went out with the sun,
travelling straight and slowly between the hulls.

To the lads, thus being drawn to the danger-zone, a send-off would be given
in salvos of cheers from the sides of the anchored vessels, the bands of the Navy
sometimes playing them out with the old airs of England. And the lads themselves,
enjoying their evanescent triumph, and feeling like the applauded heroes on a car-
nival car, would shout back a merry response, or pick up the chorus of the tune
rendered by the distant band.

Many a still evening Doe and I watched their departure, knowing that soon
we should go out of the port like that in the red of a sunset. And Monty, hearing
the cries of "Good Luck," "Love to Johnny Turk," "Finish it off quickly," "Hi, put
yer trust in Gawd, and keep your 'ead down," and the faint strains of "Steady, boys,
steady, we'll fight and we'll conquer again and again," would bewail the fact that he
was too far off to cheer, and give vent to rising and choking feelings. He wanted to

pat these departing lads on the back. For in the Green Room they had dressed for their parts, and were now going through the door on their way to the stage.

Sec.3

Were we really winning on the Peninsula or losing? August, in spite of that black remark of the O.C. Rest Camp, decided that all was well. The fresh arrivals on the troopships brought with them like a breeze from the homeland that atmosphere of glowing optimism which prevailed in England in the early August days. The same news came from the opposite direction. For the streams of wounded, who in the weeks following the Suvla invasion poured into our Mudros hospitals, told us that the Turk was fairly on the run. "It can't last long," they said. "We've only to climb one of them two hills—either Sari Bair on the Suvla front, or old Achi Baba at Helles—and the trick's done. From the top of either of 'em we shall look down upon the Narrows, and blow their forts to glory. Up'll go the Navy, and there y'are!" It would be over by Christmas, they believed; for Christmas was always the pivot of Tommy's time.

So spoke August, drinking deep from cups overflowing with confidence. September detected a taste of doubt in the cheery optimism of the Green Room, and like a loyal British September, spat out the unpalatable mouthful. But the taste remained.

Nothing but stagnation seemed to be prevailing on the Peninsula. The incessant roll of guns could no longer be heard at Mudros. The old-time shifts of wounded ceased to pour into our hospitals. In their stead came daily crowds of dysentery, jaundice and septic cases. And these men told a different tale from the wounded, who, a month before, had returned from the stage like actors aglow with triumph. All reported "Nothing doing" on Gallipoli.

And the Big Rains were fast drawing due. The time was at hand when the ravines and gorges that cracked and spliced the Mudros Hills would roar to the torrents, and the hard, dust-strewn earth would become acres of mud, from which our tent-pegs would be drawn like pins out of butter. We remembered Elijah on Mount Carmel, and looked at the sky for rain.

But we looked in alarm and not hope. For, if the Narrows were not forced before the rains and sea-storms began, the campaign, we understood, would be doomed to disaster. The rain would turn our great Intermediate Base, Mudros, into a useless lagoon, and the sea-storms would beat on the beaches of the Peninsula, smash the frail jetties built at Suvla and Helles, and, by preventing the landing of supplies, condemn the Suvla army and the Helles army to annihilation or surrender.

"Surely, oh surely," said Monty, looking up one day at a cloudy sky, "something largely conceived will be attempted before the rains work havoc among the communications on land, and the storms slash at the communications by sea. We ***must*** be going to win."

"O Lord, yes," echoed I.

But September with its dry weather began to wane, the rains started a pla-guy pelting, and the winds commenced to excite the placid AEgean, while we still awaited big movements and final things.

Sec.4

Then the evil Peninsula sent straight to Monty's feet something that seemed like a direct message of scornful warning to our little ***Rangoon*** group. It was such a message as defiant kings have sent to banter those who contemplated an invasion of their realms. This is how it came.

Day after day (you must know) in the early morning, the dead, sewn up in their blankets, were landed from the ships that had picked them up in a dying condition at Suvla and Helles. They were laid in rows on the little landing-jetty, the "Egyptian Pier." After awhile the men would put them by in a mortuary tent, where they rested till the evening, when a G.S. waggon conveyed them to the cemetery.

Generally Monty, whose duty it was to bury them, would sit on the driver's seat and ride to the cemetery, after persuading Doe and me to ride with him.

On a certain September evening Monty glanced at the Camp Commandant's "chit," and read it aloud to us: "'Seven bodies for burial at 1700.' Are you coming?"

Doe turned towards me. "Coming, Rupert?"

"No. I'm too tired."

"Oh, rot, you scrimshanker. You've been hogging it all the afternoon."

"Yes, come on," said Monty. "We'll drive on the waggon."

The G.S. waggon with its seven blanketed forms was outside waiting for Monty. It was drawn by two teams of mules with mounted drivers. The driver's seat was therefore vacant, and on to it Monty, Doe and I climbed. The waggon started, as Monty whispered: "It's rather like the Dead Cart in the days of the Great Plague, isn't it?" We never spoke loud with that load behind us.

The waggon jolted along the straight white road to the cemetery, which was a little dusty acre on a plain between the hills. We halted at the gate, and Monty, getting down from his seat, robed by the front wheels. And, when the seven bodies had been removed in their stretchers from the waggon and laid in a line upon the road, the corporal of the Burial Party saluted Monty, and said:

"One's an officer, sir. Will you take him first?"

"I'll go in front," answered Monty. "Then the seven bodies, one after another, the officer's body leading. Feet first, of course."

"Very good, sir." The corporal, seeing that the bearers stood ready at the head and foot of each stretcher, said quietly:

"Bearers, raise!"

All the bearers bent in simultaneous motion, and lifted the stretchers from the road.

"Slow—march!"

The procession moved off, Monty in front picking his way between the graves towards those open to receive the day's dead. The Greek grave-diggers rested on their spades, and bared their heads. Some stray French soldiers sprang to attention, and saluted. A few curious British and a tall brown Sikh copied the Frenchmen, remaining at the salute till the procession had passed. And, when the open graves were reached, all these stragglers gathered round to form a little company of mourners.

Having seen the bodies laid by the graves, the corporal bent over the form of the dead officer, and removed from his breast that small piece of paper, which was always pinned to the blanket to state the man's identity: in this case it happened to be a government envelope, marked "On His Majesty's Service." The corporal handed it to Monty.

I recall the moment of his action as the last quiet moment before an unexpected shock. I seem to remember that it was a very graceful body, long and shapely, that lay there, outlined beneath the tightly-wrapped blanket. It looked like an embalmed

Egyptian.

Monty read the envelope, and frowned. He read it again, crumpled it up, and looked down at the long, slender form of the dead officer. Then, glancing round for Doe and me, and catching our eyes, as we watched him in curiosity, he handed the envelope to us. We smoothed out its crumpled folds, and read: "On His Majesty's Service. Lieut. James Doon."

This was the message that the Peninsula had contemptuously tossed to us.

Monty began the service, but I scarcely heard him. I was staring at the blanketed form, and thinking of Jimmy as he had been: Jimmy with all his bitter jests about death; Jimmy grumbling on the *Rangoon* because he would have to stay at Mudros "till the end of the world"; Jimmy leaving for the Peninsula with the words that he would be back soon. I thought how strange it was that we should have been sitting on that G.S. waggon, without knowing that we were taking a last ride with Jimmy Doon. I pictured again Jimmy being borne into the cemetery, feet first, at the head of his six dead men.

"Man that is born of a woman—" Monty was saying, and, as the words fell, the bearers raised with ropes the corpse from off its stretcher, and began to lower it into the grave.

"Earth to earth, ashes to ashes, dust to dust—" At this point the kindly French and British onlookers and the tall brown Sikh picked up their handfuls of earth, and threw them upon the body as their compliment to the dead.

The sight of Jimmy going down into his grave on the lengthening ropes started in me a real grief, and, when the strangers paid their simple respect to the unknown dead, I felt momentarily stricken, and shivered with pride that I had known him whom they thus honoured. But all this passed away, and left a dull indifference. The war was fast teaching me its petrifying lesson—to be incapable of horror. I tried to recover my sorrow, thinking that I ought to do so, but I could feel no emotion at all. "This sort of thing," ran my thoughts, "seems to be the order of the day for the generation in which we were born. It's all very fine, or all very unfair. I don't know. The old Colonel and Monty said it was very glorious, so no doubt it must be. But, whatever it is, we're all in it. Poor old Jimmy."

So I fell into a mood that was partly the resignation of perplexity, partly a sulkiness with fate. With the same blunted mind, perceiving no pain, I watched the

Greek diggers, at the end of the service, as they began to shovel the earth on to my friend's body. First they tossed it so that it fell in a little pile on his breast; then they threw it, dust and clods, over his feet, till at last only the head, hooded in its blanket, was uncovered. They turned their attention to that, and the earth fell heavily on Jimmy Doon's face. I turned unfeelingly away.

Poor Jimmy, a mere super in the Gallipoli drama, had played his trifling part on the stage, and was now sleeping in the Green Room.

Was it all very fine, or all very unfair? In my tent that evening I worried the problem out. At first it seemed only sordid that James Doon should have his gracious body returned by that foul Peninsula, like some empty crate for which it had no further use, to be buried without firing party, drums or bugles. But every now and then I caught a glimpse of my mistake. I was thinking in terms of matter instead of in terms of spiritual realities. I must try to get the poetic gift of the old Colonel and Monty, whose thoughts did not prison themselves in flesh but travelled easily in the upper air of abstract ideals like glory and beauty and truth. But it was difficult. Only in my exalted moments could I breathe in that high air.

And I could not climb to-night. Perhaps if they had but sounded the "Last Post" at Jimmy's burial, I should have lost sight of its grossness and caught the vision of its glory. I was wondering if this would have unveiled the hidden beauty, when, very strangely, the bugles in all the camps rang out with the great call. It was dark, and they were sounding the "Last Post" over the close of the day's work. But for those who preferred to think so, it was blown over the day's dead.

CHAPTER IX
PROCEEDING FORTHWITH TO GALLIPOLI

Sec.1

L ook here, Doe," said I, with my finger on a map of the Island of Lemnos. "If you've guts enough to walk with me over these five miles of hills to this eastern coast, it strikes me we shall actually see a distant vision of the Peninsula itself."

Doe looked learnedly at the map.

"With a clear sky and field-glasses we might make out the fatal old spot," said he. "Come on—we'll try."

So we turned our faces eastward through the afternoon, unaware that we were about to take a last bird's-eye view of the great Naval and Military Base of Mudros, and a first peep at the Gallipoli Peninsula, where in less than a hundred hours we should be digging ourselves a home.

We bent our backs to the task of toiling up the hillsides. We found the slopes carpeted with dry grass and yellow thistles, and sprinkled with loose stones and large lumps of rock. Long-haired sheep with bells a-tinkle, sleepy black cows, and tiny mules browsed among the arid thistles, or scratched their backs against the broken rocks.

Down into the valleys we went, and up and over the summits. It was dull prose in the valleys, but fine poetry on the summits. For, whereas in the valleys we saw nothing but thistles and stones, on the summits we enjoyed extensive views of lap-like hollows nursing little white villages; we caught distant specks, brilliantly lighted in the sun, of the encircling sea; and we wondered at the blood-coloured rocks which suggested volcanic disturbances and lava streams.

After dipping into several depressions and surmounting several yokes, we suddenly overtopped the last ridge and looked down upon a tableland, which bore, like a tray of tea-things, the white buildings of a little village. The plateau was the edge of Lemnos, and ran to the brink of a jagged cliff. Beyond lay the empty waters.

"Look," said Doe, a little dreamily; "now we shall see what we shall see."

We lay down on the cliff-edge in the attitude of the sphinx, and brought our powerful field-glasses into play. And through them we saw, in the far-off haze, things that accelerated the beating of our hearts.

There, right away across forty miles of blue Ægean, was a vague, grey line of land. It was broken in the middle as if it opened a channel to let the sea through. The grey land, west of the break, was the end of Europe, the sinister Peninsula of Gallipoli. The break itself, bathed in a gentle mist, was the deadly opening to the Dardanelles. Presumably, one of those hill-tops, just visible, was old Achi Baba, which had defeated the invaders of Helles; and another, Sari Bair, beneath which lay the invaders of Suvla, wondering if they, too, had been beaten by a paltry hill.

The entrancing sight was bound to work upon Doe's nature. Still looking through his glasses, he asked:

"I say, Roop, what's the most appealing name that the War has given to the history of Britain—Mons, or Ypres, or Coronel, or what?"

"Gallipoli," I replied, knowing this was the answer he wanted.

"Just so. And shall I tell you why?"

"Yes, thanks. If you'll be so obliging."

"Well, it's because the strongest appeal that can be addressed to the emotional qualities of humanity is made by the power called Pathos—"

"Good heavens!" I began.

"And there, my boy," pursued Doe, "in picture-form before you, this humid afternoon, is the answer to your question."

"But it was your question," I suggested.

"Don't be a fool, Rupert. Ask me what I mean."

"What the deuce do you mean?"

"I mean this: that the romantic genius of Britain is beginning to see the contour of Gallipoli invested with a mist of sadness, and presenting an appearance like a mirage of lost illusions."

I told him that he was very poetical this afternoon, whereupon he sat up and, having put his field-glasses in their case, made this irrelevant remark:

"Do you remember the central tower of Truro Cathedral, near my home?"

"Yes."

"Well, do you think it's anything like a lily? For mercy's sake say it is."

"Why?" I demanded.

"And it does change colour in the changing light, doesn't it, Rupert? Say 'Yes,' you fool—say 'Yes.'"

"Why?"

"Oh, because I've written—I've written some verses about it—when I was a bit homesick, I s'pose—and I'd like you to tell—"

"Hand them over," sighed I.

"I will, since you're so pressing. They're in the Edgar Doe stanza."

Doe gave me a soiled piece of paper, and watched me breathlessly. I read:

TRURO TOWER

> Stone lily, white against the clouds unfurled
>   To mantle skies
>   Where thunder lies,
> White as a virtue in a vicious world,
> Give to me, like the praying of a friend,
> White hope, white courage, where the war-clouds blend.

> Stone lily, coloured now in sunny chrome,
>   Or washed with rose,
>   As long days close,
> And weary English suns go west'ring home,
> Look East, and hither, where there turns to rest
> A homing heart that beats an English breast.

> Stone lily, first to catch the shaft of day,
>   And first to wake

For dawns that break
While lower things are steeped in gloaming grey,
Over my banks of twilight look and see
The breezy morn that fills my sails for thee.

"Oh, you've felt like that, have you?" said I. "So've I. Your poem exactly expresses my feeling, so it must be absolutely IT."

"Rupert, you ripping old liar!" answered Doe, aglow with pleasure.

"No, I mean it; honestly I do."

"Well, anyhow," said Doe, getting up and brushing thistles off his uniform, "don't you think that now, as 'this long day's closing,' it's time we two 'weary English *sons* go west'ring home'?"

I assured him that this was not only vulgar but also void of wit; and he sulked, while we turned our faces to the west and retraced our former path. Once again the summits of the hills, as we stepped upon them, showed us the lofty grandeur of the Ægean world. We halted to examine the wonderful sight that loomed in the sky-spaces to the north of Lemnos. This was the huge brows, fronting the clouds, of the Island of Samothrace. To me they appeared as one long precipice, from whose top frivolous people (such as Edgar Doe) could tickle the stars.

"St. Paul left Troas," ventured I, "and came with a straight course to Samothrace," a little blossom of news which angered Doe, because he had not thought of it first. So, after deliberate brain-racking, he went one better with the information:

"The great Greek god, Poseidon, sat on Samothrace, and watched the Siege of Troy. It looks like the throne of a god, doesn't it? I wonder if the old boy's sitting there now, watching the fight for the Dardanelles."

As he spoke the sun was falling behind the peaks of Lemnos and nearing the Greek mainland, which revealed itself, through the evening light, in the splendid conical point of Mount Athos. And, at our feet, the loose stones and broken rocks had assumed a pink tint on their facets that looked towards the setting sun. The browsing sheep, too, had enriched their wool with colours, borrowed from the sunset. Everywhere hung the impression that a day was done; over yonder a lonely Greek, side-saddle on his mule, was wending home.

"The sun's going west to Falmouth," said Doe, inflamed by my recent appreciation of his poem. "It'll be there in two hours. Wouldn't I like to hang on to one of its beams and go with it!"

"Don't stand there talking such gaff," I said, "but get a move on, if you want to be back in Mudros before nightfall."

We pursued the homeward journey, and suddenly surprised ourselves by emerging above a hill-top and looking down over a mile of undulating country upon the long silver sheet of water that was Mudros Harbour. To us, so high up, its vast shipping—even including the giant *Olympic*—seemed a collection of toy steamers. And all around the harbour were the white specks of toy tents.

"Our mighty campaign looks, I s'pose, even smaller and more toy-like to Poseidon, sitting on Samothrace," mused Doe. "What insects we are! 'As flies to wanton boys are we to the gods; they kill us for their sport.'"

Just at that moment "Retreat" was blown in the camps below. It was with the bugles as with the bells of a great city. One took the lead in proclaiming its message; then another, and yet another joined in, till at last all corroborated the news. And the trumpets and rifles of the French told the same story.

We hurried on, but within a few minutes darkness dropped a curtain over all that we had seen from the hills.

Sec.2

We got home in time to be late for dinner, and as we sheepishly entered the mess the O.C. Rest Camp cried:

"Oh, here you are! Where have you been? Frantic wires have been buzzing all the afternoon for you—priority messages pouring in. You're to proceed forthwith to the Peninsula. Headquarters had forgotten all about you, so they are thoroughly angry with you."

We sat down and began the soup at once, intending to have dinner, even if it involved the loss of the campaign. Monty explained across the table that he was included in this urgent summons.

"Yes, rather," endorsed the O.C., who was very full of the news, "all East Cheshire Details. Apparently the East Cheshires are holding an awkward position on a place called Fusilier Bluff, and being killed like stink by a well-placed whizz-bang gun. They've got about fifty men and half an officer left per company. They're screaming for reinforcements. Salt and pepper, please. Thanks."

"Where is this Fusilier Bluff, sir?" asked I. "At Suvla or Helles?"

"Haven't the foggiest!" answered the O.C. "The Cheshires always used to be at Helles, but I daresay they were moved to Suvla for the new landing there, along with the 29th Division. Fusilier Bluff has only just become notorious. Poor young Doon got his ticket there—same gun."

"We've a score to settle with that gun, Rupert," said Doe.

Next day we dressed for our part on the Peninsula. Doe smiled grimly as he swung round his neck the cord that dangled two identity discs on his breast. " ***Now*** there's some point in these things," he said. We filled all the chambers of our revolvers and fixed the weapons on to our belts, wondering what killing men would feel like, and how soon it would begin. "It'll be curious," Doe suggested, "going through life knowing that you killed a man while you were still nineteen. Perhaps in Valhalla we'll be introduced to the men we've killed. Jove! I'll write a poem about that."

A fatigue party of Turkish prisoners carried our kit down to the "Egyptian Pier," whence we were ferried to the Headquarters Ship ***Aragon***. Once aboard, Monty took the lead, seeking out the cabin of the Military Landing Officer and presenting to him our orders. He was an attractive little person, this M.L.O., and, having glanced over our papers, said: "East Cheshires? Oh, yes. And where are they? Are they at Suvla or Helles?"

Monty said that he hadn't the slightest idea, but imagined it was the business of Headquarters to have some notion of a division's whereabouts.

"East Cheshire Division? Let me see," muttered the M.L.O., chewing his pencil.

We let him see, with the satisfactory result that he brightened up and said:

"Ah, yes. They're at Suvla, I think."

"How nice!" commented Monty. It seemed a suitable remark.

"Well, anyhow," proceeded the M.L.O., in the relieved manner of one who has chosen which of two doubtful courses to adopt, and is happy in his choice, "there's a boat going to Suvla to-night. The ***Redbreast***, I think. I'll make you out a passage for the ***Redbreast***."

He did so, and handed the chit to Monty, who replied:

"Thanks. But supposing the Cheshires are *not* at Suvla?"

"Why, then," explained the M.L.O., smiling at having an indubitable answer ready, "they'll be at Helles."

And he beamed agreeably.

Just then there entered the cabin a middle-aged major with a monocle, none other than our old friend, Major Hardy of the *Rangoon*. He fixed us with his monocle and said: "Well, I'm damned! Young Ray! Young Doe! Young Padre!" Immediately there followed a fine scene of reunion, in which Monty explained our delay at Mudros; Major Hardy told us that he had been appointed Brigade Major to our own brigade, his predecessor having been killed on Fusilier Bluff by the whizz-bang gun; and the M.L.O. shone over all like a benignant angel.

"Ah! Another for the East Cheshires," said he. "Can I have your name, Major?"

"Hardy," came the answer.

"'Hardy'—let me see," and the M.L.O. ran his finger down a big Nominal Roll. "Harris, Harrison, Hartop, Hastings—no 'Hardy' here, Major. Are you sure it's not Hartop?"

The owner of the name declared that he was bloody sure.

"Well, I may be wrong," acknowledged the M.L.O. "Why, yes—here we are, 'Hardy.' Well, you left yesterday, and are with your unit." And he put the Nominal Roll away, as much as to say: "The matter's settled, so, as you're there already, you won't need a passage."

"I beg your pardon, damn you," corrected the Major. "I'm in your filthy office, seeking a chit to get to the East Cheshires."

"I don't see how that can be," grumbled the M.L.O., so far as such a delightful person was capable of grumbling. "But, of course, there may be a mistake somewhere."

"Well, perhaps you'll be good enough," suggested Major Hardy, "to give me a chit to proceed to the East Cheshires to look into the matter."

"Oh, certainly," agreed the M.L.O., with that prepossessing smile which came to his lips when he had discovered the solution of a problem. "There are two boats going to the Peninsula to-night, one to Suvla and the other to Helles. The *Redbreast* is the one that's going to Suvla, I fancy, and the *Ermine* to Helles. At any rate, try the *Redbreast*, Major."

"Yes," interrupted the Major, "but supposing the *Redbreast doesn't* go to Suvla—*what*?"

"Why, then," replied the M.L.O., promptly and brightly, "it'll go to Helles."

This enlightened remark produced such a torrent of oaths from Major Hardy as was only stemmed by the M.L.O.'s assurance that there was no real doubt about the *Redbreast's* going to Suvla. We left the cabin to the sound of a long "Ha-ha-ha!" from its engaging occupant, who had been tickled, you see, by the Major's outburst.

We were ferried on a steam-tug to the *Redbreast*, and climbed aboard. She seemed a funny little smack after the huge *Rangoon*. We could scarcely elbow our way along, so packed was she with drafts of men belonging to the Lovat Scouts, the Fife and Forfarshire Yeomanry, and the Essex Regiment.

I was standing among the crowd on her deck, when there was a sound of a rolling chain and a slight rocking of the boat, which provoked an indelicate man near me to take off his helmet and pretend to be sick in it. There was a rumbling of the engines as their wheels began to revolve, and a throbbing of the *Redbreast's* heart as though she found difficulty in getting under way with such a load. Then a sudden and alarming snort from her siren drew cries of "Hooter's gone!" "Down tools, lads!" "Ta-ta, Mudros!" "All aboard for Dixie!" "Hurry up, hurry up, get upon the deck, Find the nearest girl, and put your arms around her neck, For the last boat's leaving for home."

With cheering from the anchored ships that we passed; with a band playing somewhere "The Bonnie Banks of Loch Lomond"; with greeting and banter from the *Ermine*, which was steaming out with us on her voyage to Helles; and with all these things under an overcast sky that broke frequently into rain, we left Lemnos, the harbour and the hills, going out through a dulled sunset.

"Put trees on those hills," said Doe, approaching me, "and in this bad light you could imagine you were going out of the estuary of the Fal to the open sea."

"Do you wish you were?" asked I, looking at the hills we had climbed the day before.

"No. I like the excitement of this. It's the best moment in the war I've had.

This is life!"

From the sunset and sounds of the harbour we steamed into the stillness and dark of the open seas. No lights were allowed on the decks, for the enemy knew all about these nightly trips to Turkey. Singing and shouting were suppressed, and we heard nothing but the noise of the engines, the splatter of the agitated water as it struck our hull, and the sound, getting fainter and fainter, of the *Ermine* ploughing to Helles.

"The stage is in darkness," whispered Doe in his fanciful way. "It's the changing of the acts."

The rain began to fall in torrents, and the sky periodically was lit by flashes of an electric storm. And then we suddenly became conscious of new flashes playing among those of the lightning.

"The guns?" I murmured.

"Sure thing," answered Doe.

A sharp shiver of delight ran through both our bodies. Our eyes at last were watching war. To think of it! We were off the world-famous Peninsula!

And it was pitch-darkness, with flashing lights everywhere! From Navy and Army both, searchlights swept the sea and sky, shut themselves off, and opened anew. Signals in Morse sparkled with their dots and dashes. From the distant trenches star-shells rose in the air, and seemed to hang suspended for a space, while we caught the rapid tick-tick of far-away rifle fire.

"It's a blinkin' firework show," said a Tommy's voice; and Doe announced in my ear: "Rupert, I'm inspired! I've an idea for a poem. Our lives are a pantomime, and the Genius of the Peninsula is the Demon King; and here we have the flashes and thunder that always illumine the horrors of his cave.... Jumping Jupiter! What's that?"

A tremendous report had gone off near us; a brilliant light had shown up the lines of a cruiser; a shell had shrieked past us and whistled away to explode among the Turks; and a loud, and swelling murmur of amazement and admiration, rising from the *Redbreast*, had burst into a thousand laughs.

"Fate laughs at my poem," grumbled Doe.

The rain raced down: and, at about ten o'clock, we learned that, for the first time in the history of the *Redbreast*, it would be too rough for anyone to land. We must therefore spend the night aboard, and take the risk of disembarking under the enemy's guns in the morning. So, wooing sleep, we huddled into the chairs of the saloon, and wished for the day. We slept through troubled dreams, and woke to a gathering calm on the sea. As our eager eyes swept the view by daylight, we found that we were in a semicircular and unsheltered bay, whose choppy water harboured two warships that were desultorily firing. Near us a derelict trawler lay half submerged.

The truth broke upon us: we were floating at anchor in Suvla Bay.

CHAPTER X
SUVLA AND HELLES AT LAST

Sec. 1

The morning sun was up as we lay in Suvla Bay. It lit the famous battlefield, so that we saw in a shining picture the hills, up which the invading Britons had rushed to win the steps of Sari Bair. From over Asia it had risen and, doubtless, beyond the unwon ridges that blocked our view, the Straits of the Narrows were glistening like a silver ribbon in its light. We would have been dull fools if we had gazed otherwise than spellbound at this sunlit landscape, where the blood of lost battles was scarcely dry upon the ground.

What surprised us most was the invisibility of the warring armies. On the beaches, certainly, there were tents and stores and men moving. But the rolling countryside beyond seemed bleak and deserted. Only occasionally a high-explosive shell threw up a spout of brown earth, or a burst of shrapnel sent a puff of white smoke to float like a Cupid's cloud along the sky. And yet two armies were hidden here, with their rifles, machine-guns, and artillery pointed at each other.

Yes, and yonder invisible Turk had behind him a sun whose rays were pouring down upon our guilty troopship. Any moment we might expect to hear a shell, addressed to us, come whistling down the sun-shaft. We had reached at last the shell-swept zone. From now onwards there could be no certainty that we would not be alive one moment and dead the next. We shivered pleasantly.

It was not till noon that a lighter came alongside, and, having taken us all aboard, proceeded to make for the beach. All the while the Turk left us unmolested, causing us to wonder whether he were short of ammunition, or just rudely indifferent to our coming to Suvla or our staying away. Two shells or three, we thought, would have had their courteous aspect. But without greeting of any kind from the enemy our lighter rose on the last wave and bumped against the jetty. We gathered our equipment, and with egotistical thrills stepped upon the Gallipoli Peninsula. For the first time we stood in Turkey. We felt in our breasts the pride of the invader.

Monty, as spokesman of our party, led us into the office of the M.L.O., and assured the gentleman that we had come to Suvla to find the East Cheshires.

"The Cheshires aren't at Suvla," said the M.L.O., with the acerbity of an overworked staff-officer. "They never were, and never will be at Suvla."

"Oh," answered Monty brightly, seeing a vision of his friend, the M.L.O. of the *Aragon*, "then they'll be at Helles."

The Suvla M.L.O. blasted Monty with a look, and said: "That's the remark of a fool."

"Exactly," agreed Monty; "it was the remark of an M.L.O."

And he explained how, all along, he had conjectured that the pleasant creature on the *Aragon* had blundered in sending us to Suvla.

"Well, why the devil did you come?" inquired the M.L.O.

"Because," answered Monty, imperturbably, "I wanted to see the world, and Suvla in particular; and I might not have had another opportunity of visiting your delightful bay."

"You mean to say," said the M.L.O., with his eyes on the badges of the Army Chaplains' Department, "that you deliberately traded on a mistake in order to get a holiday trip to Suvla? And still—ha—still you expect us to go to church."

If he was anxious to discuss the question why men didn't go to church, nobody was more ready to meet him than Monty, who therewith sat down upon a box, so as comfortably to do justice to a really interesting topic, I admit I felt a sudden horror lest he should hold forth on the Mass and Confession. I went quite cold with apprehension. It's dreadful the embarrassment you elders cause us young people lest you say something completely out of place and impossible. In very fact, youth is the age of embarrassing adults.

What Monty would have said remains a mystery, for at this moment Major Hardy, who had come in our wake, exploded into the discussion.

"Be damned to you, sir!" he said to the M.L.O., wiping his eyeglass furiously. "Be damned to you—***what***! I see nothing funny in being sent to the wrong front by a simpering, defective idiot on the ***Aragon***. Kindly give me a chit to proceed to Helles to-morrow by some bloody trawler, or something."

"With the utmost pleasure," said the M.L.O.; "Suvla can well be rid of you. You can go to Helles, or Hell, by the 6 A.M. boat to-morrow."

Bless these M.L.O.'s! Were we not indebted to them? The mistake of one conceded us a visit to Suvla Bay, and the discourteous dismissal of another ensured that we should bear down upon Cape Helles, not, as normally, in a dead darkness, but in the bright light of an October morning. I began to understand Monty's unscrupulous opportunism. It would be a wonderful trip, skirting by daylight the coastline of the Peninsula, till we rounded the point and looked upon the Helles Beaches, the sacred site of the first and most marvellous battle of the Dardanelles campaign. It was a pilgrimage to a shrine that stretched before us on the morrow. The pilgrim's route was a path in the blue AEgean from Suvla Bay to Helles Point; and the shrine was the immortal battleground. Enough; let us make the most of Suvla this day, for to-morrow we should see Helles.

Leaving the office, we sought out some shelter for the night. We found a line of deserted dug-outs—little cells cut in the sloping hillside, and scantily roofed by waterproof sheets. It was now late in the afternoon, and no sooner had we thrown down our kit into these grave-like chambers than the Turk wiped his mouth after his tea and opened his Evening Hate. There was the distant boom of a shell. Before we could realise what the sound was, and say "Hallo! they've begun," the missile had exploded among the stores on the beach. That was my baptism of fire. Without the least hesitation I copied Major Hardy and Monty, and went flat on my face behind some brushwood. Only Doe, too proud to take cover, remained standing, and then blushed self-consciously lest he had appeared to be posing.

"Does this go on for long?" asked Monty of a man who, being near us, had hurled himself prone across my back.

"Don't know, sir," answered he, cheerily, as he picked himself up. "Yesterday they sent down seventy shells, and killed six men and four mules.... Oh! there it is again."

And our informant took up a position on his stomach, while a second shell shrieked into the stores.

"They've the range all right," said Monty, as we all got up again.

"Yes, sir. But they can't have many shells left after yesterday's effort. They're so starvation short that we reckon last night they had a surprise camel-load arrive. But ain't it plain, sir, that if the Germans could get through to the Turk with ammunition, they could send down ten thousand shells in a day and blow us into the sea? That's why the 'Uns are thundering along through Servia to Turkey now, sir. They're coming all right.... Oh! there it is again."

Once more the soldier stretched his length on the ground, and a third shell tore towards us.

"As I was saying, sir," continued our new friend, now on his hind legs again, and brushing dust from his clothes. "This Suvla army, unless it can get to the top of Sari Bair, is faced with destruction, and they tell me the Helles army is just the same, unless it can get to the top of Achi Baba. It never will now, sir. And how can we quit without being seen from those hills? The 'Uns know they've got us trapped. That's why they're coming through Servia, ammunition and all. They'll be on us soon."

"But we'll win," suggested Monty, tentatively.

"O Lord, yes, sir. But not here. Things are going to be interesting here.... God knows how it'll all end.... Oh! there it is again."

The gun boomed, and the speaker kissed the dust.

I had just decided that it was best to remain recumbent, and Doe, too, had sat down rather sheepishly, when the Turk either ran out of ammunition or felt that he had done all that formality required of him, and returned to his hookah in peace.

Knowing that night would fall quickly, we hastened to make ourselves some supper. Its last mouthfuls we finished in darkness; and, having nothing further to do, determined to go to bed in our little dug-outs on the hillside. Standing in the blue darkness outside these narrow dwelling-places, like lepers among our tombs, we wished each other good-night and a good sleep. Then we crawled into our graves. Wrapping my knees in my British warm, I disposed myself to rest.

But I could not sleep. My mind was too active with thinking that I was lying in the historic ground, over which the battle had rolled. As a light in a room keeps a would-be sleeper awake, so the bright glow of my thoughts kept my brain from rest. Here was I on that amazing Peninsula, towards which I had looked in wonder from the cliffs of Mudros. Around me, and in the earth as I was, the dead men, more successful than I, were sleeping dreamlessly. On higher slopes the tired army held the fire-trenches, with its faces and rifles still turned bravely landward and upward. Above them the Turks hung to the extremities of their territory with the same tenacity that we should show in defending Kent or Cornwall. Behind the Turk ran the silver Narrows, the splendid trophy of the present tourney. And, as I had been reminded that afternoon, far away the German armies were battling through the corridors of Servia that they might come and destroy the invaders of Suvla and Helles.

To increase my wakefulness the rapid fire of rifle and machine-gun, which had been almost unheard during the day-time, began with the fall of darkness, and continued sporadic through the night. Like the chirp of a great cricket, it was doubly insistent in the silent hours. The artillery, too, was more restless than it had been in the light of day. Seemingly all were nervous of the dark.

It is ever difficult to sleep in a strange bed. I found myself opening my eyes and looking up at my oil-sheet roof. So scanty was it that it left apertures, through which I could see the stars shining in a perfect sky. I shut my eyes and gave rein to my thoughts, gradually elaborating the wild dream of a thinker who was unaware that he had at last dropped off to sleep. It seemed to me that the whole army at Suvla was that night storming the hills that intervened between us and the silver Narrows. I was rushing with the attackers, while the shells roared and pitched harmlessly among us, and at length I was standing on the summit of Sari Bair, which showed the Narrows under the moon and stars. The Narrows seen at last! There, look, was the waterway to Constantinople. I waited patiently to see the Navy pour up it in triumphant procession. Beside me was the stranger who had spoken to us in the afternoon, and I said to him: "The coast seems clear. Let's go down and swim the Hellespont, where Leander and Byron swam." But at that moment there was a loud explosion near us, and a sound as of particles of earth falling upon an oil-sheet roof.

Conscious that this tremendous report was not the creation of a troubled dreamer, but something real, which had worked itself into the texture of my dreams, I lifted heavy eyelids, and learned that a stray night-shell from the Turkish lines had burst very close to my dug-out, and the debris was tumbling on the roof.... And we were still low down on the slope to victory.

After that, sleep passed from me, and I watched the dawn break.

Sec.2

At six o'clock the next morning we were all on the little trawler, due to leave for Cape Helles. Helles! The stirring, pregnant name was a thing to toy with. Suvla was a great word, but Helles was a greater. So farewell to Suvla now. We must also see Helles.

"To Helles," said the hardened skipper, with the same dull unconcern that a cabman might show in saying "To Hyde Park."

The workmanlike boat got under way. As I gazed from its side towards the Suvla that we were leaving, the whole line of the Peninsula came into panorama before me. The sun, just awake, bathed a long, waving skyline that rose at two points to dominant levels. One was Sari Bair, the stately hill which stood inviolate, although an army had dashed itself against its fastnesses. The other, lower down the skyline, was Achi Baba, as impregnable as her sister, Sari Bair. The story of the campaign was the story of these two hills.

For perfect charm, I recall no trip to equal this cruise betimes in the sparking AEgean. Our trawler was travelling with the smoothness of a gondola on a Venetian canal. And the voyage, sunny and refreshing in itself, was given an added glamour, by reason of the shrine to which it was a pilgrimage. For, whether I could believe it or not, we were steaming fast to Helles.

My sensations, as we gaily bore through the sea upon the hallowed site, were those of one who awaits the rise of a curtain upon a famous drama. I sprang my imagination to the alert position, that I might not miss one thrill, when we should enter the bay whose waters played on W Beach. Conceive it: there would meet my gaze a stretch of lapping water, a width of beach, and a bluff hill; and I must say: "Here were confused battle, and blood filtering through the ground. There was agony here, and quivering flesh. Here the promises of straight limbs, keen eyes, and clear cheeks were cancelled in a spring morning. Our schoolfellows died here, Stanley, and Lancelot, and Moles White. Hither a thousand destinies converged upon the beach, and here they closed."

The boat was approaching a rounded headland. In a second the vision would be before me. Come now, could I think all these things—could I realise them, as we entered the bay? I found not. Before I had gripped half the thrilling ideas that were the gift of the moment, we were moored against the jetty at W Beach, and I was stepping ashore to take my part in the last chapters of the Gallipoli story.

CHAPTER XI
AN ATMOSPHERE OF SHOCKS
AND SUDDEN DEATH

Sec.1

One evening, three days later, I was sitting, inconceivably bored, in my new dug-out on the notorious Fusilier Bluff. This dug-out was a recess, hewn in damp, crumbling soil, with a frontage built of sand-bags. Its size was that of an anchorite's cell, and any abnormal movement or extra loud noise within it brought the stones and earth in showers down the walls. Indeed, the walls of my new home so far resembled the walls of Jericho that it only required a shout to bring them down upon the floor. In the sand-bag front were two apertures, called the door and the window, which overlooked the Ægean Sea. For this reason the name "Seaview" had been painted above the door in lively moments by the preceding tenant, whose grave was visible lower down the Bluff. I watched the night gathering on the sea, while over my home the whizz-bang gun—that evil genius of the place, and the murderer of Jimmy Doon—spat its high-velocity shells.

I was alone. The C.O. of the East Cheshires, who did not seem to have grasped that Doe and I were friends, had attached me to D Company, which was in reserve on the slopes of Fusilier Bluff, and Doe to B Company, which was holding the fire-trenches. The man was a fool, of course, but what could a subaltern say to a colonel? And Monty, too, had gone to live by himself. Finding that his new parish was extensive and scattered, he had abandoned Fusilier Bluff, and, choosing the most central spot, had built himself a sand-bag hovel somewhere in the Eski Line. Struth!

Everything was the limit.

I went to bed. And it was after I was deeply submerged in dreams that I awoke with a start, for someone seemed to be telling me to get up and dress, as there was an alarm afloat. A voice was saying: "All the troops have been ordered to stand to, sir. There's an attack expected. The Adjutant sent me to call you."

"Who are you?"

"Adjutant's orderly, 10th East Cheshires, sir."

"Thanks." Hurriedly dressing, I went out and found that the Bluff, now white in the moonlight, was lined with men in full equipment. Orders were being shouted, and telephones were buzzing.

"D Company, fall in."

"See that there are two men to every machine-gun at once."

D Company, with myself attached to it, left the Bluff and filed through a communication trench to the firing line. Here every man was a silent sentry, his bayonet shining in the moonlight. Doe, whose eyes were bright with excitement, was walking hastily up and down the company front, looking over the parapet, giving orders in a fine whisper, and pretending in a variety of ways that he was uncommonly efficient at this sort of surprise attack. I touched his sleeve and asked:

"What's it all about?"

"Heaven knows! A sergeant spotted some trees waving in front of the moon, thought they were Turks, and gave the alarm. He saw trees as men walking. Sorry. Can't stay."

I wandered along the trench, seeing the men of my platoon properly disposed so as to stiffen the resistance of B Company. Then I returned for the latest news of the crisis to where Doe was conversing with an unknown officer. They were recalling how they had once travelled in the train together from Paddington to Falmouth, and never seen each other again till this moment. Doe was praising the lovely country through which the Great Western Railway passed—Somerset, and the White Horse Vale, and the beautiful stretch of water at Dawlish; or the red cliffs of Devon, where the train ran along the coast. Some of the red earth of Gallipoli, he said, reminded him of Devon's red loam.

Evidently the Turkish attack was not going to materialise. I stood upon the firing-step and looked over the parapet. In the moonlight I could see the black sand-bags of the Turks' front line, and the desolate waste of No Man's Land.... Then my hand sprang to the butt of my revolver. Something **had** moved in No Man's Land. "Look out!" I said. "They're coming!" just as from behind a bit of rising ground a figure rose on to its hands and knees. I pointed my revolver at it, and pulled the trigger. The figure collapsed, and rolled forwards till its progress was arrested by a rocky projection, over which it finally lay, doubled up like a bolster. As it fell my heart gave a sickening leap, either of excitement or of fright.

At once the whole of the company front opened rapid fire. A few things seemed to fall about in No Man's Land, and I saw some figures pass across the moon as they scurried back to their trenches.

"Cease fire!" ordered the O.C. firing line. "Merely a reconnaissance raid. Silly trouts, these Turks."

And Doe came up to me, saying almost enviously:

"You've killed your man, Rupert. Congratulations."

Without answering I stood on the firing-step again, and looked at the limp form of my victim. It was dead beyond question, shapeless and horrible.

I took my platoon back to the Bluff, dismissed it, and going up to my dug-out door, stood there for a moment thinking. Since leaving it an hour ago I had killed a man.

"You mustn't rest till you've slaughtered a Turk," our new C.O. had said, for he was an apostle of the offensive spirit. "Then, if they kill you, you'll at least have taken a life for a life. And any more that you kill before they finish you off will be clear gain for King George."

Not wishing to go to bed yet, I went back to the firing line, and looked over our sand-bags once more. The body was still there, shapeless and horrible, and as limp as a half-empty sack of coals.

Sec.2

Some of the officers of B and D Companies were drinking together the following day in a hole on the Bluff, when the Brigade Bombing Officer burst in among us, and seized a mug.

"Thanks. I will," he said. "Just a spot of whisky. Well, here's to you.

Cheerioh!"

He drank half the mug, and addressed me.

"Ray, you have found favour in the sight of the General. He wants you for his A.D.C., and won't be happy till he gets you. He thinks you a pretty and a proper child and fairly clean. ***What abaht it?***"

"Good Lord," said I. "I don't know what an A.D.C. is! What do I do?"

"Oh, see that the old gentleman is fed. And cut out the saucy girls from 'La Vie Parisienne,' and decorate the mess walls with them. And—and all that sort of thing."

"Go on, Ray," urged Doe. "Of course you'll be it. Put him down for the job. I wish the old general had fallen in love with *me*.'

"I don't mind trying it," I said. "Anything for a change."

"Right," replied the Bombing Officer. "Ray, having been four days with a company of the East Cheshires, feels in need of a change. He desires to better himself. Now for the next point. I'm chucking this Bombing Officer stunt. It's too dangerous. Both my predecessors were killed, and yesterday the Turk threw a bomb at *me*. Now, is there anybody tired of his life and laden with his sin? Anyone want to commit suicide? Anyone feel a call? Anyone want to do the bloody hero, and be Brigade Bombing Officer?"

Doe blushed at once.

"I'll have a shot at it.... Anything for a change," he added apologetically.

"That's the spirit that made England great!" said the Bombing Officer. "I do like keenness. Splendid! Ray goes to the softest job in the Army, and Doe, stout fellow, to the damnedst. Thanks: just another little spot. Cheerioh!"

In name my new character was that of Brigade Ammunition Officer, but it amounted, as the Bombing Officer had said, to being A.D.C. to the Brigadier. I was entirely miserable in it. Painfully shy of the old general and his staff-officers, I never spoke at meals in the solemn Headquarters Mess unless I had carefully rehearsed before what I was going to say. And, when I said it, I saw how foolish it sounded.

And Major Hardy—who, you will remember, was our Brigade Major—used to be unnecessarily funny about my youth, fixing me with his monocle over the evening dinner-table and asking me if I were allowed to sit up to dinner at home. I imagine he thought he was humorous.

Grand old Major Hardy! I must not speak lightly of him here. It is only because I have now to finish his story that I have mentioned my regrettable declension on to the staff.

Major Hardy had not been ten days on the Peninsula before he made his reputation. His monocle, his "what," and his rich maledictions were admired and imitated all along the Brigade front. From Fusilier Bluff to Stanley Street it was agreed that Major Foolhardy was a Sahib. Twice a day every bay in the trench system was cursed by him. "God! give me ten Turks and a dog, and I'd capture the whole of this sector any hour of the day or night," and his head was over the parapet in broad daylight, examining the Turkish peepholes. It was a common saying that he would be hit one fine morning.

The morning came. The Signal Officer and I were sitting in the Headquarters Mess, sipping an eleven o'clock cherry brandy, and wondering why the General and the Brigade Major had not returned from their tour of the trenches. Headquarters were situated in Gully Ravine, that prince among ravines on the Peninsula. From my place I could see the gully floor, which was the dry bed of a water-course, winding away between high walls of perpendicular cliffs or steep, scrub-covered slopes, as it pursued its journey, like some colossal trench, towards the firing line. Down the great cleft, while I looked, a horseman came riding rapidly. He was an officer, with a slight open wound in his chin, and he rode up to our door and said: "Hardy's hit. A hole in the face."

He was followed by the General, whose clothes and hands were splashed with Major Hardy's blood. The General told us what had happened. He had been talking to Hardy and some others on Fusilier Bluff, when the infamous whizz-bang gun—that messenger of Satan sent to buffet us—shot a shell whose splinters took the Major in the face and lungs. He dropped, saying "Dammit, I'm hit, *what*," and was now being taken in a dying condition down Gully Ravine to the Field Ambulance.

It surprised me what an everyday affair this tragedy seemed. There were expressions of sorrow, but no hush of calamity. Jests were made at lunch, and all ate as heartily as usual. "Well, he lasted ten days," said the Brigadier, "which is more than a good many have done."

Personally, I found myself repeating, in my wool-gathering way, the word "Two." Already two out of the five who sat down to lunch together that first day on board the *Rangoon* had been killed—and, for that matter, by the same gun. "Two." "The knitting women counted *two* ." Ah! that was what I was thinking of. The knitting women had knitted two off the strength of that little company. Monty, Doe, and myself were left. I wondered which of those would have fallen when the knitting women should count "Three."

It was not difficult to prophesy. Monty, though he was as venturesome as any combatant, could never quite share the dangers of the men who lived in the trenches. His dug-out, back in the Eski Line, was safe from everything but a howitzer shell. And I—ye gods! I was comparatively secure, loafing about in the softest job in the Army. Everything pointed to Doe as Number Three.

I thought of our unbroken partnership, and decided—as much in rash defiance as in loyalty to my friend—that I would ask to be relieved of my position as Ammunition Officer and allowed to return to my battalion. The permission was granted. And oh! I cannot explain it, but it was good to be back with my company after the enervating experience of staff-life. And, better still, now that Doe was no longer a platoon commander but Brigade Bombing Officer, he could live where he liked, and had arranged to share my dug-out—that delectable villa on Fusilier Bluff known as "Seaview." Really, under these conditions, the Peninsula, we felt, would be quite "swish."

CHAPTER XII
SACRED TO WHITE

Sec.1

On a certain morning Doe and I in our dug-out on Fusilier Bluff felt the pull and the fascination, coming over five miles of scrub, of the magical Cape Helles. It was but a score of weeks since the first invaders had stormed its beaches: and we wanted to drink again of the romance that charged the air. So, being free for a time, we walked to the brow overlooking V Beach, and stood there, letting the breeze blow on our faces, and thinking of the British Army that blew in one day like a gale from the sea.

The damage wrought by that tornado was everywhere visible. Near us were the ruins of a lighthouse. In old days it had glimmered for distant mariners, who pointed to it as the Dardanelles light. But, at the outbreak of war, the Turk had closed his Dardanelles and put out the lamp. He would never kindle it again, for the **Queen Elizabeth**, or a warship of her kidney, had lain off shore and reduced the lighthouse to these white stones. Across the amphitheatre of the bay were the village and broken forts of Seddel Bahr; and, aground at this point, the famous old hulk, the **River Clyde**. You remember—who could forget?—how they turned this vessel into a modern Horse of Troy, cramming its belly with armed men, running it ashore, and then opening square doors in its hull-sides and letting loose the invaders—while the plains of Old Troy looked down from over the Hellespont. What a litter old Mother Clyde carried in her womb that day! From where we stood we could see those square doors, cut in her sides, through which the troops and rushed into the bullet-hail: we could see, too, the semicircular beach, where they had attempted to land, and the ribbon of blue water in which so many, weighted with their equipment, had sunk and died.

And what was that thing a few cable lengths out, a rusty iron something, rising from the water, and being lapped by the incoming ripples? It was the keel of the old *Majestic*, which lay there, deck downwards, on the ocean bed.

"It's too pathetic!" exclaimed the sensitive Doe. "Let's go and visit the *Clyde*. Fancy, old Moles White was in that boat."

We dropped down from the headland into V Beach Bay, and, in doing so, passed the limit of the British zone and trespassed upon French territory. The slope, from the beach upward, was as alive with French and Senegalese as a cloven ant-hill is alive with ants. The stores of the whole French army seemed accumulated in the neighbourhood. There was an atmosphere of French excitability, very different from the stillness of the British Zone. Stepping from the British Zone into the French was like turning suddenly from the quiet of Rotten Row into the bustle of the Boulevard des Italiens. It was *prenez-garde* and *attention la! depeches-vous* and *pardon, m'sieu*, and *sacre nom de dieu!* before we got through all these hearty busy-bodies and drew near the hull of the *Clyde*.

With unwitting reverence we approached. I'll swear I was within an ace of removing my hat, and that, had I talked to Doe, I should have spoken in a whisper. It was like visiting a church. Look, there by the square doors were the endless marks of machine-gun bullets that had swept the men who tried to leave the boat for the shore. God! they hadn't a dog's chance. If those bullet indentations meant anything, they meant that the man who left the square door was lucky if he got ashore with less than a dozen bullets in his flesh.

We stepped on to the gangway that led to the nearest of the doors and hurried up to it, catching something of the "Get back—get back!" sensation of those who had been forced by the bullets to withdraw into the hold. A huge hold it showed itself to be when we bowed our heads and stepped into it through the square door. Yes, they could cram battalions here. What a hive the *Clyde* was when they hurled it ashore! And what a swarm of bees it housed! In this hold, now so silent and empty, what emotions throbbed that day!

"Poor old White!" murmured Doe. "He got ashore well enough, and wasn't killed till the fighting on the high ground. By Jove, Rupert! we'll search the Peninsula from here to Fusilier Bluff for his grave. Come on."

We left the comparative darkness of the hold, and stepped through the square door, that had been so deadly an exit for hundreds, into the bright daylight. At once there was given us a full view of V Beach, with the sea sparkling as it broke upon the shingle. The air all about was strangely opalescent. Seddel Bahr shone in the sun, as only a white Eastern village can. The hills rising from the beach looked steep and difficult, but sunlit and shimmering. Everything shimmered as a result of the sudden contrast from the darkness of the hold. Even so must the scene have flashed upon the eyes of the invaders as they issued from the sides of the *Clyde*. For many of them, how quickly the bright light went out!

We had hardly entered the ruined streets of Seddel Bahr before a shell screamed into the village and burst with a deafening explosion in a house, whose walls went up in a volcano of dust and stones.

"Asiatic Annie!" we both said, at once and in unison.

For all of us knew the evil reputation of Asiatic Annie—that large gun, safely tucked away in the blue hills of Asia, who lobbed her shells—a seven-mile throw—over the Straits on to the shores of Cape Helles—a mischievous old lady, who delighted in being the plague of the Beaches.

"If Asiatic Annie is going to begin," said Doe, "we'll have important business elsewhere. Hurry on. We're going to find White's grave."

To get from Seddel Bahr to Fusilier Bluff it was necessary to cross diagonally the whole of the Helles sector. There lay before us a long walk over a dusty, scrub-covered plateau, every yard of which was a yard of battlefield and overspread with the litter of battles. This red earth, which, when the Army first arrived, was garnished with grass and flowers, groves, and vineyards, was now beaten by thousands of feet into a hard, dry drill-ground, where, here and there, blasted trees stood like calvaries against the sky. The grass resembled patches of fur on a mangy skin. The birds, which seemed to revel in the excitements of war, soared and swept over the devastated tableland. Northward from our feet stretched this plateau of scarecrow trees, till it began to incline in a gentle rise, and finally met the sky in the summit of Achi Baba. That was the whole landscape—a plateau overlooked by a gentle hill.

And here on this sea-girt headland the land-fight had been fought. No wonder the region was covered with the scars and waste of war. Our journey took us past old trenches and gun-positions; disused telephone lines and rusting, barbed wire; dead mules, scattered cemeteries, and solitary graves.

And not a grave did we pass without examining it to see if it bore the name of White. Our progress, therefore, was very slow, for, like highwaymen, these graves held us up and bade us stand and inquire if they housed our friend. Whenever we saw an isolated cross some distance away, we left our tracks to approach it, anxious not to pass, lest this were he. And then, quite unexpectedly, we came upon twenty graves side by side under one over-arching tree, which bore the legend: "Pink Farm Cemetery." And Doe said:

"There it is, Rupert."

He said it with deliberate carelessness, as if to show that he was one not easily excited by sudden surprises.

"Where—where?" I asked.

"There—'Lieutenant R. White, Royal Dublin Fusiliers.'"

"Good Lord!" I muttered: for it was true. We had walked right on to the grave of our friend. His name stood on a cross with those of six other officers, and beneath was written in pencil the famous epitaph:

> "Tell England, ye who pass this monument,
> We died for her, and here we rest content."

The perfect words went straight to Doe's heart.

"Roop," he said, "if I'm killed you can put those lines over me."

I fear I could not think of anything very helpful to reply.

"They are rather swish," I murmured.

CHAPTER XIII
"LIVE DEEP, AND LET THE LESSER THINGS LIVE LONG"

Sec.1

One thing I shall always believe, and it is that Doe found on the Peninsula that intense life, that life of multiplied sensations, which he always craved in the days when he said: "I want to have lived."

You would understand what I mean if you could have seen this Brigade Bombing Officer of ours hurling his bombs at a gentleman whom he called "the jolly old Turk." Generally he threw them with a jest on his lips. "One hundred and *two*. One hundred and *three*," he would say. "Over she goes, and thank the Lord I'm not in the opposite trench. BANG! I told you so. Stretcher-bearers for the Turks, please." Or he would hurl the bomb high into the air, so that it burst above the enemy like a rocket or a star-shell. He would blow a long whistle, as it shot skyward, and say "PLONK!" as it exploded into a shower of splinters.

For Doe was young and effervescing with life. He enjoyed himself, and his bombers enjoyed him as their officer. Everybody, in fact, enjoyed Edgar Doe.

In these latter days the gifted youth had suddenly discovered that all things French were perfect. Gone were the days of classical elegancies. Doe read only French novels which he borrowed from Pierre Poilu at Seddel Bahr.

And why? Because they knew how to live, *ces francais*. They lived deeply, and felt deeply, with their lovely emotionalism. They ate and drank learnedly. They suffered, sympathised, and loved, always deeply. They were *bons viveurs*, in the intensest meaning of the words. "They live, they live." And because of this, his spiritual home was in France. "You English," said he, "*vous autres anglais*, with your damned un-emotionalism, empty your lives of spiritual experience: for emotion is life, and all that's interesting in life is spiritual incident. But the French, they live!"

He even wrote a poem about the faith which he had found, and started to declaim it to me one night in our little dug-out, "Seaview":

> "For all emotions that are tense and strong,
> And utmost knowledge, I have lived for these—
> Lived deep, and let the lesser things live long,
> The everlasting hills, the lakes, the trees,
> Who'd give their thousand years to sing this song
> Of Life, and Man's high sensibilities—

"Yes, Roop, living through war is living deep. It's crowded, glorious living. If I'd never had a shell rush at me I'd never have known the swift thrill of approaching death—which is a wonderful sensation not to be missed. If I'd never known the shock of seeing sudden death at my side, I'd have missed a terribly wonderful thing. They say music's the most evocative art in the world, but, *sacre nom de dieu*, they hadn't counted the orchestra of a bombardment. That's music at ten thousand pounds a minute. And if I'd not heard that, I'd never have known what it is to have my soul drawn out of me by the maddening excitement of an intensive bombardment. And—and, *que voulez-vous*, I have *killed*!"

"Hm!" muttered I. He was too clever for me, but I loved him in his scintillating moments.

"*Tiens*, if I'm knocked out, it's at least the most wonderful death. It's the *deepest* death."

I laughed deprecatingly.

"Oh, I'm resigned to the idea," he pursued. "It's more probable than improbable. Sooner or later. *Tant va la cruche a l'eau qu' a la fin elle se casse.*"

"*Tant*—'aunt,'" thought I. "*Va*—'goes.' *La cruche*—'the crust.' *Qu' a la fin elle se casse.*" And I said aloud: "I've got it! 'Aunt goes for the crust at the water, into which, in fine, she casts herself.'"

"No," corrected Doe, looking away from me wistfully and self-consciously. "'The pitcher goes so often to the well that at last it is broken.'"

Sec.2

About this time the great blizzard broke over Gallipoli. On the last Sunday in November I awoke, feeling like iced chicken, to learn that the blizzard had begun. It was still dark, and the snow was being driven along by the wind, so that it flew nearly parallel with the ground, and clothed with mantles of white all the scrub that opposed its onrush. This morning only did the wild Peninsula look beautiful. But its whiteness was that of a whited sepulchre. Never before had it been so mercilessly cruel. For now was opening the notorious blizzard that should strike down hundreds with frost-bite, and drown in their trenches Turks and Britons alike.

It was freezing—freezing. The water in our canvas buckets froze into solid cakes of ice, which we hewed out with pickaxes and kicked about like footballs. And all the guns stopped speaking. No more was heard the whip-crack of a rifle, nor the rapid, crisp, unintelligent report of a machine-gun. Fingers of friend and foe were too numbed to fire. An Arctic silence settled upon Gallipoli.

And yet I remember the first day of the blizzard as a day of glowing things. For on the previous night I had read in Battalion Orders that I was to be Captain Ray. And so, this piercing morning, I could go out into the blizzard with three stars on my shoulders. With Gallipoli suddenness I had leapt into this exalted rank, while Doe, a more brilliant officer, remained only a Second Lieutenant. For him, as a specialist, there was no promotion. For me, no sooner had my O.C. Company been buried alive by the explosion of a Turkish mine, and his second-in-command gone sick with dysentery, than I, the next senior though only nineteen, was given the rank of Acting Captain. And Doe, always most generous when most jealous, had been profuse in his congratulations.

I confess that not even the hail, with its icy bite, could spoil the glow which I felt in being Captain Ray. I walked along my company front, behind parapets massed with snow, to have a look at the men of my command. All these lads with the chattering lips—lads from twenty to forty years old—were mine to do what I liked with. They were my family—my children. And I would be a father to them.

And when, at the end of my inspection, a shivering post corporal put into my hands a letter addressed by my mother to 2nd-Lieut. R. Ray, I delighted to think how out-of-date she was, and how I must enlighten her at once on the correct method of addressing her son. I would do it that day, so that she might have opportunities of writing "Capt. Ray." For one never knew: some unpleasantly senior person might come along and take to himself my honourable rank.

I seized the letter and hurried home to our dug-out. Doe was already in possession of his mail, so, having wrapped ourselves in blankets to defeat the polar atmosphere, we crouched over a smoking oil-stove and read our letters.

I was the first to break a long silence.

"Really," I said, "Mother's rather sweet. Listen to this:—

> "'Rupert, I had such a shock yesterday. I heard the postman's
> knock, which always frightens me. I picked up a long, blue
> envelope, stamped "War Office." Oh, my heart stood still. I
> went into my bedroom, and tried to compose myself to break the
> envelope. Then I asked my new maid to come and be with me when
> I opened it. After she had arrived, I said a prayer that all
> might be well with you. Then I opened it: and, Rupert, it was
> only your Commission as 2nd Lieutenant arriving a year late.
> Oh, I went straight to church and gave thanks!'"

Doe gazed into the light of the oil-stove.

"The dear, good, beautiful woman!" he said.

And so it is that the famous blizzard carries with it two glowing memories: the one, my promotion to Captain's rank; the other, the sudden arrival of my mother's letter like a sea-gull out of a storm. Her loving words threw about me, during the appalling conditions of the afternoon, an atmosphere of England. And, when in the biting night our elevated home was quiet under the stars, and Doe and I were rolled up in our blankets, I was quite pleased to find him disposed to be sentimental.

"I've cold feet to-night," he grumbled. "Roll on Peace, and a passage home. Let's cheer ourselves up by thinking of the first dinner we'll have when we get back to England. *Allons*, I'll begin with turtle soup."

"And a glass of sherry," added I from my pillow.

"Then, I think, turbot and white sauce."

"Good enough," I agreed, "and we'll trifle with the wing of a fowl."

"Two cream buns for sweets," continued the Brigade Bombing Officer, "or possibly three. And fruit salad. *Ah, mon dieu, que c'est beau!*"

"And a piece of Stilton on a sweet biscuit," suggested the Captain of D Company, "with a glass of port."

"Yes," conceded the Bombing Officer, "and then cafe noir, and an Abdulla No. 5 in the arm-chair. *Sapristi*! isn't it cold?" He turned round sulkily in his bed. "If it's like this to-morrow I shan't get up—no, not if Gladys Cooper comes to wake me."

So he dropped off to sleep.... And, with Doe asleep, I can say that to which I have been leading up. Always before the war I used to think forced and exaggerated those pictures which showed the soldier in his uniform, sleeping on the field near the piled arms, and suggested, by a vision painted on the canvas, that his dreams were of his hearth and loved ones. But I know now of a certain Captain-fellow, who, on that first night of the blizzard, after he had received a letter from his mother, dreamt long and fully of friends in England, awaking at times to find himself lying on a lofty wild Bluff, and falling off to sleep again to continue dreams of home.

CHAPTER XIV
THE NINETEENTH OF DECEMBER

Sec. 1

The grand incident in the last act of the Gallipoli Campaign—the grand *motif*—was the Germans' successful break through Servia. They had driven their corridor from Central Europe through Servia to Constantinople; and, for all we knew, the might of Germany in men and guns were pouring down it. Of course they were coming; they must come. Never had the generals of Germany so fine an opportunity of destroying the British Divisions that languished at Suvla and Helles. What chance had the Haughty Islanders now of escaping? The wintry storms were already cutting their frail line of communications by sea, and smashing up their miserable jetties on the beaches. The plot should unravel simply. The German-Turk combine would attack in force, and the British, unable to escape, would either surrender or, in good Roman style, die fighting.

We knew the Germans were coming. When the blizzard rolled away and left behind a glorious December, we began to hear their new guns throbbing on the distant Suvla front. Doubtless more guns were rumbling along the streets of Constantinople, and troops concentrating in its squares. They were out for the biggest victory of the Central Empires since Tannenberg. Six divisions from Suvla and four from Helles would be a good day's bag. Perhaps the Turks were not without pity for the tough little British Divisions that, depleted, exhausted, and unreinforced, lay at their mercy on the extremities of the Gallipoli Peninsula.

We knew they were coming, and joked about it.

"It's getting distinctly interesting, Captain Ray," said Doe, as we sat drinking tea in Monty's dug-out in the Eski Line. "I say, give me a decent funeral, won't you?"

"We shan't bury you," answered Monty unpleasantly. "We shall put you on the incinerator."

"If the worst comes to the worst, I shall swim for it," said I, always conceited on this point. "It'll only be a few miles easy going, in this gorgeous December weather, from Gully Beach to Imbros."

"But, *au serieux*," continued the picturesque Doe, "do you realise that this is December, 1915, and we shall probably never see the year of grace 1916? Damned funny, Captain Ray, isn't it?"

"Don't be so romantic and treacly," retorted Monty. "You'll do nothing heroic. You'll just march down to W Beach and get on a boat and sail away. There's going to be some sort of evacuation, I'm sure. They've cleared the hospitals at Alexandria and Malta, and ordered every hospital ship in the world to lie off the Peninsula empty. They are prepared for twenty thousand casualties."

"Yes," agreed I, "and, as there are no reinforcements, it can't mean a big advance, so it must mean a big retreat. There's nothing to bellyache about. We're going to evacuate, praise be to Allah!"

"Oh, try not to be foolish, Captain Ray," returned Doe impatiently. "Have you been so long on this cursed Peninsula without knowing that we couldn't evacuate Suvla without being seen from Sari Bair, nor Helles without being seen from Achi Baba? And, directly the jolly old Turk saw us quitting, he, and the whole German army, and Ludendorff, would stream down and massacre us as we ran. We'd want every man for a rearguard action to hold them off. The bally thing's impossible."

"Well, we did the impossible in getting on to the Peninsula," put in Monty, "and we shall probably do the impossible in getting off. Besides, not even Turks can see at night."

"That's all very fine," rejoined the lively youth. "But the impossible landing was done by the grandest Division in history, when they were up to full strength. Now our divisions are jaded and done for. Besides, only one army could get away. Even if the Suvla crowd did effect a surprise escape, the Turk would see to it that the Helles mob didn't repeat the performance. Our Staff would have to sacrifice one army for the other. And, as the Suvla army is bigger than ours, they'd sacrifice us for a certainty. So cheer up, and don't be so damned miserable."

"Oh, well," said Monty, refilling Doe's cup. "Let us eat, drink, and be merry, for to-morrow we die."

Doe lifted up the mug to toast his host.

"*Morituri te salutamus*," he said, and out of his abounding spirits began to sing:

> "The Germans are coming, oh dear, oh dear,
> The Germans are coming, oh can't you hear?"

Sec.2

And amid all this speculation on Helles, there came suddenly a rumour that, so far from the Turks attacking us, our whole line was about to assume the offensive and move forward. This was a mere angel's whisper one morning: by the afternoon it had blown like a dust-drive into every dug-out.

It's a good rule, my friends who shall fight the next war, if you want to know the secrets about a forthcoming attack, always to ask the padre. He is the rumour-merchant of the fighting army. And Monty was no exception. Directly the strange rumour reached the Eski Line, Monty busied himself tapping every source for more detailed information.

First he inquired of the Battalion Intelligence Officer whether there were anything reliable in this talk of an imminent attack. Intelligence nodded its head, as much as to say: "I've promised that not a breath of it shall leave my lips, but—" Well, Intelligence nodded his head.

Then, on another occasion, the Quartermaster, having just returned from Ordnance (where they know everything), looked a profoundly sinister look at Monty, and said:

"They're going to keep *you* busy shortly."

"What, a show on?" asked Monty hypocritically.

"Yes, some stunt—some stunt. But don't know anything about it."

Next Monty was at Divisional Signals (always a well-informed and oracular body), who said they supposed he knew there would be very little opportunity for Divine Service on Sunday.

"You mean," said he, with brutal plainness, "that this beastly attack is fixed for Sunday."

"Now, nobody said that," was the reply. "But take it from us that on Sunday your men will be too busy parading for other purposes than for Divine Service. Strictly on the Q.T., of course."

The same day at the Bombing School Monty found but one subject of conversation.

"It'll be the stickiest thing we've had for some time, as ourselves, the Scotties, and the French are all involved in it. Your people, the East Cheshires, are going over at Fusilier Bluff, after we've blown up a huge mine. Their Brigade Bombers are going to occupy the crater. But, of course, mum's the word."

Lastly, Monty held mysterious communion with my sergeant-major, a wonderful cockney humorist, who possessed the truth on all points. As far as Fusilier Bluff was concerned, said he, the attack was an effort to reach and destroy the terrible whizz-bang gun. It was believed that the gun's location was in a nullah where its dump of ammunition was inaccessible to our artillery. Only bombers could reach it. So they were going to blow up a mine of 570 pounds of ammonel, and the bombers, supported by the infantry, were going to rush for the crater. From the crater they would sally forth and reach the gun. "And glory be to Gawd," concluded the sergeant-major piously, "that I ain't a bomber."

Sec.3

On the eve of the attack Doe and I were in our dug-out discussing what part the C.O. would allot us in the operation, when an orderly appeared at the door.

"Brigade Bombing Officer here, sir?" he asked, saluting.

"Sure thing," said Doe.

"The C.O. wants to see you at once, sir."

Doe shrugged his shoulders. " *Quand on parle du loup, on en voie le queue.* Now we shall hear something." And he followed the orderly.

A trifle jealous, I awaited his return. He came back with joy sparkling in his eyes—how far assumed I know not—and, flinging himself down on a box, cried: "Rupert, the show in this sector is *my* show! They're going to blow up the jolly old mine; and the minute it goes up I've got to take the bombers over the top and occupy the crater. Then, if I think it possible, I'm to go further forward to the whizz-bang gun and blow it into the middle of the next war. **Voyez-vous**, they know they've a competent young officer in charge of the bombers. Rupert, we shall not stay long in the crater. And, if you please, the C.O. wishes to see Captain Ray immediately."

"Which means I'm for it too," said I, as I went out.

The C.O. explained my share. I was to take over all my company and capture the trenches on the right of the crater. On capturing them, I was to open a covering fire to enable the bombers to go further forward. A similar move was being made by B Company on the bombers' left. In short, a wedge was being driven into the Turkish line, and the point of the wedge—Doe's bombing party—was to penetrate to the gun-position. Both my task and Doe's were dam-dangerous, said the Colonel, but Doe's was the damnedest. On the effectiveness of my flanking support might depend his life and the success of the raid. Did I see?

"Yes, sir."

The hour of the attack was not known, he explained. Since the whole Helles line was moving, the final order must come from G.H.Q. But everybody was to be armed and ready in the trenches by dawn.... And ... well, good evening, Ray.

It was about dusk. I returned to the dug-out, and by candle-light wrote out my company orders. Then Doe and I decided that we ought to put together a few letters. And Doe tossed his pencil gaily into the air and caught it. The action was to cover with a veneer of merriness a question which it embarrassed him to ask.

"Oughtn't we to make a jolly old will?"

"Sure thing," agreed I, in imitation of him. "It'll be rather fun."

Sec.4

Soon after Battalion Orders were out, Monty came and sat down in our dug-out. We had known he would come, and our reception of him was planned. Doe, whose affected gaiety had begun to give place to a certain wistfulness as the darkness fell, spoke first:

"D'you remember telling us one night on the **Rangoon** about some fellows who—who—gave you their wills the day before an attack?"

Monty turned his head, and started to frown through the dug-out door at the still AEgean Sea.

"Yes," he said.

"Well, Rupert and I thought that we'd—that p'raps you'd look after these envelopes, in case—"

"Oh, damn!" said Monty. I had never heard him swear before, but I knew that in the word his big heart spoke. Doe still held our envelopes towards his averted face, and at last he took them silently.

"Thanks, awfully," said Doe.

"Thanks," said I.

"Oh, for Heaven's sake, shut up!" Monty grumbled, and started whistling unconsciously. Immediately in my mind the words "Dismiss me not thy service, Lord" framed themselves to the tune, and conjured up a vision of the smoking room of the *Rangoon* and its decks by starlight. Abruptly Monty broke off, and said, still frowning at the sea:

"Since those days you've been fairly loyal sons of the Church. Aren't you going to use her before to-morrow? To-night's a more literal Vigil than that voyage. Can't I—aren't you going to use me?"

It was the old Monty of the *Rangoon* speaking.

"We'd thought about it," answered Doe, reddening.

"I so want," murmured Monty, "to be of use to all the fellows who are going over the top to-morrow. But they don't understand. They don't think of me as a priest with something to do for them that nobody else can do. They think I've done my job when I've had a hymn-singing service, and preached to them.... And all the time I want to absolve them. I want to send them into the fight—white."

No word came from us to break a long pause. We had become again those listening people of *Rangoon* nights.

"But *you* understand," he recommenced. "And, if you'll come to your Confession, I'll at least have done something for somebody before this scrap. Rupert, you can thank Heaven you don't feel as I do—that you've nothing positive to do to-morrow—that you're not pulling your weight. I shall just skulk about, like a dog worrying the heels of an attack."

"Rot!" said Doe. "You've done wonders for the men."

"No, I haven't, except for those who come to their Mass and Confession. I've held no services a layman couldn't hold, and done nothing for the sick a hospital orderly couldn't do. And I want to be their priest."

"Well, we'll both come to-night."

Monty ceased frowning at the sea, and smilingly turned towards us.

"You may think," he said, "that I've been of some help to you; but you can never know of what help you two have been to me."

"Oh, rot!" said Doe, tossing a pencil into the air.

Sec.5

It was about ten o'clock when I came away from Monty's home in the Eski Line, where I had made my Confession. I retain an impression of myself, as I walked homeward through the darkness, moving along the summits above Y Ravine. I was listening to the nervous night-firing of the Turk, who was apprehensive of something in the morning, and hearing in my mind Monty's last words: "Forget those things which are behind, and press towards the mark of your high calling."

Walking along the Peninsula at night being always a gloomy matter, I was glad to arrive at the dug-out, where Doe was already under his blankets. I lay down and spent a long time battling with my mind to prevent it keeping me awake by too active thinking. For, if only I could drop off into unconsciousness, I had the chance of sleeping till an hour before the dawn.

Sec.6

There is something depressing in being called while it is still dark, and being obliged to dress by artificial light. As I laced my boots by the flame of the candle in the dusk before the dawn, I felt a sensation I used to experience at school, when they lit the class-room gas in the early twilight of a winter afternoon—a sensation of the sadness and futility of all things.

I awoke Doe, and could tell, as he sat up, rubbing his eyes and yawning, that returning memory was filling his mind with speculation as to what unthinkable things the morning might hold in its womb. With the feigned gaiety of the day before he flung off his blankets, and said:

"Well, Roop, it's 'over the top and the best of luck' for us this morning."

"Strange how quiet everything is," I replied. "The bombardment ought to have started before this."

"Yes, it's a still and top-hole morning." Saying this, Doe went to the dug-out window to look at the dawn. The moment that his face framed itself in the square of the window, dawn, coming in like an Ægean sunset with a violet light, lit up his half-profile, throwing into clear relief the familiar features, and dropping a brilliant spark into each of his wide, contemplative eyes. The effect was a thing of the stage: it lent him an added wistfulness, and I felt a pang of pity for him, and a throb of something not lower than love. He walked back to his bed, whistling, while I completed my preparations by fixing my revolver to my belt.

"Well, I'm ready," I said. "I must go and look at my braves."

"Don't s'pose I shall see you again, then, before the show," said Doe, pulling on his boots nonchalantly.

"No. We'll compare notes in the captured trenches this evening."

"Right you are. Cheerioh!"

"Chin-chin."

I went out, reviewing painful possibilities. In the trenches I found my company "standing-to," armed and ready. Knowing that idle waiting would mean suspense and agitation, I went about overhauling ammunition, and instructing my men on the exact objectives and the work of consolidation. My restlessness brought back vividly that day when I had suffered from nerves before the Bramhall-Erasmus swimming race. The same interior hollowness made me chafe at delay and long to be started—to be busied in the excitement of action—to be looking back on it all as a thing of the past.

The morning wore on. There was bustling in the communication trenches, pack-mules bringing up ammunition, and men shouldering cases of bombs. At ten o'clock the C.O. came round the line. Now that the imminence of the attack had made unpleasantly real his duty of sending us over the top, he had grown quite fatherly. "Don't get killed," he said. "I can't spare any of you—battalion dam-depleted already.... Is there anything you wish to ask, my boy?"

"Yes, sir. I want to know what time it begins, and what exactly it's all about."

"At two o'clock," he replied. "The mine goes up then. But what it's all about

I know no more than you do. Personally, I think it is to cover some operations at Suvla. The Staff is obviously so dam-anxious to let the Turk know we're going to attack, that I'm sure this is a diversion intended to keep the Turk's Helles army occupied, and prevent it reinforcing Suvla. Go and have a look from the Bluff out to sea, and observe how well the show is being advertised. There may be reason for this ostentation, but it's dam-awkward for my lads, who'll have to run up against a well-prepared enemy."

"But s'posing it means they're going to evacuate Suvla, and leave us to our fate, what'll be our position on Helles then, sir?"

"Well, we shall be like the rearguard that covered the retreat at Mons—heroes, but mostly dead ones."

"Good Lord!" thought I, as the C.O. turned away. "We shall be lonely on Helles to-night if we hear that the Suvla Army has left for England."

I went, as he suggested, to glance at the preparations on the sea. I saw a string of devilish monitors, solemnly taking up their position between Imbros and our eastern coast. Destroyers lay round the Peninsula like a chain of black rulers. A great airship was sailing towards us. From Imbros and Tenedos aeroplanes were rising high in the sky.

The Turk, wide awake to these preliminaries, was firing shrapnel at the aircraft overhead, and hurling towards the destroyers his high-explosive shells, which tossed up water-spouts in the sea. The whizz-bang gun spat continuously.

"You won't spit after to-night," I mused, "if Doe reaches you."

And, from all I knew of Doe and his passion for the heroic, I felt assured that he would never stay in the crater like a diffident batsman in his block. He would reach the opposite crease, or be run out.

"He'll get there. He'll get there," I told myself persistently.

Sec.7

The attack having been postponed till two o'clock, Monty held an open-air Communion Service in Trolley Ravine. The C.O., myself, and a few others stole half an hour to attend it. This day was the last Sunday in Advent, and a morning peace, such as reminded us of English Sundays, brooded over Gallipoli. Save for the distant and intermittent firing of the Turk, everything was very still, and Monty had no need to raise his voice. The Collect was probably being read thus softly at a number of tiny services dotted about the hills of Helles and Suvla. Never shall I hear it again without thinking of the last pages of the Gallipoli story, and of that Advent Sunday of big decisions. "O Lord, raise up thy power, and come among us ... that, whereas we are sore let and hindered in running the race that is set before us, Thy bountiful mercy may speedily help and deliver us." Like an answer to prayer came the words of the Epistle: "Rejoice.... The Lord is at hand. Be anxious for nothing. And the peace of God which passeth all understanding shall keep your hearts and minds." Read at Monty's service in Trolley Ravine, it sounded like a Special Order of the Day. I remembered what the Colonel had hinted about Suvla, and wondered whether at similar services there it was being listened to like a last message to the Suvla Army.

Not long had I returned to my fire trenches before our bombardment opened. The shells streamed over, seeming about to burst in our own trenches, but exploding instead the other side of No Man's Land. Distant booms told us that the Navy had joined in the quarrel. The awful noise of the bombardment, lying so low on our heads, and the deafening detonations of the shells disarrayed all my thoughts. My temples throbbed, my ears sang and whistled, and something began to beat and ache at the back of my head. My brain, crowded with the bombardment, had room for only two clear thoughts—the one, that I was standing with a foot on the firing-step, my revolver cocked in my hand; the other, that, when the mine gave the grand signal, I should clamber mechanically over the parapet and rush into turmoil. Hurry up with that mine—oh, hurry up! My limbs at least were shivering with impatience to be over and away.

A great report set the air vibrating; the voice of my sergeant-major shouted: "It's gone up, sir!" a burst of rapid rifle and machine-gun fire, spreading all along the line, showed that the bombers had leapt out of the protection of the trenches and gone over the parapet—and, almost before I had apprehended all these things, I had scrambled over the sand-bags, and was in the open beneath a shower of earth that, blown by the mine into the air, was dropping in clods and particles. Confound the smoke and the dust! I could scarcely see where I was running. The man on my right dropped with a groan. Elsewhere a voice was crying with a blasphemy, "I'm hit!" Bullets seemed to breathe in my face as they rushed past. I stumbled into a hole. I picked myself up, for I saw before me a line of bayonets, glistening where the light caught them. It was my company; and I must be in front of them—not behind. Revolver gripped, I ran through and beyond them, only to fall heavily in a deep depression, which was the Turkish trench. An enemy bayonet was coming like a spear at my breast just as I fired. The shadowy foe fell across my legs. From under him I fired into the breast of another who loomed up to kill me. Then I rose, as a third, with a downward blow from the barrel of his rifle, knocked my revolver spinning from my hand. With an agony in my wrist, I snatched at his rifle, and, wrenching the bayonet free, stabbed him savagely with his own weapon, tearing it away as he dropped. Heavens! would my company never come? I had only been four yards in front of them. Was all this taking place in seconds? One moment of clear reasoning had just told me that this cold dampness, moving along my knee, was the soaking blood of one of my victims, when a Turkish officer ran into the trench-bay, firing backwards and blindly at my sergeant-major. Seeing me, he whipped round his revolver to shoot me. My fist shot out towards his chin in an automatic action of self-defence, and the bayonet, which it held, passed like a pin right through the man's throat. His blood spurted over my hand and ran up my arm, as he dropped forward, bearing me down under him.

"Hurt, sir?" asked the sergeant-major, kindly. "We've got the trench."

"Man the trench," said I, an English voice bringing my wits back, "and keep up a covering fire for the bombers."

At the mention of the bombers I thought of Doe. Getting quickly up, I stood on the piled bodies of my victims to see over the top. As I looked through the rolling smoke for the position of the bombers, I heard my sergeant-major saying to a man in the next bay:

"Our babe's done orl right. He's killed four, and is now standin' on 'em."

Without doubting that he was speaking of me, I yet felt no glow at this rough tribute, for I was worried at what I saw in the open. In the fog of smoke I descried a figure that must be Doe's. He was still out on the top, his party straggling and bewildered. It perplexed me. Why was he not under cover in the crater of the mine? Had all my blood-letting work only occupied the time it took him to run from his trench to the lips of the crater?

Seeing his danger, I rushed along my company, shouting: "Curse you! Double the rapidity of that fire. Do you want all the bombers killed?" till I reached our extreme left, where we had been in touch with Doe. Jumping up again, I watched his movements. I saw him running well in front of his bombers, who were now going forward, as if to a definite object. "Good—good—good! He'll get there." The words were mine, but they sounded like someone else's. Then, almost before the event which provoked it, I heard my own low groan.

Doe stopped, and staggered slightly backwards. His cap fell off, and the wind blew his hair about, as it used to do on the cricket-field at school. He recovered an upright position; he smiled very clearly—then folded up, and collapsed.

I saw his party retire rapidly, but in orderly fashion, under the command of their sergeant. Beyond them B Company, whose right flank had been left hanging in the air by the withdrawal of the bombers, began to execute a similar movement.

"Tain't the bombers' fault, sir," exclaimed my sergeant-major. "The mine failed to produce a crater. They'd nowt to occupy."

Sick with misery and indecision, I was realising that I must retire my company, its left flank being exposed—I was taking a last look at the huddled form that had been my friend, when I saw him rise and rush forward. Excitedly I cried: "Fire! Fire! Keep up that covering fire! Be ready to advance at any moment." Ha, there were no tactics about the position in front of Fusilier Bluff that minute. Doe was tumbling forward alone. A company, firing furiously to keep down the heads of the Turks, was "in the air"—and ready to advance.

"Message to retire at once, sir," reported my sergeant-major.

Look! Doe had something in his hand. He hurled it. A distant thud and a small report merged at once into a great explosion, which reverberated about the Bluff. Doe laughed shrilly. He fell. But it could only have been the shock which knocked him over, for he was on his feet again, and staggering home.

"Gawd!" screamed the sergeant-major. "He's bombed the gun and exploded the shell-dump. Finish whizz-bang!" And he bellowed with triumphant laughter.

"I knew he would," cried I. "I knew he would. This way, Doe!"

He was going blindly to his right.

"Message from C.O. to retire at once, sir."

"This way, Doe!" I roared at him, laughing, for I thought he was well and unhurt.

But no. He pitched, rolled over, and lay still.

I gasped. What was I to do? Ordered to retire, I wanted to jump out and fetch him in. In those few seconds of indecision, I saw a figure crash forward, pick up Doe's body, and run back.

"The padre! The padre!" exclaimed the sergeant-major.

"No? Was it?"

"Gawd, yes! The gor-blimey parson!"

"Pass the word to retire," I commanded. "Hang it! We seem to have done the job we set out to do."

Sec.8

Covered with blood and dust, my jacket torn, I came half an hour later upon Monty, where he was sitting wearily upon a mound. I had but one question to ask him.

"Is he dead?"

"No. Hit in the shoulder the first time. Then, after he got up and bombed the gun, hit four times in the waist."

"Will he die?"

"Of course."

I walked away, as a man does from one who has cruelly hurt him.

"O Christ!" I said, just blasphemously, for in that moment of tearless agony all my moral values collapsed. "O Christ! Damn beauty! Damn everything!" Then there came a disorder of the mind, in which I could only repeat to myself: "The Germans are coming, oh dear, oh dear. The Germans are coming, oh dear, oh dear. The Germans—Oh, drop it, for God's sake, drop it!"

A night and a morning passed: and the next afternoon I was sitting on the Bluff, glumly watching a destroyer flash and smoke, as she hurled shells over my head to Achi Baba. An officer came up, and with grim meaning handed me the typed copy of an official telegram.

"Here's the key to yesterday's riddle," he explained.

I took it and read: "Suvla and Anzac successfully evacuated. No casualties."

The officer waited till I had finished, and then said:

"Well, what's our position on Helles now? A bit dickey, eh?"

Scarcely interested, I looked along the coast of the Peninsula and saw two great conflagrations, the smoke ascending in pillars to the sky, at Suvla and Anzac, where the retiring army had fired the remaining stores.

CHAPTER XV
TRANSIT

Sec.1

Then Monty approached me, as I tossed stones down the slope on to the beach.

"I've seen him," he said. "He's in No. 17 Stationary Hospital, the 'White City.' Are you coming?"

"Of course," replied I uncivilly. Did he think *he* would visit Doe and *I* wouldn't—I who had known him ten years? The man was presuming on his six-months' acquaintance with my friend.

"Well, come down to the dump, and we'll find you a horse."

"How is he?" asked I, not choosing to be told what to do.

"Bad. Come along. There's no time to lose."

"All right—I'm coming, aren't I? I don't need to be ordered to go."

In silence we went down Gurkha Mule Trench into Gully Ravine, where the horse lines were.

"Saddle up Charlie," said Monty to his groom, "and get the Major's chestnut for Captain Ray."

The groom brought the horses, and, as he tightened up the girth on Monty's dark bay Arab, asked me:

"Are you going to see Mr. Doe, sir?"

I turned away without answering. I hadn't spoken to him, and there was no occasion for him to speak to me.

"Yes, we are," said Monty promptly.

"Sad about such a nice young gentleman. He's packing up, they say."

"The damned alarmist!" thought I. "He relishes the grim news."

But I knew in my heart that I was only grudging him his right to be sorry for Doe. Who was *he* to grieve? Three months before he had not heard of us. On all the Peninsula there was only one just claim to the right of grieving: and that was mine.

Monty mounted. Seizing the reins carelessly, I put my foot in the chestnut's stirrup. As I rose, the bit pulled on the mare's mouth and she wheeled and reared, shaking me awkwardly to the ground.

"Damn the bloody horse," I said aloud.

Monty stroked his bay's silk neck, as though he had heard nothing.

"You've got his rein too tight, sir," the groom told me.

"All right! I know how to mount a horse."

I swung into the saddle, and, ignoring Monty, set the mare, which was very fresh, at a canter towards Artillery Road. Artillery Road was a winding gun-track that climbed out of Gully Ravine up to the tableland beneath Achi Baba. Much too fast I ran the chestnut up the steep incline, and emerged from the ravine on to the high level ground. Straightway I looked across two miles of scrub to the sea-ward point of the plateau, where stood a large camp of square tents. It was No. 17 Stationary Hospital, the "White City." ... I wondered which of those tents he was in.

The chestnut, anxious for a gallop through the scrub, and excited by the noise of Monty cantering behind, pulled hard. My heart was in sympathy with her, and I let her open into a stretch-gallop. For I was absurdly thinking that, if once I allowed Monty to draw abreast of me, I should yield to him a share of my position as chief mourner. I wanted to be lonely in my grief.

At a point in front of me on the beaten road shells were dropping with regularity. Savagely grieving, I let the mare race the shells to the danger zone. What cared I if shell and mare and rider converged together upon their destruction?

I rode through a rush of confused impressions. At one moment I was passing Pink Farm Cemetery, which had two of its crosses nearly broken by a shell-splinter. I was wondering if they would bury him there, alongside of White, under the solitary tree. At another, I was galloping through the lines of the Lowland Division, where a band of pipers was playing "Annie Laurie," and an officer cried out to me: "Stop that galloping, you young fool." In answer I put heels to the mare's flanks and urged her on. And all the while the "White City" was growing nearer and larger, and my heart beginning to beat with anticipation and fear. I shouldn't know what to do or to say. Never shy of Doe living, I was shy of Doe dying.

Having pulled the excited mare into control and dismounted, I looked round, sneakily sideways, for Monty. I wanted his company now, for I feared what was coming. Too proud to appear to wait for him, I shammed difficulty with the animal's head-rope, and delayed long over the task of tethering her securely. And the time, during which Monty arrived and dismounted, I killed by unloosening girth and surcingle.

"Come along, Rupert, old chap."

Monty led the way to Doe's tent. And the chief mourner followed humbly behind. As we dipped our heads to pass under the porch, we went out of the glare of the open air into the subdued and gentle light of the tent. At once a coolness like that of evening displaced the warmth of the afternoon. And a strange quiet fell about our ears. It seemed to me that the eight cots were empty.

The orderly on duty greeted Monty with a soft whisper: "He's quite conscious, sir, but won't last long."

Following the glance of the orderly, I saw Doe's wide eyes fixed upon me.

"Hallo, Rupert."

I hurried to his bedside, feeling, even in that moment, a triumphant joy that his affectionate welcome had been for me and not for Monty.

"Hallo, Doe."

He looked very beautiful, lying there. His complexion, always as flawless as a little child's, had assumed a new waxen loveliness, no touch of colour varying its pale and delicate brown. And his eyes were brilliant.

"Well—we did in the old gun, Rupert, that killed—Jimmy Doon—and Major Hardy.... The *Rangoon* proved too strong for it, after all!"

How characteristic of our dear, dramatic Doe his words were!

"Yes," I said, and could think of nothing more to say.

He moved his body slightly, and I, cudgelling my mind for some remark, asked:

"Were you hurt much?"

"I was wounded—in the shoulder—and then hit four times, after I—the doctor seems to think it's pretty bad—but oh, it's nothing."

As he spoke I could see that he was rather pleased with the picturesqueness of being "Dangerously Wounded," and that, while he wished to inform us how interesting he had become, he wished also to appear to be stoically making light of his pain. And I loved him for being the same self-conscious heroic character up to the last.

The brilliant eyes sought out Monty, who was standing just behind me. Doe gazed at him, and, after a thoughtful pause, laughed nervously.

"I wonder if I shall be—here—to-morrow, when you come. I dare say I shan't."

Again I saw the thought behind his words. Probably my love for him was blazing up, in these farewell moments, brighter than it had ever been, and illuminating all things. I saw that he wanted to live, but feared he was going to die. I saw that he had gambled everything upon his last remark, and was waiting to see if he would draw life or death.

Had he said it to me I should have answered hurriedly: "Of course you will," but Monty was cast in more courageous metal. Boldly he seized this moment to convey the truth. He offered no denial to Doe's daring suggestion that the end was near: instead, he laid his hand very gently on the boy's wrist, as if to tell him that he wished to help him through with a difficult thought.

Throughout my life, till someone shall tell me that my time has come, I shall remember Doe's look when he saw that Monty was not going to dispute his statement. His wide eyes stared inquiringly. Then they filmed over with a slight moisture, for they belonged to a boy who was not yet twenty. He dropped his eyelids to conceal the welling moisture, but raised them a few seconds later, revealing that the tears had gathered still more abundantly, and his lashes were wet with them. Nevertheless he smiled, and said:

"Well, it can't be helped. If I'd known when I started that it would end like this—I'd have gone through with it just the same. I haven't got cold feet."

Sec.2

"It's an end to all the ambitions and poems," said Doe later, when the window-less tent seemed to be getting dark, though the afternoon was yet early. "P'raps you'll be left to fulfil yours, Rupert. Do you remember you said in Radley's room—all those hundreds of years ago—that you wanted to be a country squire?"

"Yes," answered I, with a quivering lip.

"And Penny wanted—to be a Tory.... And I wanted to lead the people. Oh, well. I'd like just to have known—whether we won the war in the end. P'raps you'll know—"

"We're winning," said I feebly.

"O Lord, yes," agreed Doe, dreamily echoing an old memory.

It grew darker, though not yet three o'clock; and my brain seemed to be receding from me with the light. I felt tired and frightened. There was a long pause, till at last I said:

"Well, I s'pose I must be going now."

God! The futility of the words! And they were the last I could utter to Doe!... I grasped his wrist. If I couldn't speak, I could pass all my abounding love and misery through the pressure of my hand.

"Good-bye," he said. "Thanks for coming to see me."

The boyish words broke me up. My brows contracted in pain. My eyes burned, and misery filled my throat. I even felt a smile at the tragedy of it all pass over my face. Then with an audible moan I rushed away.

I went out to my horse without waiting for Monty. I could have waited for no-body. I wanted motion, action, something to occupy my hands and feet and mind. As I mounted the mare she began to walk away. But walking was not action enough. Impatiently I urged her to a canter and a gallop. And, while she galloped, increasing her distance from the "White City," I asked myself if I realised that I was riding away from Doe for ever.

The spirited mare, knowing that she was going home to her lines, opened out like a winner racing up the straight. The extravagance of her speed exactly fitted my extravagant mood. I promised myself that, just as I was letting my animal have its head, so I would slacken all moral reins, and let my life run uncontrolled. There was ***not*** more beauty in things than ugliness, nor more happiness in life than pain. Have done with this straining after ideals!... The horse gathered pace.

Then, as I rode savagely and thought savagely, a strange thing happened. I was gripping the mare with my knees, and, now that she was attaining her highest speed, I leaned forward like a jockey, throwing my weight on her withers. The wind rushed past me; the exhilaration of speed filled me; that invigorating sensation of strong life pulling upon my reins and springing between the grip of my knees ran through my veins; my lungs tightened; a pleasing weariness set in below the heart; and for a moment I almost felt the unconquerable joy of youth in life!

Instantly I pulled the wild animal in, and dropped into a melancholy walk. I felt as if I had been trapped. Not yet would I be disloyal to Doe by admitting beauty in creation or joy in living. I walked the lathering mare to the lines, like a tired jockey who has run his race. Then I wandered home to Fusilier Bluff—home to a dug-out for two! I couldn't enter the dug-out yet. I lay down on the Bluff, watching the late sun nearing the hills of Imbros.

The misery possessing me was of that passionate kind which embraces self-torture. I wilfully excavated the ten past years for memories of Doe, though, in so doing, I was pressing upon my wound to make it hurt. I watched him as a boy, getting into the next bed in the Bramhall dormitory, or rowing in the evening light up the river at Falmouth. I saw two young khaki figures, his and mine, setting out at midnight to sin and sully ourselves together. I heard him quoting on the hilltops of Mudros his haunting couplet:

> "As long days close,
> And weary English suns go west'ring home."

The memories made my breath come fast and jerkily. With madly exalted words I addressed that slight fair-haired figure, which must now for ever be only a memory. "***My*** friend," I said to it; "***mine, mine!***" In the freshness of my loss, I thought no lover had ever loved as I did. "I loved you—I loved you—I loved you," I repeated. And I even worked myself up into a weary longing to die. Pennybet had led the way, and Doe now was following him. And why should not I complete the story? Why not? Why not?

My brain was pulsing thus tempestuously when Monty drew near me. I affected not to notice his coming, but when he sat down beside me I decided to speak
first. I felt it would be a supreme relief to hurt him with the news that I had abandoned his ideal, and let my spiritual life collapse. So, without looking at him, I said
angrily:

"There's no beauty in it."

"Rupert, you're wrong," he answered, "and you'll see it when you are less unhappy." He paused. "Doe—Edgar used to worry himself because he thought that
any really good thing that he did was spoiled by a desire for glory. He often said
that he wanted to do a really perfect thing. And, Rupert, this afternoon he told me
that, when he went forward to put out that gun, he felt quite alone. He seemed
surrounded with smoke and flying dust. And he thought he would do one big deed
unseen.... He did his perfect thing at the last."

"There's no beauty," I repeated dully.

"Rupert, Edgar is dead.... And there's only one unbeautiful thing about his
death, and that is the way his friend is taking it."

Monty stopped, and both of us watched the sun go down behind Imbros. It was
throwing out golden rays like the spokes of a wheel. These rays caught the flaky
clouds above Samothrace, and just pencilled their outline with a tiny rim of gold
and fire. And the hills of Imbros, as always in the AEgean Sea, turned purple.

"There's no beauty in death and burial and corruption," I said.

"Yes, there is, even in them. There's beauty in thinking that the same material
which goes to make these earthly hills and that still water should have been shaped
into a graceful body, and lit with the divine spark which was Edgar Doe. There's
beauty in thinking that, when the unconquerable spark has escaped away, the material is returned to the earth, where it urges its life, also an unconquerable thing,
into grass and flowers. It's harmonious—it's beautiful."

This time I forbore to repeat my obstinate denial.

"And your friendship is a more beautiful whole, as things are. Had there been
no war, you'd have left school and gone your different roads, till each lost trace of
the other. It's always the same. But, as it is, the war has held you in a deepening
intimacy till—till the end. It's—it's perfect."

"It'll be more perfect," I answered, in a low, hollow voice, "if the war ends us both. Perhaps it will. There is time yet."

At so bitter a sentence Monty gave me a look, and broke through all barriers with a single generous remark.

"Rupert, old chap, the loss of Edgar leaves *me* numb with pain, but I know I'm not suffering like you."

A dry sob tore up my frame.

"Oh, I don't know what I feel," I gulped, "or what I've said. I think I've been a self-centred cad. I'm—I'm sorry."

Monty muttered something gentle, and left me reclining on the Bluff and look-ing out to sea. I didn't turn my head to watch him go. But I was thinking now less stormily.

Yes, I had been behaving like a fool: but I had been mad, as though everything had snapped. To-morrow I would recover my mental balance and resume moral effort. My last loyalty to Doe should be this: that I would not let his death destroy his friend's ideals. That, as Monty said, would spoil the beauty of it all. And I, least of any, should spoil it! But to-night—just for to-night—my fretful, contrary mood must play itself out. To-morrow I would begin again.

So I lay watching the changing lights. Darkness came close behind the sun-set, and there, yonder, Orion hung low in the sky. I tossed a few stones down the Bluff, but soon it was too dark to see them after they had travelled a little distance. Overhead the sky deepened to the last blue of night, but along the western horizon it remained a luminous sea-green. Against this bright afterglow the hills of Imbros stood almost black. I stared at them. Then the luminous green turned to the blue of the zenith, and the hills were lost. And the cold of the Gallipoli night chilled me, as I lay there, too indolent and despairing to seek warmth.

CHAPTER XVI
THE HOURS BEFORE THE END

Sec.1

On the following day we buried Doe at sundown. In a grave on Hunter Weston Hill, which slopes down to W Beach, he lies with his feet toward the sea.

The same evening the medical orderly abused my confidence and informed the doctor that I was running a high temperature; and the doctor told me to pack up, as he was sending me to hospital. I refused.

I pointed out to him that if I, as a Company Commander, were to go sick at this juncture of the Gallipoli campaign, I could never again look the men of my company in the face. I tried to be funny about it. I asked him if he knew that Suvla had been evacuated; and that the Turks had therefore their whole Suvla army released to attack us on Helles—to say nothing of unlimited reinforcements pouring through Servia from Germany. I offered him an even bet that a few days hence we should either be lying dead in the scrub at Helles, or marching wearily to our prison at Constantinople. How, then, could I desert my men at this perilous moment? "The Germans are coming, oh dear, oh dear," I summed up; and then shivered, as I remembered whose merry voice had first chanted those words.

All this I explained to the doctor, but I did not tell him that, when I discovered my abnormal temperature, I had felt a quick spring of joy bubbling up, for here was an excuse for getting out of this Gallipoli, of which I was so sick and tired; and then I had remembered how, in loyalty to Doe, I had replaced my old ideals, and by their light I must stay. I must only leave the Peninsula when I could leave it with honour of holding Helles for the Empire.

In the end the doctor and I compromised. He said he would not send me to hospital, but that I must go down to the dump, and take things easy for a few days. From there I could be summoned, since I took myself so devilish seriously, to die with my men when the massacre began. I told him that the dump was too far back, but that, if he liked, I would go and live with Padre Monty in the Eski Line.

So a few days before Christmas I arrived with my batman and my kit at Monty's tiny sand-bag dug-out. He gave me a joyous welcome, stating that he would order the maids to light the fire in the best bedroom and air the sheets. Meanwhile, would I step into his study?

Sec.2

"I'm glad," said I to Monty at breakfast the next morning, "that I shall spend Christmas alone with you here. I couldn't have stood just now a riotous celebration with the regiment."

"Of course not," he agreed, and we both kept a silence in honour of the dead.

"Though I doubt if it'll be a riotous Christmas for anyone," I resumed. "Probably the last most of us will ever know."

"Stuff!" murmured Monty.

"'Tisn't stuff. Have you seen the Special Order of the Day that has been printed and stuck up everywhere, congratulating us on our attack of December 19, which, it says, 'contributed largely to the successful evacuation of Suvla,' and telling us that to our Army Corps 'has been entrusted the honour of holding Helles for the Empire'?"

"Heavens!" he muttered. "We can't do it."

"Of course we can't; and we can't quit."

"Not without being wiped out," he agreed.

"Exactly. I wonder what it'll feel like, having a Turco bayonet in one's stomach."

"Rupert," said Monty suddenly, "we've had a bad jar, and we're getting morbid. Cheer up. Muddly old Britain will get us out of this mess. And now we're jolly well going to make all we can out of this Christmas. It'll certainly be the most *piquant* of our lives. *Adams!*"

"Sir?" Monty's batman appeared at the dug-out door in answer to the call.

"Get your entrenching tool. We're going to dig up a little fir for a Christmas tree."

So we spent the next days making our Christmas preparations, determined to keep the feast. We decorated the sand-bag cabin—oh, yes! Over the pictures of our people, pinned to the sand-bag walls, we placed sprigs of a small-leaf holly that grew on the Peninsula. We planted the little fir in a disused petrol-tin, and, after a visit to the canteen, decorated it with boxes of Turkish delight, sticks of chocolate, packets of chewing-gum, oranges, lemons, soap, and bits of Government candles. It was a Christmas tree of some distinction. And mistletoe? No, we couldn't find any mistletoe, but then, as Monty said, it would have no point on Gallipoli, there being no—just so; when we should be home again for Christmas of next year, we would claim an extra kiss for 1915.

"Pest! Rupert," exclaimed Monty, "we've forgotten to send any Christmas cards. To work at once!"

We sat down at the tiny table and cut notepaper into elegant shapes, sticking on it little bits of Turkish heather, and printing beneath: "A Slice of Turkey" (which we thought a very happy jest); "Heather from Invaded Enemy Territory. Are we downhearted? NO! Are we going to win? YES!"

And by luck there arrived a parcel from Mother with a cake. Of plum pudding we despaired, till one fine morning there came a present (half a pound per man) of that excellent comestible from the *Daily News* (whom the gods preserve and prosper).

"All is now ready," proclaimed Monty.

Christmas Day dawned beautiful in sky and atmosphere. It would have been as mild and gracious as a windless June day had not the Turk, nervous lest these dogs of Christians should celebrate their festival with any untoward activity, opened at daylight a prophylactic bombardment.

We stood in the dug-out door and watched the shells dropping.

"Does it strike you, Rupert," asked Monty, making a grimace, "that Old-Man-Turk has more guns firing than ever before?"

"Yes," I answered. "The guns from Suvla have come."

The words were no sooner out of my mouth than a shell shrieking into our own cookhouse, drove us like rabbits into the dug-out.

"Does it strike you, Rupert," said Monty, "that Turk Pasha has some pals with him who are firing heavier shells than ever before?"

"Yes," said I. "The Germans have come."

Sec.3

The afternoon we devoted to preparations for the feast of the evening. We laid the table. There was a water-proof ground-sheet for the cloth. There were little holly branches stuck in tobacco tins. And there were candles in plenty (for they were a Government issue, and we could be free with them). At Monty's suggestion, who maintained that the family must be gathered at the Christmas board, we placed photographs of our people on the table. There was a picture of Monty's sister and (for shame, Monty! fie upon you for keeping it dark so long) the picture of somebody else's sister. There was the portrait of my mother, and oh! in a silent moment, I had nearly placed on the table the dear face of Edgar Doe, but, instead, I put it back in my pocket, saying nothing to Monty, and feeling guilty of a lapse.

We were glad when the darkness came, for we wanted to try the effect of the candles, both those on the table and those on the Christmas tree. And truly the darkness, the candles, the flying sparks from our Yule log, and the smell of burning wood made Christmas everywhere.

Then we sat down to the meal. The menu said: "Consomme Gallipoli, Stew Dardanelles, Plum Pudding, Dessert, Lemonade a la Tour Eiffel." The soup was very good, even if it was only the gravy from the next course. And the stew in its plate looked almost too fine to disturb; the very largest onion was stuck in the middle—was it not Christmas Day? The pudding we set on fire with the Army rum issue. And the dish of dessert was a fine pile of lemons and oranges—the lemons not being there to be eaten, of course, but to make the show more brave.

Then the batmen were fetched in and given the presents from the Christmas Tree. And we drank healths in lemonade a la Tour Eiffel. We toasted the King, the Allies, "Johnny Turk beyond the Parapet," and, above all, "Our People at home, God bless 'em!" We sang "For they are jolly good fellows," and it was wonderful what a fine thing two officers and their soldier-servants made of it. Somebody, warmed up by this lively chorus, raised his glass and suggested "To Hell with the Kaiser!" But this toast we disallowed, on the ground that it would spoil our kindly feeling, and besides, as Monty observed compensatingly, he would be toasted enough when he got there.

And, when it was all over, I went out into the darkness to walk alone for a little, and to get the chill night air blowing upon my forehead. It was as clear and fine a night as it had been a day—cloudless, still, and starlit. And—forgive me—but I could only think of him whom we had left on Hunter Weston Hill, with his feet toward the sea, lying out there in the cold and the quiet. O God, when should I get used to it?

CHAPTER XVII
THE END OF GALLIPOLI

Sec.1

Wandering down the Gully Ravine one morning, I encountered a long line of men marching up it in single file. I passed as close to them as possible, so that, by a glance at their shoulder-straps, I might ascertain their regiment. No sooner had I learned who they were than I turned about and hurried back to Monty's dug-out. This life holds few pleasures so agreeable as that of conveying startling news.

"Who do you think's marching up the Gully?" I demanded.

"I don't know. Who?" asked Monty.

"The Munster Fusiliers!"

"What? The immortal 29th Division? From Suvla. The dickens! What does it mean?"

Before we could decide what it meant my batman came back from a visit to the French canteen at Seddel Bahr.

"They're landing hundreds of troops at V Beach, sir," said he. "The Worcesters are here, and the Warwicks."

"The 13th Division," exclaimed Monty. "Also from Suvla."

"They're reinforcements," said I. "It's all in accordance with the Special Order of the Day that we are to 'hold Helles for the Empire.'"

Monty was just about to pulverise me with a particularly rude rejoinder, when a voice outside called "Hostile aircraft overhead," and we were drawn at a run to the door by the unmistakable sound of anti-aircraft guns, followed by the bursting out of rifle and machine-gun fire, which grew and grew till it sounded like a mighty forest crackling and spluttering in flames. We glanced into the sky at the shrapnel puffs, and immediately discovered two enemy aeroplanes flying lower than they had ever done before. We could almost see the observers leaning over the fuselage to spy out if the British on Helles were up to the monkey tricks they had played at Suvla. So low were they that all men with rifles—the infantry in their trenches, the A.S.C. drivers from their dumps, the transport men from their horse-lines—were firing a rapid-fire at the aeroplanes and waiting to see them fall.

"Cheeky brutes!" I shouted, and, observing that our batmen were hastily loading their rifles, ran for my revolver, determined to fire something into the air.

"It's like us," growled Monty, "to land reinforcements under the very eyes of the enemy aeroplanes—" He paused, as though a new idea had struck him. "Rupert, my boy, did you say that the Special Order about holding Helles was *extensively* published?"

"Yes, rather. Hung in the very traverses of the trenches."

"I thought so." He nodded with irritating mysteriousness. "What fools you and I are! Stop firing at those Taubes. Or fire wide of them—fire wide."

"Why?"

"Because our Staff will want them to get home and report all that they've seen. That's why."

Of a truth Monty was quite objectionable, if he was excited with some secret discovery, and thought it amusing not to disclose it. And when, later that afternoon, a message came round saying that irresponsible units were not to fire at hostile aircraft, owing to the danger of spent bullets, he bragged like any pernicious schoolboy.

"I told you so. O Rupert, my silly little juggins, you're as dense as a vegetable marrow. I mean, you're a very low form of life."

Sec.2

The weather broke. Two days of merciless rain turned the trenches into lanes of red clayey mud, and the floor of the Gully Ravine into a canal of stagnant brown water. And one evening Monty returned from his visitations, limping badly. He had slipped heavily, as he paddled through the ankle-deep mud, and had hurt his back. I sent him at once to bed, and on the following morning announced that I was going to no less terrifying a place than Brigade Headquarters to insist on his being given a pair of trench-waders. He enjoined me not to be an ass, and I rebuked him severely for speaking to his doctor like that, and, going out of the dug-out, broke off all communication with one so rude.

Reaching Brigade Headquarters, which were on the slope across the Gully, I asked the least alarming of the Staff Officers, the Staff Captain, for a pair of trench-waders.

"Sorry," answered he, "we've had orders to return them all." He looked most knowing, as he said it, and seemed to think it a remark pregnant with excitement.

"Oh, I see," I replied, quite inadequately.

"Yes," he continued, staring whimsically at me, "we've been ordered to shift our quarters to-night."

"Good Lord!" I said, still confused.

"Yes, we leave—*by ship*—at midnight. It's the Evacuation. The other two brigades of our Division have already gone, and we go to-night!"

"The devil!" exclaimed I. "Then I'll go and pack."

"Of course; and tell the padre to meet the battalion at W Beach at ten o'clock."

Down the hillside I went, across the Gully, forging like a steam-pinnace through the water, and up the face of the opposite hill. Full of the glorious bursting weight of good news, I looked down upon our batmen at work in the cookhouse, and roared: "Pack the valises. We're off to-night." I rushed into the dug-out. "Get up," I commanded Monty; "we leave by ship at midnight."

Never did an invalid with a broken back leap so easily out of his bed, as did Monty. He assured me, however, in an apologetic way, that he had been feeling much better even before he had the news.

"Now you know," said he, "what the Special Order about holding Helles was for—to deceive old Tomfool Turk; and why those regiments from Suvla were landed here—to appear to the Turk like reinforcements, but really to conduct the evacuation at Helles, having learnt the job at Suvla; and why we wanted the Turkish aeroplanes to get back with news of our landing of troops—but, my bonny lad, for every two hundred we land by day, we'll take off two thousand by night!"

After a morning of hurried packing we decorated the dug-out walls with messages for Johnny Turk to find, when he should enter our deserted dwelling. "Sorry, Johnny, not at home"; "Au revoir, Abdul."

"Really," said Monty, "we possess a pretty wit." And, having placed a mug of whisky on the table with a bottle of water, so that Old Man Turk could pour it out to his liking, he wrote: "Have this one with me, John. You fought well."

"Get my kit down with yours," said I. "I'll meet you at W Beach at ten pip-emma."

"Why?" he asked in surprise. "Aren't you coming with me?"

"No," I replied, playing scandalous football with the cookhouse; "I'm going to join my company and lead my braves to safety. Good-bye."

"For Heaven's sake, don't be rash," he called after me as I set off. "There may be dangerous work."

"Meet you at W Beach at ten pip-emma," cried I, now some distance away.

"But you haven't the doctor's permission to return."

"Damn the doctor!" I yelled, and disappeared.

Sec.3

It was quite dark in the fire-trenches by seven o'clock. My men, with every stitch of equipment on their backs, stood on the firing-step and kept up a dilatory fire on the Turkish lines.

"Maintain an intermittent fire," I ordered, as I walked among them. "Not too much of it, or the Turk will think we're nervy, and begin to suspect—not too little, or he'll wonder if we're moving."

In silence the relief of my company was effected. The men of the 13th Division, who were taking over our line, replaced one after another my men on the firing-step, and kept the negligent fire unbroken. With a whisper I officially handed over my sector to their company commander.

"You'll follow us to-morrow, probably," I said, to comfort myself rather than him. I didn't want the man who relieved me to be among the killed.

"What *will* happen, *will* happen," he murmured. "Good luck."

"We shan't be sure we're really going," I prattled on, lest silence became morbid.

"I simply can't believe it. Either we shall be killed, going from here to W Beach, or our orders will be cancelled at the last moment."

"Pass the word to Captain Ray," whispered a voice, "to march his men out."

"Word passed to you, sir, to march," said the sergeant-major.

"From whom?"

"Pass the word back—who from?"

"From Commanding Officer."

I walked to the head of my company. "File out in absolute silence," said I, not remembering at the moment that this was the great order of evacuation. I watched my company file past me—twenty-eight men. Then I followed, wishing it were lighter, for man never quite outgrows his dislike of utter darkness—and this was a nervous night. We threaded guiltily through the old trench system, and emerged into the Gully Ravine, hardly realising that we had bidden the old lines good-bye.

Since dusk the Turk, as apprehensive as ourselves, had been shelling the Gully. And now, as we splashed and floundered along it, shells screamed towards our column, making each of us wonder dreamily whether he would be left dead by the wayside. We reached Artillery Road, and discerned the shadowy form of the remainder of the battalion.

A figure appeared from somewhere, and I recognised the voice as the C.O.'s.

"I shall take the other companies by the road under the cliffs. Take your men over the tableland, and wait for me at W Beach. We shall get there more quickly and less noisily that way."

"Yes, sir," said I, saluting. But under my breath I swore. I had no desire to take my men along the plateau, because, whereas the road under the cliffs was well sheltered, the tableland was exposed to all the guns on Achi Baba, every one of which—so jumpy was the Turk—seemed manned and firing. And I had set my heart on getting my company—all twenty-eight of them—off the Peninsula without the loss of a single man. The route, too, lay over Hunter Weston Hill, and I wanted to avoid seeing and thinking of Doe's grave to-night.

So, worrying anxiously, I gave the order "D Company—march!" and led the way up Artillery Road, while the men, observing that the other companies were proceeding in comparative safety along the Gully, began to sing quietly: "I'll take the high road, and you'll take the low road ... and we shall never meet again," and to titter and to laugh.

"Silence!" I commanded.

Hearing only the padding of our feet as they marched in step, and keeping our eyes on the ground that we might not miss the beaten track and wander into the heather, we tramped along the trail which I had taken on my wild ride to Doe's bedside. We passed Pink Farm Cemetery, barely distinguishing the outline of its solitary tree. We left the "White City" on our right. It was brilliantly lit, that the Turk might think everything was as usual on Helles. We reached the summit of Hunter Weston Hill, and looked down upon a still grey plain, which was the sea.

On the slope of the hill, not fifty yards from where Doe was lying, I had halted my men and was making them sit down, when a voice out of the darkness asked:

"Who's that?"

My heart bounded with fright. A sense of the eerie was upon me, and for a second I thought it was Doe's voice.

"D Company," I called hollowly, "10th East Cheshires."

"Ah, good!" repeated the voice, which was Monty's. And he stepped out of the night, giving me another nasty turn, for it was like some unexpected presence coming from the darkest corner of a room. He sat down beside me, and began to talk.

"The moon is due up about midnight. They want to get us off before moonrise, so that the Turk may not shell us by its light. His aviators are expected to try night-flying."

"Oh!" said I. I was thinking of other things.

"But they've been shelling us pretty effectively in the dark. Asiatic Annie is very busy troubling the beaches."

"Oh?" I said again.

And at that moment a flash illuminated the eastern sky like lightning.

"There you are," said Monty. "She's fired."

No sound of a gun firing or a shell rushing had accompanied the flash. Only alarm whistles began blowing from different points on the hillside.

"They're blown by special sentries," explained Monty, "who are posted to watch the hills of Asia for this flash, and warn the troops to take cover."

"Take cover," I said to my men.

The shell was on its way, but, as it had a journey of seven miles to make across the Dardanelles, a certain time must elapse before we should hear the shriek of the shell as it raced towards us. It seemed an extraordinary time. We knew the shell was coming with its destiny, involving our life or death, irrevocably determined, and yet we heard nothing. The men, under such cover as they could find, were silent in their suspense. Then the shell roared over our heads, seeming so low that we cowered to avoid it. It exploded a score of yards away. A shower of earth rained upon us, but no splinter touched anyone. The men whistled in their relief and laughed.

"Does this happen often?" I asked Monty, when I found I was still alive.

"Every few minutes. It's ten o'clock. We embark at midnight."

"I'm moving my men, then. Asiatic Annie has the range of this spot too well."

I marched my company down to the beach, and told them to take shelter under the lee of the cliff. We had scarcely got there before Annie's wicked eye sparkled from Asia, the warning whistles blew, and, after crying "There she is!" we waited spellbound for the imminent shriek. The shell burst in the surf, scattering shingle and spray over every one of us.

"You'd think they'd seen us move," I said, listening for the groans of any wounded. None came, but I heard instead the sound of muffled voices and marching feet, and saw men moving through the darkness along the brink of the sea like a column of Stygian shades. It was the battalion arriving, with other units of the East Cheshire Brigade.

"I know what'll happen, Rupert," said Monty, when these men had crowded the beach and the hill-slope. "Some drunken Turk will lean against that old gun in Asia, and just push it far enough to perfect its aim."

And he looked round upon the mass of men and shuddered.

It was getting cold, and we huddled ourselves up on the beach. Some of us were indifferent in our fatalism to the shells of Asiatic Annie; if our time had come—well, Kismet. Others, like myself, waited fascinated. I know I had almost hungered for that meaning flash in Asia, the terrible delight of suspense, the rush of thrills, and the sudden arresting of the heart as the shell exploded.

Sec.4

Then, about one o'clock, the moon broke the clouds and lit the operations with a white light. It should have filled us with dismay, but instead it seemed the beginning of brighter things. The men groaned merrily and burst into a drawling song:

> "Oh, the moon shines bright on Mrs. Porter,
> And on her daughter,
> A regular snorter;
> She has washed her neck in dirty water,
> She didn't oughter,
>   The dirty cat."

And Monty, hearing them, whispered one of his delightfully out-of-place remarks:

"Aren't they wonderful, Rupert? I could hug them all, but I wish they'd come to Mass."

The moon, moreover, showed us comforting things. There was the old *Redbreast* lying off Cape Helles. There were the lighters, crowded with men, pushing off from the beach to the waiting boat.

"You could get off on any one of those lighters," said I to Monty. "Why don't you go?"

"Why, because we'll leave this old place together."

After he said this I must have fallen from sheer weariness into a half-sleep. The next thing I remember was Monty's saying: "Look alive, Rupert! *We're* moving now." Glancing round, I saw that my company was the last left on the beach. I marshalled the men—twenty-eight of them—on to the lighter.

"Now, get aboard, Rupert," said Monty.

"You first," corrected I. "I'm going to be last off to-night."

"As your senior officer, I order you to go first."

"As the only combatant officer on the beach," I retorted, "I'm O.C. Troops. You're simply attached to me for rations and discipline. Kindly embark."

Monty muttered something about "upstart impudence," and obeyed the O.C. Troops, who thereupon boarded the rocking lighter, and exchanged with one step the fatal Peninsula for the safety of the seas.

On the ***Redbreast*** we leaned upon the rail, looking back. The boat began to steam away, and Monty, knowing with whom the thoughts of both of us lay, said quietly:

"'Tell England—' You must write a book and tell 'em, Rupert, about the dead schoolboys of your generation—

> 'Tell England, ye who pass this monument,
>   We died for her, and here we rest content.'"

Unable to conquer a slight warming of the eyes at these words, I watched the Peninsula pass. All that I could see of it in the moonlight was the white surf on the beach, the slope of Hunter Weston Hill, and the outline of Achi Baba, rising behind like a monument.

CHAPTER XVIII
THE END OF RUPERT'S STORY

Sec.1

Let Monty have the last word, for he spoke it well. He spoke it a few days ago, in the late autumn of 1918, that is to say, as the war breaks up, and nearly three years after we slipped away in the moonlight from W Beach. In those intervening years the game losers of Gallipoli had avenged themselves at Bagdad, Jerusalem, and Aleppo. In every field the Turkish Armies had been destroyed: and now the forts of the Dardanelles were to be surrendered, and the Narrows thrown open to the Allies. One wished that the dead on Gallipoli might be awakened, if only for a minute, at the sound of the old language spoken among the graves, to see the khaki ashore again, and British ships sailing in triumph up the Straits.

Many of the old Colonel's visions of the emancipation of the Arab world, and the control of the junction of the continents, had thus been realised. And a nobler crusade than that which he saw in the Dardanelles campaign had been fought and won by the army which entered Jerusalem. And, note it well, the men who won these victories were in great part the men who escaped from Suvla and Helles. For, like the Suvla Army, the whole Helles Army escaped. And the Turk was a fool to let them go.

But, before I give you Monty's last word, let me tell you where I am at this moment. It is early evening, and I am writing these closing lines, in which I bid you farewell, sitting on the floor of my kennel-like dug-out in a Belgian trench. There is a most glorious bombardment going on overhead. It has thundered over our trench for days and nights on to the German lines, which to-morrow, when we go over the top, we shall capture, as surely as we captured the one I am sitting in now. Yes, Turkey is out of the game; Bulgaria is out of it; Austria is crying for quarter; and Germany is disintegrating before our advance.

Our bombardment is the most uplifting and exciting thing. So fast do the shells fly over and detonate on the enemy ground that it is almost impossible to distinguish the isolated shell-bursts; they are lost in one dense fog of smoke. Just now we ceased to be rational as we stood watching it. "That's the stuff to give 'em!" cried a Tommy in his excitement. "Pump it over! Pump it over!" and, as some German sand-bags flew into the air: "Gee! Look at that! Are we downhearted? NO! 'Ave we won? YES!" And I wanted to throw up my hat and cheer. There seized me the sensation I got when my house was winning on the football-ground at school. "We're on top! On top of the Boche, and he asked for it!"

I have now returned to my dug-out, feeling it in my heart to be sorry for the Germans. I am impatient to finish my story, for we go over the top in the morning.

Sec.2

It is in a letter just arrived from my mother that we find Monty's last word—his footnote to this history. She describes a ceremony which she attended at Kensingtowe, the unveiling of a memorial in the chapel to the Old Kensingtonians who fell at Gallipoli. Monty, as an old Peninsula padre, had been invited to preach the sermon. My mother writes in her womanly way:

"He preached a wonderful sermon. We all thought him like a man who had seen terrible things, and was passionately anxious that somehow good should come of it all.

"Calvary, he said, was a sacrifice offered by a Holy Family. There was a Father Who gave His Son, because He so loved the world; a mother who yielded up her child, whispering (he doubted not): 'Behold the handmaid of the Lord'; and a Son Who went to His death in the spirit of the words: 'In the volume of the Book it was written of me that I should do Thy will, O my God; I am content to do it.'

"And, in days to come, England must remember that once upon a time she, too, was a Holy Family; for there had been years in which she was composed of fathers who so loved the world that they gave their sons; of mothers who whispered, as their boys set their faces for Gallipoli or Flanders: 'Behold the handmaid of the Lord' (and oh, Rupert, I felt so ashamed to think how badly I behaved that last night before you went to Gallipoli—how rebellious I was!). He went on to speak of the sons, and what do you think he said? He spoke of one who, the evening before the last attack at Cape Helles, asked him: 'Will you take care of these envelopes, in case—' He declared that this simple sentence was, in its shy English way, a reflection of the words: 'It was written of me that I should do Thy will; I am content to do it.'

"That boy, an old Kensingtonian, was mortally hit in the morning. There was another with him, also an old Kensingtonian, who was still alive, and might yet come marching home with the victorious army.

"I lost his next words, for there I broke down. But I seem to remember his saying:

"'All men and all nations are the better for remembering that once they were holy. England's past, then, is holy; her future is unwritten. But Idealism is mightily abroad among those who shall make the England that is to be. And all that remains for the preacher to say is this: Nothing but Christianity will ever gather in that harvest of spiritual ideals which alone will make good our prodigal outlay; for, after all, we have sown the

world with the broken dreams and spilled ambitions of a
generation of schoolboys....

"'All you who have suffered, you fathers and mothers, remember
this: only by turning your sufferings into the seeds of
God-like things will you make their memory beautiful.'

"Oh, Rupert, I was elevated by all he said, and I prayed that
you might go on with willingness and resolution to the end,
and that I might face the last few weeks of the war with
courage. I thought of the remark of your old Cheshire Colonel,
that, instead of wandering during these years among the
undistinguished valleys, you have been transferred straight to
the mountain-tops. Do you remember how I used to call you 'my
mountain boy'? The name has a new meaning now. Even if you are
in danger at this time, I try to be proud. I think of you as on
white heights."

Sec.3

"Only by turning your sufferings into the seeds of God-like things will you
make their memory beautiful."

As I copied just now those last words of Monty's sermon, I laid down my pencil
on the dug-out floor with a little start. As in a flashlight I saw their truth. They created in my mind the picture of that AEgean evening, when Monty turned the moment of Doe's death, which so nearly brought me discouragement and debasement,
into an ennobling memory. And I foresaw him going about healing the sores of this
war with the same priestly hand.

Yes, there are reasons why such wistful visions should haunt me now.
Everything this evening has gone to produce a certain exaltation in me. First, there
has been the bombardment, with its thought of going over the top to-morrow.
Then comes my mother's glowing letter, which somehow has held me enthralled,
so that I find sentences from it reiterating themselves in my mind, just as they did in

the old schooldays. And lastly, there has been the joyous sense of having completed my book, on which for three years I have laboured lovingly in tent, and billet, and trench.

I meant to close it on the last echo of Monty's sermon. But the fascination was on me, and I felt I wanted to go on writing. I had so lost myself in the old scenes of schoolroom, playing-fields, starlit decks, and Grecian battlegrounds, which I had been describing, that I actually ceased to hear the bombardment. And the atmosphere of the well-loved places and well-loved friends remained all about me. It was the atmosphere that old portraits and fading old letters throw around those who turn them over. So I took up again my pencil and my paper.

I thought I would add a paragraph or two, in case I go down in the morning. If I come through all right, I shall wipe these paragraphs out. Meanwhile, in these final hours of wonder and waiting, it is happiness to write on.

I fear that, as I write, I may appear to dogmatise, for I am still only twenty-two. But I must speak while I can.

What silly things one thinks in an evening of suspense and twilight like this! One minute I feel I want to be alive this time to-morrow, in order that my book, which has become everything to me, may have a happy ending. Pennybet fell at Neuve Chapelle, Doe at Cape Helles, and one ought to be left alive to save the face of the tale. Still, if these paragraphs stand and I fall, it will at least be a *true* ending—true to things as they were for the generation in which we were born.

And the glorious bombardment asserts itself through my thoughts, and with a thrill I conceive of it—for we would-be authors are persons obsessed by one idea—as an effort of the people of Britain to make it possible for me to come through unhurt and save my story. I feel I want to thank them.

Another minute I try to recapture that moment of ideal patriotism which I touched on the deck of the *Rangoon*. I see a death in No Man's Land to-morrow as a wonderful thing. There you stand exactly between two nations. All Britain with her might is behind your back, reaching down to her frontier, which is the trench whence you have just leapt. All Germany with her might is before your face. Perhaps it is not ill to die standing like that in front of your nation.

I cannot bear to think of my mother's pain, if to-morrow claims me. But I leave her this book, into which I seem to have poured my life. It is part of myself. No, it *is* myself—and I shall only return her what is her own.

Oh, but if I go down, I want to ask you not to think it anything but a happy ending. It will be happy, because victory came to the nation, and that is more important than the life of any individual. Listen to that bombardment outside, which is increasing, if possible, as the darkness gathers—well, it is one of the last before the extraordinary Sabbath-silence, which will be the Allies' Peace.

And, if these pages can be regarded as my spiritual history, they will have a happy ending, too. This is why.

In the Mediterranean on a summer day, I learned that I was to pursue beauty like the Holy Grail. And I see it now in everything. I know that, just as there is far more beauty in nature than ugliness, so there is more goodness in humanity than evil. There is more happiness in life than pain. Yes, there is. As Monty used to say, we are given now and then moments of surpassing joy which outweigh decades of grief, I think I knew such a moment when I won the swimming cup for Bramhall. And I remember my mother whispering one night: "If all the rest of my life, Rupert, were to be sorrow, the last nineteen years of you have made it so well worth living." Happiness wins hands down. Take any hundred of us out here, and for ten who are miserable you will find ninety who are lively and laughing. Life is good—else why should we cling to it as we do?—oh, yes, we surely do, especially when the chances are all against us. Life is good, and youth is good. I have had twenty glorious years.

I may be whimsical to-night, but I feel that the old Colonel was right when he saw nothing unlovely in Penny's death; and that Monty was right when he said that Doe had done a perfect thing at the last, and so grasped the Grail. And I have the strange idea that very likely I, too, shall find beauty in the morning.

THE END

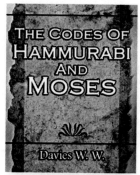

The Codes Of Hammurabi And Moses
W. W. Davies

QTY

The discovery of the Hammurabi Code is one of the greatest achievements of archaeology, and is of paramount interest, not only to the student of the Bible, but also to all those interested in ancient history...

Religion   **ISBN:** *1-59462-338-4*

Pages:132
MSRP $12.95

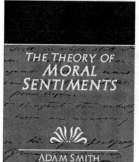

The Theory of Moral Sentiments
Adam Smith

QTY

This work from 1749. contains original theories of conscience amd moral judgment and it is the foundation for systemof morals.

Philosophy **ISBN:** *1-59462-777-0*

Pages:536
MSRP $19.95

Jessica's First Prayer
Hesba Stretton

QTY

In a screened and secluded corner of one of the many railway-bridges which span the streets of London there could be seen a few years ago, from five o'clock every morning until half past eight, a tidily set-out coffee-stall, consisting of a trestle and board, upon which stood two large tin cans, with a small fire of charcoal burning under each so as to keep the coffee boiling during the early hours of the morning when the work-people were thronging into the city on their way to their daily toil...

Pages:84

Childrens   **ISBN:** *1-59462-373-2*   *MSRP $9.95*

My Life and Work
Henry Ford

QTY

Henry Ford revolutionized the world with his implementation of mass production for the Model T automobile. Gain valuable business insight into his life and work with his own auto-biography... "We have only started on our development of our country we have not as yet, with all our talk of wonderful progress, done more than scratch the surface. The progress has been wonderful enough but..."

Pages:300

Biographies/   **ISBN:** *1-59462-198-5*   *MSRP $21.95*

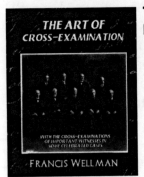

The Art of Cross-Examination
Francis Wellman

QTY

I presume it is the experience of every author, after his first book is published upon an important subject, to be almost overwhelmed with a wealth of ideas and illustrations which could readily have been included in his book, and which to his own mind, at least, seem to make a second edition inevitable. Such certainly was the case with me; and when the first edition had reached its sixth impression in five months, I rejoiced to learn that it seemed to my publishers that the book had met with a sufficiently favorable reception to justify a second and considerably enlarged edition. ..

Pages:412

Reference   ISBN: *1-59462-647-2*   *MSRP $19.95*

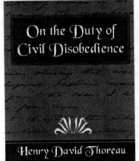

On the Duty of Civil Disobedience
Henry David Thoreau

QTY

Thoreau wrote his famous essay, On the Duty of Civil Disobedience, as a protest against an unjust but popular war and the immoral but popular institution of slave-owning. He did more than write—he declined to pay his taxes, and was hauled off to gaol in consequence. Who can say how much this refusal of his hastened the end of the war and of slavery ?

Pages:48

Law   ISBN: *1-59462-747-9*   *MSRP $7.45*

Dream Psychology Psychoanalysis for Beginners
Sigmund Freud

QTY

Sigmund Freud, born Sigismund Schlomo Freud (May 6, 1856 - September 23, 1939), was a Jewish-Austrian neurologist and psychiatrist who co-founded the psychoanalytic school of psychology. Freud is best known for his theories of the unconscious mind, especially involving the mechanism of repression; his redefinition of sexual desire as mobile and directed towards a wide variety of objects; and his therapeutic techniques, especially his understanding of transference in the therapeutic relationship and the presumed value of dreams as sources of insight into unconscious desires.

Pages:196

Psychology   ISBN: *1-59462-905-6*   *MSRP $15.45*

The Miracle of Right Thought
Orison Swett Marden

QTY

Believe with all of your heart that you will do what you were made to do. When the mind has once formed the habit of holding cheerful, happy, prosperous pictures, it will not be easy to form the opposite habit. It does not matter how improbable or how far away this realization may see, or how dark the prospects may be, if we visualize them as best we can, as vividly as possible, hold tenaciously to them and vigorously struggle to attain them, they will gradually become actualized, realized in the life. But a desire, a longing without endeavor, a yearning abandoned or held indifferently will vanish without realization.

Pages:360

Self Help   ISBN: *1-59462-644-8*   *MSRP $25.45*

www.bookjungle.com *email: sales@bookjungle.com fax: 630-214-0564 mail: Book Jungle PO Box 2226 Champaign, IL 61825*

QTY

The Rosicrucian Cosmo-Conception Mystic Christianity by *Max Heindel* ISBN: *1-59462-188-8* **$38.95**
The Rosicrucian Cosmo-conception is not dogmatic, neither does it appeal to any other authority than the reason of the student. It is: not controversial, but is: sent forth in the, hope that it may help to clear.. New Age/Religion Pages 646

Abandonment To Divine Providence by *Jean-Pierre de Caussade* ISBN: *1-59462-228-0* **$25.95**
"The Rev. Jean Pierre de Caussade was one of the most remarkable spiritual writers of the Society of Jesus in France in the 18th Century. His death took place at Toulouse in 1751. His works have gone through many editions and have been republished... Inspirational/Religion Pages 400

Mental Chemistry by *Charles Haanel* ISBN: *1-59462-192-6* **$23.95**
Mental Chemistry allows the change of material conditions by combining and appropriately utilizing the power of the mind. Much like applied chemistry creates something new and unique out of careful combinations of chemicals the mastery of mental chemistry... New Age Pages 354

The Letters of Robert Browning and Elizabeth Barret Barrett 1845-1846 vol II ISBN: *1-59462-193-4* **$35.95**
by *Robert Browning* and *Elizabeth Barrett*
Biographies Pages 596

Gleanings In Genesis (volume I) by *Arthur W. Pink* ISBN: *1-59462-130-6* **$27.45**
Appropriately has Genesis been termed "the seed plot of the Bible" for in it we have, in germ form, almost all of the great doctrines which are afterwards fully developed in the books of Scripture which follow... Religion/Inspirational Pages 420

The Master Key by *L. W. de Laurence* ISBN: *1-59462-001-6* **$30.95**
In no branch of human knowledge has there been a more lively increase of the spirit of research during the past few years than in the study of Psychology, Concentration and Mental Discipline. The requests for authentic lessons in Thought Control, Mental Discipline and... New Age/Business Pages 422

The Lesser Key Of Solomon Goetia by *L. W. de Laurence* ISBN: *1-59462-092-X* **$9.95**
This translation of the first book of the "Lemegton" which is now for the first time made accessible to students of Talismanic Magic was done, after careful collation and edition, from numerous Ancient Manuscripts in Hebrew, Latin, and French... New Age/Occult Pages 92

Rubaiyat Of Omar Khayyam by *Edward Fitzgerald* ISBN:*1-59462-332-5* **$13.95**
Edward Fitzgerald, whom the world has already learned, in spite of his own efforts to remain within the shadow of anonymity, to look upon as one of the rarest poets of the century, was born at Bredfield, in Suffolk, on the 31st of March, 1809. He was the third son of John Purcell... Music Pages 172

Ancient Law by *Henry Maine* ISBN: *1-59462-128-4* **$29.95**
The chief object of the following pages is to indicate some of the earliest ideas of mankind, as they are reflected in Ancient Law, and to point out the relation of those ideas to modern thought. Religion/History Pages 452

Far-Away Stories by *William J. Locke* ISBN: *1-59462-129-2* **$19.45**
"Good wine needs no bush, but a collection of mixed vintages does. And this book is just such a collection. Some of the stories I do not want to remain buried for ever in the museum files of dead magazine-numbers an author's not unpardonable vanity..." Fiction Pages 272

Life of David Crockett by *David Crockett* ISBN: *1-59462-250-7* **$27.45**
"Colonel David Crockett was one of the most remarkable men of the times in which he lived. Born in humble life, but gifted with a strong will, an indomitable courage, and unremitting perseverance.. Biographies/New Age Pages 424

Lip-Reading by *Edward Nitchie* ISBN: *1-59462-206-X* **$25.95**
Edward B. Nitchie, founder of the New York School for the Hard of Hearing, now the Nitchie School of Lip-Reading, Inc, wrote "LIP-READING Principles and Practice". The development and perfecting of this meritorious work on lip-reading was an undertaking... How-to Pages 400

A Handbook of Suggestive Therapeutics, Applied Hypnotism, Psychic Science ISBN: *1-59462-214-0* **$24.95**
by *Henry Munro*
Health/New Age/Health/Self-help Pages 376

A Doll's House: and Two Other Plays by *Henrik Ibsen* ISBN: *1-59462-112-8* **$19.95**
Henrik Ibsen created this classic when in revolutionary 1848 Rome. Introducing some striking concepts in playwriting for the realist genre, this play has been studied the world over. Fiction/Classics/Plays 308

The Light of Asia by *sir Edwin Arnold* ISBN: *1-59462-204-3* **$13.95**
In this poetic masterpiece, Edwin Arnold describes the life and teachings of Buddha. The man who was to become known as Buddha to the world was born as Prince Gautama of India but he rejected the worldly riches and abandoned the reigns of power when... Religion/History/Biographies Pages 170

The Complete Works of Guy de Maupassant by *Guy de Maupassant* ISBN: *1-59462-157-8* **$16.95**
"For days and days, nights and nights, I had dreamed of that first kiss which was to consecrate our engagement, and I knew not on what spot I should put my lips..." Fiction/Classics Pages 240

The Art of Cross-Examination by *Francis L. Wellman* ISBN: *1-59462-309-0* **$26.95**
Written by a renowned trial lawyer, Wellman imparts his experience and uses case studies to explain how to use psychology to extract desired information through questioning. How-to/Science/Reference Pages 408

Answered or Unanswered? by *Louisa Vaughan* ISBN: *1-59462-248-5* **$10.95**
Miracles of Faith in China
Religion Pages 112

The Edinburgh Lectures on Mental Science (1909) by *Thomas* ISBN: *1-59462-008-3* **$11.95**
This book contains the substance of a course of lectures recently given by the writer in the Queen Street Hall, Edinburgh. Its purpose is to indicate the Natural Principles governing the relation between Mental Action and Material Conditions... New Age/Psychology Pages 148

Ayesha by *H. Rider Haggard* ISBN: *1-59462-301-5* **$24.95**
Verily and indeed it is the unexpected that happens! Probably if there was one person upon the earth from whom the Editor of this, and of a certain previous history, did not expect to hear again... Classics Pages 380

Ayala's Angel by *Anthony Trollope* ISBN: *1-59462-352-X* **$29.95**
The two girls were both pretty; but Lucy who was twenty-one who supposed to be simple and comparatively unattractive, whereas Ayala was credited, as her Bombwhat romantic name might show, with poetic charm and a taste for romance. Ayala when her father died was nineteen... Fiction Pages 484

The American Commonwealth by *James Bryce* ISBN: *1-59462-286-8* **$34.45**
An interpretation of American democratic political theory. It examines political mechanics and society from the perspective of Scotsman James Bryce Politics Pages 572

Stories of the Pilgrims by *Margaret P. Pumphrey* ISBN: *1-59462-116-0* **$17.95**
This book explores pilgrims religious oppression in England as well as their escape to Holland and eventual crossing to America on the Mayflower, and their early days in New England... History Pages 268

QTY

The Fasting Cure *by Sinclair Upton*   ISBN: *1-59462-222-1* **$13.95**
In the Cosmopolitan Magazine for May, 1910, and in the Contemporary Review (London) for April, 1910, I published an article dealing with my experiences in fasting. I have written a great many magazine articles, but never one which attracted so much attention... New Age/Self Help Health Pages 164

Hebrew Astrology *by Sepharial*   ISBN: *1-59462-308-2* **$13.45**
In these days of advanced thinking it is a matter of common observation that we have left many of the old landmarks behind and that we are now pressing forward to greater heights and to a wider horizon than that which represented the mind-content of our progenitors... Astrology Pages 144

Thought Vibration or The Law of Attraction in the Thought World   ISBN: *1-59462-127-6* **$12.95**
by William Walker Atkinson   Psychology/Religion Pages 144

Optimism *by Helen Keller*   ISBN: *1-59462-108-X* **$15.95**
Helen Keller was blind, deaf, and mute since 19 months old, yet famously learned how to overcome these handicaps, communicate with the world, and spread her lectures promoting optimism. An inspiring read for everyone... Biographies/Inspirational Pages 84

Sara Crewe *by Frances Burnett*   ISBN: *1-59462-360-0* **$9.45**
In the first place, Miss Minchin lived in London. Her home was a large, dull, tall one, in a large, dull square, where all the houses were alike, and all the sparrows were alike, and where all the door-knockers made the same heavy sound... Childrens Classic Pages 88

The Autobiography of Benjamin Franklin *by Benjamin Franklin*   ISBN: *1-59462-135-7* **$24.95**
The Autobiography of Benjamin Franklin has probably been more extensively read than any other American historical work, and no other book of its kind has had such ups and downs of fortune. Franklin lived for many years in England, where he was agent... Biographies/History Pages 332

Name	
Email	
Telephone	
Address	
City, State ZIP	

☐ **Credit Card**   ☐ **Check / Money Order**

Credit Card Number	
Expiration Date	
Signature	

Please Mail to: *Book Jungle*
PO Box 2226
Champaign, IL 61825
or Fax to: *630-214-0564*

ORDERING INFORMATION

web*: www.bookjungle.com*
email*: sales@bookjungle.com*
fax*: 630-214-0564*
mail*: Book Jungle PO Box 2226 Champaign, IL 61825*
or PayPal *to sales@bookjungle.com*

Please contact us for bulk discounts

DIRECT-ORDER TERMS

**20% Discount if You Order
Two or More Books**
Free Domestic Shipping!
Accepted: Master Card, Visa,
Discover, American Express

Lightning Source UK Ltd.
Milton Keynes UK
19 January 2010

148837UK00001B/76/P